The Tomb of El
By
Christopher Cartwright

CW01467647

Copyright 2019 by Christopher Cartwright
This book is protected under the copyright laws of the United
States of America. Any reproduction or other unauthorized
use of the material or artwork herein is prohibited. This book
is a work of fiction. Names, characters, places, brands, media
and incidents either are the product of the author's
imagination or are used fictitiously. All rights reserved.

Prologue

Magdalena River, Colombia – 1535

The *Santa Rosa Celeste's* sails billowed open with the gust of wind and she sailed south along the ancient river.

It was the only means of penetrating the foreign jungle, so dense that its trees stood like the buttress of a sinister fortress. The river was dwarfed by two enormous mountain ranges on either side of its banks as it formed a secret pathway into the heart of the jungle and the secret land beyond. A place where legends, were they to be believed, had foretold of a city full of gold. A city ruled by an extraordinary man…

El Hombre Dorado

Felipe Ferdinand thought about the near mythical story. The name translated into *The Golden Man*. According to conquistadors who had journeyed into the region and traded with the local Muisca people, their city was ruled by a man who would paint himself in gold and wash in a lake high up in one of those nearby mountain ranges. It was believed that the man had come from El Dorado, an ancient city made of solid gold.

Felipe knew the stories were exaggerated.

They had to be, there wasn't enough gold in the entire world to build a city. Even so, if the rumors were even slightly based on truth, he was going to be a rich man. That much he could believe. If a savage native man could afford to wash precious gold into a lake as part of some sort of ritual to the gods, then it was fair to say that gold was nearly superfluous wherever that man had come from.

It was because of that belief that Felipe Ferdinand had sold the house his once noble father had owned and risked everything he'd owned in order to sponsor this expedition. A risk that would ruin him, or make him richer than Charles V, the king of Spain.

He thought about the bet he'd made. He was set to lose everything – including his life – if the expedition failed. He either needed to return with gold, or not at all. He thought back to the promises that he couldn't keep.

And lastly, he thought about the man he'd murdered to acquire the map.

A strong, northerly wind gusted through the steep valley. It had been constant for the past three days, allowing them to make some of their best progress against the slow-moving current of the river.

How many miles inland had they traveled?

It was a difficult question to answer. The river, like all rivers, meandered and snaked around, instead of traveling in a straight line. At a guess, they had traveled somewhere in the vicinity of five hundred miles since leaving the Atlantic.

The *Santa Rosa Celeste* was a Spanish carrack, purpose built for the expedition. It had a large aftcastle and a slightly smaller forecastle. The aft-castle was used for steering and as a platform to attack other ships during boarding actions with the use of muskets and small cannonades. The forecastle was used for defense and tended to make navigation somewhat difficult. The stern was rounded, and the main deck was large to support a large crew and appropriate cannon armament. Such an arrangement made the carrack a little top heavy but, as mentioned, she was primarily constructed for long voyages at sea and not naval combat. The quarters below were expectedly cramped as much of the hull was dedicated to the storage of supplies and any present cargo.

The wide beam measured in at twenty-five feet and her length was approximately seventy-five feet. These measurements related to the design concepts of the day and her purpose of being a long-range ship. The sailing warships and cargo ships of the future would eventually reduce the width of the beam as compared to the length of the ship in an effort to streamline the vessel for the purpose of improved speed.

It had a shallow draft, allowing it to reach the upper ends of the river and navigate obstacles that rose from the riverbed.

The Magdalena widened and a large tributary opened up to the east.

Captain Rodriguez José ordered the helmsman to turn them into the wind and for the sails to be furled.

Felipe turned to the captain, his brow furrowed. "Is that the river?"

Captain José's lips thinned into a hard line. "It's hard to say. We only have the basic notes of last year's expedition, which were intentionally indistinct in case they were to fall into the wrong person's hands."

Felipe grinned. "Those notes and maps did fall into the wrong hands. I paid a fortune and had to pull a lot of strings, which will ultimately cost me my life if I fail to deliver the gold, so I'll ask again, do we have the right river?'

The captain nodded. "It's the first major river we've seen since we entered the valley."

Felipe nodded. He knew the navigational notes by heart.

Sail south, through a valley lined by snowcapped mountains, into the heart of the jungle. When the river widens and a large tributary enters the river from the east, follow the tributary until navigation becomes impassable. Follow the river as it climbs into the mountain range to a great waterfall. Follow a series of steps carved in the mountain to reach the top, and then follow the river to its origins.

Felipe asked, "How do you want to do this?"

The captain said, "I've ordered the sails furled and the rowboats lowered. We'll ease the *Santa Rosa Celeste* in as far as we can."

Felipe's eyes narrowed. "And then?"

Captain José grinned. "Then you're on your own. Your men will need to continue on horseback. We'll wait for you on the ship."

*

The *Santa Rosa Celeste* didn't travel far into the tributary.

Despite its shallow draft, the ship beached on a gravelly sandbar within minutes. The crew rowed an anchor out to aft of the ship and then went through the laborious process of winching the ship off the sandbar.

By midday, the *Santa Rosa Celeste* was floating again and at rest on her anchor in the middle of the tributary. It was a good location. Along the wide river, the crew who remained behind on board would be well positioned to defend the ship if the local Muisca people attacked.

Felipe Ferdinand led a small army of fifty conquistadors up the tributary toward the distant mountain ranges. They tried using rowboats, but were unable to go any farther upriver. Instead, they would need their horses.

It was a delicate process bringing horses ashore.

The warhorses were brought out of their stalls in the ship's hold. In order to prevent the horses from panicking, they were blindfolded and carefully raised from below deck by hoists attached to slings surrounding the horses' bodies. In these early days before wharves were built, the horses were lowered into the water and made to swim ashore, led by men in row boats.

Felipe rode a majestic Andalusian purebred warhorse, named *Victory*.

The Spanish stallion was strongly built, and compact yet elegant. It had a thick coat as black as the night's sky, with a long, thick mane and tail. The breed was known for its intelligence, sensitivity and docility. Standing at fifteen and a half hands, the beast would make a formidable impression on any native people of the region, who had never seen a horse until Christopher Columbus first reached the shores of South America and still believed that horse and man were one and the same.

On horseback, they headed east, moving quickly despite the thick tropical jungle. They hacked their way into the heart of the mountain, each day gaining more altitude. The region was close to the equator making very little seasonal changes to the weather. Instead, Felipe observed, the climate changed on altitude. The tropical jungle thinned as they climbed above the rainforest into a more temperate environment, with the thick vegetation and dense forest thinning the higher they climbed.

It took days to climb and with each day of progress they appeared to step into a new season. Felipe made notes, describing each of the zones as he witnessed them.

Tierra caliente – hot land – for the jungle rainforest near sea level.

Tierra templada – temperate land – for the region above the canopy of the jungle. The weather might as well have gone from summer to fall.

Tierra fría – cold land – at an altitude of more than six thousand feet, the mountain become shrouded in cloud forests.

Tierra helada – frozen land – where snow became a common sight.

The tributary river they had been following ran through a deep valley. Towering walls of stone lined either side.

Up ahead, Felipe ordered his men to stop…

Because a massive waterfall, more than four hundred feet high, rose to the sky like a castle parapet, and told him they were on the right path.

*

Felipe stared through the telescope. His mind forming a mental image of the path to Guatavita – the golden lake – according to the map he'd stolen.

They were on the right track.

The giant waterfall confirmed that. The route up the mountain was to the right about half a mile back from the waterfall. Felipe closed his left eye and looked through the telescope. He traced the narrow rock shelf that ran along the southern end of the valley. It disappeared beneath a steep pass, and then up through a spur that disappeared into the clouds above.

Felipe put the telescope down. He motioned to his men the route they would take, before, like all good leaders, he led the way.

It took them the better half of a day to overcome the waterfall and another to follow the river to the lake high above.

The sparse tundra opened to a large altiplano – a wide plateau surrounded by mountainous regions. Felipe imagined the place a highly cultivatable site and powerful Spanish city one day, and for a moment wondered if that was indeed the gold and wealth really hidden in the region.

Over the next day they crossed the altiplano and climbed the mountains to the east. Hot water flowed from nearby natural springs. He climbed down from *Victory,* his eyes darting between the map that he'd stolen and the strange new inhospitable landscape. The boiling water of the thermal pools bubbling like some sort of medieval cauldron, a crucible for new life, where strange creatures evolved ten times faster than those at sea level.

To the east, mountain peaks filled their vista.

According to the man he'd killed for the map, the golden city of El Dorado was somewhere at the base of those mountains, between the burning lakes and the high peaks.

He studied the distant backdrop through his telescope.

Staring at the mountains in the distance, he scanned the leveled ground of the mesa, before fixing on a crater shaped lake in the foreground.

Something caught his eye. He bit his lower lip and grinned. His heart thrummed in his chest at the sight.

A man was on a ceremonial raft, drifting toward the center of the lake.

The dark clouds above shifted and a single beam of crepuscular sunlight shone down upon the man, turning him and the raft to gold.

Felipe's eyes narrowed and he swallowed hard.

The man on the raft wasn't turning gold beneath the sun's ray. He was covered in gold dust and was carrying several intricately carved golden items on board. A moment later, the man, threw the golden items of jewelry into the lake.

Felipe swore.

The man on the ritual raft jumped into the icy lake, and proceeded to bathe the heavy gold off.

Greed and anticipation rising in his chest, Felipe lowered his telescope, climbed onto *Victory* and beckoned his men onward.

They rode their horses hard along the mesa. The Spanish warhorses, sensing their riders' enthusiasm became energized, running free at a gallop.

At the edge of the crater, Felipe pulled up his horse and dismounted. There was no doubt in his mind that they could slaughter the primitive tribe, but then what would they do? There was no gold left near the lake, so they would need to find out where it had come from. No, they needed to follow the man back to his village, to a place where Felipe now believed gold was plentiful.

They waited until the golden ceremony on the lake was completed, and the strange tribe began their journey to their village, before Felipe and his men followed at a distance.

It took them until late in the evening to reach it.

A small city, surrounded by large wooden poles nearly twenty feet high and driven into the earth to form a protective barrier like that of a castle.

Their minds went wild at the thought of what such a barricade might be protecting.

Felipe thought they should wait until the morning to pillage it, but his men were overcome with greed and desire after witnessing the local chieftain throw gold into the lake. Against Felipe's better judgement, and unable to restrain his men any longer, he gave a curt nod of approval – and he and his men rode wildly into the golden city of El Dorado.

*

There was bloodshed of course.

How could there not be? His men had been promised riches beyond their wildest dreams.

Instead, they had found nothing more than a primitive village.

Unlike the other pre-Columbian civilizations encountered by the Spanish conquistadors, such as the Aztec, Maya and Incas who constructed large temples of stone, the Muisca tribe's architecture was rather modest and made of non-permanent materials such as wood and clay.

The entire village was surrounded by tall wooden poles joined together to form a protective enclosure, with a single gate on the southern end. Inside, the houses were constructed around a central square with the house of their chieftain in the center. The houses of the Muisca, called bohíos or malokas, were circular structures made of poles of wood and walls of clay, with a conical reed roof. A long beam of wood supported the roof in the center of the round structure and was attached to the wooden poles. The interior of the roof was decorated with cloths with thin strokes of different colors.

Felipe cursed and dismounted his warhorse. He was breathing hard, the sound and fury of battle – even if it was one sided – still rung loudly in his ears. There was blood on his Toledo sword. He wiped it with a leather cloth before inserting into his clean scabbard.

He sat down and had a drink while one of his men reported the outcome of the battle. As he could tell at glance, it was needless slaughtering of the native Muisca tribe. All were killed with the exception of two, whom his translator was interrogating now to see if they know where the gold had been found. Three of his men were injured, but none of the injuries were life-threatening.

Over the course of the next hour, his men murdered any remaining survivors, including the two who had been interrogated after they provided nothing of use and declared they had never heard of any city fitting the descriptions of El Dorado. What little of apparent value that could be found was taken from the Muisca village, and Felipe's party commenced the long and arduous journey down the mountain range, back to the ship.

The *Santa Rosa Celeste* made the slow journey north along the Magdalena.

There was a somber mood on board. Men had wasted years of their life on this expedition and had spent their fortunes on equipment and horses to do so. Now all that was lost. They would return to Spain as failures. Not just failures. Some would lose what possessions they had to pay off incumbent debts.

Felipe glanced up at the distant storm clouds and tried to imagine his next move. He would lose everything he owned, and when that wasn't enough, he would lose his life. He was almost certainly better off remaining in the foreign land, where his backers would find it difficult to extract their revenge for his financial losses.

The Magdalena flowed into the Caribbean Sea.

The *Santa Rosa Celeste* passed the headlands, turned east, and set its sails for a long journey across the Atlantic to Spain, where Felipe would await his imprisonment and execution.

Sometime later, a loud bang erupted, as the *Santa Rosa Celeste* scraped along the outer reef.

From down below, a sailor shouted, "We're taking on water!"

*

Captain Rodriguez José swore a vicious oath.

He and his men fought for nearly forty-eight hours to keep the *Santa Rosa Celeste* afloat while they ran out of every piece of sailcloth in an attempt to reach the nearest shore. The region northeast of the mouth of the Magdalena River was surrounded by jagged rocks and deadly reefs, making it impossible to come to shore to make repairs.

Instead, they ran for a sandy bay he'd noted farther east along the coastline.

Ropes were tied to a pair of large trees and the *Santa Rosa Celeste* was winched up onto the dry sand. An inspection of the portside hull revealed a six foot by four-foot scar where the ship had ripped across the reef. The crew went to work felling local trees to make the repairs. It was a local breed of dark mahogany. The strong hardwood, unique to that section of the coast, was a godsend.

After nearly three days of repairs were made, the *Santa Rosa Celeste* was pulled off the beach and into the bay. It took another two days to re-provision the Spanish four-masted carrack with fresh water from a nearby creek, and make it ready for its long sail across the Atlantic, home to Spain.

That was the first time they spotted the strange local people.

They were dark skinned, with long black hair and matching eyes. A friendly people and happy to trade with them for fresh provisions. They spoke a language similar to the Muisca people, whose language a few of his men had learned to speak some words. Already those men were talking to the people and trading iron carpentry nails in exchange for delicate and intricate ceramics, precious emeralds, and polished pearls made of pure gold. The local people were eager to exchange gold for the iron nails. They seemed almost indifferent to the precious stones they were trading, as well as large emeralds.

José met with Felipe who had a wry grin on his face.

José asked, "What is it?"

"Look at this," Felipe handed him what appeared to be a golden pearl.

José arched his eyebrow in incredulity and examined the stone.

It was enough to fit snugly in the palm of his hand. Despite its size the stone felt disproportionately heavy. It was perfectly smooth and roundish, but not a complete sphere. More of a misshapen ball or distorted musket shot. He let the stone run delicately through each of his fingers, the same way a gambler might shuffle a casino chip, giving him an intrinsic feel for the stone. It was smooth, but there was no sign of it having been polished. Instead, it was almost as though the gold had been forced to develop that way, the same way a pearl might start off as a piece of sand in an oyster shell.

"What is this?" José bit his lower lip. "It looks like a golden pearl!"

"That's what I thought," Felipe replied, his eyes wide with greed. "And these natives are trading it like they're worthless."

José's eyes narrowed. "How many do they have?"

"I don't know. A lot. Enough that they appear more worried that we might run out of nails than we are that they'll run out of gold."

"Did they say where they got it from?"

Felipe shook his head. "No. We've asked, but they're refusing to answer the question."

"Refusing?" José licked his lips. "Or just unable to understand what's being asked of them?"

"Refusing," he said without hesitation. "They said its forbidden."

"What's forbidden?"

"Everything to do with these damned golden pearls. Talking about where they came from, what they are, why they have so many of them, everything is forbidden."

José grinned. "Except trading them for worthless iron nails?"

Felipe nodded. "That's something at least."

"But if you can find out where they're getting them, we'll be the richest men in Europe."

"Exactly."

José asked, "Are you certain they can't be persuaded?"

"Yes. One of my men kidnapped one of them and threatened to kill him if he didn't tell us where the golden pearls had come from. The man looked frightened at first, but as soon as he was pushed to tell where the gold had come from, he appeared downright terrified. In fact, at that point, he tried to kill himself."

José arched an eyebrow. "He wanted to commit suicide instead of reveal the truth?"

"It would appear so."

Felipe saddled *Victory*.

Captain José asked, "Where are you going?"

Felipe grinned. "To find El Dorado of course."

*

Captain Rodriguez José frowned.

He'd waited nearly two weeks for Felipe and his men to return. He knew that by now they were probably all dead. He should have left them. They weren't supposed to be gone for that long. By now the men would most likely be dead.

Besides, Felipe had taken a third of the men with him. Even if they had been attacked, what was he supposed to do? If the natives had somehow overcome Felipe and his men, then there was nothing he could do about it.

Against his better judgement, he decided to go after them.

He asked for a list of volunteers. Men who were willing to risk their lives to rescue Felipe and his men. In the end, he had twenty-four volunteers. Less than he needed and more than he wanted. Felipe had fifty men and now he was going to attempt a rescue with roughly half of that. Worse still, it left the problem of what would happen to the *Santa Rosa Celeste* if something went wrong? He still needed to leave enough men to protect her and, given the worst-case scenario, someone needed to return to Spain for reinforcements.

In the end, he'd ridden into the jungle with just twenty men.

There was a well-defined trail through the dense forestry of the jungle where Felipe's horses had clearly made their way. About two miles in, José and his party reached the fresh water spring where his crew had first encountered the strange and mythically rich natives. The spring looked like something out of the Garden of Eden. A small blue-green lagoon lay beneath a canopy of jungle foliage. Fresh water bubbled from a nearby spring, flowing out of the ground to feed it on one end, and a slow flowing stream on the other. The forest had been cleared by regular foot-traffic so that one could walk right around the lagoon without difficulty.

José's eyes darted across the lagoon.

He had brought a tracker but didn't think he'd need the man. After all, Felipe had fifty men on horseback – that's a hard thing to hide in a dense jungle. Yet now, there was no sign the horses had ever been there, let alone ridden past the lagoon.

José glanced at his tracker. "Well?"

The tracker's eyes narrowed. He squatted down. "This area has been intentionally swept since the horses were here."

"The natives have tried to conceal the presence of Felipe and his men?"

The tracker shrugged. "It would appear so."

"But the horses… they came up this way, didn't they? I mean, that couldn't have been a ruse, could it?"

"No. I'm confident the horses came this way."

"But you can't see where they went?"

The tracker ran his hands through the surface of the muddy trail. The creases in the man's face deepened, but he didn't answer.

José watched the tracker.

The man's glazed eyes seemed to be taking in the entire place, seeing things that simply weren't there. He was fixated as though he were in a trance. The whole thing lasted more than fifteen minutes.

The tracker turned to him, his lower lip curved upward in a half-grin.

Losing patience, José snarled, "Well, do you see anything?"

The tracker nodded and pointed to a dense section of forest on the opposite end of the lagoon, the side closest to the rising mountain. "Through the doorway, right there."

José sighed with relief.

His eyes darted toward the dense forest where his tracker was pointing. There was a variety of rich evergreens growing so close to make it impossible to walk through, let alone ride fifty horses. "There's a doorway down there?"

The tracker nodded. He walked slowly around the lagoon. José climbed down from his horse and followed him.

The tracker stopped at the hidden doorway.

José frowned. "I don't see anything."

"It's here."

The tracker gripped one of the thick vines that seemed to connect several plants together into one colossal enmeshed piece of forestry.

He pulled on it, but nothing moved.

José said, "Are you sure this is the spot?"

The tracker nodded. "This is it."

He tried a second vine, but it didn't move.

José knelt down and filled his leather flask with water from the spring. He sat down and took a swig of it.

The water was sweet and icy cool.

He leaned back against the rocky ledge behind him, expelled a deep breath and considered his next step, when something moved.

The stone he'd leaned upon was a secret lever.

Gentle vibrations shook the face of the rock-wall and were followed by the sound of heavy machinery making progress. José imagined the series of intricate mechanisms moving within. The finely-toothed wheels of the sprockets inside, turning multiple roller chains, and multiplying the force of his hand more than a hundred-fold, through a succession of complex gear ratios.

The sound finally ceased, and everything was still once more.

And behind the tracker, a large section of the forest, nearly ten feet wide, slowly retracted – revealing a stone trail, carved into the otherwise impenetrable jungle.

*

José and his men rode their horses hard.

Over the course of the next two days they followed the ancient stairway through the jungle, as it zigzagged and jutted in some sort of invisible maze beneath the forest's dense canopy. It was impossible to know how far they had gone, or in what direction for that matter.

Had they simply rounded the mountain ranges, or climbed it?

The question was moot. At the end of the day, there was only one way to go and they had to follow that ancient path wherever it led through the jungle.

And wherever it had taken them in the process, it now led through a small pass between two large rockfaces. The entrance was so narrow that had it not been for the ancient path carved into the rock, they would not have spotted it at all.

The slender opening meant they needed to dismount to walk their horses single file through the entrance. The chasm opened up to a large cave which extended deep into the mountain through a long tunnel.

It was cold and damp, with no light penetrating from above.

José stared at the slight dot of light, like fire, in the distance, suggesting the place opened up on the opposite side of the mountain.

They followed it through and the place opened to the large remnants of an ancient sinkhole.

José had seen them before, but normally from above and never from directly below. He reflected on what he knew about sinkholes, trying to apply it to his surroundings. The sandstone quartzite had most likely been eroded over eons from an underwater river system, before the weight of the rock above became too much, and it all collapsed, leaving a large, sun filled sinkhole. The dry cavern through which they had entered must have been the remnants of that ancient subterranean river system.

They stepped into the opening.

It was a rough circle with a diameter of two hundred feet. His eyes drifted upward. The dense jungle appeared to have continued to grow to form a healthy canopy above. Beams of sunlight dappled through the canopy vegetation and lit the unique world enclosed by sandstone.

Here, they discovered a small village, presumably of the natives who Felipe had traded with for the golden pearls, and a few of the local people went about their daily tasks. One sharpened the head of a spear on deep grooves in the sandstone, another boiled water in a golden pot, while kids played.

The natives looked up at them, startled by their presence, but not aggressive.

The tracker, who had been able to speak parts of their language earlier when they had traded, now spoke to them.

José watched as his tracker talked slowly, making use of hand gestures and drawings of horses in the soil to fill in the gaps. The natives and the tracker exchanged various forms of communication. They all seemed happy, and their body language didn't suggest any harm or concern. Maybe Felipe and his men hadn't been attacked, after all? Maybe they had simply become lost in the impenetrable jungle?

José told his tracker to ask them if they could look around and see if there were any signs of their lost companions.

The chieftain, recognizing José as the leader, smiled and opened the palms of his hands outward in a gracious sign of acceptance.

José nodded back, thanking the man in Spanish.

They searched the strange village. It didn't look dissimilar to the one they had found near the golden lake, all the way up the Magdalena River. There were seventeen houses in total with the largest being in the center. The architecture was nearly identical, with an array of circular structures made of poles of wood and walls of clay, with a conical reed roof. A long beam of wood supported the roof in the center of the round structure and was attached to the wooden poles. The interior of the roof was decorated with cloths with thin strokes of different colors. The only obvious difference being that instead of large wooden poles circulating the village, this one had the protection of a hundred-foot-high sandstone quartzite enclosure.

And although the village might not be made of gold, there was certainly plenty of evidence that gold was plentiful.

The cooking utensils, pots, and knives were all made from gold.

José was about to ask his tracker to find out where the villager had gotten it from when Felipe stumbled into the village.

The man looked exhausted and disheveled, but alive and unharmed.

José asked, "Good God! Felipe, what happened to you and your men?"

Felipe said, "We were attacked."

José arched his eyebrows. "By the natives?"

"No. Something else. Something inhuman. Like a wraith it came at us with such ferocity that no one knew what to do."

"What are you talking about, a ghost killed the rest of your men?"

"Killed?" Felipe shook his head. "No. But whatever it was, it spooked the horses. My men and I were separated and, in the process, *Victory* took a fall and me with him. I must have hit my head in the fall, because I blacked out."

José frowned. "Are you badly injured?"

"No. Just my pride. But when I came to my men were nowhere to be seen." Felipe turned his gaze to meet José's eyes. "I assumed they had returned to the *Santa Rosa Celeste*?"

José shook his head. "Afraid not my friend."

"They're all missing?"

"Yeah. Maybe they got lost trying to find their way back to the ship."

"Unlikely. They were good men. Reliable navigators. They would have found it by now."

"What are you suggesting?"

"I don't know. But I find it hard to believe that any of these natives could have killed fifty men wearing armor on horseback."

"Then what happened to them?"

"I have no idea." Felipe glanced at his surroundings for the first time since entering the sink hole. "What is this place?"

José said, "This is where the natives live. I thought you knew."

"No. I've never been here before. I only stumbled upon it because I came looking for water and then spotted the hoofprints, and assumed I had found my men." Felipe raked the strange world with his greedy eyes. "Did you find the gold?"

"No. There's some, but no more than the Muisca people had. We should go, the *Santa Rosa Celeste* is being defended by little more than a skeleton crew."

"All right." Felipe grinned. "But we will come back with reinforcements. Mark my words, the gold's here… we just have to find it."

José agreed. "We'll head back to the Spanish settlement at Maracaibo, show anyone there a handful of those golden pearls, and we'll have an army eager to return with us."

Felipe nodded as they made their way out of the sinkhole through the dark cave.

They were about to leave through the narrow slot in the rockface when José spotted a kid picking up golden pearls from the floor at the entrance to what appeared to be a mineshaft.

José's men grabbed the native child.

He looked frightened. The tracker tried to question the boy, but the kid refused or was unable to speak.

When José threatened the small boy with his sword, the kid offered his leather bag filled with golden pearls in an attempt to appease the Spanish conquistadors. The captain took it, but then tried to enter the mine.

That's when the kid screamed.

José wasn't discouraged. He didn't have a large army. Just twenty-one men in total, but they were all armed and with the exception of Felipe, all were on horseback. Inside the cave, they could defend themselves against an army for a month. Felipe watched as the tracker held the boy, and then he followed José, and they entered the labyrinthian mine.

Long, narrow tunnels, barely large enough for the men to crawl through followed the quartz seams. The tunnels zigzagged, sometimes raising in elevation and at other times descending steeply. After twenty minutes they found another round piece of gold. This one larger than the last two. But likewise, it had been perfectly smoothed out. Clearly, someone had gone to great lengths to polish it. No stones were naturally so perfect in nature.

José started to pick up the gold, placing it in the already heavy leather pouch he'd been gifted by the child, when he heard the beast.

"What is that?" he asked.

Felipe swallowed. "I don't know what it is, but that's the same sound the creature made that startled the horses."

José's eyes narrowed. "This is your wraith?"

Both men drew their swords.

Whatever it was, it wouldn't get through their swords. Spanish Toledo steel was the strongest in the world. Nothing the natives on the new continent might have built could defend against it. And in the narrow passageway, not even a small child could get through the two blades without being speared.

José's heart raced with anticipation, but he wasn't frightened.

Wraiths were to be feared by children, not men. Besides, whatever was making that sound was clearly alive.

José clutched the leather satchel containing the golden pearls. He was damned if he would lose it in a fight with the strange creature.

A moment later, he spotted the beast.

It was no wraith, but nor was it like anything he'd ever seen. The creature looked like some sort of oversized armadillo – much larger than a fully-grown man – with a leathery armor shell and long sharp claws like a predator's talons.

Its upper lip rose in a snarl and then the creature made a high-pitched trilling sound. It had fiery red eyes which glowed like the devil. A second later, the beast charged at him, its short legs allowing it to run fast like a wraith in the night.

José dropped his bag of golden pearls and used both hands to brace the hilt of his sword.

He opened his mouth to scream…

But he was dead before any sound came out.

*

Felipe watched in horror as the near mythical beast grabbed José and retreated into the mine shaft as fast as it had appeared. It moved at the lightning speed of an overgrown trapdoor spider attacking. A predator, disappearing with its prey in the blink of an eye.

There was nothing he could do.

He grabbed the leather satchel, filled with gold. It was heavy, but there was no chance in hell he was going to come all this way just to leave the gold where it was. The gold inside was enough to justify the expedition without even taking into account what they would discover when they returned with a large army.

Felipe turned and raced as fast as he could out of the mine shaft.

Outside the mineshaft the men waited and watered their horses in the nearby creek that ran along the cavern.

Felipe burst into the main cavern. "Run!"

It took a second for anyone to react. Then, swords were drawn, but no enemy was in sight.

The tracker asked, "What is it? What happened to José?"

"He's dead! A strange beast took him."

The tracker raised his eyebrows. "A beast?"

Felipe lifted his sword. "It was some sort of tunneling creature, with armored skin like an armadillo, and razor-sharp talons. This isn't a mine shaft! I'm certain that damned beast made it."

"It's solid rock!" the tracker protested. "No animals dig their burrows in solid rock."

Felipe was about to argue the point when the tracker fell backward, smashing his face on the rocky ground.

An instant later, he saw the cause.

The native people, upon hearing the beast's trilling sound, had all gathered and banded together near the cave's entrance.

They were using slingshots, poison darts, and spears.

A single stone had struck the tracker on the side of his temple. Felipe glanced at the man. He was lying perfectly still, his chest was no longer raising or falling. The slingshot was a popular weapon of choice among many of the ancient tribes of the New World, but he'd never seen them work such devastation before.

Next to the tracker's bloodied head, was a single gold pearl. Its weight must have amplified the weapon's force, turning it as deadly as musket shot, and probably more accurate.

They killed him with a single stone!

Felipe shouted, "Everyone out!"

The men tried to climb onto their horses, hacking away at the natives with their swords. Blood rained from the clash of weapons. The Spanish conquistadors were better equipped and wore expensive plate armor made from Toledo steel, but they were outnumbered by the previously peaceful inhabitants of the village, who were now stirred into a violent frenzy like Viking Berserkers, driven by a higher power for revenge.

Felipe ducked behind one of the horses, using it for protection, and made his way toward the entrance. A mesh of warriors drifted toward the opening into the jungle. As they reached the narrow section at the entrance, they bottlenecked, and their movements slowed to a standstill. The creek that trickled through the ancient waterway which had once formed the tunnel, now flowed red – where blood mingled from both conquistador and villagers alike.

He tried to climb onto a horse, but a villager threw a spear into the animal's chest and the beast fell to the ground as soon as Felipe pulled on the saddle.

Three conquistadors tried to force their way through the barricade using their powerful warhorses.

The first two horses were pulled down by the villagers and the third rider was killed by a slingshot. Felipe's eyes took in the battle at a glance. They were being beaten. Trapped inside the cave, they had taken a defensive stance, using horses and shields to protect themselves, but they could never hold it.

Felipe watched the last rider get knocked off his horse by a club.

He didn't wait to see if the rider was alive.

Instead, driven mad by his desire to survive, he clambered onto the horse, kicked it hard – and galloped through the remaining barricade of natives, through the narrow opening in the cave, and out into the jungle.

He didn't check to see if the villagers were following.

Felipe didn't need to entice the warhorse. After the ambush the horse wanted to get away as fast as possible, too. Felipe gripped the reins and tried his best not to fall off.

They continued riding as fast as the warhorse dared until they reached the *Santa Rosa Celeste*.

Felipe informed the crew of the attack, and lied that there were no other survivors. He showed them the bag of golden pearls and promised to return with an army. Within minutes of reaching the ship, they set sail with no more than a skeleton crew.

The Santa Rosa Celeste followed the coast, heading east, toward the nearest settlement at Maracaibo. Two days into the sail they were met by a large fleet of Spanish ships heading west.

They heaved to and Felipe talked to the commander of the fleet, a man named, Gonzalo Jiménez de Quesada.

De Quesada said that he was heading down the Magdalena in search of the fabled golden city and that he was leading an army to make claim to the land.

Keen to send the treasure hunter off on a tangent as far away from the golden city as possible, Felipe told the man about El Hombre El Dorado – the golden man – who he'd seen in the lake, where the Muisca people discarded gold. For further proof, he handed De Quesada a single golden pearl and descriptions of the location of the golden lake.

De Quesada eyed him cautiously. At a glance, his face registered doubt. After all, if Felipe had indeed found the golden city, why was he telling him at all? De Quesada said, "Don't you want to lay claim to the gold yourself?"

"No. We already tried that. It cost me more than two thirds of my crew and the captain of this ship." Felipe smiled. "I have enough gold to more than recompense my crew and myself for the expedition. I'm an old man. I have family in Spain I'd like to see. Good luck to you."

De Quesada shook his hand warmly. "Thank you and congratulations."

"On finding El Dorado?" Felipe asked.

"No. On knowing when you have enough gold to live out the rest of your existence in comfort and in happiness. Wise men, given the same situation, have failed to see reason, and have instead, risked their lives and died in the name of greed. Good for you. Where are you heading, surely you must not be trying to cross the Atlantic with just a skeleton crew?"

"No, we're heading for Maracaibo. I was hoping to find enough men to help crew the *Santa Rosa Celeste* home to Spain."

"Then I'm afraid you will be waiting a while."

"Really? Why?"

"The settlement at Maracaibo has been deserted for nearly six months now. I thought you would have heard?"

"About what?"

"They were attacked and the settlement disbanded."

Felipe frowned. He knew several good men who had been living there. "Do you know where the next permanent settlement is that we might find crew to return to Spain?"

De Quesada answered without hesitation. "São Vicente."

Felipe took a deep breath. It was a long journey for a skeleton crew, but what other choice did they have? They couldn't hand over El Dorado to De Quesada. He nodded. "All right, São Vicente it is."

They wished each other good fortunes, and went in opposite directions.

Over the course of the next week the *Santa Rosa Celeste* slowly made its way east and then south along the coastline of the New World.

Felipe was starting to feel good about his chances.

He'd spent the afternoon making drawings of the strange beast that only he had seen. As he recollected on what he'd witnessed inside the tunnels of El Dorado, Felipe found himself second guessing his memories.

When he was finished, Felipe stared at the drawings. What are you?

He hadn't told anyone about the strange creature. What would he say? An oversized armadillo, with body armor impervious to Toledo steel and tunneled through solid stone, had snatched José and what... devoured him like an oversized predator?

Felipe dismissed the thought.

Instead, he headed all the way down into the lowest deck of the *Santa Rosa Celeste* and secured the drawings in the ship's treasure chest.

He carefully locked the drawings inside and smiled.

It wouldn't be long now and they would reach São Vicente.

Felipe knew that all his dreams were about to come true.

Until he heard a loud bang... where the repairs to the hull had failed...

And all his dreams were about to be shattered.

*

They had to make landfall.

There was no question of continuing on until they reached São Vicente.

The repairs hadn't set properly. They were pumping water, but with a skeleton crew, it wouldn't be enough to keep them afloat much longer.

A typical three-masted carrack had six sails: bowsprit, foresail, mainsail, mizzen sail and two topsails. But with the limited crew they had left, only the bowsprit, foresail, and mizzen sail had been set, meaning the *Celeste* was struggling to achieve six knots. At that speed, they would never reach São Vicente while the *Celeste* was still afloat.

In an uncivilized, unmapped section of the South American coast, Felipe hated the idea of making landfall to make repairs, but there was no other option. It was risky, but they had to try. So, with a heavy heart, he ordered the ship brought into the mouth of a large, unnamed river.

There was a large sandy bay in the shape of a half-crescent, surrounded by thick jungle, with mountains in the distance.

Felipe ordered the *Santa Rosa Celeste* up the river which carved its way through the foreign land. It was dark along the river, and there was a strange sense of evil as the trees encroached on the river, constricting the last of the sunlight from penetrating.

He felt uneasy as they anchored next to a sandbar in the deep water along the oxbow of the river, roughly a mile upriver from the bay.

A small team of men went to shore to fell the trees needed to make the repairs.

What remained of the skeleton crew manned the pumps and carried buckets, trying to keep the ship afloat until the repairs could be made.

Six hours later, the *Santa Rosa Celeste* swung round on its anchor, marking the change of tide.

Felipe watched as a large crocodile entered the water.

His gaze traced the massive reptile as it swam toward the opposite shore. Its yellow eyes seemed fixated on something, but Felipe couldn't make out what it was.

Felipe's eyes narrowed as he realized there were native people on the opposite bank of the river. They wore a simple leather loincloth and nothing above their waists, including the women, who carried their children.

A moment later he heard voices coming from the men in the jungle. "We're being attacked!"

The next few events unfolded faster than Felipe could have ever imagined.

Men with bows and arrows fired at any on the deck of the *Santa Rosa Celeste.*

Felipe used an axe to cut the anchor rope.

The tide was coming in and the wind was running from the seas, using the channel of the river as a funnel to focus the wind. There was no way they could sail out under these conditions. Their only hope was to sail farther upriver.

He and the last few men aboard hoisted the foresail.

The sail billowed as it caught wind and the *Celeste* pulled away from the deadly oxbow bend.

The tribal warriors, undeterred, clambered into their dugout canoes and quickly followed them. The men onboard the *Celeste* fired musket shots at their attackers, but they were too abundant.

Felipe knew in an instant that the *Santa Rosa Celeste* was never getting out of that river. The crew would never survive. Maybe they could keep the natives from boarding for some time, but soon their sheer numbers would overcome them.

But perhaps he didn't have to die?

He was nothing if not a survivor. Greedy and selfish, loyal only to gold and the power it brought. Felipe entered the aft castle, and descended three decks to where the treasure chest was located. He quickly opened the locked chest and retrieved the leather satchel of golden pearls, leaving the drawings of the near mythical beast he'd seen in the mine inside the chest.

He closed the chest and locked it again out of habit.

Felipe, armed with an arquebus ran to the forecastle. He rushed into his cabin and frantically searched for a blow-gun he'd taken as a souvenir from one of the Muisca people he'd killed. The weapon consisted of a three-foot-long hollowed out reed, through which a poison dart could be projected.

His plan was to jump overboard, and use the hollowed reed as a breathing pipe, while he waited for his attackers to pass.

It was a good plan.

And it would have worked.

Except that he was struck by an arrow as soon as he reached the deck. The arrow pierced his right shoulder.

Felipe yelled and it hurt like hell, but it wasn't fatal.

He fired the arquebus at the closest tribal warrior. The shot struck the man in the chest, killing him instantly.

He searched for the rest of his crew.

But they were all dead.

He was all alone.

And already there were more than a dozen tribal warriors on board.

His heart thumped in the back of his head. His hands shook. Holding onto the bag of golden pearls, he tried to bribe the natives.

A man with a painted face and a large knife examined the bag with minor interest, before knocking it out of Felipe's hand, where the golden pearls spilled across the deck.

Felipe's voice stumbled, but he said, "They're yours! I give them to you, as a gift!"

The warrior didn't seem to understand or care.

Instead, the warrior drove the blade straight into Felipe's gut. The warrior removed part of one of his organs, grinned, and immediately took a bite of it.

Afterward, the tribesmen disembarked.

Choking on blood and struggling to breathe, Felipe watched in horror as the *Santa Rosa Celeste* continued sailing up the unnamed river, nothing more than a ghost ship – taking with it, all knowledge of the existence of El Dorado.

Chapter One

**Butterbox Canyon – Blue Mountains, Australia –
Present Day**

They arrived in the early morning, shortly after dawn as
the Australian heat baked off the chill of the night in a sunrise
filled with blues, reds, and ochre. They had parked the Toyota
Landcruiser in the open parking lot at the end of the fire-trail
and unpacked their gear, before making the long trek into the
entrance of the canyon. Once there, they worked their way
through the main slot of the ancient canyon, opened from
millions of years of water slicing through the thin skins of
stone, until they reached the first of the vertical descents.

Nathan Sanchez carefully zipped up his full body
wetsuit.

It was a sort of obligatory ritual. He connected the chin
strap to his helmet, slowly slid each leg through his climbing
harness, tightened the belt, and fed the safety cord back in on
itself to be certain. After all, his life depended on it. He then
fed the static canyoning rope through the two steel ring bolts
permanently fixed into the sandstone along the canyon wall.
He took a bite out of the doubled rope, forming a small loop,
and attached it to the figure eight descender. With his thumb
and forefinger, he rotated the locking mechanism on the
carabiner until it was locked shut.

At five foot ten, with a wiry and muscular build, Nathan
Sanchez was the fittest he'd ever been in his life. He had dark
hair, olive skin which betrayed his Spanish heritage, and
intelligent dark brown eyes that scanned the entrance to the
first abseil into the canyon.

This was how he'd spent the past two years of his life, offering private tours of some of the world's most remote and exotic locations – caving in Madrid, blackwater rafting in New Zealand, rock climbing in Yosemite, cave diving in the Mexican Cenotes, and now, canyoning in the Blue Mountains.

It was a good life.

He sometimes wondered if it was time he grew up and got a real job.

Listening to the trickle of water as it slowly carved a rift into the sandstone, continuing to deepen the canyon that had taken millions of years to form, and preparing to enter a world unchanged since the dinosaurs, Nathan shook his head emphatically. He could get a real job when he was old. Right now, this was what living was all about.

Nathan took a final inspection of his equipment set up and knew with certainty that he was ready to go.

He switched on his helmet flashlight, gave a curt nod to his client, grinned, and said, "I'll see you on the other side."

Churn nodded. He'd been through the routine more than a dozen times with Nathan over the previous week and was becoming a formidable canyoner in his own right, despite paying a small fortune for the private tour of all the main canyons. He grinned. "You'd better."

Nathan's eyes glanced up, taking in the sun-soaked, dry heat of the Australian summer. His eyes traced the movement of the icy cold stream as it filtered along the sandstone, before disappearing down the narrow chasm into the pitch-black void. He leaned back, released the pressure on the twin abseiling ropes, and descended into the dark canyon below.

The piercing blue sky inverted into solid rock.

Nathan Sanchez swung beneath the lip of the cave, descending quickly through the narrow constriction, exchanging the dry, hot world above, for the frigid confines beneath the Earth. Icy water slammed into his face and onto his back, taking the breath from his lungs. What appeared to be little more than a trickle of water from above, now turned into a thunderous roar, as its sound amplified within the narrow confines.

He released the pressure on his right braking hand, and the double ropes quickly slid through, as he descended roughly sixty feet.

The thunderous roar of the waterfall filled his ears.

His fingers gently tightened across the rope, bringing himself to a complete stop. He swung to the left on the chockstone – a large sandstone rock, wedged between either side of the narrow canyon wall, forming a natural platform to stop.

Nathan secured himself to the twin ring bolts next to the chockstone with a PAS – personal anchorage system – and tugged twice on the rope, signaling to his client that he was off the rope, and now he could come down.

He watched as Churn rappelled with the speed and dexterity of a seasoned expert.

The sight added to the man's mystery. He was an anomaly. Nathan had been told that Churn had come to Sydney to confirm the validity of an old family legend that had been in his family for generations. But when questioned about what he might find in an old canyon, the Chinese man had bridled and clammed shut. Since then, they had trekked through a multitude of canyons every day, carrying heavy geological surveying equipment, including ground penetrating radar and sonar, yet still he'd refused to say what he was looking for.

Not that it really mattered to Nathan.

What did matter was the fact that the man was well financed.

It started to make Nathan wonder if the man knew something about an old gold mine. Perhaps his great grandparents had come out on the old gold rush? It was surprisingly common during the 19th Century rush for Chinese people to flock to the country in search of gold. Maybe they had found gold within a canyon, but had never made it home to strike a claim? Maybe he had a map of an old canyon filled with gold. Who knows? One thing was certain, he wasn't going to tell him anything about it.

In fact, on the few times Nathan had tried to question Churn about it, the man's eyes had flashed with anger, and the man had shut him down. More than that, something about the man's façade became removed, and what was left appeared to be a dangerous man. Nathan could imagine the man being an enforcer for an organized crime cartel, or a fixer for a rich unscrupulous boss, willing to do anything to get the job done.

Of course, none of these possibilities went any further to explain why someone would spend a fortune searching remote canyons that were millions of years old. In the end, it didn't matter to Nathan. What did he care if one of his clients wanted to spend a small fortune searching for gold in a remote region of the Australian Outback, searching for gold that most likely had never existed? Or, if it had, he'd sure as hell never heard about it in all the time he'd been guiding in the region.

Churn squeezed the brake hand, arresting his descent, while simultaneously kicking off the rocky ledge to reach the chockstone.

The man had swung short of his desired outcome, and like a pendulum had started his return swing. He slammed his back hard against solid rock in the darkness.

Nathan made an involuntary grimace. It looked painful. Churn didn't make a sound. For a second, Nathan thought the man might have knocked himself out, but he started to run along the canyon wall again, trying to make the swing.

This time he got close, but missed the chockstone by inches.

Nathan leaned out and caught Churn's outstretched hand, pulling him in immediately and clipping his PAS to the ringbolts.

Churn was breathing hard, but said nothing.

Nathan said, "Are you okay?"

Churn nodded. "Fine. Let's keep going."

Nathan saw fear in the man's eyes, but a hardened resolve in his face. And why not? Anyone perched on a ledge barely wide enough for two men to stand side by side, and more than sixty feet from the rocky ground below, with the constant threat of flood waters raging overhead killing them instantly, needed to be afraid. Those who weren't were delusional or insane.

Nathan fed the bottom of the rope through the new anchoring system, pulled the rope through, and prepared the final rappel. He secured the rope to through the twin ringbolts and then repeated his earlier actions until he'd rappelled all the way to the icy water below.

From there, he waited for Churn to complete the abseil, coiled the rope and made the hundred-and-fifty something odd foot swim out through the flooded cave and into the opening along the valley floor.

They'd hit the bottom of the canyon.

His client made the same thorough exploration he'd done in every other canyon they'd seen, methodically unpacking the LIDAR scopes and radar equipment. Nathan had thought he knew his way around geological equipment; he'd been around rocks and canyons all his life. But he'd never seen anything like the maps this man produced. He had felt like he was in a sci-fi film the first time Churn had shot the LIDAR laser at the ground to measure the reflected pulses with the sensor, making detailed 3D maps of the canyon.

Churn swept the targeted area relentlessly, leaving no trace unseen. He did the same thing with ground penetrating radar. And the same thing with sonar. He reminded Nathan of a hunter stalking a nervous prey, one he desperately wanted. But what could he possibly be hunting that lived beneath the canyon floors?

Sitting on a dry sandstone boulder, enjoying the blistering rays of sunshine, Nathan watched as his client set up what appeared to be expensive geological surveying equipment, installing it onto a purpose-built floatation device, which he then slowly pulled through the water, as though searching for something hidden in its deepest recesses.

Nathan grinned as he watched the man work.

There was something about him that reminded Nathan of a Pitbull. He was solid and muscular, his face set with mulish obstinacy. His mind was sharp, too. The man professed to have never abseiled before, but he picked it up quickly, performing the skill with military precision.

Churn made a couple laps of the deep pool of water, before exchanging his floating surveying equipment for a type of sampling anchor, which he used to lower into the water and retrieve samples of the soil at the bottom of the canyon. He took several samples and then returned to the shore, where he ran the samples through the precious metal analysis machine and waited.

Nathan watched the man work and grinned. It was like watching a treasure hunter search for gold using a metal detector – the likelihood of any real success was practically non-existent, but all the same, the hunter's eyes were riveted with greed.

He swallowed. The only difference here, was he still didn't have a clue what his client was searching for.

Only that he'd been paid a fortune to help find it.

When Churn was finished, Nathan asked, "Any luck?"

"What?" Churn replied, his face unreadable.

Nathan smiled. "Did you find what you were looking for?"

Churn shook his head. "No. Are there anymore pools of water like this one, farther down?"

"No. The canyon opens up into the Grose River."

Churn frowned. "Where do we go from here?"

Nathan pointed toward a small ledge, roughly three hundred feet up the sandstone cliff behind them. "There's a narrow pass over there."

Churn squinted. "It looks steep."

"Yeah, there's an exposed ledge, followed by a forty-five-foot rock climb."

"That's the only way out?"

"Afraid so."

Churn turned his narrow gaze to Nathan. "So that's it then?"

Nathan wiped his sweat, hiding his irritation. "That's it, sir. We've descended every last canyon in the area…"

Churn's lips thinned. Despite the exertion, he maintained an Eastern cool Nathan envied, and made him wonder what the man did on his days off that kept him so cold. "So that's it. The expedition has been a failure?"

Nathan said, "Hey, if you want to tell me what you're really looking for, I might be able to help you find it?"

"I doubt it. No, if that's it, I guess there's only one thing left to do." Churn' s hand drifted to his pocket with the lazy certainty of a hired hit man.

Nathan watched it, terrified.

Then Churn pulled out a granola bar, opened it with surgical precision, and ate half in one bite.

Nathan wiped his hands on his pants, trying to calm his nerves. The whisking of the Tyvek was loud in the quiet of water the trickle, and it made him jumpy. "There is still one more place to try..."

The man's eyes zeroed in like a snake. There were no granola crumbs. "Where's that?"

Nathan pulled his collar from his throat in the building heat of the morning. "It's called Claustral Canyon – and it's as beautiful as it is deadly."

Chapter Two

Ubatuba, Brazil

The world outside was a wall of water.

Torrential rain streamed down the windows, obliterating the shining streets and the mountainous forests in the distance. The city vendors raced to close up their umbrellaed carts, just blurs of color beyond the streaming glass. Locals drove boats through the flooded streets. The rain had come out of nowhere and had fallen so fast that the drainage system couldn't keep up.

Inside the warm glow of the small cafe, safe from the tempest, Sam Reilly touched the handle of his cafe de leche and smiled at the woman sitting across from him. She had blonde hair, intelligent gray eyes, and an impish smile that looked like it was in a permanent state of being restrained. The woman was strikingly beautiful. "Nice day for a picnic."

Catarina Marcello smiled back. "I'm sorry. We should have gone yesterday."

Beyond the rain, the green of the city's parks sulked, heavy and wet. He and Catarina had been planning on exploring the city's vast natural park, but the weather gods had other plans.

He squeezed her hand affectionately. "You were working."

"I had finished giving my speech on memory databanks two days ago. I promised you a vacation. I just got caught up listening to a German researcher's discussion on synthetic neuron development."

Sam said, "Sounds riveting."

"Hey, I've listened to some of your long stories…"

Sam took a sip of his hot drink and put it back down on the table. "I'm kidding. I like to hear you talk. You're so passionate about your work, I can't help but want to listen to you. Besides, you've piqued my interest now, what are people planning to do with these artificially grown neurons?"

She arched an eyebrow. Skeptically, she said, "Seriously? You want me to explain it to you?"

"Sure, why not?"

"For a starter, people with brighter minds than you, who have dedicated their lives to neurosciences, still struggle to grasp some of these concepts…"

"You don't think I'm smart enough?"

"I didn't say that…"

"Good. Because in my experience, most people can learn anything, given the right teacher."

She grinned. "And you think I'm the right teacher for you?"

"You bet."

"All right."

Sam leaned back in the chair and asked, "So why are they growing artificial neurons?"

"Somewhere in the future the flow on technology being developed will likely help people who have permanently damaged part of their brains, such as those who have had a stroke, or even those who have severed part of their spinal cord. But that wasn't why expensive grants were given to universities all around the world to produce artificial neurons."

Sam nodded. "Obviously. So what do we need them for currently?"

"Computer chips."

"Computer chips," Sam repeated, his face skeptical. "Why?"

"The need for speed. You see, superconducting computing chips modelled after neurons can process information faster and more efficiently than the human brain."

"We're doing this research to power AI?"

"Ah ha… Artificial intelligence software has increasingly begun to imitate the brain. Algorithms such as Google's automatic image-classification and language-learning programs use networks of artificial neurons to perform complex tasks. But because conventional computer hardware was not designed to run brain-like algorithms, these machine-learning tasks require orders of magnitude of more computing power than the human brain possesses."

"Why does this sound scary to me?"

"Because it is scary. What they're doing is creating super computers, powered by artificial intelligence, that uses biomimicry to develop human neurons and the biological pathway of human brains."

"They're going to rewrite humanity out of existence!"

Catarina smiled. "They're a fair way off doing that, but one day it's a question someone's going to need to ask."

Sam's eyes narrowed. "What's your particular interest in it?"

Her lips parted into a smile, and Sam thought he could listen to her talk forever when she got like this. She was in her element, talking about a field of her expertise, and a topic that she loved. "For me, I've spent my adult life trying to map out how the human brain stores data. Imagine the opportunities for human and artificial integration?"

"Cyborgs?"

"Technically, yes. But not like the science fiction films might have you believe. Instead, I'm talking about repairing a brain after trauma or degenerative disease. Imagine giving someone the gift of their memories after spending years suffering with Alzheimer's disease?"

Sam grinned. "Having recently lost some of my memory, I'm in a uniquely capable position to understand how good that would be."

She smiled, bemused. "How is your memory doing?"

"Fine. I'm back to normal. Like you said, it would most likely all come back to me eventually."

She folded her arms across her lap. "Everything? Even the day that it happened?"

"No. That's remained nothing more than a blur. It's like watching a movie and someone deleted a single scene. It's not perfect, but at least it's only a small part of the film."

Catarina laughed. "Your life in film… what an adventure, hey?"

Sam bit his lower lip and suppressed his grin. "Some adventure…"

His cell phone rang.

He picked it up, spoke to the person for a minute, and ended the call.

Catarina met his eye. "What is it?"

"That was Elise. She says the storm has damaged the Ubuntu Airport."

"How bad is it?"

"It will be another week at least before the airport's been repaired and commercial flights are reinstated."

Catrina's lips curved into a lascivious grin. "We might just get that romantic vacation I promised, after all."

Chapter Three

The next morning Sam and Catarina emerged from the Praia Grande hotel after the breakfast of croissants and coffee straight into hell. The city looked like a war zone. Power lines sagged in the flat gray sky, huge branches lay cracked and jagged over the streets. Signs and awnings ripped from their moorings flapped like the wings of broken birds. The Rio Itamambuca, the river that wound through the heart of the city, had flooded, wreaking havoc. Vendors and city workers shouted as they attempted to salvage their livelihoods.

Sam and Catarina wandered along the ravaged river bank through the struggling city until they emerged at the delta near the sea. They were confronted with a sight not uncommon in Brazil, but less common in the pristine paradise of Ubatuba – a mountain of trash. Millions of tons of debris had been swept down the raging torrent yesterday, only to be deposited by the buildup of a sand bar and their own inertia. Downed trees, grills, broken benches and tables, bicycles, shoes... Sam saw a straggling cat climb on top of a rusted oil drum, leap to a bent sign post, and scamper away.

Together he and Catarina strolled the beach along the carnage, an odd boundary to the wild, open sea. He squinted into the blinding gray sky.

Far in the distance other figures combed the beach with the timing of disasters everywhere. "And the vultures descend."

Catarina laughed. "And you're different?"

Sam suppressed a smile. "I'm a treasure hunter."

They combed the beach for almost an hour, setting aside trinkets. But it was more a way to spend time together than any real desire to plunder. As Sam stooped and bent, he watched Catarina in her green dress and sandals, hair a riot in the damp air.

A piece of wood sticking out of the sand bar caught his eye.

The grain was dark and looked like it had been in the water for a very long time. He pulled on it, slowly working it back and forth until the sand relinquished it, abruptly, causing Sam to fall backward.

Catarina attempted to suppress her laugh. "You okay?"

Sam bit his lower lip and smiled. "Yeah, never better."

"What did you find?"

He shrugged. "I don't know. Some old placard… possibly from a ship?"

Sam scraped some debris off the piece of wood idly. It looked like a boat transom, and he wondered idly at the luck of its owner. Last night was no night to be on the open sea.

Catarina headed over, seeing what he was doing. She smiled at him, the smile that had started everything.

Sam smiled back. "We all take life for granted, don't we? And then, in one instant, it can all…"

Sam frowned and cleared the debris further.

The words "*SA CELESTE*" emerged in faded, chipped paint.

"No," Sam said, cutting himself off. "It has to be a coincidence."

Catarina blinked, then leaned over. "What does?"

Sam swept further, clearing the whole piece of wood now. It was large, and looked like it could have been the width of a boat's stern.

The antique letters, *SANTA ROSA CELESTE* watched him regally.

They were faint and barely legible, but they were there.

Was it possible?

Sam squinted into the sea. He always thought better around water. That would mean the *Santa Rosa Celeste* had survived. If it had gotten away from Colombia… what if a storm forced them to take refuge on the big river? They weren't expecting the storm, they expected to be safe… but they'd underestimated the power of the weather, didn't know the navigation of the inland waterways… and got stuck – maybe killed because of it.

Sam turned to Catarina. "Don't you see the importance of this!"

Catarina suppressed a smile and leaned back, folding her arms. "Ah, no. All of that deduction went on in your head, Dr. Jones." She peered at the words. "What is it? The name plate for some Spanish boat?"

Sam waved her off. "First off… it's called a transom, where ships traditionally display their name, and not a name plate…" She rolled her eyes and he pulled his focus back to the discovery. Catarina Marcello was the only woman he knew who was beautiful, even when she was sarcastic. "And it wasn't just any Spanish vessel. That's the *Santa Rosa Celeste!*"

Catarina stared at him in silence, her face set with vacant recognition. One slender brow rose.

Now it was Sam who rolled his eyes. "As in the ship that carried the last Spanish Conquistadors to ever lay eyes on El Dorado!"

She laughed. "I'm sorry, Sam. Shipwrecks, dead king's expensive toys… Secret treasure maps are more your kind of thing. I'm more interested in the ancient maps of the human mind."

Sam grinned. "Then this might interest you. The *Santa Rosa Celeste* was sent to investigate the existence of El Hombre Dorado – The Golden Man."

The intelligence he loved sparked behind her eyes. "They were looking for a man?"

"No. By the time the *Santa Rosa Celeste* joined the expedition, the European conquerors no longer believed in the man. Instead, El Dorado had become synonymous with an elusive city of gold."

"Which they obviously never found." Off his silence, she frowned. "Did they?" She swiped at his suspense. "What did they find?"

"The crew of the *Celeste* traded with the local tribal people in what was most likely modern-day Bogotá in the Colombian Andes. The Muisca people – again, the most likely first people who lived in the region at the time, who lived in the mountain tops at the tip of present-day Colombia…" Sam paused for dramatic effect.

Catarina wasn't buying it. "And?"

"The local people exchanged small nuggets and trinkets of solid gold for iron nails. The crew kept asking where they were getting the gold, but the local tribespeople refused to say, telling them that it was forbidden to talk about."

Catarina arched her eyebrows. "Forbidden?"

Sam turned the palms of his hands skyward. "Hey, I'm just telling you the story that I've heard."

"What you know could fill books, Sam… probably fictional, over-the-top adventure books… but hey, they'd probably sell all right? I sometimes wonder if there's any truth to your stories."

Sam bridled. "Hey…"

She waved her hand. "Go on. What happened next?"

Sam set his voice low and steady, as though he were telling a campfire ghost story. "Legend has it, the crew followed some of the local people back to El Dorado, a city made of solid gold."

Catarina rolled her eyes. "Solid gold?"

He shrugged. "Hey, people like to embellish these things. The conquistadors probably just meant the local people had so many golden trinkets that it felt like the place was made of gold."

"Go on. So what happened to all that gold the conquistadors found?"

"Nobody knows for certain. Apparently, it was loaded onto the *Santa Rosa Celeste*, where it set sail for its home port in Spain."

Catarina leveled her eyes at him. Her lips were set in a wry grin, and her intelligent face plastered with doubt. "There's just one fault with your story?"

"Oh… just one, that's not too bad," he said. "What don't you believe, the fact there was a city made of solid gold, or that, having found it, no one has ever been able to locate it again in the past six centuries?"

"Those are good points too," she admitted. "But no, I was referring to the fact that if the crew of the *Santa Rosa Celeste* were the only ones to ever lay eyes on the hidden city and they were lost at sea somewhere between Colombia and Spain, how did anyone ever hear of the legend? Do you have an explanation for that?"

"Gonzalo Jiménez de Quesada," Sam said flatly.

Catarina made a bemused smile. Her face studying him with an expression of mixed curiosity and professional interest that he figured she generally reserved for the patients she was assessing. "And who would that be?"

Sam grinned. "In 1536 De Quesada commanded an expedition to explore the interior of New Granada – modern day Colombia – hoping to discover the location of El Dorado."

"Why?"

Sam's eyes widened. "Because in 1535 De Quesada's fleet pulled alongside the *Santa Rosa Celeste*, which at that time was slowly making its way east along the northern coast of South America, on its way back to Spain."

Her eyes narrowed. "De Quesada talked to the crew of the *Celeste*?"

"Yes. He spoke to its expedition leader, a man named Felipe Ferdinand. He informed De Quesada that the crew had found El Dorado. He even gave De Quesada a map and small golden pearl as evidence of the vast gold supplies."

"Why on Earth would he do that?"

"Why not keep it secret, you mean?"

"Exactly."

Sam shrugged. "Apparently, the *Celeste* was running on a skeleton crew. Ferdinand explained that on their way home they had struck a reef and needed to pull into the coast to make repairs."

She arched her eyebrow, finally drawn into the story. "Go on…"

Sam said, "The repairs were made, but at a high cost. An unknown tribe in the region had taken a certain disliking to Ferdinand's crew cutting down trees to make repairs and had attacked. Ferdinand and his men won the battle, but he'd lost nearly two thirds of his men in the process by the time the *Celeste* was underway at sea again."

Catarina set her jaw firm. "So why not return to Spain, gather more men for a second expedition, and return to claim the rewards of El Dorado?"

Sam's lips turned into a half-grin at her mercenary viewpoint. "Why didn't he keep El Dorado a secret?"

"Exactly. It's like winning the lottery and then handing over a map to where you hid your ticket. It wouldn't happen."

"No. Unless you thought you were about to lose your ticket anyway, and so you reached out for the only help you could get."

She suppressed a smile. "You think Ferdinand was reaching out to De Quesada?"

Sam nodded. "I think De Quesada was already on his way into the heart of New Granada and it was only a matter of time before he reached El Dorado. The man had a small fleet of six ships and more than nine hundred men. In contrast, Ferdinand had less than thirty men, and was on his way across the Atlantic. It could have taken him more than a year to establish funds to mount a second expedition."

"So he cut De Quesada in on the deal."

"Yes. The story goes that, on his deathbed, De Quesada admitted to signing a deal with Ferdinand, agreeing to give him a percentage of the gold retrieved when they took El Dorado."

Catarina said, "But they never did…"

"No, which means, Felipe Ferdinand lied. The question is, did he lie because El Dorado was nothing more than an elusive myth? Or, did he lie because he knew the truth about its hidden location, and, worried that De Quesada was close to finding it on his own, Ferdinand sent him on a wild goose chase?"

Catarina smiled. "And no one knows what happened to the *Santa Rosa Celeste*?"

Sam grinned. "No one knows. The ship never reached Spain. It was presumed shipwrecked and sunk. There have been nearly as many searches for the *Celeste* as there have been for El Dorado."

"And none of them provided any answers?"

"No. There's a lot of water between Colombia and Spain. The ship could be anywhere out there. I always thought they'd at least cleared the coast of South America and probably sunk out in the Atlantic, but now…"

"You think the *Celeste* is out there, shipwrecked somewhere in the Ubatuba Bay?"

Sam shook his head. His blue eyes widened, excitement burning in him like fire. "No. Not out there."

She allowed her lips to crease upward in a half-smile. "Where then?"

Sam gestured to the still-raging river, spilling out across the delta like some vengeful god from the tangled woods beyond. "Somewhere up the Rio Itamambuca."

Chapter Four

Sam watched Catarina's eyes drift across the Ubatuba Bay, across the river that penetrated the jungle, before settling on him.

She said, "You think the *Santa Rosa Celeste* made it up the river?"

He gestured to the river, sweeping his hand across the path of debris. "Don't you see? The river overflowed during the storm. It flowed downriver, where it naturally wanted to go. If the transom had gotten this far, it had to come from somewhere. Who knows what that water knocked loose? The ship itself must be somewhere, and that somewhere… must be upstream."

Catarina followed his gaze, her beautiful face closed. But she was a scientist and she liked problem solving as much as he did. "If a large conquistador's ship had indeed floundered somewhere up the river, wouldn't someone have noticed by now?"

Sam thought about that for a second. "Not necessarily."

"Why not?"

"Because there's a lot of river and even more jungle for it to become lost in."

She smiled. "And there's been a long time for someone to stumble across it. I mean, we're talking centuries…"

"Sure, but let's consider for a moment, if the *Celeste* did become grounded, or sunk somewhere upriver, it might have been buried or lost in an unmapped deep section of the river – of which, the Rio Itamambuca has plenty."

"So what changed today?"

"The storm brought it up."

Catarina wasn't going to accept that so easily. "Are you saying in the last five centuries there hasn't been a storm like this?"

Sam bit his lower lip, shrugged. "No. Of course not. Ubatuba is known for its heavy rains. That said, hunting lost treasure ships is a unique art and far from a science. Sometimes a ship simply relinquishes her secrets when she's ready..."

Catarina laughed. "You think the *Santa Rosa Celeste,* after waiting all this time, has finally decided to release her secrets?"

"Sure. Why not? It probably just knew I would be here, waiting around, looking for something fun to do."

"Like hunt for the lost treasures of El Dorado?"

He smiled. "Hey, even you said it was time I got back into doing what I normally do. You said doing routine, regular activities from my past, might help fill in any gaps I still have in my memory."

"First off... your memory is already performing better than most! Second, when I told you it was time to return to routine activities to improve your cognitive function and memory, I was thinking about you returning to the *Tahila* and working with your crew again, in whatever function and performing whatever tasks you normally perform."

Sam grinned. "My dear Catarina, searching for lost cities of gold, is just the sort of thing that I do on board the *Tahila.*"

She turned to him. A faint smile played at her lips. "I can see I don't have any chance of persuading you this is a fool's errand?"

"Not even a slight one."

Catarina nodded. "All right, why do I get the feeling that I'm not exactly dressed for a river cruise?"

Her green cotton dress clung to her body.

Sam grinned. "You're perfect."

Chapter Five

Sam and Catarina spent the next few hours picking their way through the city of Ubatuba, which was still trying to recover from the rain. Locals set up their street side tables, the Cerveza umbrellas a bright defiance against the gray sky and skewed signs.

As they hunted down somewhere to rent a small motorboat, Sam inquired about old sea legends of a large Spanish ship that sailed up river. But five centuries is a long time, and most people had come to the city to get away from all that. He got a diatribe on the slave trade, he got a brief report about when the conquistadors arrived and many offers to be his guide up the river, take him wherever he wanted to go – for a price.

The last of these stored their luxury motorboats in purpose-built lofts, high above the Rio Itamambuca. As such, their boats were the only ones not to have been damaged when the river swelled, and flooded her banks.

"Twenty minutes, sir," the man promised, gesturing to the men still sweeping up inside from the recent chaos that had ripped all the boats stored at ground level out of their cradles. He frowned, "Twenty minutes, and she's yours." He glanced at the sky. "Maybe thirty."

Sam nodded. "Take your time. Thank you."

They stopped across the street for a beer and a snack of mixed fried seafood, salty and full of lemon, at one of the ubiquitous street cafes while they waited for the eager shop attendant to clean his shop and make the boat ready after the storm. Their afternoon of detective work had worked up an appetite, and breakfast of croissants felt like a lifetime ago.

As the crisp white suited waiter poured their frosty beer in the sticky humid air, Sam leaned back and said, "I was hoping you could help me with something."

The waiter bowed with an easy smile, scenting American opportunity and American pocketbooks. "Anything, sir. Of course."

"I'm a historian doing some research on the European arrival in Ubatuba, and came across a reference to a Spanish galleon that actually sailed up the river." Sam smiled self-deprecatingly at the man's too-bright expression. "I was wondering if you knew anything about that?"

The man grinned. "I'm sure there were plenty of Spanish galleons that sailed up the Rio Itamambuca at one time. What makes this one so special?"

Sam said, "It sailed up the river, but it never sailed back down again."

"You're saying it was sunk?"

"Yeah."

The waiter stopped drying glasses for a moment, met his gaze and asked, "Did this ship have a name?"

Sam nodded. "The *Santa Rosa Celeste*."

The waiter closed his eyes as though searching his childhood memory banks for legends. In the end, he opened his eyes and shook his head. "Afraid not. I've never heard that name before. I'll ask around for you."

Sam paid him for the beers and thanked him for his time.

An old captain bussing the table nearby lifted his head. He had a piercing, unsettlingly direct gaze. His mouth set in a straight line and he placed the dirty dishes on his tray with military precision. He crumbed the table as if he was scraping someone's flesh.

The waiter returned a few minutes later. He shrugged, deflating a little. He hitched his smile up. "I'm sorry, sir. I really have no idea. I'm from Minas myself, just work here in the summer."

Sam sipped his beer. "That's all right. I was just hoping you might know someone who could point us in the right direction."

"I can ask around, some of the staff if you want…" The waiter hid his thoughts with a server's practiced mask, but Sam was good at reading people, and this one was an open book: keep these gringos drinking beer. They're here for treasure like everyone else. If they think it's real, who am I to disabuse them of that notion?

Sam smiled, leaned back and sipped. "Thank you." He gestured to their empty glasses. "We'll have another round."

The waiter nodded. "Of course, sir."

The waiter went away, but the old captain lingered. He was in his sixties, a career restaurant worker, a hard, noble man. He had the lined, weathered face of someone who had lived in the region their entire life, more a part of the land than a part of humanity. They were a dying breed. Sam noticed and held his gaze.

The captain approached their table. "You're looking for the ghost ship?"

Sam leaned forward. "Sure, if that's what people are calling it."

The man made the sign of evil, spat. He was from the jungle and had no love for the missionaries. The First People had long memories. "There was a ship and it did sail the river. The river swallowed it. It will swallow anyone who pursues it. The gods are not to be disturbed."

Sam said, "Okay, thanks for your help. We'll take your advice into consideration."

The captain's faced hardened. "I mean it. No good will come of searching for the *Santa Rosa Celeste*."

Sam wanted to ask how the man knew he was searching for the *Celeste*, but a single glance made him reconsider the notion. Instead, he said, "I understand. It was just idle curiosity. We didn't mean to offend anyone."

"None taken, sir. I'm just offering you some friendly advice," the captain replied, his voice anything but friendly.

Catarina finished her beer and stood up. "Shall we go see about this boat?"

Sam placed his empty glass on the table with a tip. "Let's go."

They stepped outside and walked to motorboat rental shop.

Catarina crossed her arms and waited while the owner unlocked the door and took off the boards on his window, which he'd put up in the face of the storm.

She glanced at Sam. Opened her mouth to speak and closed it again.

Sam caught her expression. "What is it?"

She shook her head, as though dismissing her own concerns. "It's nothing really."

Sam said, "Go on. What is it?"

"The locals are telling you that pursuit of the boat will swallow anyone who goes after it, and of course that's just where you want to go?"

Sam grinned. "Of course." At her eyebrow, he relented. "Legends have power to propel the curious. No more. We're not going to get swallowed by the river, Catarina."

"Good thing we didn't go yesterday."

Sam grinned. "Well, yes. If we'd gone up river yesterday the Rio Itamambuca would have indeed swallowed us whole."

A few minutes later the owner lowered the motorboat from its loft into the river, using a small crane, and tied it up alongside the jetty.

Sam paid the man for a forty-eight-hour hire excursion with the promise to return the vessel by tomorrow nightfall. The man looked glad for the business. Clearly only this American was crazy enough to go out on the water after last night's tempest.

They rented a Corsair 27 named *Emerald Princess*.

It was a stunning, sleek, luxury motorboat made by the high-end handcrafted shipbuilding company, Chris-Craft. At twenty-seven feet, its deck was covered in a sea of teak, polished chrome features, and luxuriant svelte upholstery. The boat was gloriously overpowered, with a single Mercury V8 8.2L engine, capable of producing 430 Horse Power.

Sam grinned with pleasure as he stepped aboard, taking Catarina's hand with a roguish smile. "Welcome aboard."

Catarina squeezed his hand affectionately, her eyes taking in the expensive boat. "Well, it's good to see you've got your taste in expensive toys back despite your memory loss."

"What do you think?"

"About what?"

"The *Emerald Princess*, of course!"

Catarina shrugged. "She looks nice. Chris-Craft seems a strange name though for a ship brand."

Sam's eyes narrowed accusingly. "What's wrong with the name, Chris?"

"Nothing." She made a sheepish smile. "I dated a Chris once... that's all."

"What happened to him?"

"Nothing. He wasn't really going anywhere in life. That's all."

"What did he do?"

"I don't know. I think he was trying to be a writer..."

"Ah... good to see you got rid of him. You can't trust a writer."

She laughed. "Why not?"

Sam met her eye and replied, "Anyone who makes their living making things up can't be trusted!"

"Unlike a treasure hunter..."

Sam nodded. "Unlike a bona fide treasure hunter."

Sam took a seat at the helm and started the engine with the press of a button. It came alive with a deep, gravelly sound. It was something straight out of a James Bond film. Despite having enough room for only a handful of people, and a small overnight cabin for two beneath the bow, the boat retailed for more than an inner-city apartment.

Catarina threw off the lines and Sam opened the throttle gently as he eased the *Emerald Princess* out of the small harbor.

Outside the break wall, he opened the throttle up and cruised across the bay heading toward the river. Sam couldn't help but grin. He had the open water, the promise of adventure, and a beautiful woman by his side. The sun glinted on the rippling waves as the wind ruffled them into a shimmer of light; seagulls and parrots wheeled and shrieked above. Beside him Catarina fixed her sunglasses, the wind from the speed of their crossing pressing the green dress to her body like a mythical figure head, muse of adventure. Sam worked the throttle a little more and the boat purred and groaned, leaping forward eagerly at his touch.

Across the bay, the wild green jungle beckoned, the water a startling, otherworldly blue. Huge boulders guarded the river's mouth like ancient sentries. Parrots swooped across the sky, jewel bright.

Sam grinned. "Tell me I don't know how to show a girl a good time."

Catarina suppressed a smile. "That remains to be seen."

Sam lifted his sunglasses to meet her gaze directly. "How so?"

She laughed. "On whether you can find this so-called treasure ship…"

Chapter Six

Catarina settled back into the svelte seats and enjoyed the journey up the Rio Itamambuca.

Branches hung over the wide expanse, dappling their passage. The boat was too high to trail her hand in the water as she had as a child, but Catarina reached out to touch the spray anyway. If she kept her gaze just ahead of the ripples caused by their passing the water was a deep, dark blue green, so clear in spots that she could see the sandy bottom with perfect clarity. She had no idea how deep it was.

The river system rose into the jungle at a steep gradient, meaning that, despite the recent downpour and flooding, the river had drained quickly, returning to its normal depth. Sandbars had shifted and the river was behaving differently than it would have a week ago, but the clarity of the water was astonishingly clear.

Sam didn't seem worried, though.

Catarina glanced at him from behind the safety of her sunglasses. He wasn't watching her anyway. He was in his natural element – on the hunt for some hidden secret, on the water, surrounded by toys. Catarina suppressed a grin. Sam Reilly was an uncomplicated man. Give him a mystery to solve, a person to defend, and some gadgets to do it with and his life was good. It was one of the reasons she liked him. Because of her job as a neuroscientist, Catarina had the tendency to get bogged down in the small pieces, the insanely complicated invisible world. Sam had a way of reminding her to be human. That was, when he remembered to be human himself, and not get obsessed by some other treasure hunt.

She shook her head. Maybe he was complicated, after all.

As if Sam felt her gaze, he turned his head and smiled at her. The wind ruffled his hair, his shirt whipping in the breeze.

She smiled back, and felt herself relax. She was in good hands.

They'd been traveling about an hour, Catarina lost in the glory of the untamed wild, when the boat started to slow.

She looked at Sam. "Did you find something?"

Sam shook his head, and pointed to the boat's digital fish finder display, which gave a 3D image of the seabed below, along with any fish, debris, or tree branches. "No. Just some debris from the recent storm."

Catarina's eyes swept the widescreen display unit, while Sam expertly navigated past the bulk of the built up debris, taking the *Emerald Princess* to an idle.

They continued on upriver.

A dark canopy of green foliage enshrouded the banks of the river like a sinister shadow. Catarina's eyes narrowed and her mind drifted to the past, as she tried to imagine what it would have been like trying to sail up the unnamed river on board the *Santa Rosa Celeste* in the 16th century. Despite being a wide river, she couldn't imagine being on a large sailing vessel trying to navigate its unmarked, natural channels with nothing more than a lead-line to mark its depth and wind to keep it moving.

The depth sounder made an alarm and her mind returned to the present. Sam, standing at the helm, eased the throttle back to idle, reached over and silenced the alarm.

Her mind returned to the present. She wrapped her arms around his slim waist and kissed the back of his neck. "What is it?"

Sam bit his lower lip. "I don't know yet. Probably just more debris. Maybe an uprooted tree, dragged into the middle of the river?"

Catarina dialed the frequency on the sonar transducer all the way up. A few seconds later, the image on the monitor became more defined. The first one looked like a white cloud of small sonar pings, the second one more like the outline of something definitely manmade, and the third sweep produced a clear image of a boat.

Sam shifted the throttle past neutral and into reverse, pulling the *Emerald Princess* up until it stopped dead in the water.

Catarina smiled, feeling her heart beat faster. "Do you think it's the *Santa Rosa Celeste*?"

Sam shook his head. "Not unless Felipe Ferdinand had access to a modern motorboat in 1535."

She stared at the image displayed on the fish finder depth sounder. It was much clearer than the original one, but still just looked like the basic outline of a boat. There was nothing to show what sort of boat it was. "You can tell all that at a glance?"

"I've spent my life staring at bathymetric imaging. That's a modern motor yacht down there, I'm certain of it. Most likely sunk during the storm." Sam depressed the marker on the GPS to make a note of the location, and continued motoring farther upriver. "I'll notify the authorities when we get back. I'm sure someone's insurance company will be interested in whatever boat that is down there, even if we aren't."

Once underway again, Sam said, "Hey, take over here for a minute will you while I go organize the snorkeling gear."

Catarina stepped behind the helm, taking control of the wheel with a confidence she didn't quite feel. "Hey, I'm not sure what I'm supposed to be doing here…"

Sam smiled and kept heading to the aft of the vessel. "What are you talking about? There's a steering wheel and an accelerator. It's no different from driving a car. Besides you've used a boat before…"

"That was a rubber zodiac with a tiller!"

"You've steered the wheel of a power cruiser when we were diving at the Whitsundays!"

"That was fifteen years ago! And it was out in the ocean with nothing to hit."

"This is in a river, there's not a lot to hit."

"Besides, I'm not even sure where I'm going."

"Upriver. Try not to hit the bank. You'll know when you get it wrong because the boat will be out of the water…"

"All right all right…" she said making small movements of the wheel to test her control of the *Emerald Princess*.

Behind her, Sam lifted the teak transom – similar to a small trunk of a car – and began to remove snorkeling equipment. The owner of the boat had assured him that the *Emerald Princess* came with snorkeling gear for two.

Catarina glanced over her shoulder and said, "Wait… you forgot to tell me where the brake is?"

"Brake…" Sam grinned. "Boats don't have brakes."

"What do I do if I'm going to run into something?"

"Use the steering wheel, try and maneuver your way around it. The river's still pretty large, isn't it?"

"That's great. But what if the river comes to an end?"

Sam continued searching for a pair of dive fins. He looked up. "Sorry, what?"

"What if the river comes to an end and I need to stop quickly?"

"Just take your hand off the throttle, about five minutes ago."

"I'm serious!"

"Why?"

She pulled the throttle back to idle. The Chris-Craft dropped off the aquaplane, but still kept its forward momentum. "Because something's coming up ahead of us…"

Sam looked up, his eyes darting between hers and the wide river. The water looked flat, and open, almost half a mile wide. There was nothing for her to hit. "Like what?"

"I don't know... the depth sounder's alarm is going off."

Sam casually walked up behind her.

Catarina turned the wheel hard to starboard, but the depth alarm kept going off. She looked at Sam, expecting him to take over or do something, but instead she saw his face was plastered with unconcerned curiosity and the same sort of irritating insouciance he'd displayed ever since she'd met him.

The depth alarm kept going off.

She felt the thrill of fear rising. "What's going on?"

"I don't know," Sam replied casually.

"I'm serious. Should I keep steering to starboard?"

Sam shrugged. "I don't know."

The alarm changed to three loud buzzes.

It meant a collision with something underwater was imminent.

She shouted, "Sam!"

He wrapped his left arm around her waist, pulling her protectively in toward his chest. With his right hand, he shoved the throttle into reverse, and the *Emerald Princess* slowed to a stop... with her bow resting on a shallow sandbank...

Catarina glanced off the side of the boat.

The sandbar was no more than a foot below the waterline.

She turned to Sam. "Where the hell did that come from?"

Sam grinned. "I have no idea."

Chapter Seven

Sam slowly reversed the *Emerald Princess*.

His eyes narrowed as he made minute adjustments to the wheel, slowly surveying the sandbar. His eyes swept the water just ahead.

Catarina watched him, and asked, "What do you think it is? The sandy shallows of a shipwreck?"

"Maybe. See that lighter spot up there?"

She nodded. "It's just a sandbar, right?"

Sam said, "That's right, but it doesn't look natural."

Catarina stepped to the front of the bow, her scientist's sense of adventure piqued at the promise of a problem with no clear solution. She shaded her hands against the glare. "What makes a sandbar unnatural?"

"Normally, a sandbar forms when a river reaches a hard point, like stones or a natural impediment, so the sand builds up in that section, forcing the river to widen as its waters searches for a clearer path to the ocean."

"But not here?"

Sam gestured to the banks, the possible river routes. "No. Not here… Instead, here it looks like the river has a clear path, but suddenly decided to deviate."

They looked at each other. "It looks like it has been heading in that direction for a long time."

He grinned. "Yeah. I'm just hoping about since 1535…"

Catarina, sharp as he'd ever known her, asked, "If this sandbar was caused by the shipwreck of the *Santa Rosa Celeste* since the 16th century, why doesn't anyone know about it?"

Sam turned his palms upward. "You mean, why isn't it marked as a navigational hazard on the map?"

"Yeah."

"Well. There's two possible reasons that come to mind."

Catarina smiled. "Go on."

"The first one is that the maps we have are old. I can't imagine Raymarine surveying the river regularly."

"No…" she rolled her eyes. "But I can't believe they would put out a map of a river that hadn't been surveyed, either."

"I agree."

"So what's the second option?"

Sam grinned. "The second option is that a shipwreck, or other large sunken object has caused a natural sandbank here, deep underwater… where boats have happily passed over the top of it for centuries… until the storm shifted sand down river."

Catarina imagined the turbid water, causing sand to run down the river, and smiled. "Which means the sand ran free until its progress was obstructed by the shipwreck, causing sand to bury it, and create a large sandbar."

Sam grinned. "Exactly."

He pressed the anchor button, and an electronic winch rapidly lowered an anchor into the water. Sam waited until the Danforth anchor – designed for sand and mud – to bite into the seabed and swing the *Emerald Princess* around.

Confident that it had, Sam switched off the engine. His face was set with joy and anticipation.

Catarina's intelligent and beguiling gray eyes stared at him. She smiled. "So how do we find out what's below the sand?"

Sam grinned. "The easiest way is to head down there and take a look. See what we have."

Catarina waited at the helm as Sam rummaged in the dive box. He pulled out a mask and some flippers, then attached the snorkel. He handed a second pair of snorkeling gear to her. "Are you coming?"

She grinned. "I bet I'll find it first!"

He smiled. "I'll take that bet…"

And a moment later he was over the side with a grin and a splash.

Catarina donned her own snorkeling gear and dipped backward into the river.

She was amazed by how clear the water was despite the recent rains. Instead of being murky and dark, the river was crystal clear. The steep gradient of the Rio Itamambuca meant that the water that flooded the river emptied out into the Ubuntu Bay as quickly as it had appeared, leaving the river clean from any debris.

Catarina snorkeled around the sandbar. She took a couple deep breaths and then dived down to try and reach the bottom of the sandbar along the deep end, but it was too deep for her to reach. She surfaced about forty-five seconds later, and caught her breath lying on her back.

After catching her breath she tried a few more free dives but found nothing but sand. She floated for another few minutes and then climbed on board the *Emerald Princess* and dried herself.

She watched Sam drift along the surface, scanning as he searched the sandbar. Then he kicked down, down… He became just a blur, obliterated in the slow current ripples and the sand drifted up by his passing.

Catarina watched closer and held her breath.

She didn't let it out until he broke the surface, panting, streaming with the clear, crystalline water. He was triumphant, frustrated.

Despite herself, she felt giddy as a school girl.

Catarina said, "Well?"

Sam climbed the two small rungs of the ladder, pulling himself onboard the Chris-Craft motorboat. "I think I found a ship!"

"The Santa Rosa Celeste?"

Sam's eyes widened, the blue sparkling with wonder in the dappled light through the forest canopy. He expelled a deep breath and stopped. "Maybe... but we're going to need a lot of help to reach her, because she's buried in sand."

He kissed her on her lips.

Her lips parted and his tongue touched hers, tasting the water on their lips. She kissed him hungrily.

When they stopped, she asked, "Now what?"

Sam grinned. "Now, we're going to need something to clear that sand."

Chapter Eight

Morning dawned clear and bright over the mouth of the Rio Itamambuca.

Local fishermen in battered, colorful boats cast their nets as they'd done for generations, calling good naturedly over the calm water, inquiring about daughters, sons, and wives. The men discussed their favorite football teams, who was going to advance to the finals, and the latest scandals in local TV shows. The morning had been a good haul for the fishermen, who had returned to the sea early after the recent storm only to be rewarded with nets full of fish.

The floats on the nets rose under an incoming bow wave.

Next to the fishermen, a behemoth of modern naval engineering motored around into the bay. She was an awesome machine – a unique combination of beauty, raw power, and seafaring capabilities. She had a long black hull and narrow beam tapering in to a razor-sharp bow. As she glided by the fishermen she looked like an oversized shark or a bullet, until an anchor was finally dropped and the evil-looking beast from the sea finally came to rest. She stayed there, ominous and benevolent, like some ancient guardian of the river's mouth.

Shouts and speculation echoed across the water through the call of birds and a small Chris-Craft motorboat pulled up alongside the ship's massive bulk like a guppy by a shark.

On board the *Tahila* everything was jovial.

Tom grinned and shook Catarina's hand in greeting. "Hey, Catarina. Still letting Sam drag you into trouble I see?"

Catarina laughed. "What can I say? He just keeps showing up."

"Hey," Sam defended himself with raised hands. He should have known the crew would tease. "It's not my fault we happened to be in the same city. She was the one with the conference. I was on vacation..."

Genevieve shook her head. "And somehow you landed yourself in a massive storm that unearthed a potential mystery buried for centuries..."

Sam grinned and shrugged. "Hey, secrets like to reveal themselves to me."

Genevieve shook her head, smiling sideways at Tom. "I don't know how you find this stuff, Sam. It's like the adventure gods just lay garlands of flowers in your lap."

Sam laughed. "Someone has to make your life interesting."

Everyone sat down to a smorgasbord of churrasco, feijoada, pao di queijo, and chicken heart pate on crusty bread, with plenty of beer to wash it down, in thick stemmed glasses for breakfast while Sam filled them in.

On one side of the table was Sam and Catarina, directly opposite him was Tom, his director of operations and Genevieve, his jack of all trades. To his right was Matthew, the *Tahila's* skipper, and Veyron, the ship's engineer and submarine expert. To his left, Elise, his resident genius, and computer expert.

Sitting next to Elise was a dog. A golden retriever named Caliburn.

It was why he could never really stay off the job, he reflected, as he thought about the way his "vacation" had gone. His team was the best and the brightest, and his boat was a joy. Why would he ever stay away?

Sam filled his team in over the events of the past few days, the discovery of the Santa Rosa Celeste's transom on the beach after the storm, the trip up the Rio Itamambuca, before finally settling on his belief that the *Santa Rosa Celeste* was most likely buried beneath several tons of sand roughly six miles upriver.

When he was finished, Matthew said, "Well, I've already looked at the charts, and I can tell you unequivocally that there's no way in hell you're going to be able to bring the *Tahila* up the Rio Itamambuca."

Sam met his skipper's worried eye. "It's all right, Matthew, I wouldn't dare."

Tom said, "Which means we're going to have to move the portable dredger onto a runabout to bring up the river."

"We don't need to move the sand far, so we won't need a barge." Sam said, "The *Emerald Princess* will do the job."

Veyron nodded. "I'll go dismantle the dredger and set it up onboard the run about as soon as we're finished here."

Sam said, "Thank you, Veyron."

Matthew grinned. "I wonder how the rental company will feel about you shifting several tons of sand from the back of their Chris-Craft luxury motor yacht?"

Sam's lips curled into a half-grin. A *what they don't know they won't care about* expression plastered on his face. "It will be fine. It's just a large pump that can sit on the aft deck. It's not like I'm planning on pumping sand onto the boat, but don't worry, we'll take good care of it."

"I knew you would," Matthew replied.

Sam turned to Elise, "Can you please find anything you can on El Dorado?"

She smiled. "Anything in particular you want to know?"

Sam shrugged. "Its location would be a great start…"

"I'm serious," Elise said. "There are going to be millions of articles on line about the legend of El Dorado, so you might want to be a little more specific about what you want me to find."

Sam paused, giving it some thought, and then said, "All right. Let's see how much you can find about the *Santa Rosa Celeste* – a description of its naval architecture, any information on her crew, where she had been on expeditions, anything you can get your hands on – also I want to know about De Quesada. He was the first to document the story of the Zipa – that's the new chief of the Muisca by the way – in a ritual at Lake Guatavita near present-day Bogotá, where the Zipa covered himself in gold and washed in the lake. De Quesada went on to form a government at present day Bogotá, Colombia. I want to know any reference you can find in the history books to a meeting between De Quesada and Felipe Ferdinand."

Elise nodded. "I'll see what I can do."

Sam said, "Any other questions?"

Tom asked, "When do you want to start?"

Sam grinned. "Right away."

Chapter Nine

It was a little after lunch by the time Sam anchored the *Emerald Princess* above the hopeful wreck site, with Catarina, Tom, and Genevieve on board.

A childish part of him felt like he was double dating again.

And what a great way to double date?

SCUBA diving for sunken treasure!

The dredging device was fairly simple. It consisted of a large diesel engine, an impeller – which drew water into the pipe, creating a suction – a hand held and operated suction pipe that could be used to draw sand from the seabed, and then deposited the sand twenty feet behind the *Emerald Princess*, which was positioned a farther twenty feet away from the sandbar and downriver to avoid the sand being carried back to the bar.

In addition to the dredger, they floated a series of sonar buoys and ground penetrating radar antennas around the suspected wreck site, which provided a detailed bathymetric image and an outline of the ground beneath the riverbed.

Sam switched on the two monitors.

The bathymetry showed a large sandbar that looked no different than any other sandbar. It was large, wide, and covered in sand and debris.

He flicked on the ground penetrating radar – GPR.

It used radar pulses to create images of the subsurface. More specifically, the nondestructive method used electromagnetic radiation in the microwave band – UHF/VHF frequencies – of the radio spectrum to detect the reflected signals from subsurface structures.

Sam's eye's focused on the monitor.

It worked slower than bathymetry.

GPR used high-frequency radio waves, usually in the range 10 MHz to 2.6 GHz. A GPR transmitter and antenna emits electromagnetic energy into the ground. When the energy encounters a buried object or a boundary between materials having different permittivities – responses to electromagnetic fields – it may be reflected or refracted or scattered back to the surface. A receiving antenna can then record the variations in the return signal. The principles involved were similar to seismology, except GPR methods implement electromagnetic energy rather than acoustic energy, and energy may be reflected at boundaries where subsurface electrical properties change rather than subsurface mechanical properties as is the case with seismic energy.

An image finally became displayed on the monitor.

Sam's heart raced. Everything he'd hoped for could either be made or shattered by the truth in the next few seconds.

The image was of poor quality at first, but a few seconds later, the shape improved, as more details were added, with each transmission of radio pulses.

Sam held his breath. His eyes narrowed on the final image and he grinned. "Well, would you look at that?"

Tom, Catarina, and Genevieve leaned in to look at it.

There, on the second monitor was a clear outline of a wooden ship.

Chapter Ten

Like the dredging equipment, the plan was a simple one.

They had four sets of SCUBA gear, and would take it in rotating one-hour shifts, to operate the dredging suction head. In doing so, they would keep one person in the water at all times, while the other scanned from the surface and directed the diver via underwater radio communications.

Tom asked, "Who wants to go first?"

"I'll make a start. There's a section over here," Sam said, pointing to the bathymetric map on the computer monitor, "where I first spotted a part of the ship's deck."

"And I'll have a turn after you," Catarina said, insisting that if she was going to go on a treasure hunt, she wanted to get her hands dirty and do right.

Sam grinned. "Agreed."

With that he attached his buoyancy control device to his air tank and regulator. The water ranged between twenty to thirty feet, making it a shallow dive. Thus, they would dive on good old-fashioned air tanks. The water was a balmy 78 degrees Fahrenheit, which meant he could leave the wetsuit at home and dive in board shorts. He grabbed his weight belt, carefully removing two pounds of lead to adjust for the loss of the buoyant wetsuit. At last he slid his feet into the dive fins, pulled the radio equipped full-face dive mask over his face, gripped the dredger suction head like a fireman, and slipped into the warm water below.

He made the all okay sign by touching his head with his hand to form a "Q" symbol.

A moment later, he expelled air from his buoyancy control device until he started to sink. At ten feet, he paused his descent, shifting his jaw side to side and making a couple swallowing movements to relieve the slight air squeeze in his middle ear.

Once the pressure equalized, he continued his descent.

He found the location he'd originally seen part of a wooden ship when he'd free dived the spot the day before, but already the place seemed to have been covered in another layer of sand.

Sam placed the dredger suction head on the surface of the sand and said, "All right, Tom… switch it on."

The drone of the diesel engine resonated through Sam's ears as the first pieces of sand were sucked into the dredging pipe.

By the time his air tank was nearly depleted, he had created a small crater in the mountain of sand. Catarina tapped him on the shoulder and continued the project.

It would take days to clear enough sand to positively identify the *Santa Rosa Celeste*, and longer still to find anything that might shed some light on the legend of El Dorado.

It was hard, loud, dirty going.

They kept working through the day and into the night. It was slow, laborious work, but it needed to be done to clear the sand.

On the second day, Sam decided to take a metal detector down with him in between rotations.

Tom grinned. "Aren't you getting ahead of yourself?"

Catarina said, "No, he and I have a bet that if El Dorado's gold is down there, I'll find it first."

Sam adjusted the settings on his metal detector. "No, I'm pretty confident treasure hunting's my area of expertise."

She kissed him and said, "Suit yourself. We'll see."

Sam put his regulator in his mouth and dived into the water.

He quickly made his descent to the clearing in the shape of the shipwreck below. Genevieve was in the process of using the dredger to remove the sand that covered the ship's deck. She was following a rectangular grid pattern in order to evenly remove the sand and reduce the risk of disproportionate weight cracking the ship's hull.

They had already found the aft castle and the opening to the decks below, but before they could enter the wreck, it was imperative that they cleared the bulk of the sand away first. Otherwise, the weight would have been enough to collapse the centuries old wood as soon as the sand inside the ship was removed.

Sam started toward the bow.

He switched on the metal detector.

Despite what Tom and Catarina had said, he wasn't looking for gold. There was no reason for gold to be on the deck anyway. If Felipe Ferdinand did in fact find El Dorado, the gold would have been stored down below, deep in the bowels of the *Santa Rosa Celeste*, where it could not only be better protected from thieves, but if the legends were to be believed, that amount of gold would have weighed so much that the bilge would have been the only place it could have been stored without damaging the ship's ballast.

Sam grinned as the LCD screen on the handheld metal detector flashed with multiple targets. They were all small, mostly irrelevant. More like little dots scattered across the deck of the forecastle. Maybe from old nails or something, but nothing big enough to be what he was looking for.

What he was searching for was the metal bell, a bronze bell that would hopefully provide the definitive name of the ship. Sailing bells were an intrinsic necessity to seafaring safety in bygone years before the introduction of blowhorns. They were used to mark the various times during watches and for safety to other vessels during foggy conditions. The bronze bell itself normally had the ship's name engraved or cast on it.

That's what Sam Reilly was hunting for.

He turned and headed toward the center of the ship's deck, to an area where the main mast would have once rested, and from which the bell of the *Santa Rosa Celeste* would have hung.

That was, if they had indeed found the *Santa Rosa Celeste*.

For the next ten-minutes Sam continued the grid search in a counter-clockwise direction over the sandy mound that represented the center of the buried shipwreck. On the first pass, he didn't find anything, but on the second round, the metal detector began to fire off loud beeping sounds, indicating a large target had been identified.

Sam shifted his position, narrowing in on the target, until he was certain he was right above it – and stopped. A small grin creased his lips beneath his dive mask. His heart raced. Five centuries of mystery were about to be revealed. He expelled some air out of his buoyancy control device until he was heavily negatively buoyant, letting his knees rest into the sand below.

He then removed a small, handheld spade, and began to dig.

The sand was easy to shift and within a few minutes he'd carved a hole deep enough that he needed to stretch to reach all the way to the bottom.

And that's when he hit something.

The tip of the small spade stopped, resonating a distinctive metal-on-metal sound.

Sam grinned and dropped the spade next to the hole. Then, with his hands, he dug around the metal object, delicately removing the sand until it came free.

The bell was covered in five centuries of tarnish as well as sand and would need to be brought to the surface and cleaned before it would reveal its secrets.

Sam shifted the bell back and forward until it broke free from the suction imposed by centuries of compressed sand.

He tried to lift it.

The bell was heavy, but not so much so that he couldn't lift it by hand. The problem was that doing so made him so negatively buoyant that it would be impossible to reach the surface on his own.

That didn't matter, there were plenty of other ways to bring something to the surface.

Sam tied a nylon rope through the bell's crown – the upside-down U-shaped piece of brass originally used to anchor the bell to the mast – and then back in on itself to form a knot. He reached around into a small Velcro pocket on buoyancy control device and removed a hundred-pound lift bag, attaching it to the nylon rope.

It was basically a balloon shaped bag with an opening at the bottom. He unfolded the bag and then used his second stage regulator – safety occy – to fill the lift bag with air from his own dive tank. Within seconds, its synthetic bladder inflated like a hot air balloon, with a single nylon rope running to the bell below.

Sam continued filling it until the ship's bell became neutrally buoyant.

He then depressed a couple bursts of air into his own buoyancy control device, and slowly made his way to the surface. On his way up, as he decreased water depth and the air volume increased, he intermittently released air from the lift bag, to avoid it shooting toward the surface like a runaway railway cart.

As he broke the surface, he inflated the lift bag fully, until the bell was almost above the surface of the water. He then surface-swam until it reached the *Emerald Princess*.

A few seconds later Tom reached in, gripped the tether and pulled the diving bell onto the aft deck of the Chris-Craft motorboat.

Tom grinned and offered his hand. "Hey, you found the ship's bell! That's great news. Well done."

Sam took his hand, and clambered onboard. "Thanks. Yeah, it's a bit of luck. The question still remains, what name does it say?"

"Let's find out."

Sam ran his eyes across the boat. Tom was by himself. "Has Catarina already started her next dive?"

Tom nodded. "Yeah, she's just taking over from Genevieve."

Sam stripped his diving gear, while Tom hosed the bell with fresh water, removing centuries worth of sand and tarnish.

Tom switched off the hose, glanced at Sam, and said, "You're not going to believe this."

Sam looked at up. "What?"

Tom said, "We've got the wrong ship."

Chapter Eleven

Sam stared at the ship's bell.

It was heavily tarnished, but the engraved lettering of the name of its ship was still clearly readable. His eyes locked on the ship's name…

SANTABUENAVENTURA

"The *SantaBuenaventura*!" Sam cursed. "All of this for some random Spanish carrack! I can't believe it."

Tom suppressed a grin. "Maybe the *Buenaventura* was even more valuable than the *Celeste*? I don't suppose you've ever heard of the ship before?"

Sam shook his head. "No. But that doesn't mean much. There must be thousands of Spanish shipwrecks strewn along this coast, the majority of which, have little of value on board and represent nothing more than a historical note."

"Still, it's not every day you find a Spanish carrack that's been sitting beneath the sand for centuries…" Tom said, trying to be helpful.

"I know." He grinned. "Thank you, Tom. We still might find something interesting on board. Who know?"

"So you're going to keep going on the expedition?"

Sam smiled. "We've come this far, no reason not to clear the rest of the debris and see what we've got. I'm sure the Brazilian government will be interested in its historical value."

Tom patted him on the back. "Good man. Besides, you never know what we might find inside?"

Sam bit down a retort that whatever it was, it could hardly compare to the gold of El Dorado. He nodded, then picked up his cell phone and called Elise.

Elise answered immediately. "Have you found a map to El Dorado, yet?"

"Not yet," Sam replied. "And what's more, it's unlikely I'm going to."

"How come?"

"We just pulled up the ship's bell…"

Elise put it together before he'd finished. "It's not the *Santa Rosa Celeste,* is it?"

Sam said, "Afraid not."

"What ship did you find?"

"I'm hoping you can tell me. Her name's the *SantaBuenaventura.*"

"And you're hoping I can search the international database of shipwrecks, both lost and found, to see if I can find a match?"

"Yes please."

"I'm on it," Elise replied.

In the background, Sam heard her fingers tapping the keyboard in a rapid fire staccato. He said, "Can you call me back as soon as you know anything about the *SantaBuenaventura?*"

Elise said, "I don't have to…"

"Why?"

"Because I've already got the answer."

Sam felt his heart race. "Really? That was fast. What is it?"

"The *SantaBuenaventura* was the second ship in the fleet that went in search of El Dorado in 1535."

"Second ship? Owned by who?"

"Not owned," Elise corrected him. "Hired on a percentage of bounty reward basis…"

Sam said, "For who, Elise!"

He pictured her smiling as she teased him. "Felipe Ferdinand."

Sam's eyes widened. "There were two ships on the expedition?"

"In fact, there were three to begin with. The first one clipped a reef as it passed through the Strait of Gibraltar."

Sam frowned. "And the other one ended up at the bottom of the *Rio Itamambuca*."

"Wrong."

Sam bit his lower lip. "It didn't?"

"No. The second one sank somewhere along the Magdalena River on its way into the jungle of New Grenada, AKA, present day Colombia, causing devasting and irreparable damage to her hull."

The edge of Sam's lower lip curled upward with incredulity. "The bell was saved!"

"Yes," Elise confirmed. "And, was possibly being taken back to Spain on board the *Santa Rosa Celeste...*"

Sam frowned. "Or any other Spanish ship..."

"Or any other ship," Elise agreed.

"Which means, we still don't know if this is all for nothing."

"Not nothing. It's still holds the enormous historical value of..."

Sam didn't hear Elise finish her sentence. Instead, he heard Catarina's excited squeal resonating loudly from the radio, as though she was being attacked.

He ended the call from Elise, and picked up the dive radio's transmitter. "What is it? Are you all right?"

There was a long pause... then, Catarina said, "Sam, you're not going to believe this... I just found gold... a lot of gold!"

Chapter Twelve

Sam and Tom grabbed their dive gear and jumped in the water within minutes.

Only Genevieve remained on board, cursing that she had already exceeded her no-decompression-limit and would need to wait another hour before her surface interval would allow her residual nitrogen levels to fall within the limits of a second dive.

Sam dropped his head, diving nearly straight down toward the shipwreck. His heart pounding in his ears. Next to him, Tom kicked his fins, and raced to reach the now visible deck.

At thirty feet, they reached the now visible deck of the shipwreck.

Catarina looked up, her white teeth grinning back at them, holding a dive bag full of small golden pearls. "I told you I'd find the gold first!"

Sam's eyes widened at the sight. His lips twisted into a giant grin. "Beginner's luck."

In a small frenzy, the three of them quickly picked up every piece of gold.

Back on the deck of the *Emerald Princess*, all four of them counted the small pieces of gold.

There turned out to be more than a hundred small, golden pearls scattered across the open deck of the forecastle.

Sam removed a small electronic scale. "Let's put it on the scales and see what it weighs."

Catarina placed the bag on the scale.

Sam watched the digital scale clock in at 30 pounds even. He did the mental arithmetic, for the value of the gold. 30 pounds equated to 480 ounces. Gold was currently trading at 1,391.65 US dollars an ounce. He grinned. "That's roughly 667,000 US dollars at today's trading rates."

Tom expelled a deep breath. "That's a lot of gold to be left lying around on the deck. Just imagine what we might find down below!"

Sam glanced at Genevieve, and Catarina's faces.

Their eyes were all wide with gold fever, and the primal wonder of a treasure hunt. There was no doubt in his mind, they didn't need to be asked to imagine it. Already, they were picturing a king's fortune stored deep below the hull.

Sam nodded. "All right, now that we've all enjoyed that thought, we'd better keep going until we reach the ship's hold."

Once their nitrogen levels had lowered to the level that they could continue to dive, the four of them resumed their rotations using the suction dredger. It was slow, time-consuming work. As night time approached, Veyron and Elise turned up in the *Tahila's* runabout with oxygen tanks and closed-circuit rebreathers so that the crew could increase their dive times from an hour up to four to six hours.

Elise and Veyron took the next two rotations. Despite everyone's desire to simply empty the sand from the two main hatches, and race to the lower decks of the ship in search of its treasure filled motherlode, it was imperative that the slow and arduous task of removing the surrounding sand took priority first. Failure to do so, could very easily see the ship – whatever ship it turned out to be – crushed by the extreme pressure of so much sand.

All six of them continued working through the night and into the next day, with each diver rotating through a work cycle of resting, sleeping, eating, and working.

Little by little, the boat emerged.

Its outward appearance became easily recognizable and enough of it became visible to positively identify it as a Spanish carrack from the sixteenth century, but still there was no evidence of the ship's name.

On the third day, Sam discovered a previously damaged and repaired section of the portside hull. He stopped his work on the suction dredger, and fixed his flashlight on the old wound.

The inspection revealed a six foot by four-foot scar to the portside of the hull.

It was most likely caused when the ship clipped a hidden reef. Judging by the size and scale of the damage, Sam was amazed that the crew of the unidentified ship had managed the reach the shore in time to salvage her, and eventually make repairs.

He fixed the beam of his flashlight on the wound.

It bore the stain of a dark mahogany.

The hardwood was in direct contrast to the lighter Spanish Oak used in the rest of the hull and most commonly found in the Iberian Peninsula, where a highly prized timber used for shipbuilding during the fifteenth and sixteenth centuries had been found.

After all these centuries, the nails used to attach the mahogany repair patch to the hull, as one would a band aid, had rusted and come free, leaving the two types of wood to separate. As Sam removed the last of the surrounding sand, using the suction dredger head, the patch came free.

He and Tom worked to bring the wood to the surface. They would be able to send a portion of the timber to a dendrologist in California who might be able to shed some light on where the trees originated from which the timber was derived. It would take time, but if they could find the rough location where such a forest grows, maybe they could get a lead on where the ship had originated, or at least, where it had its accident. Presumably, no ship crossing the Atlantic, would have attempted to do so with such a large scar on its hull. Therefore, the damage had occurred somewhere along the coast of the New World.

Possibly, somewhere near the mythical city of El Dorado.

Below the water, Sam instructed his team to focus on extracting sand from inside the hull, suctioning it out from within the now open scar along the portside hull. Working in teams of two, they tunneled into the deepest bowels of the shipwreck.

On the fourth day, they hit pay dirt.

Sam was standing in the cockpit in the mid-afternoon lull, his bones shaking from the omnipresent hum of the dredger. Through the dredger monitor he glanced upon something that looked like any old crewman's clothes or mess box.

He picked up the underwater radio mike. "Hey Tom, what is that, to your right?"

Tom maneuvered the camera to his right, focusing in on the object.

Sam's eyes narrowed. It became clear that, while it was definitely a container, the shape was different – it had a domed lid and rusted bands wrapping around the circumference.

Fastened by a lock.

Sam couldn't help the ridiculous, childish grin from spreading across his face as Tom whooped in delight. "Friends, we've got ourselves a bona fide treasure chest."

Chapter Thirteen

The excitement died down as it became clear it would likely be another twenty-four hours before they could complete the complex process of extracting the chest from where it was lodged into the sand, silt, and debris and more than five centuries beneath the water.

Sam and Tom worked the vacuum dredge inside the wreck's hull together, trying to clear the sediment from around the chest to free it. The vacuum dredge churned the water into a murky, sand-filled sludge.

In front of Sam, the rusted tip of a metal chest jutted out of the sediment.

Beneath his dive mask he grinned. They'd found it. Now was the delicate part – balancing their excitement with the caution needed to unearth the chest. After a few more minutes of excavation, a good three-quarters of the chest lay in plain view.

A rush of dopamine hit his brain, and Sam shuddered with excitement. All of the hard, waterlogged days and grit in places there should be no grit fell away as if they'd never existed. This was what he lived for. Here lay the culmination of his efforts in a bronze chest crusted in bluing tarnish. The chest was unassuming, aside from the imposing and ornate seal stamped onto the metal body.

He couldn't wait to get it open on the *Tahila*.

On the sides of the strongbox were two rows of metal hoops that seemed to have rusted less than the actual chest itself. Sam tested their integrity with a quick tug at them, and assessed they would be enough to secure the chest on its journey to the surface and onto the boat. Veyron had already prepared a complex system of pulleys and air bags to prepare for the delivery of the cargo up to the surface.

The contagious buzz reached a fever pitch on the surface, as Sam and Tom attached the lift bags to the chest.

The two men grunted and heaved and cursed, but eventually they got the heavy iron chest free from the sand that had held it for centuries. Once it was free, Sam swam behind it and fixed three sets of airbags underneath the chest as Tom helped him heave the bulk up enough to wedge the bags under. Though they were empty now, Tom would fill them up with air from a separate tank designed for this purpose, and it would float the chest to the surface.

Tom procured a small, hand-size tank of compressed air from one of the various pockets in the scuba suit and latched it to the small opening on one of the air bags. In an audible hiss, the bag expanded, and with each hiss of air, the chest began to float upward like some kind of heavenly figure. Sunlight filtered through the surface of the water, dropping swooping beams of light onto their prize.

Sam floated, motionless, in the water for a few moments to assess the currents. The small grains of sand drifted aimlessly, in no particular direction, and Sam knew that these were calm waters. Compared to the turbulent and rocky voyage to this point, the calmness seemed unusual, and was almost as if the currents knew to respect the ghostly wreck.

A large grinding sound snapped him back to attention. Tom was expertly guiding the net through the hole at the top of the shipwreck. Sam's heart was beating out of his chest over the implications of this discovery. People had been searching for the *Santa Rosa Celeste* for centuries. What was in this box?

In less than five minutes, together they let all their hands go off the chest and allowed the contraption of ropes and nets to carry the treasure to the *Emerald Princess*.

Genevieve and Catarina hauled the chest onto the aft deck by pulling on a rope which wove through an intricate set of pulleys on a tripod.

Sam and Tom climbed on board seconds later.

Resounding whoops and cries of excitement echoed through the Brazilian jungle. The excitement and energy coursed through the team like electricity, and it made all the hairs on Sam's body stand straight, even under the suit.

He stood there dripping and shaking as the others hurried to detach the chest from the net. Sam took the towel Catarina handed him, and sponged the river water off his body. She tousled his hair, damp up to her elbows. She was grinning as widely as him.

They fought the urge to bust the chest open immediately to see what was inside and instead waited until the *Emerald Princess* reached the *Tahila*. If it was filled with gold, the last thing they wanted to do was find themselves on a small motorboat on a South American river with enough gold to raise an army. And if it wasn't gold, but other artifacts, they would need some specialized equipment to keep it from being damaged by the change in its environment.

An hour later, they reached the *Tahila* and transferred the chest on board.

Genevieve opened a bottle of champagne to celebrate.

And Sam, looking around at the excited faces of his crew, said, "All right, let's open it."

Chapter Fourteen

Sam's spine tingled and gooseflesh spread up his forearms in the baking sun.

He smelled the saltwater of the river, the tang of the rust from the chest, and the sunbaked carbon fiber of the *Tahila's* deck.

Elise adjusted a digital camera, set on a tripod, to record the potentially historic opening, while Tom rummaged through the pile of gear and ceremoniously handed Sam a brick chisel and his lump hammer. Sam lined up the chisel on the inside edge of the non-hinged side of the lock and raised his right hand with the lump hammer held tightly.

He paused. A moment such as this deserved some drama. He smiled at the team gathered around. Without them, they never would have come this far. They grinned at him back.

Genevieve shouted, "Enough already! Give us the goods!"

Sam swung the hammer down in a mighty blow, which instantly shattered the weathered lock into pieces.

Sam pried open the lid. It was heavier than he'd thought, made worse by the water trapped inside that seemed to suck it closed, as if in a last gasp attempt for the river to keep her secrets.

The crew crept forward, tight in the elbows. All eyes fixed on the trunk.

With a grunt, Sam heaved the lid off. With a gush of rusty water, it hit the deck.

A gasp rose on the tranquil air. When Sam cleared his eyes from the spray, he stared.

The was no gold inside.

The crew stared.

Elise swore.

Matthew remained in silent observation.

Genevieve stilled on the wire twist of the champagne, totally stunned.

Tom frowned.

It was Catarina who noticed the anomaly, as she was trained to do. "There. Look at the lid. Is that…"

Sam cleared away some of the rust debris that had built up over time. When he saw what he was cleaning, he went even slower. It was a folio wedged into the hollow, full of old papers that had been almost destroyed by the water.

Sam wedged them out carefully, holding his breath.

Artifacts recovered from underwater sites needed immediate stabilization to manage the process of removal of water and conservation. The artifact either needed to be dried carefully, or the water replaced with some inert medium. Artifacts recovered from salt water, particularly metals and glass need be stabilized following absorption of salt or leaching of metals.

In this case, being made of paper, bound by leather, the folio needed to remain wet until specific cleaning and preserving processes could be put in place.

Beside him, Sam had a clear plastic sluice with shallow, slow running clear water from a hose at one end. The idea was that the folio could be placed inside and cleaned from salt and debris without causing further damage to the image inside. Then, Elise could perform the delicate task of drying and preserving the materials.

He carefully lifted the leather-bound folio and placed it into the water sluice.

The packet of papers hit the deck with a wet thump. "Elise. Hose?"

Elise nodded. "Not too much though. I'll keep it gentle. I don't want to tear the paper."

A nervous grimace crossed Sam's lips, as he delicately positioned the pages in the water sluice.

Elise ran the hose at a slow trickle over the pages and Sam pulled them apart with infinite care. Most of them looked like ship's diaries, but there was one toward the bottom that was very different.

"There. There."

Elise nudged out the page he pointed to, and Sam stared.

Revealed as the hose sprayed the sludge cleared was a drawing of the strangest animal he'd ever seen.

It looked like an oversized armadillo, with heavily armored skin, and large claws.

Chapter Fifteen

At the heart of the Tahila, everyone took a seat at the Round Table.

Matthew, the ship's skipper, Veyron, the ship's submersible engineer, Elise, a computer whiz, and Genevieve, a retired Russian assassin whose unique skill set had been appropriated for the team, and Sam Reilly.

The Round Table was Sam's idea. He liked the concept that each person brought their unique wealth of knowledge and experience to any mission. Given that they all had, in previous events, risked their lives for each other for the greater good, he felt that the concept of a Round Table, with the voice of each person seated there being given equal weight and consideration, was good strategy. Tom liked the symbolism of the Arthurian ideal, and he always tried to keep it in the back of his mind when he took over the director position at any time.

Symbolism was where the Round Table's similarities to its Arthurian predecessor ceased. The table itself was a three-dimensional touch-screen projector, which allowed them to bring up 3D images, expand those images, and search through in-depth 3D renditions of buildings, ships, locations, mine tunnels, and anything else the human mind could imagine and engineers have once built.

The computer room looked like a control room. Papers spread out, phones linked to the net with cables and wireless screens popped up. In the background, Genevieve laid out a tray of snacks on the sleek leather-topped wooden table nestled into the crew mess.

Elise worked her magic on the Round Table at the heart of the *Tahila*'s Mission Room.

The delicate leather journal was removed from its submersion and placed on a large bed of paper towels. As with all porous material, it was necessary for her to remove the bulk of the soluble salts present in leather recovered from marine environments.

Prior to conservation, archaeological leather must be washed in order to remove any ingrained dirt. Ideally, leather needed to be washed in water alone. Elise employed a variety of mechanical cleaning techniques, including the use of water jets, ultrasonic cleaners, and dental tools.

She carefully turned each individual page, making certain to take a digital photograph of it, before turning the next one, until she had a digital image of every page in the journal. She then set about to preserve the journal.

Elise removed a bottle of fifty percent sterile water and fifty percent ethanol and poured it into a plastic rectangular box that was large enough to store the leather journal. She then added a further ten percent glycerin and roughly five drops of formaldehyde. They were embalming drugs, which at its most basic form, was exactly what she was trying to do to the leather journal.

Sam, Elise, Tom, and Catarina crammed into the mission room, locked onto the screens where Elise worked her magic. She'd been hard at work using digital reconstruction to undo the damage that five hundred years of water damage had done to the folio pages. Now, they all clustered around looking for a ship's log, maps… anything that might help them unravel the mystery of the *Santa Rosa Celeste*.

What they found instead was something far stranger.

Tom leaned in. He touched Genevieve's arm, but his attention was riveted on the screen. "What the hell do you think it is?"

Sam stared at the screen as he'd been doing for the past twenty minutes. Finally he shook his head. "No idea." He snagged one of the tiny slices of bread coated in liver pate and munched. The retrieval had been hard work, and he realized breakfast had been a long time ago. Genevieve must see it in his face – she didn't scold him as she usually did whenever he got so absorbed in the hunt that he started eating around technology. Now, he felt tired, keyed up from his exposure to the elements and the mysteries of the past. Fresh air poisoning, his mother had called it, he thought, dusting his hands of crumbs, returning to the screen. "Looks like some sort of armadillo… crossed with a oversized worm?"

They shot him looks.

He held up his hands. "I don't know! Maybe it's an image of one of their gods?"

Elise was busy running the scan through a database of unique animal images from around the world. She shrugged, doubtful. "Maybe… but from what I'm seeing, what it looks like doesn't exist."

Catarina looked interested. "You mean it's extinct?"

Elise shook her head. "No, not extinct. I mean it's not even real. There's no record of such a creature ever existing."

Sam felt himself deflate.

But Elise was frowning at the screen. "There is good news, though…" She indicated another screenshot of the pages. "This one looks like it's very real. And it's a map."

It was true. Sam's sense of victory soared.

Matthew arrived from charting course, keeping one half of his attention focused on the navigation system. When he caught sight of the screen and heard their conversation, he threw up his hands. "Hey, that's great! I've signed off on the cost of an expedition to find a mythical lost city of gold, and a creature that doesn't exist."

Sam shot him a grin, but was preoccupied with the map. "Matthew, it's definitely a map to somewhere. You got anything better to do with that pension Our Lady General is paying you to steer this beauty?"

Matthew held up his hands. Sam thought he was conceding defeat, then realized the skipper was asking for the map.

He studied it when Sam offered him the ancient parchment. "Huh. Looks like it's in Colombia."

Sam blinked. "How do you know that?"

Matthew gestured to some random numbers. "Lat and long. Wouldn't make sense to a layman-" Sam took the teasing in stride – "but we experienced seafolk would know these numbers in our sleep."

Sam grinned. "That's why I let you on board, mate. Best and the brightest." He clapped Matthew on the shoulder and turned to Catarina with a grin. "You speak Spanish. Want to come on a treasure hunt?'

A slender eyebrow rose and she folded her arms. "With you?"

"Well. Yeah." Sam suddenly felt like a fourteen year old boy. It was ridiculous. He clapped his friend on the shoulder. "With Tom and I…"

Catarina grinned, seeing straight through the act. "Sorry, boys… I'd love to, but I have real work to do."

Chapter Sixteen

Magdalena River, Colombia

The *Tahila* sailed through the Caribbean Sea before turning south and entering the mouth of the Magdalena, the largest river in Colombia. The Andes Mountain Range stretched the length of South America, but between Ecuador and Colombia it splits into three parts called Cordilleras. The Magdalena runs down between the central and the western Cordilleras.

They made the nearly week long journey down the Magdalena River, following the same route identified in the journal that they had found in the treasure chest stored inside the *Santa Rosa Celeste*. Following in Felipe Ferdinand's footsteps – or at least, sailing record – Sam Reilly hoped that he could retrace the route to El Dorado. Using a map and satellite imaging to compare against the journal notes, he was confident that the map would lead to one of the many villages once occupied by the indigenous Muisca people in the region near Bogotá.

When Felipe Ferdinand sailed the *Santa Rosa Celeste* down the Magdalena River, none of the rivers or topographical landmarks were yet named. Using a modern map, it would be easy to follow the journal entries down an erroneous path. Besides, the fact remained, everywhere near Bogotá had been searched, and no sign of El Dorado had ever been uncovered.

No, Sam was happy to spend the time following the journey from its original known entry point along the Magdalena River. It would take time, but there were things that one's eyes, scanning the horizon from the deck of a ship, could see that no amount of zooming in on satellite images could ever achieve.

At Girardot, a Colombian municipality known for its tourism and as a vacation hotspot, they turned left, taking the small tributary of the Bogotá River and following it as far as the *Tahila* could go. Motoring past agricultural fields, the river narrowed as it entered a thick jungle. When the river became no longer navigable, Matthew anchored the *Tahila*, and Sam and Tom boarded the Eurocopter armed with the digitalized version of Felipe Ferdinand's journal.

Tom sat in the pilot's seat, while Sam took the copilot seat. Tom flicked the power switches to on and together they methodically made his way through a series of checklists.

"Good to go?" Tom asked.

"Good to go," Sam confirmed.

Tom met his eye. "The journal said Felipe rode horses from here, you sure you don't want to ride?"

Despite being able to pilot just about anything mechanical, Sam struggled to ride anything that had a mind of its own. His eyes flashed with pain as he remembered spending more than a week in the saddle of an unwavering and pugnacious camel in the Saharan Desert.

He grinned. "No, I'm good to use the copter from here on in, thank you very much."

Tom nodded. The rotors whined and a moment later he pulled the collective upward, and the black Eurocopter AS350 took to the skies.

Chapter Seventeen

The black Eurocopter traced the Bogotá River, flying low and fast.

At Sam's request, Tom alternated between flying low – just a few feet off the water – and flying high above the tree lines. As the vivid scenery raced by, Sam felt like a navigator in a rally car, trying to match up topographic and natural landmark notes in Ferdinand's journal with what he was seeing at ninety miles an hour outside the cockpit's windshield.

Up ahead he spotted a large waterfall.

Sam said, "That must be Tequendama Falls."

Tom glanced at the topographic map – displayed on the windshield on a heads-up display – which identified the river as such. "That's the one. You want me to take a hovering position here?"

"Yes please."

He glanced at Ferdinand's notes. "If this is the same waterfall the Spanish conquistadors used in 1535, his men had found a small pass to the right of the valley to climb up from the river. Can you see anything?"

Tom stared at the four hundred foot plus sandstone cliffs that lined the river valley. They had been well overgrown by jungle, but still appeared impassable. Tom shrugged. "If they did, they were made of tougher things than I am!"

Sam swept the forbidding landscape.

The Bogotá River fell from the Tequendama Falls – a 433 foot high waterfall of the Bogotá River, located twenty miles southwest of Bogotá in the municipality of Soacha. Established in approximately 10,000 BCE, El Abra and Tequendama were the first permanent human settlements in Colombia.

According to local legend, during the Spanish conquest and evangelization of the Americas, in order to escape the new colonial order indigenous people of the area would jump off the Salto Del Tequendama and become eagles to fly to their freedom.

On the southern side of the river, perched along the clifftops was an old, colonial style mansion that overlooked the Tequendama Falls. Now a museum, it was built as a mansion by architect Carlos Arturo Tapias, as a symbol of the joy and elegance of the elite citizens of the 1920s. To Sam Reilly, it looked like an ancient fortress, watching over the majestic waterfall.

The building itself looked like it might have been built over the very pass that Felipe Ferdinand referred to in his journal.

Sam bit his lower lip. "I don't know. The pass may have been built over when that mansion was constructed. I don't know."

Tom said, "Or, Maybe they backtracked… or there is indeed a pass over there, but it's no longer visible from the air?"

"Yeah… anything's possible."

"You want to keep going?"

Sam nodded. "Yeah, there can't be too many waterfalls in the region that fit this height and description. Keep following the river until we reach Bogotá."

Tom brought the helicopter up another five hundred feet and over the waterfall.

They flew over Bogotá, Colombia's sprawling, high-altitude capital, taking in its Spanish sights. La Candelaria, its cobblestoned center, featured colonial-era landmarks like the neoclassical performance hall Teatro Colón and the 17th-century Iglesia de SantaFrancisco. It was also home to popular museums including the Museo Botero, showcasing Fernando Botero's art, and the Museo del Oro, displaying pre-Colombian gold pieces.

Tom banked, and gave Sam a grin. "Do you want me to put down in the city?"

Sam shook his head. "No thanks. Another time we'll come to visit."

Tom pulled the helicopter up to a hover. "Where to?"

"Head northeast. According to Ferdinand's journal, there's a series of hot springs nearby."

Tom nodded. He'd studied the topographical maps well before taking off. "In the municipality of Sesquilé, which means "hot water" in the now-extinct language of Chibcha, once spoken by the local indigenous people, the Muisca."

"That would be the one."

Tom brought the nose of the Eurocopter into a straight and level attitude, flying slow and an elevation of a hundred feet off the ground, allowing them to try and recreate Ferdinand's trail from the air.

The landscape had changed dramatically since leaving sea level. They had risen above the thick canopies of tropical jungle.

Sam spotted the rising steam in the distance well before he saw the thermal pools. They passed the burning waterfall, where hot water rolled down the hill carving a well-defined hole in the surrounding vegetation.

He double checked the image that Ferdinand had drawn in his journal. Despite the introduction of a commercial section of the hot pools, the shape of the thermal pools and the thermal waterfall appeared surprisingly unchanged.

Sam bit his lower lip, glanced at Tom. "This is definitely it."

"All right, you want me to head toward Lake Guatavita."

"Yes please," Sam replied, placing the journal on his lap. "According to Ferdinand, his men spent time recovering here, but then headed for the circular lake."

Tom made a few adjustments on the helicopter's controls, and the lake came into view.

Sam studied the lake. It was circular and according to the guidebook its surface area was just below twenty hectares. The earlier theories of the crater's origin being a meteorite impact, volcanic cinder, or limestone sinkhole had now been discredited. The most likely explanation being that it resulted from the dissolution of underground salt deposits from an anticline, resulting in a type of sinkhole.

Lake Guatavita was located in the Cordillera Oriental of the Colombian Andes in the municipality of Sesquilé in the Almeidas Province.

Spanish colonizers and Conquistadors knew about the existence of a sacred lake in the Eastern Ranges of the Andes possibly as early as 1531. The lake was associated with indigenous rituals involving gold. However, the first conquistador to arrive at the actual location was Gonzalo Jiménez de Quesada, possibly in June 1537, while on an expedition to the highlands of the Eastern Ranges of the Andes in search of gold. This brought the Spanish into first contact with the Muisca inhabiting the Altiplano Cundiboyacense, including around Lake Guatavita.

Tom made a slow counterclockwise reconnaissance of the lake.

Sam took some photos for mementoes more than science or reference. The fact was, Lake Guatavita had been nearly drained by the Spanish in the sixteenth century and again by the French thirty years later, while modern day SCUBA divers had combed its seabed. One thing was certain, despite the Muisca mythology and rituals involving gold in the lake, it wasn't the location of El Dorado.

Tom said, "Do you want me to head toward the site of the massacre?"

"The Muisca village Ferdinand and his men slaughtered?" Sam asked.

"Yeah. I mean, that's the last reference in the journal to reaching El Dorado. So, they must have found it somewhere between Lake Guatavita and Muisca's village."

Sam frowned. "I doubt it. I mean, how does something like that stay hidden all this time?"

"You want me to head back to the *Tahila*?"

"No. It's a stretch, but even so, I want to see it from the ground."

"You want me to land here and then walk there?"

"No." Sam glanced out the window to the west. "There's a cathedral built into a salt mine in Zipaquirá. It's meant to be something quite spectacular."

"You want to go religious sightseeing?"

"No. I have a local friend who told me he'd meet us there and drive us into the archeological remains of the Muisca villages."

Tom set the new coordinates on the GPS. "All right, to the salt mine it is."

Chapter Eighteen

Salt Cathedral of Zipaquirá

The black Eurocopter landed in the middle of the carpark.

It took up four individual parking spots. Sam opened the side door and got out. Several bystanders glanced up at the helicopter, but they all gave him a wide berth. There was every chance that he was the mine's owner, or a drug lord.

Tom locked the helicopter, his face set questioningly, as though asking if it was such a good idea leaving a helicopter in a public carpark in Colombia. "You want me to stay with the helicopter?"

Sam shrugged. "No, my friend says it will be all right here."

Tom nodded. What did he care? He wasn't paying for it. "All right, where are we meeting your friend?"

"Down in the mine."

"The mine?"

"Technically, he wants to show me a cathedral."

Tom laughed. "Obviously. We're here to find El Dorado, the lost city of gold, and we're going to start with a salt mine."

Sam grinned. "I'm glad you can see the connection, because I couldn't."

They headed to the main entrance, and Sam paid for the self-guided entrance fee of US 18 dollars for each of them and was, in return, given a map of the underground mine.

He ran his eyes across the map.

The place looked like one giant labyrinth of salt tunnels leading to and throughout the Salt Cathedral of Zipaquirá, before spreading out deeper into the halite mountain, where the mine itself was worked even to today.

Tom glanced at the map from over Sam's shoulder. "Your friend couldn't meet us on the surface?"

Sam made a half-grin. "Apparently not."

The entered the first tunnel.

For about a hundred feet, small floodlights embedded in the floor next to the walls set the crimson-red arches ablaze in the dim light. The effect was striking. The entrance to the Salt Cathedral looked more like the gateway to hell than a pathway to heaven.

As they descended no steel arches were needed to reinforce the tunnel, as the salt was compressed and fused into solid rock that geologists called halite.

They descended nearly 650 feet to reach the underground Roman Catholic church. It was a well-known tourist destination and place of pilgrimage in the country, but Sam was surprised the effect the sight had on him.

The temple at the bottom has three sections, representing the birth, life, and death of Jesus. The icons, ornaments and architectural details are hand carved in the halite rock.

Fourteen crosses along the route were the Stations of the Cross, representing the events of the *Via DoloRosa*, which was Jesus' journey to crucifixion and each ripe with its own subtle symbolism, before opening into a massive chamber – at the end of which, a towering forty-five-foot crucifix glowed in electric blues, fading into majestic purples.

Sam guessed the cross must have weighed twenty or thirty tons, until he drew nearer and discovered it weighed nothing…

In fact, it was a giant hollow carving.

Sam's eyes swept the landscape, silently taking in the entire chamber. To the left of the glowing, carved crucifix was a stone replica of Michelangelo's *Creation of Adam*.

Above, a ceiling swirling with the spiral patterns of salt, reminding him that the entire mountain had once been battered by the sea, during an era when the mountain was below the sea. Those same rocks were 135 million years old, a relic of the vast Tethys Ocean that once covered the entire region. Sam turned and glanced at the dome, surrounded by stone angels that a nearby guide informed a group of tourists, was where the choir sings.

Behind them, a man said, "This place... it's quite extraordinary, almost magical, isn't it my friend?"

"It is really something," Sam agreed, before recognizing his friend, and shaking the man's hand. "El Gordo Rojas!"

"Sam Reilly... as I live and breathe. It is good to see you again."

"Likewise," Sam said, and he meant it, running his eyes across his friend. The man was of average height, with wiry muscles stretched over an almost gaunt frame. He was in his late forties, but his hair remained a dark black. He introduced Tom. "This is a good friend of mine, Gustavo Rojas. El Gordo Rojas, this is Tom Bower, a world leader in underwater exploration and a friend since school."

"Pleasure to meet you, Tom," Rojas said, shaking his hand firmly.

"Likewise," Tom grinned. "Sam called you El Gordo... doesn't that mean... fat?"

El Gordo Rojas nodded. "Yes, I'm afraid it was a childhood name, and it sort of stuck."

Tom suppressed a grin. "You were the fat kid at school?"

"No," El Gordo replied. "The opposite. My family were very poor, I remember spending much of my youth starving."

Tom bit his lower lip. "And, so people called you fat?"

El Gordo shrugged. "No one ever said that nicknames needed to make any sense."

Sam said, "Tell me, why did you bring us down here?"

El Gordo frowned. "You don't like it?"

"Sure, I do," Sam said. "I like it very much, it's brilliant, but we didn't come here for a religious or even cultural journey, we're looking for history about the Muisca people and we're searching for El Dorado."

Now El Gordo's lips were twisted upward in a thousand-watt grin. "Isn't everyone? Many people before you have come to this land having heard tales of a city born from gold, but all they discovered was a mountain of salt."

Sam nodded. "You brought us down here to remonstrate me for searching?"

"Not at all," Gordo folded his lanky arms across his chest. "No, I brought you here to show you evidence that you're looking in the wrong place."

Sam said, "You think El Dorado doesn't exist?"

"No, in fact, I know for certain El Dorado does exist."

"Really?" Sam asked, "How?"

El Gordo ignored the question, and returned to his original statement. "There's nothing but salt in this region. The Muisca people were expert craftsmen with gold, but they didn't mine it."

Tom's eyes narrowed, "If the Muisca didn't mine gold, where did they get it?"

El Gordo's face lit up. "That's the million…okay, billion-dollar question, isn't it?"

Sam kept him focused. "What's the answer?"

El Gordo said, "It's it obvious?"

"No," Sam and Tom replied in unison.

El Gordo grinned. "They traded for it with El Dorado."

Chapter Nineteen

Sam met his friend's eye with incredulity. "How do you know the Muisca people traded directly with the people of El Dorado?"

El Gordo said, "I could try and explain it, but it's much better if I just show you both."

"Show us?" Tom asked.

El Gordo nodded. "Look, years before the underground church was built in the 1930s, the miners carved a sanctuary, as a place for their daily prayers asking for protection from the saints before starting to work. In 1950, the construction of a bigger project had begun, and the Salt Cathedral, which was inaugurated on August 15, 1954 and dedicated to Our Lady of Rosary, Patron saint of miners."

"We read the guidebook," Sam said, somewhat confused where his friend was going with his story.

El Gordo said, "Most people read that, but what they don't realize is that most of the galleries down here were in fact carved out by the ancient Muisca."

A slight smile creased Sam's lip. "You're kidding."

"What's more," El Gordo continued, "The halite mines were exploited already by the pre-Columbian Muisca culture since the 5th century BCE."

"Okay," Sam said, "but what does any of this have to do with El Dorado?"

El Gordo nodded again. "Come with me and I'll show you."

Sam asked, "Where?"

"The Salt Cathedral of Zipaquirá shares the mountain with a working salt mine located several hundred feet below the sanctuary complex."

All three men climbed into El Gordo's Jeep and he drove them down into the dark depths of the actively working tunnels of the salt mine.

The Zipaquirá mine was still working beneath the cathedrals. In fact, it continued for thousands of feet below the cathedral, while hundreds of miles of it extended in every direction, like giant tendrils. But unlike the crude mining techniques employed by early Spanish conquistadors who used dynamite to collapse the halite, it had now evolved with modern mining techniques. A freshwater bath now dissolved the halite and the resulting brine is pumped to the surface where the salt is removed through evaporation.

Sam couldn't be sure how far they had traveled or how deep underground they were when El Gordo finally pulled up the Jeep, parking in a not so small alcove surrounded by walls upon walls of halite.

El Gordo said, "This is it. We're here."

Sam suppressed a grin. They appeared to be at the end of some sort of offshoot of the main mine, miles from anywhere or anything, and at least half a mile underground. "Here where?"

"You'll see," El Gordo said, as he climbed out of the jeep and patted Sam on the shoulder, handing him and Tom a pair of mining helmets. "You'll need these."

Sam and Tom exchanged glances as they switched their headlamps on. Tom looked like he was wondering if El Gordo could be trusted, or whether Sam's old friend was about to kill them. Sam nodded. El Gordo could be trusted.

Turning to El Gordo, Sam said, "Lead the way."

"It's not far," El Gordo replied, the beam of his flashlight reflecting off the walls of halite, turning them into glittering diamonds.

They walked down a horizontal shaft, which appeared to lead nowhere and serve no purpose. Unlike the large tunnels through which they had entered and had been built by extracting the surrounding halite, this one was small – not much larger than a person could comfortably walk through without hunching over – and appeared to have served as a passageway and not to extract the rich halite within its walls.

The question remained, where did it lead?

Sam took a breath. The passage was pitch dark, dank, with a faint smell of sulfur in the air. El Gordo moved with the quick and purposeful stride of a much younger man.

After nearly twenty minutes the passageway came to an abrupt ending, with a large iron door preventing any farther progress.

Sam bit his lower lip as he watched El Gordo work his way through a series of keys. "Where are you taking us?"

"You'll see," El Gordo said.

El Gordo found the key he wanted and used it to open up the steel cover that protected a keypad. He immediately inputted its code.

A moment later, the door's hydraulic arms retracted, and the heavy steel opened inward, revealing a large cavern.

On the far side of the room El Gordo fixed his flashlight on an ancient mosaic of a city on the wall. The flashlight reflected the image so brightly that it took Sam a moment to realize what he was staring at.

Then realization dawned on him like a flash of lightning.

The city depicted was made of solid gold.

Chapter Twenty

Sam made an audible gasp.

Tom suppressed a curse, his eyes wide and focused.

El Gordo folded his arms across his chest and stood silently, his face set with the resignation of someone whose views had just been vindicated.

Sam shook his head and blinked as though expecting the image to disappear like a mirage. When he opened his eyes and it hadn't, he grinned and examined the image that was nearly ten feet high and equally long.

The entire thing had been etched into a sheet of solid gold.

Houses, like those that the Muisca had used, called *Bohíos* or *Malokas*, stood at the center of the mosaic. Their circular structures made of poles of wood and walls of clay, with a conical reed roof. A long beam of wood supported the roof in the center of the round structure and was attached to the wooden poles. They were spread out in a rough circle, with the largest at the center.

Unlike the villages used by the early Muisca people, this one wasn't surrounded by a perimeter of tall wooden poles. Instead, it appeared enclosed in a solid wall of stone. Sam's eyes narrowed, as he tried to decipher what the image was depicting – was El Dorado within a cavern underground? That would explain why it had never been found despite extensive searches over five centuries.

He stepped forward and looked at the top of the image. Jagged beams of light had been etched into the top right-hand corner of the painting. It might have represented something else, but he was pretty sure it was meant to show sun warmly filtering down on the village... which most likely ruled out any chance that it was subterranean.

Sam focused on the little details within the landscape. The indigenous people who appeared to be working on small, individual tasks – cooking, cleaning, sharpening a knife or spearhead in little grooves in the stone ground. The people and their tasks, all appeared similar to the Muisca people found in the region by the Spanish conquistadors who ventured there during the fifteenth century. With the exception being that these people were all made of gold and working with tools of gold…

He leaned in, until he could see one of the person's faces. The artists had gone to the effort of making every detail in the person's face. It was incredible craftmanship. The spear sharpener was glancing at something at the other end of the frame.

At first, Sam assumed that it was merely the artist's representation of one of the villager's looking up, designed simply to put the character's facial features in the forefront of the viewer's perspective, but then he spotted that the next villager, was staring at the same thing from a different angle. Sam's eyes raced from each of the villagers until he was certain that it wasn't just a coincidence.

Every single one of them despite their position on the landscape, had the same sort of expression as they gazed toward a focal point on the mural. Sam's eyes narrowed as he considered where he'd seen that sort of expression before.

Then it hit him…

It was veneration.

But what were they looking at? Sam's gaze zeroed in on the imperceptible focal point. It was toward the left hand-side of the painting. It was an animal of some sort. He'd dismissed it at first, assuming it to be a dog or a pet of some description, but now that he was closer, Sam was able to make out its distinctive features.

His lips creased upward into a grin.

Because he'd seen the creature before.

It was a type of over-sized armadillo, short, with heavily armored plates, and powerful legs equipped with sharp claws for burrowing. The very same creature that didn't exist in any animal database on Earth…

And the identical creature to the one they'd found drawn inside the journal they had discovered inside the treasure chest on board the *Santa Rosa Celeste*.

Chapter Twenty-One

"Well… what do you think?" El Gordo asked.

Sam met his eye. "This is amazing. The first definitive proof that El Dorado exists. When was it found?"

"Nearly twenty years ago."

"How did you manage to keep it a secret for so long?" Sam asked.

El Gordo expelled a sigh. "Some miners discovered it while they were drilling exploratory shafts in search of new seams of halite. After the artwork's discovery there was an accident, and the shaft collapsed, killing most of the men who worked there. It was later discovered there was a fault in the tunnel, and the whole region was declared unsafe."

Sam said, "And consequently no one ever found out about the discovery."

El Gordo said, "That's right."

Tom asked, "How many survivors were there?"

"Just two."

Tom persisted. "Why didn't they talk?"

El Gordo unfolded his arms and leveled his eyes with Tom. "Look, you have to understand that no one chooses to work in the Colombian mines. Hell, mining conditions are the same all around the world. It is hard, dangerous, often deadly at times, work… and Colombia, particularly in the late eighties didn't have anything in the way of occupational health and safety."

Sam grinned, knowing where this was going. "They were poor kids who ended up working in the mines."

El Gordo matched his grin. "That's right. We were poor kids, working in the mines to survive. We were never going to make anything of our lives."

Sam said, "And then you came across a fortune in gold."

"That's right, and it was all ours. Only it wasn't at first…" El Gordo closed his eyes, as though remembering those painful days. "There were eight of us as part of the exploration team, set to mine the small, narrow exploratory passages. We all knew what it meant. Of course, the gold wasn't ours. It belonged to the company, didn't it?"

Sam had known a few Colombians in his time. Some of them shared a somewhat relaxed view of personal ownership. It was hard not to in a world where the divide between rich and poor was so great… and where kids as young as El Gordo once needed to work in the mines. "What happened?"

"There was a disagreement. The other men didn't believe it could be achieved. In the end, the decision was taken from us, and granted by God."

Sam said, "Go on… what did you do?"

"Not me… God."

Sam held his glare. "Go on."

"The mine collapsed. To this day I'm not sure why it did. I was the only one to get out."

Sam asked, "What did you do?"

"I falsified seismology and geology reports to ensure no one ever attempted to mine that section of the salt mine again. Then, as the recession hit at the end of the eighties, into the early nineties the mine was set to close permanently."

Sam nodded. "So, you bought it."

"That's right," El Gordo said proudly. "My idea was that I would fund my own search for El Dorado."

Tom's lips twisted into an incredulous smile. "But if you were poor, how did you afford to buy it?"

El Gordo held out his hand. In it were three golden pearls identical to the ones found scattered on the deck of the *Santa Rosa Celeste*. "With these."

Sam said, "We found some of the same mysterious pearls on board the *Santa Rosa Celeste*."

El Gordo suppressed a smile. "So now we both know that El Dorado exists."

"You never found El Dorado," Sam said. It was a statement, not a question.

"No. In the end, the price of salt changed, and we hit a new seam, and I made my fortune out of the very mine in which I had once been trapped by the circumstances of my life. I founded many searches, but if El Dorado still exists, which I'm not even so sure it does, it is so well buried that no one will ever find it."

Sam shrugged. "Sometimes treasures release their secrets when the time is right."

El Gordo laughed. "And you think the time is right now?"

"I don't know what I think. But I do know that the mysteries of the *Santa Rosa Celeste* have finally surfaced after more than five centuries, and perhaps, it might be time for El Dorado to follow."

El Gordo shot him an appraising gaze. "I believe you know something that I don't."

"I'm not sure yet. I have a map from Felipe Ferdinand. I'm hoping you might help me make sense of it. The jungle's too thick for me to search using satellite images of its topography."

"You want to share the secret of El Dorado with me?" El Gordo asked without hiding his skepticism.

Sam said, "I'm sure the Colombian government will want its share too…"

El Gordo nodded. "We'll cross that once we find it."

Sam returned his focus to the strange armadillo-like creature delineated as a God in the painting. His eyes darted back to El Gordo. "All right, now there's something I want you to share with me…"

"Shoot."

"Do you know what that creature is there?" Sam asked, pointing to the armadillo-like creature.

"The armadillo?"

"You know as well as I do that's not an armadillo."

El Gordo allowed his lips to part into a half-grin. "You're right, I do. But I'm fascinated to know how you came to know it."

Sam said, "Those golden pearls you have… they were scattered on the deck of the *Santa Rosa Celeste*, while locked in a treasure chest safely in the bottom of the ship was a journal – in it, was a series of hand drawings by Felipe Ferdinand, of that exact same creature. I had my researcher conduct a digital search for anything like it. She found nothing even close. Not extinct and certainly not extant."

"Those drawing might not be to scale." El Gordo met his eye and spoke seriously. "Maybe they were just drawings of an armadillo?"

Sam held his gaze. "You know that's not true."

El Gordo turned the palms of his hands skyward. "No. I suppose you were never going to believe that."

"So what are they really?"

El Gordo made a sort of half-shrug. "How would I know?"

"Come on, El Gordo, you still owe me one," Sam said. "What do you know?"

El Gordo made a dramatic, theatrical sigh. "All right, all right. I don't know what it's called, but I know the people of El Dorado worshiped the damned thing. And what's more, I know the strange creature was somehow responsible for producing these golden pearls."

Sam made a wry smile. He didn't hide his skepticism. "That creature made them? How?"

"I don't know. But when I first set eyes on this chamber, this wasn't the only image I found. There were others… and every one of them focused on that armadillo. One in particular had a small container made from gold, and inside, were about a hundred of those pearl-like stones."

"They could have been an offering to the creature?" Tom suggested.

"Maybe," El Gordo admitted. "But I don't think so. I think it was showing where their wealth had come from."

Sam asked, "Can I take some pictures?"

El Gordo nodded. "Sure, but if you tell anyone they were taken down here I'll deny it. This might not be a gold mine, but it's a mine just the same, and we have plenty of security – both high tech and in terms of man power. We're friends, Sam Reilly… but don't ever betray me…"

Sam brushed the not-so-idle threat away with the wave of his hand. "I get the idea. I'll use it for research purposes only and let you know if I find anything."

"Good man. I knew I could trust you." El Gordo glanced at Tom, but didn't repeat the threat. It had been made already, and besides, if Sam trusted Tom, El Gordo probably figured he did too. "Now, you said something about following a map?"

"Yes," Sam said, removing a copy of the map in the journal. "Here, according to this, Ferdinand took his men to this Muisca village, where he found El Dorado. I'd like to repeat his journey and see what we find. Can you help us?"

El Gordo ran his eyes across the map. Within a few seconds he frowned. "I'm happy to show you, but there's nothing there that you need to see. Definitely nothing that will lead you to El Dorado."

"Why?"

"Because someone's already been there. It's called Las Delicias…"

Sam repeated the name. "Las Delicias… what is it?"

"It's just another Muisca village."

"Any chance it's something more?"

El Gordo said, "No. Although the Spanish chroniclers have reported "great populations" of the Muisca territories, the people lived in small settlements, described by the Spanish conquerors as dispersed homesteads. As the Maya people, the Muisca related the smaller settlements with their effective agriculture. Houses on the Bogotá savanna were built on slightly elevated areas to prevent them from flooding from the various rivers, humedales and swamps, characteristic of the area. Each community had their own farmlands and hunting grounds surrounding their houses. The houses were constructed around a central square with the house of the cacique – that was the name of their chieftain – in the center. Two or more gates in the enclosure known as a Cercado gave access to the village."

"And that's what I would find if I followed this map?"

"Yes. Look it up. Excavations in the Las Delicias neighborhood of Bogotá, on an alluvial terrace of the Tunjuelito River in 1990, exposed six circular structures of fifteen feet in diameter. The occupation of these houses has been dated from the start of the Muisca Period until the colonial period. The living space was occupied in two stages, starting from 950 BCE, followed by a next phase dated at 750 BCE. The dating has been done based on carbon, taken from the floors of the area. Ceramics, animal bones, swindles, seeds and jewelry have all been found in this location too."

"All right, so we're all out of leads."

El Gordo said, "It appears so, unless you found something else in that shipwreck of yours?"

"Afraid not."

El Gordo nodded. "If you're finished here, I'll take you back to your helicopter."

Sam took one last glance at the golden city. "One more question."

"Shoot."

"You said before that this image proves the Muisca traded for the gold…"

"That's right," El Gordo confirmed. "What about it?"

"How did you come up with that understanding? I've studied every inch of this landscape, and to me it looks just like any other Muisca village. If anything, I'd say it proves that El Dorado exists within the confederation of the Muisca People."

"Then you would be wrong."

Sam smiled. "Why?"

"Scholars all agree that the housing of the Muisca was egalitarian. There was little, if any, differentiation between the living spaces of the caciques and the lower-class people. In this village, the center building is nearly three times those of the surrounding huts. What's more, its fortified with a series of armored spikes and at main entrance two warriors posed."

Sam gave that some thought. It made sense. He grinned. "That explains a lot."

El Gordo asked, "What?"

Sam shook his head. "No wonder no one has ever found El Dorado all this time."

"Why?" Tom asked.

Sam said, "We've been looking in the wrong spot."

El Gordo nodded in agreement. "If this village isn't Muisca it confirms that El Dorado wasn't either. But all the same, it doesn't help us much. Just because we've ruled out this small region doesn't mean that we've narrowed it down much – we still theoretically have the rest of the world still to search."

"Not the rest of the world," Sam said emphatically. "Somewhere between here and Ubatuba, Brazil."

El Gordo's eyes narrowed. "That's where we know the *Santa Rosa Celeste* traveled?"

"Yes."

"It's still a lot of ground to cover," El Gordo said. "It potentially includes the bulk of the Amazon rainforest, which you could easily spend your lifetime and your fortune searching without finding it."

Sam said, "You're right. Which is why I need to find a way to narrow the search area down somehow."

El Gordo laughed. "Good luck with that. Okay, I'm sorry I couldn't offer you any more help. I'll take you to your helicopter and wish you good luck."

On the surface, Sam shook El Gordo's hand and thanked him for the help.

El Gordo said, "Don't worry about it. I still owe you plenty."

Sam said, "Forget about it."

"All right, I will. Good luck finding El Dorado."

Tom thanked El Gordo and climbed into the cockpit of the Eurocopter.

A few minutes later and they were in the air again.

Tom glanced at Sam. "How do you know El Gordo?"

Sam said, "About ten years ago I saved a ship he owned from running aground somewhere near Panama. Its engines had died during a heavy storm that was battering the ship toward the shore. I led a team of marine engineers on board and saved the ship. No questions asked about its cargo."

Tom eyebrows arched. "What was she carrying?"

Sam shrugged. "I have no idea."

"And he was forever grateful to you for that?"

Sam said, "Yeah, that's about it…"

"Really?" Tom's voice was doubtful. "He seems highly indebted to you."

Sam bit his lower lip. "The same ship was intercepted by our Navy off the coast of SantaFrancisco. Custom official boarded and found three hundred million dollars' worth of cocaine."

"El Gordo's a drug dealer?"

Sam shrugged. "The man's rich enough to leave an entire golden etching of El Dorado sitting down the bottom of a salt mine. He owns a private island in the Bahamas, a Leah Jet, a fleet of helicopters, and a penthouse on 5th Avenue in New York. I don't know, but I can tell you I know that he didn't get that rich by mining salt."

Tom cursed. "I thought you said we could trust this guy?"

"Hell no. I only went there because I was sure if anyone could help us find El Dorado, it was El Gordo Rojas, which, by the looks of things, I was right to believe."

Tom set a course for the *Tahila*.

Sam watched the jungle race by far below them. He switched off, letting his mind wander, before his cell phone snapped him back into alertness.

Sam didn't recognize the number. He said, "Hello?"

"Hello. Sam Reilly?"

"Speaking. Who's this?"

"My name's Doctor Liia Miller. I'm a dendrologist from UCLA. We spoke a week ago."

Sam's heart raced. He knew exactly what the woman was calling about. Without preamble, he asked, "Did you find anything?"

"Yes, as a matter of fact I did." Then, before he could ask, she said, "The wood you sent me was *Cariniana Pyriformis*."

Sam frowned at the Latin name. "Can you tell me that in English, please?"

"Colombian Mahogany. Carbon dated to the 1500s give or take fifty years."

"I don't suppose you can narrow down roughly where in Colombia the wood might have come from?"

Liia answered straight away. "I took the liberty of checking for you, knowing that you would ask. It turns out, *Cariniana Pyriformis* grows widely throughout the heart of Colombia."

"What about the coastline?" Sam asked, hurriedly adding, "Somewhere a ship traveling along the Magdalena River near Bogotá through to Ubuntu in Brazil might have come across."

"In present day, there are scatterings of *Cariniana Pyriformis* all along the coast, from Colombia, Venezuela, Guyana, Suriname, French Guiana, and Brazil."

Sam frowned. "There's no way to narrow it down any further?"

Doctor Miller's voice softened. "I didn't say that. I was just letting you know that the exorbitant amount I'm billing you for my dendrology services are justified. Most of those trees have been planted since the Spanish invasion for shipbuilding. But in the 1500s, it was a very different story. There was only one place where a ship of your description might have felled *Cariniana Pyriformis* to make repairs."

Sam's heart leaped into his mouth. "Where?"

Doctor Miller said, "The Sierra Nevada de Santa Marta, Colombia."

Chapter Twenty-Two

El Gordo Rojas watched as the black helicopter took off, trailed in the distance, and finally disappeared beneath the horizon.

A moment later he picked up his cell phone and pressed redial.

A man answered immediately. "Well?"

"Sam Reilly knows the truth…"

"Really?" The man's voice was filled with admiration. "The question remains to be seen, is he good enough to find it?"

El Gordo hesitated for a second. "I believe so… but if he isn't, well… then he was never going to be useful to us, was he?"

"No. I suppose you're right."

"Do you want me to have him followed?"

"No. We'll hear about it as soon as he reaches El Dorado."

"Then what?"

"If he finds El Dorado it's almost a given that he will go in search of the Tomb."

El Gordo exhaled a deep breath. "But much less likely he will find it."

The man's voice relaxed. "If he's good enough to get this far, he'll find it."

"And if he does?"

The man's voice on the other end of the line hardened. "Then we kill him."

Chapter Twenty-Three

Sierra Nevada de Santa Marta, Colombia

Sam Reilly stared at the satellite image.

They projected onto the center of Round Table – the digital 3D projection table inside the mission room on board the *Tahila* – while the *Tahila* was anchored off the Caribbean Coast of Colombia. Sam studied the images.

The Sierra Nevada de Santa Marta formed an isolated mountain range separated from the Andes chain that runs through Colombia. Reaching an altitude of 18,700 feet, just 26 miles from the Caribbean coast, the Sierra Nevada was one of the world's highest coastal ranges – the highest being the Saint Elias Mountains in Canada. The Sierra Nevada encompassed roughly six and half thousand square miles and served as the primary source of thirty-six rivers, spanning across the Departments of Magdalena, Cesar and La Guajira.

The place looked just about as remote as any Sam could imagine.

The entire coastal region was covered in tropical rainforest made up of perennial trees, with a canopy reaching between a hundred to a hundred and thirty feet, making its natural exploration highly difficult from the air and on foot. At its higher altitude the mountain range was covered in snow all year round. Sam grinned. The place looked impenetrable even with modern technology. It was the perfect place to hide an ancient city – even one made of gold.

He picked up the dossier Elise had produced for him on the region and started to read.

The Tairona people were its indigenous rulers. Carbon dating from archeological sites showed the Tairona maintained a sedentary or semi-sedentary occupation of the Colombian Caribbean coast as early as 200 BCE. From what Sam had read about the Tairona, their history and culture were every bit as woven into mystery and legends as the story of El Dorado.

They formed one of the two principal linguistic groups of the Chibchan family, the other being the Muisca. Genetic and archaeological evidence showed a relatively dense occupation of the region by at least 200 BCE. Pollen data compiled by Luisa Fernanda Herrera in 1980 showed considerable deforestation and the use of cultigens such as Yuca and Maiz since possibly 1200 BCE.

Ethnohistorical data showed that initial contact with the Spanish was tolerated by the Tairona, but by 1600 AD confrontations grew, and a small part of the Tairona population moved to the higher stretches of the Sierra Nevada de Santa Marta. In doing so, the Tairona were able to evade the worst of the Spanish colonial system during the 17th and 18th centuries when they were eventually forcibly integrated into the Spanish Encomienda system. The indigenous Kogi, Wiwa, Arhuacos, and Kankuamo people who live in the area today are believed to be direct descendants of the Tairona.

Knowledge sources about the pre-Columbian Tairona civilization were limited to archaeological findings and a few written references from the Spanish colonial era. One of the first descriptions of the region was written by Pedro Martyr d' Anghiera and was published in 1530. The area also was described by other explorers who visited the region between 1505 and 1524. Anghiera portrays the Tairona valleys as densely populated, with extensive fields irrigated in the same way as those in Tuscany. Many villages were dedicated to fishing and traded their marine goods for the rest of their needs with those living inland. Anghiera describes how they aggressively repelled the Spanish when they attempted to take women and children as slaves in the first contacts. It appears that the Tairona were very violent and the Spanish suffered great losses, which resulted in a more diplomatic strategy from the first governor of Santa Marta, Rodrigo de Bastidas.

One of the best-known Tairona nucleated villages and archaeological sites is known as Ciudad Perdida, which translated to *The Lost City*.

Sam paused, and read the last three words again out loud.

The Lost City…

It was a major city, about thirteen hectares at its center. It was discovered by looters in 1975 but was now under the care of the Colombian Institute of Anthropology and History. Recent studies suggest that it was inhabited by approximately 1,600 to 2,400 people that lived in at least 124,000 square feet of roofed space, in about 184 round houses built on top of terraces paved with stone. In addition to this city, there were once many other sites of similar or greater size and it has been predicted that many of these ancient cities remain hidden within the dense and inhospitable jungles of the region.

A larger site, *Pueblito*, was located near the coast, containing at least 254 terraces and had a population of about 3,000 people. Archaeological studies in the area show that even larger nucleated villages existed toward the western slope of the Sierra Nevada de Santa Marta, like *Posiguieca* and *Ciudad Antigua*.

Smaller villages and hamlets were part of a very robust exchange network of specialized communities, connected with stone-paved paths. Villages that specialized in salt production and fishing, like *Chengue* in the Parque Tairona, are evidence of a robust Tairona political economy based on specialized staple production. The Tairona were known to have built stone terraced platforms, house foundations, stairs, sewers, tombs, and bridges. Use of pottery for utilitarian and ornamental or ceremonial purposes was also highly developed as a result of fairly specialized communities.

Sam scrutinized the details.

Were the Tairona capable of building El Dorado?

Tom Bower entered the Mission Room. "What do you think?"

Sam tilted his head, questioningly. "About the *Sierra Nevada de Santa Marta*?"

"Yeah, and the Tairona... do you think they were capable of building El Dorado?"

"I'm not sure," Sam answered honestly. "But I do know the *Sierra Nevada de Santa Marta* is more than capable of hiding it for the past five centuries."

Tom suppressed a grin. "Until now."

"Hopefully..." Sam's eyes widened. "You never know. Crazier things have happened."

"Are you ready to go?" Tom asked.

Sam switched off the computer. "Yeah."

"Good, because Genevieve says the Eurocopter is fueled and ready."

Sam grinned. "Then let's go find El Dorado."

Chapter Twenty-Four

The sleek Eurocopter took off from the *Tahila* and raced across the Caribbean Coast, with Genevieve at the controls, Tom in the copilot seat, and Sam manning the LIDAR instruments in the back of the helicopter.

Blue-green shades of turquoise waters streamed by the cockpit windshield, before the ground below turned a dark shade of green as they flew over the dense foliage of the jungle that reached the shore.

From the air, the jungle glittered like velvet as the sun cut through the clouds like a hallmark card, dark and light with the promise of coming storms.

From the cockpit, Genevieve said, "I'm commencing the horizontal grid search pattern."

Sam flicked on a couple switches. "All right, I'm starting the LIDAR pulse."

LIDAR is fundamentally a distance technology. From an airplane or in this case, a helicopter, LiDAR systems actively send light energy to the ground in the form of laser pulses. This pulse hits the ground and returns to the sensor.

The surveying method measures distance to a target by illuminating the target with a pulsed laser light and measuring the reflected pulses with a sensor. Differences in laser return times and wavelengths can then be used to make digital 3-D representations of the target. The name lidar, now used as an acronym of light detection and ranging, was originally a portmanteau of light and radar.

The *Tahila* had pulled into the bay at *Playo Cinto*, one of several small bays along the *National Park of Tayrona*. The idea was to run a sweeping airborne laser swath mapping of the forests along the coastlines.

If the Santa Rosa Celeste did obtain its Colombian Mahogany used to make its repairs from a forest inside the *Sierra Nevada de Santa Marta*, a stretch of fifty miles of coastline that was the most likely place Ferdinand would have come ashore to do so.

Sam stared at the LIDAR monitor intently, like a child watching a computer screen.

Tom asked, "What exactly should we be visually looking for?"

Sam said, "Well, a big golden city with the words painted in gold lettering, El Dorado, would be nice..."

Tom ignored his banter. "And failing that?"

"Keep your eyes out for any unnatural changes in the topography of the tropical rainforest canopy. You're looking for areas where the trees have been forced to grow at awkward positions and strange angles. Anything that might indicate people had once terraformed the landscape in some way."

"All right, we can do that," Tom announced.

Sam said, "Also, keep your eyes on sections where trees appear to be growing in unnaturally straight lines."

"Straight lines?"

"Yeah. The Tairona routinely built large footpaths made of stone between their cities. My guess is that Felipe Ferdinand and his crew came across just one of those paths while he was felling trees to make repairs, and decided to follow it."

"Great," Tom said, his lips twisted in a bemused grin. "So now we're looking for the yellow brick road to the Emerald City?"

"Ideally, I'm hoping it leads to El Dorado, but I'll take an Emerald City if we come across it," Sam said, missing Tom's reference to the Wizard of Oz.

They ran nearly fifty miles without coming across any stone pathways. They were just about to circle back, when Sam said, "We got it all wrong."

Genevieve smiled, keeping the helicopter low and level. "Got what wrong?"

"Everything," Sam said. "We've been looking for a stone path leading through the jungle all the way to the ocean – working on the assumption that Ferdinand and his men found it when they came to shore to fell trees and make repairs to the *Santa Rosa Celeste*."

"You don't think that's the case?"

"No. The Tairona didn't have paths leading all the way to the beaches anywhere near here. Smaller villages and hamlets were part of a very robust exchange network of specialized communities, connected with stone-paved paths. There were specific villages that specialized in fishing. Three in this region in total. They've all been identified farther east along the Colombian coast and none along this stretch."

Tom turned his head right over his shoulder and met Sam's gaze. "If the Tairona never built stone-paved paths to ocean, how did Ferdinand find El Dorado?"

"There's two possibilities," Sam said. "One. A group of Tairona people met them and invited them. Or, two, and more likely, they found the Tairona people and followed them back to El Dorado."

Tom sighed. "Sure, but Sam, that still doesn't explain where Ferdinand came across the Tairona people in the first place."

"That part just hit me..." Sam grinned. "After making repairs to the *Santa Rosa Celeste*, what was the next most important priority Ferdinand undertook before making the long journey across the Atlantic?"

Tom and Genevieve burst out the answer simultaneously. "They were trying to refill their supplies with fresh water!"

Sam nodded. "Exactly."

"Which meant the crew of the *Santa Rosa Celeste* had to venture into the jungle, until they found fresh water."

Genevieve banked right, taking the next river course, following inland until its source. There was nothing manmade seen on the LIDAR imaging, so she looped around and followed the next river. And the next two after that.

None of them showed any signs of the Tairona.

At the end of the fifth one, Genevieve turned to Sam and said, "We're getting low on fuel, we should head back soon."

Sam nodded. "Agreed. We'll refuel and return."

Genevieve banked the helicopter to the left, and prepared to set a course for the *Tahila*, still anchored in the bay.

A narrow line flicked by on the LIDAR monitor.

Sam caught little more than a glimpse of it. "Wait!"

"What is it?" Genevieve asked, bringing the helicopter to a hover.

The dense forest below billowed under the intense downdraft, as the helicopter's rotor blades spun wildly, heaving several tons of downward pressure in the form of gusts of wind.

Sam said, "Go around again, I think I just spotted a trail."

Genevieve said, "All right, but we'll need to head back shortly."

"Not a problem."

Genevieve maneuvered the cyclic control, and the helicopter came around again.

Sam said, "Stop."

There in front of them, was the yellow brick from the Wizard of Oz. Of course the bricks weren't yellow, or gold for that matter, but they were stone-pavers and they led deep into the rainforest of the *Sierra Nevada de Santa Marta*.

Sam swung the monitor around so Tom could see it. "Check this out!"

Tom grinned and made a whistle. The thing looked like a giant staircase made of stone. A grand staircase for the gods. The question remained, did it lead to heaven or hell? "There you go."

Sam asked, "Genevieve, how much flight time do we have before we need to turn back?"

"Not much. I can give you another ten minutes, but that's it."

Sam grinned. "That's all I'm hoping we'll need."

Genevieve flew the helicopter west, following the stone trail all the way up until it came to a dead end at the base of the mountain.

Tom said, "Sorry, Sam. The road looks like it goes to nowhere."

Sam stared at the LIDAR monitor and frowned.

It certainly looked like the road led all the way to the base of the mountain and then ignobly ceased to exist.

He adjusted the frequency of the LIDAR pulses, and the images turned crisp.

Sam grinned.

There, in front of him, was an almost imperceptible gap. It was formed between two forty something foot high opposing pieces of sandstone, across an otherwise vertical crag.

"That's it!" Sam shouted, excitedly. "El Dorado must be hidden inside."

Genevieve said, "All right, I'll mark the GPS coordinates. We'll can't put down here anyway, so we'll have to head back to refuel, and then you can find somewhere nearby to hike up here."

Sam said, "That jungle would take us a month to hack through."

"You got a better idea?"

"Yeah, the forest height drops to twenty feet a few clicks back that way. How about Tom and I rappel through the canopy and hike in?"

"All right, but you'd better be quick or I'm going to run out of fuel."

"We will. I promise."

Tom put a hand affectionately on Genevieve's shoulder as he shuffled through the cockpit and into the cargo area. "We'll see you soon."

"You'd better. Don't make me have to cut through that rainforest to find you."

"We won't," Sam promised.

Sam and Tom quickly loaded their backpacks over their shoulders and were about to climb out of the helicopter.

Genevieve said, "Have you got enough ammunition?"

Sam bit his lower lip. "We're heading into the jungle, not a warzone."

She persisted. "But you're armed?"

"We're armed, but I'm not expecting trouble. This place looks like it's been deserted for centuries."

"It might be," Genevieve said, holding the aircraft steady. "Then again, there might be an army of Tairona warriors protecting El Dorado – and I'm going to guess they're going to be a little pissed off to see you arrive."

Tom said, "Don't worry, Genevieve. I'll stop Sam from doing anything too stupid."

With that said, Sam and Tom fixed two separate ropes to the helicopter's rappelling rings, and attached their descenders while Genevieve held the Eurocopter in a steady hover.

Sam made a brief exchange with Tom. An instant later, they both leaned back, released the pressure on their descender, and rappelled through the canopy of the rainforest, into the dark jungle below.

Chapter Twenty-Five

As soon as Sam's feet reached the ancient stone pathway, he and Tom disconnected their descenders and pulled the ropes through the twin ringbolts on the helicopter. The ropes fell to the ground beside them. Sam crouched down, hunching over, trying to shield his head from the seven-ton downdraft of the Eurocopter's powerful rotor blades.

On his radio mike, Sam said, "You're good to go, Genevieve. We'll give you a call on the sat phone as soon as we're ready for extraction."

"Understood," Genevieve replied. "I'll be ready."

A second later, the helicopter banked north and headed toward the *Tahila*.

The ground beneath the rainforest canopy was dark, where even the speckled sun struggled to reach the ground.

It seemed sinister somehow, if a jungle could.

Sam removed his backpack and withdrew his Heckler and Koch MP5 submachinegun. He attached a full magazine and then connected the weapon to his shoulder holster. Colombia was notorious for drug lords, and guerrilla warfare associated with rival cartels, but he highly doubted any were operating out of the lost jungles of *Sierra Nevada de Santa Marta*. As for any remnants of the ancient indigenous people of the Tairona, he doubted they still existed, and if they did, it was unlikely they would want to harm him.

But that didn't mean he wasn't afraid.

According to the dossier Elise had provided, they would be far from alone in the jungle. Colombia was a mixing pot of predatory animals, including jaguars and cougars – as well as several he'd never even heard of before.

Sam pulled his backpack onto his shoulders and he and Tom commenced their long hike up to the vertical base of the mountains. The terrain was steep, feeling more like rock climbing than hiking, and the path was well covered with thick vegetation.

Tom hacked away at the growth with a machete that he had brought for that specific purpose. It was slow going. The tropical air was thick and warm to breathe.

Tom glanced at Sam, a wry smile creasing his lips. "We couldn't have rappelled another half a mile up the mountain, could we?"

Sam laughed. "I was going to suggest it to Genevieve, but you saw the terrain. It would have been too steep to get the helicopter close enough to rappel – we would have been left dangling twenty feet off the ground."

"Instead, we're going to spend the next few hours hiking through the jungle."

Sam grinned. "At least this way we'll feel we're really adventurers!"

Tom pursed his lips, breathing hard. "Hey, we are really adventurers."

Sam shrugged and kept climbing.

It was nearly two hours later, when Sam finally stopped. He glanced up at where the stone stairway reached the base of the sandstone wall of solid mountain, like a parapet of an ancient and impregnable castle. A series of thick vines covered the base of the crag, extending more than thirty feet above their heads. It was so dense that Sam struggled to see where the path might lead or if it indicated the final destination.

His heart picked up its pace. "There it is!"

Tom suppressed a grin as he looked at what appeared to be a solid wall. "There what is? All I see is a towering wall of sandstone."

Sam grinned. "Hopefully the gateway to El Dorado."

Tom wasn't willing to give in so easily. All he said was, "Maybe…"

Together they hacked away at the vines and vegetation, slowly forming an opening allowing them to pass through the overgrowth – behind which, was nothing but solid stone.

Sam placed his hand on the stone. It was cold and unyielding. He scratched away at the brush until he could see more of the stone pillar. His eyes followed the ancient stone-stairway, tracing its path, until it reached its seemingly ignoble conclusion at the base of the mountain.

He frowned, almost certain that they had found it. He removed a small knife from his belt and used it to scrape away a few centuries worth of dirt built up along the final step. It didn't take long. The dirt shifted quickly, and he was soon rewarded with a clearly visible stone, the upper lip of which, appeared to have once been carved slightly underneath the thirty-foot parapet tower of stone.

Sam and Tom exchanged a quick glance.

No words were spoken, but both knew what the other one was thinking – after everything they had found, El Dorado couldn't simply end with an ancient path that led nowhere.

They continued to clear away the rest of the vegetation to the side of the stone path. When that one yielded no signs of where the path might have once continued, they turned and made an opening in the opposite direction. Both men worked hard, in a silent, determined, trance – unwilling to give up on El Dorado.

It took nearly an hour.

Neither of the men was men willing to acknowledge their defeat, and both kept working until Sam finally called for a rest.

He stepped back a dozen or so steps to where they had left their backpacks, took a seat on a large beside the trail, and then drank from his canteen bottle. Tom followed him. They were both still breathing hard from their efforts. They were losing fluids quickly in the tropical heat.

Tom's hazel eyes fixed on the precipice of stone ahead of them. His lips were set in a hard line. After a few seconds, his lips broke into a grin.

Before Sam could ask what the hell he had to smile about, Tom began to laugh. It was big and boisterous, matching his size. At nearly 250 pounds of muscle, when he laughed, he sounded like a giant.

Finally, unable to take it any longer and impatient, Sam asked, "What?"

Tom didn't speak. Instead, his eyes remained fixated on the mountain.

Sam's gaze slowly drifted in the direction Tom was looking, landing on a small carving to the right-hand side of the tower of sandstone. He grinned incredulously, because the marking was the very same that he'd seen drawn repeated inside Felipe Ferdinand's journal.

It was a figure eight on its side known as a lemniscate symbol, representing the mathematical concept for infinity. Buried inside the larger of the two circles was a second lemniscate turned upward and perpendicular to the original one, making the overall image something of an anomaly. Elise had tried to identify any reference to it, but found nothing in any known mathematical, hieroglyphic, or linguistics database.

He went up and placed a hand on the stone, right where the unique symbol appeared.

Thirty feet high, and approximately five feet wide, the entire stone swiveled to the left, pivoting like an enormous doorway to reveal the opening to a secret chamber…

Chapter Twenty-Six

Sam switched on his flashlight and entered the cave.

The stone doorway led them through a small pass between two large rockfaces. The ancient stone-path which they had followed through the jungle continued along the tight constriction, and deep into the mountain. The air was noticeably cooler inside, and there was a dampness to it, too.

The beams of Sam's flashlight shot across the chamber, as he tried to scope out the depth and breadth of their new environment, before landing on the glistening water of a shallow subterranean creek.

Tom fixed his beam at the end of the shallow creek, where it disappeared deeper underground, along with the cavern itself. "It looks like we're heading in the other direction."

Sam nodded. "It looks like it."

They continued along the tunnel, carved over the eons by the slow-moving creek, before their progress was hindered by another wall of gardens.

Sam fought his way through a hanging curtain of vines and stared.

A city stared back at him, regal and serene.

It seemed impossible… and yet here it was.

They stepped into the opening.

It was a rough circle with a diameter of two hundred feet. His eyes drifted upward. The dense jungle appeared to have continued to grow to form a healthy canopy above. Beams of sunlight, dappled through the canopy vegetation and lit the unique world, which was enclosed by sandstone.

Sam checked their position on the GPS built into his phone. The lost city was buried at the base of an ancient sinkhole nestled between the base of the two peaks. Centuries of growth had all but completely covered the canopy of the sinkhole, forming a garden dome. Sam imagined the place would appear like one giant sea of velvet green from the air, and without the aid of highly focused LIDAR, no one would have ever imagined a ruined city lying in secret. As for those who came by foot, in the tangled jungle and oppressive heat, it would have taken an expert mountaineer to find it.

Of course, it had remained hidden for centuries.

Tom's boots crunched the ground behind him. They slowed, then stalled.

He and Sam stared at each other, open mouthed.

The two men grinned.

The abandoned city was beautiful in a ruined kind of way as they wandered in the gentle sunlight and the sounds of birds. The crumbling stone walls were overrun with ivy and jungle vines, the cracked ground shaded by the tall trees overhead. It gave the ruins the feeling of a cathedral. In the dense quiet, Sam felt like he was disturbing a sacred space.

"Look," Tom said, and pointed. He bent, and handed Sam a tiny iron spear head.

Taking it in at a glance, Sam said, "Probably used by the Tairona warriors of days gone by."

Sam scanned the ground.

What other secrets were waiting for them?

They wandered through statues and architecture. They found trinkets – iron coins, scraps of fabric, bone jewelry.

But no gold.

Sam tried to push down his disappointment. This was the find of a century and anyone would be elated. The gold was not important, he told himself. He told himself the same thing again when he thought of what Catarina would say when he told her they'd found the city, but it wasn't what they'd thought.

Tom shook his head as if he could hear Sam's thoughts. "I know that look. You've found an ancient city not on any map, unknown to the outside world, through a hike that no man in his right mind would ever be able to execute. You found the mirage city. You found the impossible. And you're going to beat yourself up because it's not swimming in gold?"

He shook his head and Sam forced himself to admit he was being childish with a small grin. "Sam. The important thing is the map. It's real. It led us SOMEWHERE. That means that the rest of it – those creatures, the stories… those are real, too."

Sam said, "I'd better call the Genevieve and let her know we're going to make camp here tonight and keep searching in the morning."

"Agreed."

Tom turned to pick up an old spear head.

Then his hand stilled.

"Um… Sam?"

The tone made Sam turn. He raised his brows as Tom beckoned him over. Sam went, ready for anything. Inscriptions, scorpions, snakes… In the dim light, mixed in with shit and guano and sticks and leaves, Tom pointed to stones.

"Look."

If it weren't for the long day, Sam would have caught on sooner. As it was, it took him a minute to realize what he was looking at wasn't some dried, ancient excrement, but solid pancakes of pure gold.

"What is that?"

He turned the pieces over in his hands, his sweaty fingers removing the grime. Tom used Genevieve's handkerchief to wipe the last of them. They gleamed in the dim light, unmistakable. They were small, but hardly worthless. Sam weighed them in his hand. He wasn't a goldsmith, but treasure hunting had given him a certain amount of finesse. These were more than a couple pounds each, at least.

Tom scanned the floor. "Where did they come from? It's like they just came out of the ground." He raised his brows. "There was so much gold here that when they left, these were just neglected? Passed over?" He fondled the expensive find.

"Maybe they were dropped on the way out." Sam was doubtful. There were no signs of a hurried evacuation, and someone would definitely notice if something of this size fell out of their pocket. Maybe their bag...?

He studied it again. "it's different from the pearls we found in the chest. These look like they haven't been worked. Or rather..." He looked closer. "They're not actually raw. They seem like they've been melted down. See here, how it's all fluid? It's like someone took the pearls and transformed them..."

Tom blinked. "Why the hell would they do that?"

Sam shrugged. "Transportation, maybe? These are definitely less conspicuous than those pearls. If you're trying to smuggle them out, or disguise where they came from..."

Tom shook his head. "It doesn't make any sense. The Muisca were known for trading these. I can see why people thought the city was made of gold if they leave it just lying around, but it doesn't make any sense –"

He stalled at a rummaging sound coming from the far side of the portico. The two men stilled, instantly alert. Stupid, Sam thought. They'd let their guard down. Just because they thought the city was undiscovered didn't mean it was, really. Anyone could be lying in wait, determined to defend their treasure. The hell with men. Animals. The Colombian jungle was no picnic. His hand crept to his belt.

The rustling stopped. He and Tom looked at each other in the quiet.

"Did you see that…"

A blur charged them from the shadows in a shower of dead leaves and grit.

Sam yelled, "Tom! At your three O'clock!"

Tom said, "I see it!"

It was unlike anything he'd ever seen. Or rather, he'd seen it exactly once. It was the creature from the drawing inside the chest.

It was real.

And it was coming straight for him, teeth bared, intent to kill.

Tom and Sam scattered. Sam pulled his Heckler and Koch MP5, aiming it ready to fire, but hesitated – it was nearly extinct, it was rare, it was legendary – the last of its kind?

No reason to kill it if they didn't have to.

At the sight of the submachinegun, the creature charged at him, faster than he could believe possible.

Sam raised and fired the MP5, releasing a sustained burst of 9mm parabellums straight into the creature's armored torso.

The bullets barely fazed it, bouncing off its seemingly impenetrable armor.

The mythical beast raged toward him.

Sam and Tom continued to open fire, letting off round after round, but the beast kept advancing. Its claws tearing on the stone, its thick tail lashed at the air, almost as if it were propelling it forward like a shark uses its tail for thrust. Sam desperately sought a defendable position, but found none. He fired again and again, deafened as the shots echoed off the ancient stone. Dimly, he was aware of Tom shouting and waving his arms, trying to distract the creature advancing.

His empty chamber clicked the same time he heard the shout.

Behind them, someone shouted, "Stop!"

The creature stopped.

In the sudden stillness, a man emerged from the shadows. He was the same color as the rock, and for a moment Sam thought he was seeing things. He wore linen pants and shirt, and he had a cultured, intelligent face.

He said something in a language Sam didn't recognize, but imagined was ancient Tairona.

The creature came when called. The man patted its shell, and then motioned for it to leave them, and it slunk into the shadows toward the leaves, leaving a trail of sand in its wake.

Sam and Tom stared at their savior.

The stranger smiled at them and said, "I'm so glad you made it. I've been waiting for you, Sam Reilly."

Chapter Twenty-Seven

Sam's lips twisted into an incredulous grin. "How do you know my name?"

"All in good time," the man replied. "Come, have a seat, you must both be tired."

They settled on a series of boulders at the center of the lost city.

It was a strange meeting place. They sat in the dusty enclosure, facing each other in feigned relaxation.

The man was of Spanish-native descent and spoke impeccable English with a cultured accent. Sam wondered where he had learned the language so well, and what the hell such a man was doing in the middle of the jungle. There was only one question that mattered, though.

"Who are you?" Sam gestured to the ruins. "And what do you mean you've been waiting for us here?"

The man settled back. "I am sorry about… before. I was not expecting visitors." He smiled, charming. "We don't get many up here."

Tom raised his brows. "I can imagine. But you said you were waiting for us. That means…"

The man spread his hands. They were long fingered, elegant. Not the kind of hands you would imagine a rough jungle man to have. They were the hands of a priest or a scholar. "Waiting for and expecting are two different things. I've been waiting for ten years. I'd almost lost hope that someone would come. And so I was not expecting you today. But here you are."

It was surreal, but Sam was getting used to it. Mythological creatures, lost cities… just another day's work. He glanced at Tom and back to their new friend. "What was that thing?"

"A *Nyia Chía*. One of the last of its kind. In the now-extinct language of Chibcha, once spoken by the Muisca and Tairona, literally translates to, *Gold God*. The ancient Tairona people have been their guardians for nearly three thousand years. Now, I am the only caretaker who remains. And this is possibly the last of its kind." His piercing black eyes bored into them, intent. "That is why I need your help."

Sam's lips twisted into a wry grin. "Our help?"

"We need to find its lost colony."

Sam and Tom exchanged a glance. Then they turned back to the man. "You'd better start at the beginning."

The man settled back on his boulder like he was in a penthouse drawing room, completely at home. "You asked who I am. I am the caretaker of the Nyia Chía. What remains of them, anyway. My name is Cristóbal Ramirez."

Sam blinked. Despite the very Spanish name, the man spoke impeccable English, with the upper-class air of an old school British aristocracy. He sized up their host, trying to be unobtrusive. This man was full of riddles.

Ramirez seemed to notice, and his pensive gaze turned into a slightly joking one. "I studied at Cambridge, then Yale, years ago. Business and law." He said this evenhandedly, as if it was of no importance.

Sam studied him, altering his assessment.

"Business and law." He spread his hands, taking in the wild jungle, the ruined city. "How did you end up here, then?"

"Fortune favors the bold?" The caretaker chuckled.

A large awkward silence settled until Tom broke it abruptly.

"Forgive me, sir, but none of this makes any sense." He pulled his Glock out and laid it in his lap. "Can you just talk plainly? Neither of us take kindly to getting mauled by mysterious beasts, or being fed lines by the man who takes care of them. If that thing tried to kill us, we've got a right to know why."

Ramirez raised his hands in surrender and smiled. "Of course, of course. I am not feeding you lines. I just... don't know where to begin."

Tom raised a brow. "The beginning? Always works for me."

Ramirez took a deep breath and began.

"This entire area –" he gestured with his arms "was the home of the Tairona people, who traded their gold with the nearby Muisca people. You probably have heard of them, given your background. They were one of the four grand civilizations in the Americas before Columbus discovered America." His lips twisted at the word. "They're famous for the legend of El Dorado, but they were more than that. They made advanced contributions to ancient art, pottery, textiles..." He gestured at the ruined city. "They weren't great architects compared to the Maya, Inca, or the Aztecs, but they were renowned, even in their age, for their skilled gold working."

Now they were getting somewhere. Sam said, "Go on."

Ramirez shrugged. "You must understand. To the Muisca, gold was simply another element of daily life. It had more spiritual importance than monetary. There was a Muisca ceremony held at Lake Guatavita. The priests covered the ruler in gold dust and then rowed him on a raft to the center of the lake. There, he leapt into the waters in an act of ritual cleansing and renewal while his subjects threw precious objects into the lake during the ceremony.

"The Spanish, on hearing this story, allowed their imagination and lust for gold to leap beyond the bounds of reality and soon a legend arose of a magnificent city built with gold. Naturally, as it never existed in the first place, the city was never found and even the lake has stubbornly refused to reveal its secrets despite several costly attempts over the centuries." He chuckled. "Even the Spanish, with their wild imaginations, could never have envisioned the truth."

Sam raised his eyebrows, inviting him to continue. "What was that?"

"The Tairona worked with the *Nyia Chía* – creatures from another world. No one knows where they came from. In the now extinct language of Chibcha, once spoken by the Muisca, and four advanced indigenous civilizations of the Americas, the name translates to the *Gold God*. The tribe revered them as spirits of the Earth made flesh. They eat silica – sand. Their armor is nearly impenetrable. And then... there is the gold."

"What about the gold? They're its... guardians?" It sounded too far-fetched to believe, but Sam was learning to suspend his disbelief.

Ramirez smiled. "It's not quite that... simple."

"The Niya Chia survive off eating minerals. They are what are known as lithotrophs – the only known macrofauna of the kind. The lithotrophs of our planet are microorganisms, but the *Niya Chia* aren't. They burrow into the mountain, making labyrinthian tunnels and passages through sandstone, quartz... eating as they go."

Sam blinked. "Eating? You mean..."

"They're the only mammals known – well, sort of known – who turn inorganic compounds into energy sources." Ramirez smiled as they tried to process this. "But certain minerals, particularly gold, can't be digested. Thus, they build up in the creature's gut, until eventually the creature regurgitates it. Into pure golden pearls."

Tom glanced in surprise at the nuggets in his hand. Sam watched him fight the urge to wipe his hand on his pants.

Watching their reactions, Ramirez grinned. "You've seen them, then?"

Sam and Tom glanced at each other. "Yes."

Ramirez nodded. "So you know. They're stunningly beautiful, aren't they? And extraordinarily rare. The gold used to be dumped somewhere in the Muisca village as a worthless waste product. They only discovered how valuable it was when the Spanish arrived and appeared to go crazy over the stuff."

"So that's how the legend of El Dorado started?"

"Exactly."

Sam shook his head. "Forgive me. But how do you fit into the picture?"

Ramirez settled back. "The *Niya Chia* needed guardians. The man who took the job was the divine link between these godly aliens and the mere Tairona mortals: the El Hombre Dorado– The Golden Man. Of course, he wasn't a Nyia Chía himself, but his status was above the Muisca and under the Nyia Chía. He represented the symbiotic relationship the two had."

At Tom's expression, Ramirez expanded.

"Think of it like the Pope. The pope connects the rest of humanity – we mere mortals – with God. He is the messenger, you could say. The El Dorado Hombre was the same."

Sam settled back. This cleared it up a little more. "How is this, this 'Golden Man' chosen?"

"The caretakers are chosen for life. When they die, the elders of the Muisca tribe select the best young men of the tribe to train and compete. They're always the bravest, strongest, smartest…" He trailed off, as if not wanting to appear vain. "You get the idea."

"They go through a hellish journey training to be one of the five selected. The elders force them to eat animal hearts, run for tens of miles at a time, among other things. Finally when the tribe deems them ready, all five men enter the arena, where the Nyia Chía enter and kill all but one man. The man chosen to be El Dorado Hombre."

The air seemed much chillier than it had ten minutes ago.

Tom raised his brows, taking in the linen slacks and shirt. "You went through such a trial?"

Ramirez smiled. "No. I am not worthy of the name caretaker, but I am all they have."

Sam shook his head. "I don't understand. Where is El Dorado Hombre now?"

"Buried in a tomb of gold. The Nyia Chía bury his body alongside funeral rituals."

"Where is this tomb?"

The caretaker shrugged. "Wherever the last El Dorado was buried. The tomb is stored at the center the Nyia Chía's colony, protected by a labyrinth of tunnels that go deeper and deeper. Without top-tier experience and intuition, anyone that dared enter would get lost and rot in the maze."

"So what happened to him? What went wrong?" Sam interjected.

"The people eventually realized how harmful it was for the Nyia Chía to farm them. They were starving. The Nyia are curious organisms. They need to be free to wander. They also need plenty of moisture, like canyons and rivers. Up here..." He gestured to the mountaintop. "There is the river, but after several years of drought, the natural ecosystem was disturbed. The muisca didn't know what to do."

Ramirez continued. "It all changed in 1421. During that year, a number of Chinese ships set out on an expedition and crossed the Atlantic. Unlike the Spanish conquistadors who followed Columbus's terror campaign in 1492, the Chinese were interested in gathering knowledge and information, not taking lives. They also had no desire to take their lands."

"That was good for the Tairona, right?"

Ramirez's brow darkened.

"The Ming Dynasty in the Far East were so intrigued by these people on the other side of the world that the emperor's ambassador convinced the El Dorado Hombre to return to China with them. No one knows if the man was bribed, or if he simply was persuaded by the chance of adventure. Either way, knowing that he was instrumental to the survival of the Nyia Chía colony, he split it in two so he could care for half while a newly elected El Dorado would take care of the other in the homeland. Naturally, the tribe was also split."

This information was far too much for Sam to digest. The thoughts sat in his head, stuck and clogging up his brain. "I'm sorry. So the Chinese convinced the caretaker to split the tribe, taking half to China? I thought you said they were dying out here. Wouldn't that be a good thing?"

"A native plant belongs in native soil." Ramirez suddenly sounded angry and hid it with difficulty. "Every blessing is a curse, and every curse a blessing. The world is mysterious. That's why I- we need your help, Mr. Sam Reilly."

Sam had not been expecting this conversation this morning. Not at all. "Why me?"

"You found El Dorado, didn't you? The stuff of legend, exploring and finding lost treasures that no other man could even hope to see?"

Sam grinned, his cheeks forming a slight dimple. "It's not much of an ancient city. It wasn't hard to find. I'm sure I'm not the first to even spot it. No one has noticed it because they think it has no value. No disrespect, sir."

Ramirez chuckled back. "None taken."

Sam spread his hands, "Given that you already know who I am, I'll ask again, why me?"

The man's dark eyes bored into his and Sam thought of the unblinking gaze of snakes. Somewhere in the distance there was a rustling, a chomping, the sound of scales on stone. Was the creature having dinner? Sam found it impossible to look away from the caretaker's penetrating gaze.

"Because you found the Mahogany Ship," he said, as if it were obvious. "Which means you've located the closest link to the last El Hombre Dorado, and the surviving colony of Nyia Chía."

Chapter Twenty-Eight

Sam met the caretaker's eye, startled by the non-sequitur. "What do you know about the Mahogany Ship?

Ramirez's dark eyes gleamed. "The Mahogany Ship was one of the Zheng He's fleet of sixty-two treasure ships that circumnavigated the globe in 1421, during the Chinese reign of Enlightenment."

The man leaned back in his brocade chair and crossed one leg over the other. "El Hombre El Dorado split the colony of Nyia Chía, taking them to China to help them survive. It was supposed to be a mutual solution. You're right – the creatures were starving in the Andes, but a part of China was known to have the right amount of silica – that's sand – and quartz to survive. And so the Golden man made the decision to move."

Things were starting to make sense, in their bizarre way, to Sam. "So they could have gone down with any Treasure Ships."

"No. Only the Mahogany Ship, the very one that you, Mr. Reilly, found in Warrnambool. The rest of the Treasure Ships reached China, where they were destroyed as part of the Haijin."

"The Haijin?" Tom managed the unfamiliar word with difficulty.

"The Chinese government restricted private maritime trading and coastal settlement during most of the Ming dynasty and some of the Qing. They claimed it was to deal with Japanese piracy and to mop up the last of the Yuan partisans. But the sea ban was completely counterproductive. By the sixteenth century, piracy and smuggling were endemic." His eyes smiled, as if he sided with the rebels. "And most of them consisted of Chinese who had been dispossessed by the policy."

"How do you know the Nyia Chía didn't reach China?"

Ramirez steepled his fingers. "Two reasons."

Sam said, "Go on."

"The first is because you found the Mahogany Ship."

Sam looked blank. "I don't understand. There were sixty-two Treasure Ships."

"Yes. But only one that was built out of mahogany. More specifically, *Cariniana Pyriformis* – AKA Colombian Mahogany. It was built on sight, specifically to transport the colony of *Nyia Chia* to China."

"I was certain all the Treasure Ship had been made of mahogany…"

"No. China didn't have mahogany forests in 1421. They were introduced later, but were never native to the region. According to the Tairona's records, they were built out of Fir trees."

Sam expelled a breath. "And the second reason?"

The man settled back with infinite patience. Sam wondered if he had a limit. "Because, if they had, these golden pearls would have started to turn up in jewelry stores throughout China, and eventually Europe, Africa, and the rest of the globe."

"But they never did."

"No. Which means, they never made it to China."

Tom glanced at Sam. "Or someone wanted to keep them hidden."

It was fully dark now, and the stars above the jungle canopy shone brighter than Sam had ever seen them. In their light, the men contemplated the hidden strangeness of the world. Finally Sam settled back. "What makes you believe they're still alive?"

The caretaker shrugged. "They're hard to kill. They don't require oxygen to breathe like we do. They can live in environments that would kill you and I almost immediately."

Sam pressed, "Still, a long time has passed since 1421. What are they… immortal?"

The man's eyes hardened. "They're still alive."

Sam's eyes narrowed. "What makes you so sure?"

The caretaker expelled a deep breath. "Well, they were alive at least until 1861."

"What happened in 1861?" Sam asked.

Ramírez said, "In 1861 a small gold merchant in Venice started selling pearls of gold."

Sam took a breath and let the information process. "Could he have somehow collected it from the first Spanish explorers?"

"Maybe a few, yes. But the merchant began selling lots of them. Hundreds."

Sam said, "Which means he had a steady supply."

"Exactly." The caretaker leaned forward to press his point. "As the colony began to die out in the Andes, the last El Hombre Dorado sent an expedition to China because it was clear niya chia were thriving somewhere." The man's expression darkened. "He was never seen again. Shortly after, the Tairona of El Dorado were slaughtered in a rampage. No one knows exactly who lay behind the massacre."

The two men processed all of this. Finally Sam shook his head. "So what happened to the tribe here? Their caretaker was gone."

Ramirez stroked his pants. "They had a caretaker."

"Who?"

"My grandfather."

They stared at him.

"He was a naturalist with roots in the tribe. He cared about maintaining his culture's legacy."

Sam and Tom looked at each other. Their glances were clear. He cared about the gold.

Ramirez caught the look. "You think he was after the riches, and perhaps he was. But it didn't matter. He discovered soon that without their true Golden Man, the colony stopped procreating. The already threatened population in South America hovered on the verge of extinction.

"When my grandfather heard of the golden pearls in the Venetian market, he knew that the colony in China had survived. But there was one catch."

"What was that?"

"He sent word to business contacts of his in Amsterdam, who had contacts in Venice for any information of the golden pearls. What came back was… startling."

"Startling?"

"He expected the shipment to originate in China." Ramirez paused, watching their reactions. "It was a British merchant. From Australia."

Sam blinked. "Australia!"

Ramirez almost smiled. "He felt the same way."

Tom leaned forward. "Was it possible the Chinese sold the pearls to the Australians, and the Australians sold the pearls to the Italians?"

Ramirez shook his head. "There was no steady trade between China and Australia until the late nineteenth century. And for private enterprises… it just didn't make good business sense. Australia isn't on major trade routes. It's at the end of the world."

Sam raised his brows. "So you think the colony of *Nyia Chía* and El Hombre Dorado are still in Australia?"

"Not just Australia. I think they're in New South Wales."

Sam grinned. "That's very specific."

Ramirez nodded. "They have the right climate. The right geological composition. It would be an ideal habitat." Ramirez's eyes dimpled. "There is stranger fauna in Australia. You have to admit, the *Niya Chia* wouldn't attract much notice. Even if they were seen."

Sam and Tom looked at each other. "Huh," Tom said, leaning back. "Australia."

"That's what we believe." The caretaker paused, his eyes darting from Sam to the single remaining *Nyia Chía*, which munched happily in the corner, turned around like a dog, and went to sleep. "Unless..."

"Unless...?"

"The current El Hombre Dorado has moved the colony again."

Chapter Twenty-Nine

Claustral Canyon, Blue Mountains

Nathan Sanchez had always had a soft spot for Claustral Canyon.

It had been the beacon his uncle had held up when he was teaching Nathan how to canyon. He'd trained and trained, all with the hopes of descending into the magical depths of the earth. One morning his uncle had woken him before dawn and told him to get his canyoning gear. It wasn't an unusual request in summer, especially since the days were brutally hot and Uncle Jack liked to beat the crowds. But when they'd pulled into the parking lot… Nathan had known. He'd descended Claustral Canyon many times since, but the magic of the first had never truly left him.

They had arrived just before sunrise, and Nathan had pulled a sharp right just past Mount Bell as he'd done many times. He and Churn had unpacked their car, and however nervous the man made him, Nathan had to admit he carried his own gear. The sun was blazing white-orange in the pale blue sky, and their footing was easy to see as they navigated the entrance gully down to Claustral Brook. A good thing, too, since the entrance wasn't always easy to find until you were on the other side of it.

When they reached the brook, Nathan was vindicated. He'd climbed this canyon many times, and more often than not he'd have to swim it. Now, there was barely a trickle, due to the extreme heat wave they'd experience. He and Churn splashed through, and Nathan pushed down the contradictory feelings to a bad omen and triumph. He wondered if Churn noticed the difference.

After they'd slogged their way through the second swim, they reached the first of the abseils. It wasn't deep – just thirty feet – and both men scrambled down through the hole. Nathan clipped his rope on the convenient ledge as if he were greeting a friend at a familiar coffee shop. The sudden swoop, and sixty feet of static canyoning rope landed him dizzyingly at the bottom into the pool.

As they swam across the pool, dragging their gear in the light dappled by the huge ferns along the edge of the brook, Nathan had to check and make sure Churn was still there. The man was quiet as a shark.

As Nathan hooked up in the ring bolt for the second abseil, he was glad he hadn't tried to combine both on a 150 feet of rope. He'd done it before, and while quicker, the pulldown was a bitch and he didn't want to risk it with an inexperienced climber.

But he wasn't sure how inexperienced Churn was anymore. The man hit the bottom at the same time he did.

Finally, they came to the third abseil, Nathan's favorite – the Keyhole. It was the longest drop yet – roughly 45 feet – taller than the house Nathan had grown up in. The hole was open today – another good omen. Nathan had been here when it was blocked by debris, in which case they'd have to swim and go over the top, and they were cold enough already, almost 100 feet inside the belly of the Earth. He'd offered to go first and rig the ropes on all the abseils so Churn wouldn't have to wait while they did it on site, but the man had refused.

Nathan thought he didn't trust him.

The feeling was mutual. Nathan pushed it away and crawled through the keyhole. As darkness shrouded him like a warm blanket, the cave was suddenly illuminated by the mystical blue light of the glowworms, which he prayed would protect him from the dangers of the canyon.

As they hit the bottom, Nathan felt some tightness ease in his chest despite their situation. It felt like coming back to his house after vacation, even though they'd been here only… what was it? Just a little over a week ago? My god, it felt like a month. The glow worms pulsed gently, peacefully, in the slight drip of the water trickling down the walls and the deep coolness was welcome after the immense heat they'd been experiencing for most of the month. Nathan rubbed his hands on his pants and started to unpack the equipment as they'd done every other time.

Unlike every other time, Churn was not helping him. Nathan looked up in surprise.

"You're not interested in surveying?"

Churn scanned the scenery skeptically. "I do not understand," he said, his tone frosty, "why you insisted on coming here again. We were here a few days ago. And my boss doesn't appreciate wasted time. Or unnecessary expense."

Nathan leaned on the sonar. "You can reassure your boss that this expedition is just as important as the one he financed three months ago. Maybe more so."

"Oh?" The man's thick brow rose sardonically. "Maybe more so. What could possibly have changed? There was nothing to find."

Nathan pulled at the zip of his wetsuit. When he'd started this expedition, it had been for the cash. Now it had become a matter of personal pride. Nathan took his passion seriously, and the implication that he was wasting his client's time rubbed him the wrong way. "Nothing to find then. Things are different now."

"In three months?" The man's brows rose. "How?"

"The heatwave." Nathan gestured to the coolness inside the canyon, a welcome relief from the past two weeks of soaring temperatures. "It's been... exceptional. And helpful, in its way." He tapped his boots in illustration. "It's left the water levels inside the canyon shallower than they have ever been for more than a century."

Churn's eyes narrowed, but Nathan had to admit, the man was quick. It had taken him a few days to come up with the theory. "You think the water height might have been different back in 1421?"

Sanchez tried not to sound smug. "I'd be surprised if it wasn't."

The man watched him with that flat black gaze, and Nathan fought to keep looking him in the eye. Then Churn came to life again and gestured sardonically toward the drop off. "Then by all means. After you."

They rappelled down the first three waterfalls without incident, the whisk of their descent echoing off the damp walls.

When they hit bottom, Nathan tied his rope to the sandstone keyhole. He attached his figure eight descender to the rope with long practice under Churn's watchful eye. The air was damp, earthy. It smelled like rain, but Nathan knew rain wasn't coming. It was with the scent of the water in his nose and the thought of the sandstone sidewalks he'd used to play as a child that he hauled himself through the keyhole, and swung down into the dark abyss far below.

Chapter Thirty

The Rocks – Sydney, Australia

The iconic Sydney Harbor bridge loomed over the quay as Sam and Tom navigated the streets. The Rocks was one of the oldest neighborhoods in Sydney, and one of the most colorful. When Sam was a teenager, the Rocks was where you went to get a drink on the sly and play some darts with your friends and eavesdrop on all the sailors who were ashore on leave, enchanted as they swore and drank and spun tales of their adventures.

Now, petunias and geraniums spilled out of window boxes of the quaint storefronts and chic, tan patrons gathered at the street side cafes, glad to soak up the sun and gossip. Sam and Tom passed art galleries showcasing work from local artists: indigenous carvings, mud paintings, impressionist landscapes of the outback. Sam shook his head as he passed a shop selling plastic didgeridoos and stuffed platypuses. Now there were more souvenir shops than pubs. With its proximity to the harbor, the Rocks had become a tourist trap, full of craft shops, clothing shops, opal shops, pearl shops, fudge shops… Still, as Sam narrowly avoided a herd of teenagers cavorting down the sidewalk, it was a little like coming home.

Tom grinned after them. "Makes you feel old, doesn't it?"

Sam laughed. "Time flies."

It was early evening, and the city was enjoying the start of the annual Vivid Sydney – a festival of light, music, and ideas – in which outdoor immersive light installations and projections were displayed on a number of prominent buildings, while local and international musicians performed.

Sam glanced up at the bridge. It was lit up in a series of bright colors.

But they weren't here to sightsee. Sam double checked the address of the shop they sought on his phone, then looked up, scanning the street names. The sandstone bricks that made up the façade of the Museum of Contemporary Art glowed with an array of blues and purples. They walked to the end of the building and turned left.

Sam stopped. He marveled at the way the human mind worked. Twenty years away and it was like he'd never left.

"Come on," he said, turning down the alley and off the main thoroughfare. "This way."

The sign outside the brick building read *RAY JEWELRY – FINE CRAFTSMANSHIP SINCE 1871,* in filigree script.

Tom whistled. "Been here a while, haven't they?" Coming straight from Colombia as he was, it took Sam a moment to realize what he meant. But Tom was right – it was one of the notable things about Australia that didn't seem obvious until you thought about it: in Colombia, something that had been around since the 1600s was commonplace. But compared to Colombia, Australia was an infant country. 1871 was around almost since the beginning of European settlement in Australia.

Sam peered inside. "That's the point." One hundred and forty odd years wasn't quite as long as the Europeans had been here, but it was long enough. "With a legacy like that, they'll know the history of any major gold discovery anywhere near these parts. And that's what we need."

He pushed the door open without waiting for Tom's reply. A small bell chimed their arrival and a man with long curly grey hair and a large nose looked up from behind the counter. He was burly but not fat, and wore a worn leather apron that made Sam think he might be the owner. The man wiped his hands on an equally worn rag and put away his tray of opals, sliding his tweezers into a cork. "Afternoon, gentlemen. Help you with anything?"

Sam smiled. The man was a clear craftsman, which he respected. "I sure hope so." He dug in his pocket and pulled out a small jewelry box with a fuzzy cover. He'd bought a pair of earrings back in Colombia for Catarina, mostly just to get the box. She'd accepted it with a wry smile like she knew what he was up to. But that night at dinner she'd worn the earrings.

Sam handed it across the counter, watching the goldsmith's face go professionally blank in anticipation of just about anything. "I was hoping you could tell me about these."

The goldsmith opened the box.

Whatever he'd been preparing himself for, it wasn't this. His mouth dropped open in slight shock at the sheer beauty of the pearls.

A hush descended over the carpet smell and streak-free glass.

After a full minute of silence, the goldsmith looked up at Sam. "This is… Impeccable work. I've…" The man trailed off and peered closer.

That was a good sign. Sam leaned forward slightly over the counter. "Have you ever seen anything like this, sir?"

The man's lip quirked at the word "sir," but he kept his eyes on the gold. "No," he admitted as he rummaged on the counter and found a monocular loupe. He polished the lens with an anti-static cloth pulled from a case and shook his head. "I'm a goldsmith by trade, gentlemen – my grandfather taught my father who taught me. I've been around this business since I was born. And I've never seen anything like this."

The goldsmith fit the loupe to his eye, laid the gold pearls carefully on a velvet tray, and examined them with the help of long forceps. Sam and Tom waited in suppressed excitement. The shop was totally silent, just the hum of the air conditioner battling the heatwave that pushed at the windows outside.

Finally, the goldsmith shook his head.

"They're amazingly pure," he said. "I'm surprised that no one put their mark on them. But then, it would ruin the aesthetics."

"Put their mark... Oh." Sam hesitated, but there wasn't anything to lose, and perhaps quite a bit to gain. "They weren't fabricated. They're... in their natural state."

The goldsmith squinted sharply at them through the loupe. His eyes narrowed. "I'm afraid you must be mistaken."

Sam shook his head. "I don't believe so."

"I've been working this trade... oh, nigh on sixty years. And I've never seen or heard of gold naturally forming in such a state. Copper, sometimes, but gold's molecular structure is different. It doesn't... do this."

"Well, these are... unique, you could say. And we have reason to believe they came from around this area."

"Not from around here, they didn't." The goldsmith's voice was hard and certain, but remained polite.

Tom and Sam glanced at each other. Sam asked, "Even if it's never been found in the area, have you ever heard of anything like it ever being sold here? Or even traded?"

"I wish I had! But no, I haven't. I'm sorry." The goldsmith slid the tray back across the counter with some reluctance. "Where did these come from?"

"We uncovered them in an archeological site in Ubuntu Brazil, and records from the site seem to indicate there might be more of them. It's not so much a treasure hunting mission as it is a historical issue, you understand."

"Ubuntu... hey?" The goldsmith's brow furrowed. "How the hell did you get from a shipwreck in Ubuntu to search here for the gold?"

Sam grinned. "How did you know about the shipwreck?"

"I didn't… until you confirmed it. But now that you mentioned it, I vaguely recall hearing about someone discovering some old Spanish ship recently… what was her name, the *Santa Rosa Celestial*?"

"Just *Celeste*," Sam replied. Improvising, he said, "And the connection to Australia is pretty thin. In fact, it was the television exposure of the discovery of the *Santa Rosa Celeste* that led to another gentlemen contacting us about these golden pearls. According to his family legend, they were found during the gold rush during the 1850s, but the original prospector who discovered them, took their secret location to the grave."

The goldsmith considered the story, his eyes darting between Sam and Tom, as if trying to determine its validity. Failing to find any evidence in any direction, he said, "It's possible the original source is still out there… but it's more likely that any of the other mainstream, you know, big production gold mines, probably gobbled it all up, and melted it down into bullion. Leaving you and your client none-the-wiser."

Sam nodded. "That's always a possibility."

Appearing to give it some more thought, the goldsmith asked, "Do you know what gold field your client's ancestor had worked?"

Sam shook his head. "I'm sorry, I don't. All my client has are the records in one of his ancestor's journals, which makes note of arriving at Sydney Cove, and planning to set off in search of his fortunes. I don't suppose that narrows it down much?"

"Not really. I mean, it's unlikely he worked the Victorian gold fields of Ballarat, Castlemaine, or Bendigo. But apart from that, the man could have prospected anywhere in New South Wales. Was there any evidence he ever hit it big?"

Sam said, "I believe so. According to the records, the man left Sydney in 1853 a rich man."

"Do you know where he went with his riches? I mean, what country had he originated from?"

Sam bit his lower lip, unsure where to take the fictional narrative. Then he recalled Ramírez mentioning that the ship was a Chinese Treasure ship, bound for Nanjing, China, and Sam was given an idea. "The lucky prospector was Chinese. I don't suppose that might help narrow down which gold fields he might have worked?"

"Not even close." The goldsmith gave Sam and Tom an appraising look, similar to the one Sam had seen when the man had evaluated the golden pearls. "You have no idea what the times were like back then, do you?"

Sam suppressed a smile, expecting a history lesson. "What were the times like during the early gold rushes in Australia?"

"The Australian gold rushes changed the convict colonies into more progressive cities with the influx of free immigrants. These hopefuls, termed diggers, brought new skills and professions, contributing to a burgeoning economy. The mateship that evolved between these diggers and their collective resistance to authority led to the emergence of a unique national identity. Although not all diggers found riches on the goldfields, many decided to stay and integrate into these communities."

"How many people are we talking about?" Sam asked, genuinely interested.

"The gold rushes caused a huge influx of people from overseas. Australia's total population more than tripled from 430,000 in 1851 to 1.7 million in 1871. Australia first became a multicultural society during the gold rush period. Between 1852 and 1860, 290,000 people migrated to Victoria from the British Isles, 15,000 came from other European countries, and 18,000 emigrated from the United States. Non-European immigrants, however, were unwelcome, especially the Chinese."

"The Chinese weren't welcome? I thought there were plenty of Chinese involved in the early gold rush?"

"They were," the goldsmith acknowledged. "The Chinese were particularly industrious, with techniques that differed widely from the Europeans. This and their physical appearance and fear of the unknown led to them being persecuted in a racist way that would be regarded as untenable today."

"How many would there have been?"

The goldsmith mulled it over. "During that time period… I'd say somewhere in the vicinity of a hundred thousand."

Sam swallowed. "That amount of people can cover a large area. All right, it was worth a try."

The goldsmith took a deep breath and asked, "Mind if I take another look at the stones?"

Sam pushed the gold pearls toward him. "Go for it. Be my guest."

Several minutes more of silence passed wherein the goldsmith studied every inch of each of the pearls, as if assessing the possibility, they could possibly be telling the truth. Finally, the goldsmith folded up his loupe and stowed it away with its cloth. "Well, they're beauties. I wish I could be more help – I'd love to have a supply for the shop. Unique pieces, to be sure." He watched Sam pack them back in their little box, a craftsman bidding farewell to the rarest of the rare and glad to have had the chance to do so. The goldsmith nudged his chin as Sam closed the box and tucked it in a small velvet bag. "You know, you might head up to the Barracks, at Hyde Park. Used to be the center of Colonial Australia."

Sam blinked. "You think there would be a connection there?"

The goldsmith shrugged. "They have several good museums, and an archeological and historical society. They've got records of everything dating back to the early settlement at Sydney Cove. Established by Governor Phillip on February 7, 1788."

Sam laughed. "You know your history."

The goldsmith grinned. "I take my grandkids. They love it." He nodded at the small box containing the treasure. "If anyone has ever found pearl shaped gold, they would have records of it."

Sam pocketed the jewelry bag. "That's a very good idea. Thank you so much for your help, sir."

The goldsmith stuck his hand across the counter. His grip was firm when Sam shook it with a smile. "Call me Keith. Keith Bell. And come back if you find anything!" he called after them as the bell clanged with their exit. Keith shook his head again as the two men turned the corner and out of sight.

He whistled to himself. "Beauties," he murmured, and went back to work.

Chapter Thirty-One

The Barracks, Hyde Park

The Barracks Museum at Hyde Park was imposing.

Appropriate, Sam thought as the jeep pulled to a stop in the small parking lot, as it had been originally built to house and control convicts. It was fenced in by high walls on the southern and western side, casting long shadows as the sun began to set.

Sam entered the museum through the front door and was greeted promptly by the attendant at the information desk. She was in her early thirties and an academic. She had long blond hair that looked like it was rarely that color, with the large glasses that were in fashion at the moment that made her look like a bug. Judging from how small her eyes looked behind the lenses, Sam guessed they were more than a fashion statement. Her nameplate read "Emily."

Sam held out his hand and smiled. "Good morning. My name's Sam Reilly, I'm doing some research in these parts. I'm hoping you can help me."

"Of course, sir. That's what we do!" Emily had been working the Barracks for the past three summers and she pegged Sam Reilly for a returned expat Aussie tracking down some convict ancestors. He had that vibe. She prepared herself accordingly as Sam dug in his pocket. She expected him to pull out a list of names, and instead was handed a small jewelry box.

Okay… so they weren't names. He was giving her an heirloom.

She grinned. "You do know the way to a girl's heart, Mr. Reilly. What's the…"

Emily opened the box and gasped. "Oh!"

Inside were three gold pearls, perfectly spherical.

Sam grinned when she looked up at him, blank-faced. "Need a minute?"

His voice seemed to bring her back to herself. "Sorry," she babbled. "I'm not being very professional. I… in fact, I think I want to propose. What –"

Sam gestured at the box. "We have some reason to believe that these came from around here, and were hoping you could help us find out if that's true or not. I have it under good authority that you have the most comprehensive archive in the state."

Emily stared at the pearls. "More than six million records," she murmured out of habit. "Then she collected herself out of sheer willpower and turned to the small office Sam could see through a partially open door behind the desk.

"Francine," she called. "Can you take over out front? I need to help the gentlemen run the fiche."

Sam, Tom and Emily were squeezed into the tiny records office which was barely big enough to hold the antiquated computer. "Sorry," she said, when she saw him looking at the ancient machine with a dubious expression. "I know. It's a dinosaur, but it stores stuff- with lots of backups and external drives – and budget doesn't deem speed as a job requirement."

She flexed her fingers and hit the keys. "Okay… so you're just looking for any record of any mention of any objects similar to these anywhere near these parts?"

Tom laughed, his bulk folded awkwardly into the tiny space. "Exactly."

"Specific. I love it." She typed in a flurry of keys that made Sam think he'd misjudged her – maybe she took her job seriously after all. She bit her lip.

"No luck on gold pearls… just a lot of images and articles about jewelry. How about gold spheres… golden balls…?"

Sam shrugged. "That might work?"

She ran through several more options, then finally lookd at them. "Sorry, gentlemen. No luck."

Sam frowned. "Can you think of anything you haven't tried?"

Emily shrugged, a frown between her brows. "I've tried everything I can think of. Unless..." She typed some more, and over her shoulder Sam saw some windows come up. "This thing is ancient, you do have to be specific, so let's see if..." Her face lit up in triumph, the screen illuminating her enormous glasses. "We have a winner! GOLDEN pearls..."

The article was brief, dating from 1854. Attached was a drawing. It wasn't fine art, but the pearls were unmistakable. Emily sat back so he could skim for himself. "Apparently some local goldsmith added them to his inventory, then set them in a ring for one of the wealthy heiresses in town."

Sam leaned closer to the screen. "Does it say where they came from originally? Where did he get them?"

Emily squinted closer to the computer screen through her bug-like glasses. She followed the line of the text with a painted nail. "It says here, that they were traded for with the indigenous population."

"Any idea by who or where?"

She spoke without looking up from the screen. "There's a suggestion here that they... were trading with the Darug People... but – hang on... a second note suggests that the Darug People had actually traded before... that they had received the gold pearls from... the Gundungurra People of the Carmarthen Hills."

Sam blinked. He'd never heard the term. "The Carmarthen Hills? Where is that?"

Emily grinned. "You're not from around here, are you."

Sam prickled. "Well, actually, I did live here for a few years when I was a boy." He shook his head. "I've still never heard of them."

Emily nodded knowingly. "You were one of those cutups in school? Never paid attention?" Her dimple deepened. "I always hated people like you."

Sam laughed. "So quick to judge."

Her eyes narrowed, appraising him. "Do you want me to fill you in?"

Sam allowed a half-grin to form. "Yes please."

"The Carmarthen Hills is what Arthur Philip, the first Governor of New South Wales, named what is currently known as the Blue Mountains." She recited the information as if she was indeed giving a book report.

Sam grinned despite himself. "You win. Okay. Let's see if we can go two for two. Do you know anything about the Darug and Gundungurra People?"

"Do I know anything about the Darug and Gundungurra People? Like I could ever forget? Mrs. Whitmer, fourth grade. She made us color the map. The Darug People lived at the base of and lower parts of the Blue Mountains – they were red on the map. The Gundugurra occupied the upper and western area of the Blue Mountains. They were marked green."

Sam smiled broadly. "Thank you, Emily. I knew we came to the right place."

"You're welcome." Emily smiled. "I have to ask, now that you've found what you were looking for, what are you going to do about it?"

"I have no idea." Sam grinned. "Maybe we'll go for a hike in the Blue Mountains… see if we can find where the Darug and Gundungurra People found them in the first place."

Emily laughed. "Good luck with that."

Sam and Tom both squinted as they emerged from the dim museum into the blinding sun. Tom laughed as Sam slung on his sunglasses and squinted into the distance toward the mountain range that dominated the distant skyline, as they headed due west, along M4.

Tom chuckled and shook his head as he opened the door to the jeep and rolled down the top to give them some relief from the heat that was already starting to settle in waves over the pavement. "Never thought you cut up in school, Sam. Always pegged you for someone who paid strict attention."

Sam raked his fingers through his hair and settled his arm on the window, gesturing to the glorious view straight through the windshield. "If the Gundugurra people found the gold pearls, and they traded with someone… if there's a record of it here… looks like we're heading to the Blue Mountains."

"It's getting a bit late. Where do you want to go today?"

"We'll stay in Katoomba tonight, and make arrangements to search some of the canyons tomorrow."

Chapter Thirty-Two

The Three Sisters, Blue Mountains

The Blue Mountains rose over the horizon in the early morning mist. Their craggy peaks dipped into low gorges hidden by the forests that blanketed their sandstone slopes. Sam and Tom took a seat at *The Avalon* – a local boutique restaurant that occupied an old theatre hall, and overlooked the Jamison Valley.

Sam sipped at his coffee from behind the large glass window overlooking the Jamison Valley where he and Tom had stopped for breakfast, judging it to have better fare than their hotel. Beyond the glass, the Three Sisters jabbed into the sky like some ancient, primal city. When he was a boy Sam had spent a lot of time turning them into things, like some boys did with clouds – he'd gone through possibilities from chess pieces, to giants turned to stone, right through to massive monkey figures furred by trees.

Tom tapped the table. "Sam?"

"Sorry." Sam grinned. "Just… admiring the scenery."

Tom grinned. "Well, you want to admire this here scenery, then?"

Sam glanced at the table. "What have you got?"

Between the pie plates, coffee mugs and crumbs, the table was covered with a series of topographical maps. He and Tom were going over what felt like the entire Blue Mountain range with a fine-toothed comb, trying to work out areas possibly high in quartz-sandstone.

Tom hunched over the map. It showed a canyon running through a remote section of national park. He pointed to a section of mountainous terrain shaded in green. "This area here has the highest deposits of quartz-sandstone in the entire Blue Mountains."

Sam ran his eyes across the geologist's report. "Is that a canyon there?"

Tom nodded. "Looks like it. I don't know much about it… there's a name here… somewhere, I don't know if you've been there before."

Sam asked, "What's the name?"

"Claustral Canyon."

Sam grinned as he repeated the name reverently, "Claustral Canyon…"

Tom asked, "You know it?"

"Hell yeah I know it. My dad and I used to race through it years ago. It's long, cold, and hard – but from memory, the place would be the perfect environment for the Nyia Chía to thrive."

A waitress asked, "Can I get you gentlemen anything else?"

Sam smiled at her. "Another cup of coffee would be great. We're working hard."

She grinned. "You got it. And it looks like it." She nodded at their maps. "Going climbing?"

"Not climbing today. Just canyoning. Thought we'd start with Claustral Canyon." He shot Tom a raised eyebrow to prove he had been paying attention and Tom threw up his hands in mock defeat, tossing down his pencil and instead tucking into his pie. "What do you think – good choice?"

The waitress grinned. "Better bring your thick wetsuit. It can get pretty cold despite the external heat this time of the year."

"Thanks. We'll keep it in mind."

Tom watched her walk back behind the counter. "She's probably right about the wet. What do you think? Do we risk it?"

"It has the highest possibility of having the highest levels of quartz sandstone in the area." Sam raised his brows. "Better start there." He leaned out of the waitress's way as she filled their cups and toasted her. "If it's a bust, we can work our way down and dry out as we go."

Sam finished his coffee and said goodbye to David and Dylan, the owners of *The Avalon*, and old friends of his.

They climbed into their jeep and headed toward the old Katoomba Airstrip.

Chapter Thirty-Three

Katoomba Airfield, Blue Mountains

The Katoomba airfield was a fifty-hectare airstrip located in Medlow Bath. It opened in 1965 as a facility for recreational flying, tourism, an emergency services operation. Its long-term lessee, Rod Hay, was killed in a plane crash near the airfield in 2016, leaving the airfield to close down while expressions of interest were sought for a new lease.

Sam pulled up along the dirt runway. At the end of it a Robinson R44 helicopter stood with its rotor blades already turning.

Tom smiled. "I thought you said this place wasn't operational currently."

Sam shrugged. "It's not."

"Where did the helicopter come from?"

"A friend of mine's offered to lend it to us for the weekend."

Tom laughed. "Where do you find these friends?"

Sam's eyes drifted away toward the helicopter, his mind locked on a distant memory. "It's a long story."

"I don't doubt it."

Before he could tell it, an older man climbed out of the helicopter and shook Sam's hand with a firm grip. He was in his early sixties, tall and wiry, with the sort of physique and tan lines more likely found on an outback farmer than a pilot in the city.

"It's nice to see you again, Brian." Sam smiled with genuine pleasure to see his old friend. His eyes turned to Tom. "Tom, meet Brian Mayo. He lives in Sydney these days and teaches people to fly out of Bankstown, but once upon a time he was just about the maddest helicopter pilot you'd ever meet."

Tom shook his hand. "Nice to meet you, Brian."

"Likewise. I've read a lot about your adventures and extraordinary exploits."

Tom let the name linger for a second. "Brian Mayo! Now I remember where I've heard that name before. You looked after Sam for a couple weeks during the summer when we were still in high school."

"That's right," Brian said, his mouth set in a broad grin, his eyes wide and distant as if focusing on a fond memory. "Sam spent the summer in his teens learning to muster cattle."

Tom said, "That's not all I heard…"

Sam grinned at the vivid recollection. "No. I had told my father I had wanted to learn to fly helicopters… then, when I persisted, he suggested I spend some of my summer vacation in Australia, learning to really fly helicopters."

Brian nodded. "You never did make much of a cattle musterer, but by the end of it, you sure as hell could fly that little Robinson R22!"

Sam bit his lower lip. "Yeah, and in some places that I wouldn't dare fly it today."

"That's probably why you're still here to talk about it after all these years," Brian said, patting him on the back.

His voice was friendly and his tone joking, but there was a crispness to his voice. The fact was, cattle mustering by helicopter was just about the deadliest form of piloting in existence. Sam had no doubt that Brian had lost plenty of friends over the years.

Sam let the silence sit there out of respect for a few seconds, and then said, "All right, we'd better get going."

"She's all yours," Brian said. "Key's in the ignition. Stay safe."

"Thanks." Sam handed the Jeep's keys to Brian. "We'll hopefully only need it for the weekend. I'll see you in Bankstown."

"Take all the time that you need. I'm billing you for it anyway..."

"Thanks."

They dropped their backpacks on the rear seats of the Robinson R44.

Sam took the pilot seat, flicked the engine master to on, and took off.

Chapter Thirty-Four

The Robinson 44 helicopter they'd hired to fly over the Grose Valley made a terrific racket and Sam and Tom had to shout to hear each other over the noise. It was still Sam's favorite way to see Australia, though – by air, the rugged rocks and dangerous, dramatic landscape somehow flattened into a sheet of pure, untouchable beauty. Made him remember his place in the scheme of things.

They banked and made another pass over the Grose Valley, which sprawled below them in abject majesty despite the gray skies and low clouds. Sam scanned the topography below. The Grose river gleamed like a silver scar far below. Most of the valley fell within the Blue Mountains National Park, so it remained pristine and untouched by man. Because of this, it was home to some unique flora and fauna – including platypus and the endangered water skink. There were any number of places in here that a colony of mythical beasts might hide in, burrowing deep into the earth under miles of stone, Sam thought. Watching the valley spread below him now, with the detachment of distance, Sam was certain they were close. The Blue Mountains gave birth to magic. This morning the whole legend of the Niya Chia seemed entirely believable.

"There," Tom said, and pointed out of the tiny window.

Sam grinned. "You want a closer view of the rock?"

The helicopter banked in a huge, sweeping curve, and they zoomed in closer to Hanging Rock, its distinctive curve cutting the sky like a scythe. The only way to properly get the scale of the thing was from the air, Sam thought. He'd climbed it several times and, despite the height and the magnificent view, he'd been unimpressed. It was now, from the window of the tiny copter, that the sheer size of the edifice came into view.

Sam grinned. "Should I put it down on the rock?"

Tom laughed. "Is that even legal?"

"I doubt it," Sam replied. "Come on, we'll follow the valley east until we reach the start of Claustral Canyon."

He banked south, and flew over the Grose Valley.

After a short flight, the large rock shelf – an outcrop of sandstone – came into view. Sam brought the helicopter down into a hover directly over the top of it, before slowly easing off the throttle, reducing the collective, and placing the R44's skids down for a spritely landing.

The place was called the Camel's Hump.

It was about a mile to the south of the township of Bell and half a mile from that of Mount Tomah. The unique and distinctive rocky outcrop was bounded by Claustral Brook and Rainbow Ravine, through which, they could enter Claustral Canyon. By flying, they were saving themselves the better half of a full day's hike.

Sam switched off the engine, and the rotor blades slowed to a stop.

He and Tom stepped out and retrieved their backpacks.

Sam's eyes swept the spectacular vista. The late morning skies had darkened to a drizzle-threatening gray. His eyes traced the outline of the Gross Valley and across the Blue Mountains, before returning to the unique rocky platform upon which they were standing. It was made from a series of hundreds of sandstone tessellations, reminding him of that old computer game that used to come standard with the original Microsoft Windows…

What was the name of it? *Mahjong Titans.* That game where you had to combine two of the same mahjong stones to remove them from the playing field, so long as the stones were free from any blocking them from above.

He had no idea what caused the strange formations, but to him it looked like some sort of mysterious giant had simply stacked them that way, gluing them together.

Tom looked around. He'd done plenty of canyoning previously, but never in Australia. He met Sam's eye and asked, "Which way?"

"We'll follow that path down into the valley below"

Tom traced where Sam had pointed and nodded. "Okay."

Sam led the way – not that there was much navigation needed – the thick heath made it nearly impossible to wander off the main trail used by canyoners.

To the right, a steady set of grinding grooves in the sandstone revealed one of the few remaining remnants of aboriginal presence in the area, where they had once sharpened spears and knives for hours.

They moved quickly over the rough terrain, descending into Rainbow Brook.

Sam took two steps into the water and stopped.

Because, coiled up along a small sandstone island in the middle of the creek, was a large Eastern Brown Snake, one of the deadliest snakes in the world.

Chapter Thirty-Five

Tom jumped back and cursed.

Sam casually stepped through the water around the island, giving the Eastern Brown plenty of room to itself. He was cautious, but indifferent to the lethal predator.

Tom swallowed and stepped back farther. "Are you crazy?"

Sam, now safely past the snake, grinned. "Since when are you afraid of snakes?"

"Since I came to Australia and discovered that just about every one of them will kill me."

"Are you kidding me?" Sam met his gaze, and spotted more fear in Tom's eyes than he expected. "Almost no one gets killed by snake bites in Australia anymore… despite what the movies and occasional tourist brochure might lead you to believe."

Tom arched his eyebrow incredulously. "Really?"

"I'm not kidding. Since 2000 just 35 people have died from snake bites! Last year there were four deaths in all of Australia, and so far this year, there's only been one."

"Wow… I had no idea." Tom backed away putting another twenty feet between him and the snake for good measure. "Still, I don't plan on becoming a statistic, no matter how unlikely. Besides, we're miles from anywhere. I doubt either of us would ever reach a hospital alive if we got bitten."

"That's not a problem, either." Sam smiled, evidently bemused by Tom's discomfort. "It doesn't quite work like that. No one in their right mind should die from an Australian snakebite… unless they're really unlucky."

Tom kept his eyes fixed on the snake, which was still curled up along the rock in the middle of the water, sunbaking. "Really? What makes you say that?"

"It has to do with how snakebites kill in the first place. Basically, despite all the different pathophysiology of most snakebites, all of the lethal ones in Australia require the movement of the lymphatic system to transfer the venom to vital organs and consequently kill the victim."

"So then… what, you just shut down the lymphatic system and the poison doesn't reach anywhere important?"

Sam nodded. "Something like that. I'm carrying a couple crepe bandages. They can be used on the bitten limb to provide pressure immobilization – in the unlucky event that either of us do get bitten by a snake – it works in two ways to save our lives. One, it stops lymphatic drainage, and two, immobilization of the bitten limb prevents the pumping action of the skeletal muscles."

"That's it?"

"Yeah. It's the contraction of muscles in your limbs that pumps the lymphatic system around. If you lie down and don't move at all after being bitten by one of these deadly snakes, in theory, even without a pressure immobilization bandage, the toxin won't be able to travel through your system and kill you."

"In theory?" Tom asked.

"Yeah, well… we won't try it out. Just in case, I brought a couple bandages. It took toxicologists until the 1980s to work that one out… but the Aboriginals have known it for some forty thousand years."

"Wait…" Tom stopped. "Are you telling me the aboriginals have known how to treat lethal snakebites for thousands of years?"

"Yeah. It's been told in their Dreamtime for as long as anyone can remember."

"Dreamtime?" Tom asked.

"The Dreamtime is the Aboriginal understanding of the world, of its creation, and its great stories. The Dreamtime is the beginning of knowledge, from which came the laws of existence. For survival these laws must be observed."

Tom hesitantly climbed around the side of the creek's rocky ledge, giving the most possible distance from the sleeping snake. As soon as Tom was past the snake, he sped up just about running along the water, as though he expected the Eastern Brown to get him at any minute.

Sam had to stop him from just about running off the next ledge. "Feel better?"

"Much. Thank you. Where you up to?"

"The Dreamtime."

"Oh, right." Tom took a drink from his water bottle. "And it spoke about snake bites?"

"Yeah," Sam replied. His eyes were wide, and animated as he spoke of the stories some of the Aboriginal Elders had told him while he was living in the outback for a Summer. "According to Aboriginal Dreamtime stories their ancestors knew that the snake bite of a brown snake would leave a person dead, unless they lay perfectly still immediately after being bitten – for five days and five nights to be exact. The victim's family and friends would bring water and food to the victim, knowing that to survive, the person would need to never move their legs. At the end of that time, the poison would be gone, and the person would be free to walk away."

Tom bit his lower lip. "It's just a story. Surely?"

"Maybe, maybe not. One thing's for certain, it's backed up by science. Early settlers in Australia documented stories of witnessing such events by the Aboriginals, in which they describe them as being able to miraculously save their own people after they had been bitten by an otherwise lethal snake. At the time, it was believed to be ancient Aboriginal medicine, but we now know the science behind the process – the lymphatic system can't pump poison without the movement of skeletal muscles."

Tom shook his head in wonder. "That's crazy. I had no idea."

Rainbow Brook split into a fork and Sam took the one on the left, descending into the start of Claustral Brook.

The water sliced a narrow fissure in the sandstone, leading to a narrow slot. Sam slowly clambered down the rocky ledge and into the shallow water below, while plumes of spray from the nearby waterfall filled the air. Making his way out of the water, his feet slipped on one of the abundant giant fern fronds. He braced himself on a giant boulder and managed to prevent himself from hitting the ground hard.

He exchanged a slight glance with Tom, and continued to walk through the shallow water, before scampering over a series of logjams.

Sam stopped at a sunny boulder, where a pair of red water dragons were soaking up the warmth above an icy pool. It was overhung with massive ferns, which allowed dappled light to penetrate, turning the emerald-colored moss, into a radiant glow. Crystal clear water flowed into an equally clear pool at the bottom of the canyon from a nearby spring. He took out his drink bottle and filled it from the fresh water, having a quick taste of the sweet, delicious water – fed by a natural spring, it had been untouched by humans. Sam put the lid back on the bottle. His eyes darted toward the deep section of the pool, where a couple large, blue-shelled yabbies clawed their way beneath the safety of a submerged rock.

189

The gradient suddenly increased, and they prepared to begin their descent into Claustral Canyon, and stopped.

Because the entrance to Claustral Canyon was surrounded by a series of Police Rescue and SOT Paramedics.

Their faces were drawn, their eyes bloodshot, and the mouths set in a hard, straight line. One thing was certain with just a glance – no one was going down Claustral Canyon today.

Sam asked, "What happened?"

A female SOT paramedic replied, "A small party of canyoners were lost down Claustral Canyon yesterday."

Chapter Thirty-Six

Sam asked, "Has a search party been sent through to locate them?"

"Of course." She gestured behind her, and Sam thought this was the search party, that things were well in hand. At least, he thought that until she deflated. "But that party's gone missing too. So too did the next one we sent."

"What? You're kidding me." Sam looked toward the entrance to the canyon he knew so well. It suddenly seemed foreboding. He shook his head, hitched his pack higher, and took a deep breath. "So, send another team. Make certain they know the canyon well." He looked her straight in the eye. "It's not like there's many places there to get lost. The whole area is restricted by giant walls of sandstone!"

She didn't back down. "We already did send another team. That knew the canyon well."

"And? What did they find?"

She must have sensed something in his posture too that indicated he was an ally, not an adversary. She spread her hands. "Nothing."

Tom crossed his arms and loomed. "What do you mean, nothing?"

"I'm not being coy, sir – that's just it. They didn't find anyone."

Sam looked at Tom. "No one? What are you telling me?"

The paramedic sighed. "That we have a total of six people lost in Claustral Canyon, and despite multiple trips through, no one can locate any of them." Her face softened. "Not even bodies."

Sam and Tom looked at each other, then to the gray sky. Tom shrugged. "I know that look. You tell her."

She frowned. "Tell me what?"

Sam turned to the paramedic. "I know this canyon well. I've done the trip dozens of times over the years in high and low water. Let us go in. If they're still down there, we'll find them."

"So we can come in after you, too?" The paramedic asked. "No way."

Sam tried to be charming. "Ma'am…"

She was not charmed. She held out her hand as if she wanted to slap the sky. "You see this rain coming down, sir?"

"This drizzle," Tom put in helpfully.

"This drizzle that looks like it's going to pour buckets any minute now. You look like a smart man, so it's a tossup in my experience whether you looked at the weather report this morning – smart men sometimes do, sometimes don't. So let me fill you in. According to the meteorologists, there's a major storm coming through. Put an end to this heat wave, which will be a blessing, but that ground is bone dry. There's no place for that water to go. And if you know Claustral like you say you do, you know it floods like the old testament under heavy rain."

Sam grinned. "Then, we'll just have to make sure to be quick."

Chapter Thirty-Seven

In the distance the sky darkened.

A crack of thunder split the horizon, and echoed as it ripped through the narrow valley. Canyon slots, by definition were carved into the mountain by the passage of water, slowly slicing its way through stone across the ages. When rain fell, there would be nowhere for it to go except the bottom of the canyon. That water, bound and compressed by the ancient and immovable walls of sandstone, would turn violent quickly – raging through the constrictions, destroying everything within its path.

The violent downpour had commenced.

It was miles away, and so far, the water at the bottom of the canyon was still a trickle – but it wouldn't stay that way for very long.

Sam and Tom moved fast.

They were now on a race against the storm, where the winners got to live, and the losers most likely ended drowned.

Sam reached the first of three major waterfalls.

He clambered down into an opening caused by two opposing boulders the size of small cars and found the first set of twin abseiling bolts. He quickly set up the rope. Peering down below, the rock was a myriad of orange, red, and green hues. White, turbid water streamed down the slick passageway of stone. The colors so vivid, and the crevasse so raw and forbidding.

Sam didn't stop to admire it.

As soon as the twin ropes reached the water below, he attached his Hydrobot descender and was rappelling down the waterfall.

Tom was next.

He moved with the speed of a professional, despite having never made his way through the canyon before.

They swam across the deep, almost black, pool of water, before clambering up over a set of narrow boulders, to reach the second set of fixed ring bolts.

Sam was about to attach his descender when he heard the roar of the first waterfall, which echoed in the narrow confines of the canyon like the Rolls Royce engines of a 747, suddenly change pitch. It was like someone had simply shifted up a gear.

His eyes darted to the first waterfall.

Its white, frothy, downpour – which was little more than a trickle a few minutes earlier – had started to increase in diameter.

It looked deceivingly modest.

But it was growing fast, and it would be impossible to outrun for much longer.

Sam said to Tom, "You go first."

Tom hesitated for a split second, his eyes meeting Sam's, and, seeing the defiance in them, didn't argue. "Don't take too long!"

"I won't!" Sam promised. "Go and set up a rope from the keystone!"

"I will." A second later, Tom had clipped in his descender and disappeared down the second waterfall.

As soon as the tension released from the rope, Sam was attached to it, and rappelling to the icy water below.

They were now nearly eighty feet beneath the ground where limited light dappled through the top of the canyon to reach them. The pool between the second and third waterfall was the darkest. It formed an almost round barrel cave roughly twelve feet in diameter, with a narrow slot – not more than a few feet – piercing the sky high above. At the far end, a large sandstone arch blocked the progress of the canyon, and underneath this, a small round keyhole – barely big enough for an adult to climb through, remained.

The water's progress was impeded by the narrow keyhole, which now formed a sort of bottleneck in the canyon, causing the water to rise with unimaginable speed. Water rampaged through the keyhole and down the final waterfall into the complete darkness below.

The echoing roar of water seemed to change up another notch or two, until it drowned out the shouts from Tom.

Instead of doubling up the rope, Tom tied a single rope off the twin ring bolts. It meant that Sam only needed to reach one rope, and not two, as he normally would. It might save him a few seconds. Enough to possibly make the difference between life and death.

Sam and Tom exchanged a quick glance.

Tom nodded. He knew that he needed to keep going if Sam was ever going to get a chance to escape.

A couple seconds later, Tom was gone.

Sam paddled, hand over hand, across the dark pool, fighting to reach the keystone. Strange currents pulled and tugged at him. He had to use almost all his energy just to stay afloat, fighting the powerful undercurrents that were trying to suck him under.

The sound of the rampaging waterfall suddenly turned silent. He turned his head to look at it, almost expecting a reprieve from the Gods.

Instead, he saw that the water level had risen so sharply, that the waterfall was no longer dropping water into the pool. Instead, it was flowing down in one giant, flooded mass.

Sam swallowed.

He was about to be hit by a deadly flashflood.

Chapter Thirty-Eight

The keyhole was no longer visible beneath the rising vortex.

Instead, Sam was dragged around in a clockwise direction around the barrel cave, the water speeding up as it rose. The swirling water gushed into a raging whirlpool as the water was forced through the keyhole under extreme pressure.

The space in the ceiling of the barrel cave decreased quickly. If the deadly undercurrent didn't drag him under soon, he would run out of breathing space up above.

He needed to act.

But right now, he was expending all his energy just trying to stay alive, as he was tumbled like a ragdoll in the washing machine like crucible of the vortex.

On the far right he saw the end of the rope Tom had used to make his descent. It was still attached to the ring bolts high on the wall to the far right.

Sam tried to reach it.

On his first-time round, he missed it by more than a foot, before the current dragged him round and past it.

He kicked hard. This time, instead of trying to stay afloat, he turned his efforts to propelling himself near the sandstone outer wall.

On the second round, he was close to it, but at the last minute the undercurrent tipped him over, so that his hands couldn't meet the rope.

He didn't even make a try for it on the third round.

Or the fourth.

Adrenaline surged in his veins, like the torrent of water in which he was now trapped. His heart pounded, his chest burned, and his muscles screamed.

Fatigue was setting it quick.

It was impossible to stop the terror rising in his throat like bile.

The beam of his headlight flashed across the dark chamber, sending subsequent rays of light and shadows scattering throughout his vision.

Until all he could see was darkness.

His mind was going crazy.

Sam's head dipped under water, and he started to drown. He fought to reach the surface again, only to take one sweet gasp of air before being sucked under once more.

He was expelling every single bit of his body's energy and resilience to reach the surface, time after time, and that strength was rapidly ebbing away – into permanent darkness.

Sam could no longer differentiate between darkness and light, between the sweet air above water, and the icy cold suffocation below.

His life, along with his consciousness was drifting away.

The current turned and jostled him about. His muscles relaxed and he no longer fought the inevitable, as he found peace with his position.

The vortex reached a single logjam and he was thrown upward, slamming his back against the rocky wall in the process, sending spasms of sharp pain through his spine.

It was enough to wake him.

If only for the very last time.

His eyes opened.

The beam of his flashlight was fixed on something.

It was long and thin, like a snake…

And incredibly valuable to him.

Although he couldn't quite recall why.

Then it hit him. That was the rope he needed. His head broached the surface and he took a great big gasp of air.

A second later, his right hand gripped the rope.

His fingers locked on, his knuckles turning white, as they gripped it like a vice.

Instead of kicking to stay afloat, he turned his head downward, and dived.

The beam of his head flashlight shot through the narrow opening of the keyhole. Sam kicked hard. One.

Two.

On the third kick, his body was captured by the flow of water being sucked through the tiny keyhole. Like air in a jet engine, Sam was forced through at speed, propelled into the vacant space on the other side.

For a split second, he was free – suspended in the forty-two feet of air that made up the third waterfall.

The rope suddenly reached its end.

Sam gripped it hard with both hands.

He gritted his teeth as the rope pulled him in a backward pendulum swing that was going to hurt, as he was hurled toward the sandstone face of the waterfall.

He braced for the hard hit against the wall.

But it never came.

Instead, he swung, seemingly endlessly – into the vacuum of empty space – inside a mysterious cave that wasn't supposed to exist.

Chapter Thirty-Nine

Sam took a deep breath and tried to blink away the haze.

There was a light up ahead, flickering from side to side. His mind was drifting in a mist, somewhere between conscious and unconscious. There was a faint roar of the movement of water but it was no longer threatening… more like the distant growl of a restrained predator. There was another sound nearby, too. But he couldn't quite make sense of it.

It was a sort of rhythmic sound.

Like the drum of a pump going up and down.

Reality failed, and confusion reigned. He felt nothing. No joy. No pain. All fear had finally left him. He was just there. Floating in the void… no longer falling, not yet at the bottom.

And then the pain started.

Right in the middle of his chest – spreading out across his ribs in shards of electricity.

He wanted to scream. He wanted to make it stop.

His arms flailed, as though he might fight off the agony, as he would an assailant.

Far in the distance, he heard Tom's voice. It was comforting and reassuring, but he had no idea what he was saying. It was as though his friend was just too far away for his voice to be properly heard.

Sam tried to scream out loud, but something was stopping him.

He tried again and again… but nothing would come out.

His eyes opened fully.

Abject terror followed in an instant.

He couldn't breathe.

He was trapped within his own body, unable to do anything.

The next thing he knew, he was breathing out.

A long, deep, exhale.

Only it wasn't air that was coming out.

It was water, and by the looks of things, a hell of a lot of it.

The arm of a giant tipped him over. He went from supine to prone in a split second, and the water gushed from his mouth.

"There you go, Sam…" Tom expelled a deep breath. "I knew it would take more than a flashflood to drown you!"

Sam felt his friend's hand, like the paw of a bear, patting his back between his shoulder blades. He tried to take a breath in. His chest rattled and gurgled. There were a few more heavy pats on his back, some more coughing.

And eventually, a deep breath.

That, too, hurt.

But soon he was sucking fresh, sweet tasting, air through his opened mouth and into his lungs.

His right hand still clasped the rope.

Sam's gaze turned to Tom, who had tears in his eyes.

He asked, "What happened?"

Tom frowned. "You took on a flashflood and it very nearly won."

Sam tried to move and noticed his chest was sore. "So what did you do, punch me until I woke up?"

Tom grinned. His eyes went wide with relief. "Your lungs were so full of water. By the time you swung through the wall of water, landing into this cave, you weren't breathing – and for the past few minutes… I'm pretty certain you were dead."

"How long were you doing CPR on me?"

"Not long. I don't know if your heart had even stopped. I just knew I needed to get rid of some of that water."

"Thank you, Tom... for saving my life."

"You're welcome. I'd really appreciate it if you took more care of it this time."

It was Sam's turn to grin. "I'll try my best."

"That's all you can do."

"About that..." Sam said.

"Yeah?"

Sam said, "Where are we?"

Chapter Forty

Tom sighed. "The short answer is, I have no idea."

Sam turned his head and the beam of his flashlight revealed a large chamber.

It was roughly eight feet wide where it met the back of Claustral Canyon's third waterfall, before opening up to more like thirty feet. At the far end of the grotto, a narrow passageway – similar to those that he'd seen in El Dorado – lead upward and deeper into the mountain.

Sam nodded. "What do you know?"

"The third abseil in Claustral Canyon is forty-two feet on average before it reaches a dark pool of water."

Sam nodded. Relieved that he could still remember that. "Not anymore..."

"No," Tom agreed. "I remember the SOT paramedic telling us that there's been a drought and that the water levels were the lowest in recorded history. When I came through the keyhole and rappelled down the waterfall, I descended nearly eighty feet before finding the cave."

A spark of understanding rose in Sam's sluggish cognition. "The cave has always been there. But since the lower pools in the canyon after each waterfall are exceedingly deep, pitch dark, icy cold, and potentially deadly – as I just found out – no one in their right mind has ever tried to swim to the bottom of them."

"Right," Tom confirmed. "My guess is that the lost party and the two rescue parties that followed, all entered this cave, too."

"So where are they?"

"I don't know. Deeper inside, I guess."

Sam swallowed. "Makes you wonder, doesn't it?"

"What?"

"If the water was low, why they didn't just climb out again."

Tom turned the palms of his hands upward. "They must have fallen, or become trapped somehow."

"Yeah, we'll come back here with more ropes and equipment. We'll take it slow. If three separate parties have become trapped down here there's no reason to make it a fourth one."

"That's a great idea, but I'm afraid it might not be possible."

"What are you talking about?" Sam's usual insouciant confidence was rising quickly. "We'll just wait until the flashflood is finished and the water settled, and then we'll swim out, and get reinforcements."

Tom sighed, "That might not be possible."

"Why?"

"The entrance to this cave is about ten feet below where we're sitting now, but the water is rising. Judging by the previous high-water mark, the pool at the bottom of the third waterfall normally sits at least thirty feet higher than this."

Sam ran his eyes across the chamber. It was the first time that he'd noticed the sandstone ceiling showed signs of permanent submersion. He expelled a painful breath of air. "And with the flashflood, this entire chamber's going to be flooded within minutes."

Tom nodded. "Afraid so."

His eyes drifted toward the strange tunnel, presumably made by the lost colony of *Nyia Chías*. It sloped gradually uphill.

The question was, would it be high enough?

And almost in response to his question, the water began to rise like a tsunami.

Chapter Forty-One

Tom asked, "Can you move?"

Sam nodded. "I'll have to."

He crawled on his hands and knees up to the passageway – partly because he didn't have the strength to rise any further and partly because the ceiling wasn't tall enough for him to stand.

Inside the tunnel, the air was damp and musty, making the walls seem closer and more claustrophobic than they actually were. The ground was covered in moss, making it difficult for Sam to gain a foothold. They systematically and stoically continued, suppressing claustrophobia and fear of the unknown to explore what was lying on the other end of the tunnel. The roar of the deluge at the mouth of the cave got dimmer as they ventured deeper, but the water continued to rise.

Despite their hope, the tunnel didn't climb much higher. Instead, it reached a plateau and then fell, sharply descending steeply into an unknown abyss.

Sam and Tom exchanged a quick glance.

A small stream had started lapping at their knees and wrists as they crawled along the tunnel. It was a good four inches thick, and steadily rising.

Tom said, "We can't stay here."

Sam turned his beam behind them. The water was rising by the second. "I know."

Tom shined his flashlight down the *Nyia Chia* tunnel. The beam disappeared in its depths. "I'll go first."

Sam protested. "No. I got us into this…"

"Yeah, you did," Tom said, with a suppressed grin. "But you're still recovering from your near drowning experience. I'll have a better chance of dealing with, whatever we might find, so I'll go first."

Sam looked up, thought about arguing against it, but one glance at Tom's hardened resolve, and he knew that he would be wasting his breath. "All right, all right... go... be careful."

Sam watched Tom go on ahead, crawling down the steep tunnel. And all he could think about was the fact that every ancient tribe, capable of building great things, often went to great lengths to defend them for eternity.

Doubt crept into Sam's mind.

What if this was a trap, laid by the Tairona centuries ago?

The Egyptians used false entry points to the pyramids to trap would-be looters and grave robbers, leaving them to rot in pre-made prisons.

And what if it was a trap?

Where could they go? The fact remained, they were going to drown if they didn't keep going. No, they needed to keep going if they were to have any chance of surviving.

It was that simple.

Sam continued on, slowly, while Tom led the way.

The beam of his flashlight flickered across the walls of the tunnel and he spotted something he hadn't noticed before. They were engraved with strange symbols. Unlike any he had seen previously. symbols had beautiful looping patterns and geometric swirls, as if the walls were a place for experimenting with the creation of new shapes. They seemed almost cosmic. It was clear from the complexity of the carvings and sacred atmosphere that this was an important place for the Tairona tribe.

As he ran his fingers over the engravings and appreciated their artistry, Sam was jolted out of his thoughts with a sharp cry from Tom.

Sam's heart thumped hard in his chest. "Tom?"

No answer.

Sam's fingers tensed on the cave wall. He called out again. "Tom, are you all right? What happened?"

No reply.

Stone carvings and the cosmic wonders forgotten, Sam compulsively began crawling faster toward the source of the sound in an effort to reach Tom. However, Sam suddenly felt the ground enter a steep descent. He attempted to anchor his feet on the floor, but to no avail thanks to the steady stream flowing underneath him. He began sliding downward as the wet moss provided no traction to hold on to at all.

Sam slid backward, lost all control, and raced down the polished tunnel like a kid on a waterslide. He tried to desperately jam his fingers into the sides of the walls, but years of submersion had left them like Teflon.

He forced himself to keep his eyes open as he rounded a series of sharp bends, before the *Nyia Chia* tunnel opened into complete nothingness.

Sam tried to prevent himself from going off the edge, but it was impossible.

A split second later, his tenuous connection to the sandstone tunnel was lost, and he was hurled into the air, free-falling into a dark void for the second time that day.

And this time, without a rope.

Chapter Forty-Two

His feet struck first.

The impact winded him. The pool of water felt like concrete, before giving way, and swallowing him whole. He penetrated the depths of the dark water like a pin.

Despite the pain, he forced himself to kick as hard as possible.

It seemed to take forever to reach the surface. Looking up, he could see the bright glow of light radiating in an unfocussed haze.

And then his head broke the surface and he gasped for air.

Tom was next to him in seconds, supporting him toward a rocky ledge so that he didn't have to keep swimming in the deep water.

Sam wiped the water from his face and opened his eyes. Multiple flashlights glared back at him. He brushed them away with the wave of his hand. A couple of the beams switched off. Those that remained, were pointed away from him, into the water.

He blinked again and let his eyes settle to the new environment.

In addition to Tom, five people stared back at him.

Sam took them in at a glance. Their faces were drawn, their skin raw from more than twenty-four hours of water submersion, but none of them appeared injured and deadly levels of fatigue were still a far way off.

There was a Spanish canyoner who he guessed was one of the civilian adventurers who had first gone missing. Sam met his eye. "You were the first to fall down the tunnel?"

The Spanish man looked sheepish. "Yeah. That was us. We found the additional cave system at the bottom of the unusually shallow pool at the bottom of the third abseil in Claustral... thought we could explore it and then climb back out."

Sam nodded. He could mentally picture making the same mistake. "Somewhere along the lines, you slipped, and kept sliding until you got trapped down here."

The man nodded.

"What about your partner?" Sam asked. "I was told there were two people who went missing first."

"Yes. His name was Churn. He was a Chinese national over here on vacation."

"Was?"

The Spanish man swallowed, his eyes turning away. "I'm afraid when we hit the ground here, I surfaced, but he didn't."

"Did you try and look for him?"

"Of course I did. But this water is deep. Deeper than I could ever duck-dive down to while holding my breath. This was almost twenty-four hours ago by the way. He's long since dead. I'm sorry. But there was nothing I could do about it."

Sam nodded. "I'm sorry."

"It's okay. I know I'm responsible. After all, I was his guide. But he was the one who spotted this cavern and decided to explore it. Still, I'll have to live with his death for the rest of my life."

Sam turned to the other four people. Two had Police Rescue wetsuits. Both men in their thirties, with a tough, and fit appearance. And two wore SOT Paramedic wetsuits. One a man in his late forties, and the other a woman in her late thirties. Sam glanced at the rescuers. "And you followed them down the rabbit hole?"

The female SOT with a name badge of Jen Campbell took offence. "Hey Lancelot, I didn't see you doing any better."

Sam grinned. "Touché."

Tom asked, "All right, all right. We all made the same damned mistake. Does this thing lead anywhere?"

Jen said, "No… maybe? It looks like an ancient sinkhole. The place reminds me of the bottom of a well. We've tried to climb out along every corner, but it's slippery and there's very little natural handholds to grip onto."

Sam turned his flashlight beam upward, taking in the full extent of their predicament. They were at the bottom of what might very well have been a sinkhole or more likely a well made by the Tairona people or dug by the *Nyia Chia*. Whoever made it no longer mattered. The fact was, they were trapped some fifty feet below the top of the well, where a series of bounded logs peered out from a dry cave above, looking remarkably like a primitive pulley system.

Another twenty feet lower than the pulley system, he could see the opening through which they had all fallen, and now a small waterfall ran free.

He started to say it how he saw it. He was speaking as much to himself as to anyone else, the same way he and Tom would bat ideas back and forth. "When we got sucked down there was a flashflood. That water is slowly overflowing the outside cavern, the waterslide-like tunnel, and will eventually run into here. Eventually, the water will rise high enough that we can float to the surface."

Jen was quick to point out the problem. "We had the same thought when the water started to flow, but the problem is for the water to keep flowing enough to raise the water level in this chamber and enough to climb out, which will still mean that the passage to come in will be flooded. Even if we waited until everything equalized, we'd never be able to swim that far underwater without SCUBA equipment."

Sam wasn't to be deterred. "So, we go higher. Wherever that cave up there leads."

"And if it doesn't lead anywhere?"

Sam shrugged. "Then I suppose we're dead. But I've been in some scrapes in my time, I'm not willing to call it quits just yet."

Over the next ten or so minutes, Sam and Tom were introduced to each of the remaining five canyoners. Nathan Sanchez, the man with a half-Spanish appearance, was the canyoning guide, who had taken down Claustral Canyon in the first place. Kyle Best and Robert Kennedy were two Rescue Police Officers from Katoomba, who had been tasked with the original search and rescue operation. Pete Bitner and Jen Campbell were the two paramedics who had been the second search party down the canyon.

With the exception of Churn, who was now gone, they were all very experienced.

Sam studied their position.

The walls of the cavern seemed to tower far above. The cavern extended wasn't big, but it felt endless, somehow. The cathedral like sides were interspersed with jagged boulders and smooth erosion, and some ledges that seemed like they had almost been carved by gods. The walls glowed with moisture and glow worms, giving the whole thing a mystical air.

There was a ledge they could just about reach a little above the water. His eyes traced the rocky wall from the ledge upward. It was almost perfectly smooth for about eight or nine feet, but then there were a couple rocky handholds. Nothing big and nothing definite, but a rock climber could probably make it if they wanted to.

Sam turned to the people he shared the well with. "I don't suppose any of you can rock climb?"

Nathan met his eye with a suppressed smile. "I can a little."

Sam's eyes narrowed. "I take it you've already tried to climb out of here?"

"Yeah. It's the first ten to fifteen feet which are impossible. There simply aren't any holds and the walls are like Teflon. But if I could get past that, I think I could reach the top."

"Good." Sam gestured toward the first ledge. "See that big jug approximately ten feet up from the ledge?"

Nathan glanced at it. "Yeah?"

"If we can boost you there, do you think you could climb the rest of the way?"

Nathan grinned. "You bet your ass I can."

Chapter Forty-Three

Nathan stood on the ledge and stared at the vertical wall above.

He focused, concentrating hard, as he mentally tried to map out a series of hand and leg movements that would eventually allow him to reach the top. It was frustratingly similar to trying to complete a complex maze as a kid, where every route would inevitably lead to a dead end.

After a few minutes, he said, "Okay, I'm ready to give it a try."

"We'll be here for anything you need," Jen said.

The new comers Sam and Tom were already on the ledge, with Tom – a giant of a man holding the coil of rope out of the water to try and reduce some of its weight, and Pete Bitner, the SOT paramedic and next biggest person taking up the remaining space on the ledge.

Tom handed him the rope. It was waterlogged, but as good as he was going to get. He looped it diagonally across his shoulder and chest, before using the tail end to tie it on. On his harness he carried a small rack of climbing hexes, nuts, and spring-loaded cams – all of which would be necessary to anchor the rope either part way up the climb, or even at the top, so that the rest of the party could make the ascent. Everything else he left on the ledge. The climb would be impossible to achieve carrying his backpack.

Sam and Pete interlocked their fingers so that Nathan could use them as a foot placement, before stepping onto Tom's shoulders and gaining the necessary height to reach the first hand-hold.

He tried to balance, but the ledge was too narrow and there were too many people already on it to lift his foot up.

Nathan shook his head after a couple tries. "It's no good. Sam, I'll get you back in the water."

Sam nodded. The man seemed to understand that it wasn't a debate about who was bigger or stronger. The fact was Nathan needed Tom's height, and Pete's size to make the jump to the first hold.

Nathan glanced over his shoulder. Already, the remaining members of the party had swam backward, leaving him plenty of room to fall into the water if he failed.

He glanced at Tom and Pete. "Ready?"

"Ready," they confirmed in unison.

Nathan took a deep breath and said, "Here we go."

He placed his hands wide across the slippery wall of sandstone and placed his left foot onto Pete's intermeshed fingers. The man made a slight grunt, but his stance was rock solid.

Nathan stepped his right foot onto Tom's shoulder.

And stood up.

His fingers were just out of reach of the big bucked hold.

"I'm going to have to jump," he warned.

Tom said, "Go for it."

He bent his legs, took a deep breath, and sprung.

His right hand connected with the hold, but he couldn't keep it. His fingers locked with a clump of green moss, ripping it free from the sandstone, and he fell backward.

Beneath him, Tom and Pete managed to push his falling body toward the water, so that he landed in the deep, maleficent black pool below.

He surfaced a couple seconds later, apologized, and tried again.

He fell the second time.

And the third.

But on the fourth time, his fingers gripped the hold – matching it with both hands – before pulling up and locking onto a deep jug above.

His fingers sunk in, appreciatively connecting to the lip of sandstone, like a ladder.

He continued without pausing for rest, maneuvering his body across a series of complex bouldering moves and riding the momentum until he reached the top.

At the top he tied the rope across what appeared to be a primitive pulley system, and threw the opposite end down to the water below.

Leaning over the edge of the cavern, he said, "You guys have to see what's up here."

Chapter Forty-Four

The Labyrinth

Sam climbed the rope next.

He used a pair of hand-held ascenders that smoothly slid along the vertical rope, but a toothed locking-cam prevented it from moving downward under tension. To climb he alternated between the right and left one while shifting his legs higher up the wall.

Through pursed lips, he began his ascent.

It was hard work, but easy enough and he was at the top within minutes.

At the top, Nathan's mouth was open, his eyes wide. Impatiently, he said, "You've got to see this."

"What is it?" Sam asked, and then stopped, because he spotted what Nathan had found.

There was a handcrafted pulley system with a wooden bucket silently hanging off the end. The system itself seemed to be made out of a dark, oak tree, with a thick brown shade that betrayed its age and wear. Sam squinted. There were no native oak trees in Australia. The pulley itself consisted of several axles and grooves attached to a fraying rope that was black with use. Though it lay quiet right now, Sam knew that if one of them were to pull the inconspicuous end of the rope near the largest axle and groove, the entire machine would come to life like a slumbering monster, bringing up water from the dark pools in which their group had barely managed to escape. A small question began forming in Sam's mind as he inspected the system with his eyes.

Who would need a pulley and well here?

As if he had read his mind, Nathan said, "It appears someone's been living here for a long time." He met Sam's eye. "Or something."

"Yeah… or something," Sam agreed, remembering the armored creature of the Nyia Chia that nearly killed them in El Dorado.

From down below, Jen shouted, "I'm on rope, ready to climb."

"Go ahead, you're free to climb," Nathan shouted back before returning to inspect the pulley and its grey-rock foundation.

Over the next twenty minutes, everyone made their way to the top of the well.

The bricks were well-worn and Sam could even see shallow footprint imprints made by the residents of the mystic caverns. The footprints led away from the well to another tunnel. Even when the entire group trained their flashlight helmets into the passageway, they could not make a dent in the seemingly all-consuming darkness.

Sam asked, "Who wants to go first?"

Without hesitation Nathan said, "I do."

Sam followed close behind.

Once fully inside the tunnel, an odd smell not dissimilar to old books in forgotten libraries filled their noses. They all noticed the smell getting gradually stronger as they continued in.

Sam began to inspect the walls for engraving and symbols similar to the ones he saw in the passages that led him to this point. However, instead of the familiar symbols, there was a pattern of a set of three deep claw marks running down the length of the tunnel walls. They did not look like anything possibly made by man, the tunnel looked like it had been dug by an animal – and Sam knew exactly what that animal was, too.

The image of the *Nyia Chia* charging at him was still raw in his memory.

They trudged on silently for five more minutes before they came to a junction. From the main tunnel they were in, three more tunnels branched out into different directions at perfect perpendicular angles.

Without a word, all five of them looked at Sam for guidance. He racked his brain to remember what he had done last time he went exploring and came to a labyrinth. China's Lost Army, The Greek Maze of Horrors… In all of these there was one rule of thumb he had followed: stay to the right side. Maybe it was superstition, but Sam, student of history, considered it wisdom passed down from all the way back from the Greeks and their story of the Minotaur and the Labyrinth of Crete. Princess Ariadne helped Theseus by advising him to only follow his right hand and unravel a string along the way so he could find his way back. Sam turned to the team, meeting everyone's eyes before speaking.

"We'll stick to the right," he said. "And we need to find a way to track our steps so we can retrace them if we meet a dead end."

At their nods, he scattered a small handful of stones in his wake, and started off down the right-hand passage. The passageway was like a maze, but no one got lost. At times they grabbed onto coats to keep from losing each other, but when they reached the cavern at the end, they all started as one.

The passageway opened up into what looked like a ruined village living inside the rock. The buildings were built of stone and wood, and were crumbling. There was a primitive power to their construction that halted the group in their tracks. Without question, and without communication, they all knew they were looking at something that had never before been seen by modern man.

Movement in the shadows made Sam spin. Wary of the last time he'd been in an abandoned city and an armored tank of a creature had tried to kill him, Sam spun, on the alert. He doubted there was a caretaker here to save them.

The movement stopped. Then continued. Sam waited, feigning as if he hadn't seen it, and then he turned his headlamp on full blast at the same time he spun and shone it toward the shadow that had moved.

Silhouetted in the bright glare was the last thing Sam expected to see.

A wiry Chinese man stood frozen in the glare. Behind him, stacked like a dragon's hoard, was a nest full of golden pearls.

Beside him, Nathan Sanchez swore.

Chapter Forty-Five

Sam watched the scene unfold and wondered what Nathan and Churn were really doing down there in the first place.

Could it be that he and Tom weren't the only ones searching for the Tomb of El Dorado and the remaining Nyia Chia?

Nathan said, "You bastard!"

The group took in the scene in bewilderment, equally astonished by the newcomer's sudden appearance and staggered by the sight of the gold. Sam felt the roar of triumph rage in his chest, despite his injuries, his soaked clothes, and bone-aching exhaustion – they'd found it.

Nathan was already moving forward. "What happened? I thought you were dead!"

Jen Campbell glanced between them. "You know each other? This was the client you lost in the tunnels?"

Nathan nodded. "We got separated in the deluge... he must have..." He stared at Churn as if he'd seen a ghost. Sam sensed a strange surge of loyalty and wondered what exactly their relationship was. "What did happen?"

Churn was short and dark, made even shorter and darker by the shadows of the cave and the low glow of the gold and the glowworms. His voice was soft, cultured, and very precise. "I got swept through to the other side. I found my way here." He gestured. "And I found... this."

Jen whistled. "This place is incredible. What is..."

But Kyle, the police officer, was glaring. "This is what you came in after, isn't it? This is why you ignored flash flood warnings, why you decided to explore an unstable cavern in an unstable drought... For what?" He gestured. "For money?"

"You can't say it's not worth it, mate." Even Nathan had to jump in. "It's not just the money. It's the history. It's Australian history, man." Again, Sam noticed that spark leap between Nathan and the Chinese man, and this time – or was he imagining it? – he caught a glimpse of surprise in the Asian man's face.

"Aussie history, huh?" Kyle asked. "What the hell is this place?"

Churn brought himself up to his short stature but seemed much taller. "I am funding this search. Money to me…" He spread his hands. "Is no object. History, however…" His eyes gleamed. "Is worth everything."

Sam jumped in. "I couldn't agree with you more, actually. Unfortunately, history might be our downfall, here." He gestured at the silence, which was loud as if listening to a shell at the beach. "We have to keep moving if we want to stay ahead of this water. There's a good chance it will flood us even in here."

Nathan gaped. "Surely it can't get much higher?"

"I don't know. Either way, I think we'd better keep going. We can always come back again for a proper archeological and historical expedition."

Jen's eyes returned to the hoard of golden pearls. "And what about the gold?"

"Leave them. They'll only slow you down. If this place floods while we're still in here, that gold isn't going to do anyone any good."

Churn cursed. "No way. I'm not leaving it."

Sam shrugged. "Suit yourself. It must weigh a hundred pounds."

"And be worth more than a hundred thousand dollars," Churn persisted, greedily shoving the gold into the bottom compartment in his backpack, until it was so heavy, the entire canvas sagged.

Sam stopped, his eyes meeting Churn's. "I thought you said it's not about the money?"

"I did. It isn't. It's about the history, but I've invested a large amount of time and resources into searching for this because of an old family legend where one of my great ancestors, who came out here during the gold rush of 1851 and found a number of these near magical golden pearls... so I'm not going to leave them here to be flooded forever."

Sam wanted to argue. "Suit yourself. You can argue your ownership of the gold once we get out of here... but first we'd better get out of here."

Returning to the practicalities, Nathan asked, "About that, I don't suppose you have an idea which way leads out of here?"

Sam said, "No. Look for something that leads upward, toward the surface."

Tom said, "Or, something that leads downward, exiting into another submerged pool or something like the one in Claustral Canyon."

"Really?" Sam asked. "I figured that was a once off... whoever lived here used that to siphon water into their well."

"Sure, but if there is an exit out into the surface, the question then remains, why hasn't anyone ever found it previously?"

Sam nodded. "Good point. All right, we'll have to spread out. The exit could be anywhere. The only other thing you should keep your eyes out for is any gust of wind."

And with that, the group spread out and searched for an exit.

Sam noticed many similarities to the Tairona city in Colombia. Despite the abundance of stone, the structures were built of clay and wood. They were miraculously well preserved for such temporary materials. The houses were conical, with small doors and windows, perfect to keep out or let in the elements at will. Though they saw relics of pottery and weavings, there were no chairs.

The others wandered in a hush, their awe and excitement overflowing like the river behind them. He shook his head. There was no doubt in his mind that this was the place where El Hombre Dorado and his group of ancient Tairona people cared for the colony of Nyia Chía. But no one lived here anymore. In fact, from what they could gather, it looked like no one had lived there for a very long time.

Sam called over to Tom. "Tom, I'll need that pack a minute. Can you bring the water?"

Tom came over, already unscrewing the top of the canteen. He raised his brows when Sam didn't drink. "Not thirsty?"

"Didn't want the echo." It was true. Even whispers had a way of sounding like shouts in this space. Tom glanced around, understanding. "You know what this means, don't you?"

Tom couldn't fight his grin. "Please don't go all mushy on me now."

Sam slapped at him. "This is it. We found it." He gestured at the cave. "You're telling me there can possibly be another place where the Tairona and the El Hombre Dorado raised the new colony of the Niya Chia?" His eyes shone, picking up the gleam of the glowworms. "Tom. We've found it. We just have to find... them."

"Well, yes. It does look like that. But how do we find them?"

Sam shook his head. "Don't know yet." He watched the preparations of the others as they made ready for another attempt to find their way out.

In the distance, Jen shouted, "Hey! I found something... there's a strong breeze coming from up here!"

Chapter Forty-Six

Sam raced to Jen.

She was standing near one of the passageways that led to the south.

He asked, "What have you got?"

Jen waved her hand in the passageway in triumph. "Feel that? Fresh air! It's coming from this direction!"

The promise of the sight of sky and the pressure of the water rising behind them was enough to push them on. Sam left the village with regret, but also with grace – glad he'd gotten to see it once in his life. The glowing blue of the glowworms, the carvings in the cavern walls, the history steeped in the ancient huts were sights he would never forget.

His reverie was interrupted by an argument.

Kyle and Pete were on the impassive Chinese man. Churn was struggling to lift his gold laden backpack onto his shoulders. They were trying to pull it down, resorting to hand gestures and fury when he stepped back out of their reach. Kyle was trying to avoid the confrontation this deep below ground. Pete Bitner looked like he'd just as happily fight the man underground as he would above ground, for risking their lives.

He glanced between the two of them. It looked like it was going to get ugly.

Sam hobbled over. "What's going on here?"

Kyle gestured furiously at the bulging pack. "This one just loaded up all the gold into his own pack."

The little man stood taller and for some reason Sam thought of the mob. "Someone must carry it out. It is evidence."

Sam held up his hands with an easy smile, hiding his distaste. Distaste had no place in life or death situations. "Be that as it may, we're not even close to out of this yet.'

Churn's voice was cold and his smile didn't reach his eyes. "I don't care, I'm taking the damned gold!"

Sam's voice went an octave colder himself. He'd risked his life to help these people, and this was the thanks he got? "That gold weighs more than a hundred pounds. And if we have to go through what we went through to get in here to get out of here, there's no way that it's not going to drag you down." He gestured at the small, bedraggled group, some of them injured, all of them hungry, wet and tired and cold. "Drag us all down. And we can't afford to get dragged down."

Churn hoisted his pack higher. "If I fall, you don't have to come after me. I know the risks."

Spare me from idiots, Sam thought. This was not at all how he'd planned this day to go. "See that you don't. I'll do a lot to save a man, but I can't save someone from their own stupidity."

Sam returned to Jen and the breeze she had found.

They climbed through the maze in silence, the cavern walls pressing in around through the scent of sweat and damp stone. Sam's knees ached from all the crawling. Just when he was certain he didn't have any skin left to lose, his thoughts were suddenly drowned by the sound of rushing water.

Not again.

But when they emerged at the end of the tunnel, they were met with a different sight.

Hope.

They stood at the edge of a fast-flowing subterranean river, rushing by in a dim, glowing blue. And on the opposite side, their first sign of light – daylight. Jen grinned and Churn let out an excited *whoop*. Glow worms lit the walls like pyrotechnics, casting their excitement in an otherworldly glow.

Nathan said, "In case you haven't noticed that opening is on the wrong side of that subterranean river…"

Sam exchanged a glance with Tom.

They had both been in a similar situation years ago.

Sam said, "I noticed."

Nathan, his voice almost pugnacious, said, "So do you have any idea how we're going to get around it?"

Sam dropped his pack, picked up his rope, and grinned. "Yeah, we'll set up a Tyrolean Traverse."

Chapter Forty-Seven

Churn, usually coy and indifferent to the group, asked, "What's a Tyrolean Traverse?"

Sam met his eye, and saw fear in his eyes. "Have you ever been ziplining?"

Churn frowned. "What?"

Sam said, "All right, it's like this. I'll tie off some rope at an anchor point up here and then swim across with the rope and secure it on the other side. Once Tyrolean Traverse is set up, you can attach yourself to it with a carabiner and shimmy across, high above the river."

Churn said, "I get the picture, but there's one thing I don't understand…"

"What's that?"

"How are you going to get across the river in the first place?"

"That's a good question. I'll tie the rope to myself and try and swim across. I can empty my dry bag and inflate it with air to use as a flotation device. If I don't make it, you can all pull me back to this side."

Pete Bitner asked, "Have you ever tried to cross fast-flowing water?"

"Yeah, I have… on the occasion…"

"How did that go?"

Sam said, "Badly."

"Yet you still want to try?"

Sam raised his brows. "Anyone have a better plan?"

No one did, which was how Sam came to knot the rope onto his harness. They tied the other end up high on one of the stalactites on their side of the bank. He had supervised the tying himself and could only hope the ancient limestone notch below the knot held. Tom manned the rope attached to the rock. He trusted Tom. Sam took a breath.

The current rushed past in the riverbed, swift and merciless. Sam pushed down his exhaustion, and the pain, pulling himself into a sort of battle mode.

There was never much to say in battle mode. He started upriver along the bank on dry land, trailing the rope like a leash.

Jen frowned. "I thought you were…"

"The current's going to sweep him back. If he times it right, the river will do most of the work for him, and drop him off on the other side." For the first time Churn sounded admiring. A challenge also burned in his words.

Sam's heart raced. "I don't know if the river will do most of the work, but hopefully it will do some."

Tom said, "Good luck."

Sam took a couple deep breaths. There was good chance the current would drag him underneath the water. The less carbon dioxide he was carrying when he began the better he would be.

On the last breath, he gripped the flotation device, and took a running jump into the middle of the subterranean river.

He plunged into the icy water, confirming what he'd expected – that the river had spent much of its life beneath the surface of the Earth, where sunlight rarely penetrated, and was never given the chance to warm the water.

The water did indeed drag him back – harder and much faster than he expected.

He shot downstream like a cork out of a barrel.

Despite being an exceptionally strong swimmer, he was little more than a passenger, riding the river. His fingers clung to the flotation device, as if his life depended upon it – which it did.

The rapids pummeled him around like a ragdoll, dragging him farther and farther downstream, until the rope went taut. That meant Tom had either realized he was never going to make it and had started to pull in the rope, or worse yet, that he'd reached the end of his seventy-foot rope. For a few seconds he swung side to side, across the river, like a pendulum.

Then, no longer able to drift freely with the river, Sam was pulled under.

He took one last gasp of air before it happened.

Try as he might to keep grip on the dry bag, the river was more powerful than his hands, and it was ripped free from him, disappearing downriver in an instant.

Sam could hear his heart pounding in the back of his ears.

He tried to swim free, but it was impossible. The current was a thousand times stronger than he was. What was worse, it seemed to be stronger than the rest of the canyoners who should have been pulling him into the shore by now.

His lungs burned and he fought down the panic that was rising quickly.

He battled the raging water, legs churning, lungs burning, heading on in pure survival instinct alone. But none of them were going to give him what he needed.

Why hadn't they pulled him to the bank?

Time ticked by. Seconds seemed like hours.

Were they going to be his last ones alive?

It was the weight of him on the rope against the fast-flowing water that was going to kill him. His body was acting like an anchor.

He tried to release the carabiner, but there was too much tension on the rope to open its locking mechanism.

Sam, driven wild with panic, and aware that he was racing toward the edge of his survivability, reached down to his ankle, where he kept a diving knife. With his thumb he popped the latch and withdrew the knife by its handle.

He sliced the rope with the razor-sharp blade, severing the rope in one swift movement.

Released from his confines, Sam rolled backward and was dragged backward. His entire world, quickly disappearing in the black water rapids.

Chapter Forty-Eight

Sam opened his eyes.

His back slammed hard against something, stopping his progress. Instinctively, his hands gripped in the dark for it, finding perch on the round stomp of stone. His helmet flashlight fixed on the base of a stalagmite. It was at the bottom of the river, and right now, it was the only thing he could use to stabilize himself with.

Despite the speed of the water, the river was surprisingly clear. The beam from his helmet flashed on the riverbed, showing its gradient slowly increasing sharply upward next to the stalagmite. It also showed the surface of the water wasn't far off.

He was lying right next to the river's bank.

Discombobulated from being rolled around the turbid water, he'd lost complete sense of all directions. There was no way to know which bank he was on. It didn't matter. He needed to breathe. Driven by the need for survival, he dug his feet hard against the back of the stalagmite, and reached up.

His hands gripped a stalactite that hung from the ceiling of the cavern.

Sam's biceps contracted with a jolt, and he pulled himself out of the water like a sprung coil, gasping for air. He climbed fully out of the water, edging his way up the river bank.

In the distance, he spotted a series of flickering lights from the opposite side of the river. Their voices undiscernible over the roar of the river.

He closed his eyes and thanked whatever gods were listening for landing him on the right side of the river.

After hauling himself out of the river and resting for a good minute, he walked back upriver until he found the location opposite the rope.

Tom coiled the rope and threw it across the river.

Sam caught it on the first go. He found a perfect outcropping to tie the rope with a double figure-eight knot. He checked the knot and then checked it again. With his numb hands, hunger, and exhaustion, it would be so easy to make a mistake. And a mistake now would mean the entire journey here had been wasted.

Sam cupped his hands and shouted across the river. Despite his full capacity, the words were barely audible over the roar of the water.

"Ready?"

They got the idea, though. One by one they all glided across, using their carabiners or ascenders to cut down on the friction of their hands, tucking their legs up toward their chests, backpacks lurching them inverted like turtles. Sam watched and counted. Cheers rose up with each successful transit. Pete. Jen. Kyle. Robert. Nathan. Tom…

Churn went last, the muscular and wiry little Chinese man almost touching the surface of the water due to his pack weighed down with the gold. Sam shouted at him to drop it, but it was too late – the man had already made the jump.

"Idiot," he muttered. "He's going to get himself…"

The rope dipped in the middle under the weight of Churn's backpack. The backpack dipped into the water, causing it to rapidly fill. The more it filled, the heavier it got, and the farther Churn sank into the water.

Churn's back, waist, and legs were all dragged under.

He was going backward, and at this rate, the backpack would pull him under water any minute now. Sam was divesting himself of his own pack and coat before he knew what he was doing, he was in the water before he could register their shouts. Sam stopped at his shins.

"Drop the pack!" Sam shouted. "You'll drown!"

The water pushed strong at his legs, and in his weakened state Sam nearly lost his balance.

He seemed in danger of it already. Tangled in the rope and in his heavy cargo, Churn floundered in the raging water. Gasps echoed up and down the line as he struggled.

"Idiot!" Tom bellowed, fighting to be heard over the roar of the water. "Drop it! You're going to die!"

Beside them, Nathan Sanchez was pure white. "Jesus," he whispered, locked on the scene like everyone else. "But he never even…"

Then he whipped off his jacket and started forward. "Shouldn't we –"

But it was too late.

Instead of relinquishing the pack, Churn cut the rope.

Falling into the fast-flowing water below.

Like a twig in the black-water rapids, he was swept downstream and disappeared into the black abyss where the river dissolved deeper underground.

Chapter Forty-Nine

Sam was haunted by the memory of Churn saying that he could look after himself.

They all accepted that Churn was dead. No one could have survived and they were in no position to try a body retrieval now, let alone ever.

Instead, in a somber mood, they continued hiking up the tunnel that appeared to lead to daylight. The trail continued for another two hundred odd feet, before opening halfway up in a spectacular gorge. The walls were overhung with massive ferns and emerald-colored moss. Crepuscular rays filtered through thick ferns, causing the whole gorge to glow.

Nathan dropped a rope down ready to rappel.

He met their gaze and said, "Welcome to the green room."

Chapter Fifty

It took nearly three hours to hike out of the canyon, climbing the spur of the mountain, before finally coming out onto the Camel's Hump.

Next to the Robinson R44 was a blue and white AS 350B Squirrel police helicopter, on its fuselage was its callsign, POLAIR 3.

There was a large debrief.

Specialist detectives had arrived to take detailed notes before anyone was allowed to leave. Even once they had finished, Sam and Tom were warned that they might need to be contactable in the coming months if and when a formal inquest was to be held.

Nathan Sanchez explained the full story about how Churn had come to him with a story that his great something grandfather had found a unique type of gold from a canyon somewhere over the Blue Mountains. It had been a family legend for nearly a hundred and seventy years.

Sanchez explained that for the first two months, Churn had refused to tell him what he was looking for, simply paying him a daily rate to take him through all the various canyons in the Blue Mountains. It was only once they had completed every one of them that Churn had finally given in and told him the full story in the hope that Nathan could identify other water sources.

Nathan went on to explain that Churn had actually returned to China having given up on the search until he'd noticed the water levels in Claustral were at their lowest since they were first explored in the 1960s. As a result of which, he convinced Churn to come back for another search.

When they had finished, Nathan asked to make a phone call and just let his family know that he was safe.

Sam and Tom provided a brief and systematic report of the events since they entered Claustral Canyon, all the way through to when Churn was dragged under water, and instead of cutting his backpack strap off, he cut the rope that made up the Tyrolean Traverse.

What none of them could answer was whether or not Churn had done so by mistake or intentionally rather than letting the gold go.

When they were all finished and free to go, Sam said goodbye and good luck to Nathan Sanchez.

Nathan held up his index finger, motioning for Sam to wait.

The athletic man turned around, reaching with both hands into his backpack. He rummaged around inside, and after a brief search he withdrew a small leather-bound notebook that was barely smaller than Sam's hand. Its cover was smooth with faint traces of the scaling of older leather. The book was clearly old, even ancient, maybe buried with a royal tomb, maybe passed on for generations in a family… who could tell?

Nathan said, "I want you to have this."

"Thank you." Sam's eyes narrowed on the book. "What is it?"

Sam opened the book and was instantly hit with the distinct dank smell of old paper. It was all written in Chinese script with elaborate curves and finishes that only could have been made with a quill. He fumbled it back and forth between his hands.

"Do you know what it says?"

Nathan shook his head. "No. But Churn said it was from his grandfather, who inherited from his grandfather, and so on. Apparently, his dad told him these crazy stories he learned from living in Australia, back before it was barely even a country. Some myths about extraterrestrials that ate sandstone and turned it into gold. Hell, even I know the story by now. It was all he would talk about."

"Was this the only place that he was searching for the origins of those golden pearls?"

"No. He told me that his father or grandfather… someone, I can't remember who, said that there was one other place they might be found. It was there that Churn was investigating when I called him and asked him to come back to Claustral Canyon."

"Do you know where it was?"

"The second search place?"

"Yeah."

"No."

Sam continued to flip through the leather book aimlessly. "Do you mind if I borrow this, and see if I can get it translated?"

Nathan said, "You can keep it. It's worthless now. Didn't bring him much luck, did it."

Sam took the book. "Thanks. Do you have any idea where Churn lived?"

Nathan racked his brain for any information he had forgotten about his doomed customer as he watched the prop on the copter start to spin.

He shrugged. "He said he was nomadic and liked to keep his distance from everyone. I spent nearly six months searching for this place with him, and he never opened up to me. He mentioned New York, Hong Kong, Finland… the Maldives. He'd been all over."

Damn. Sam nodded, but couldn't let it drop. In the distance, Tom shook hands with everyone. They were running out of time.

"You don't even have an address or name of a relative?"

A simple shake of the head was the reply. "That wasn't an aspect of my expedition with him. I'm generally fine with getting paid cold cash and doing my job. Sure, I get close with a lot of my clients, but at the root, it's a customer – service relationship. I don't ask questions about them, and they don't ask them about me."

Sam nodded. "What about his passport? He must have one if he got into the country?"

"That I have. Or a copy of it, anyway." He rummaged in his bag again. "I make copies of all of my clients. Legal reasons, and just general security." He pulled out a waterproof folder, and rifled through.

Sam raised his brows. "You keep hard copies?"

"Yeah, and digital," Nathan confessed, handing over the ragged paper. "I'm old school."

"Good thing."

Sam studied the printout and the grainy black and white photo. Inside on the left was a slightly younger version of Churn. On the right, there was a listing for what could only be his name, birthdate, and address.

He couldn't read a word of them, but he knew someone who would find out for him.

He stared at the address.

Sam and Tom said goodbye to Nathan.

Sam climbed into the Robinson R44 and switched on the engine.

As the rotors began to turn, Tom asked, "If the *Nyia Chia* have long since left this region, and the only man who knew anything about where they might have gone drowned... where do you want to go now?"

Sam handed him the copy of Churn's passport.

Tom glanced at it and read the location out loud. "Dìxià Chéng, Beijing – China."

Chapter Fifty-One

Nathan Sanchez watched the Robinson R44 takeoff.

His eyes traced the helicopter as it slowly disappeared over the horizon and then picked up his cell phone, and pressed redial.

A man on the other end of the line answered. "Did you do it?"

Nathan nodded to himself. "Yes, uncle."

"Good. Do you think he will find the truth?"

Nathan glanced at the helicopter, no more than a pinprick on the horizon. "I think he might. One thing's for certain, he's a hell of a lot more resourceful than Churn ever was."

His uncle said, "Good. And the GPS tracker?"

"It's in the book. All we have to do is let Sam Reilly find out what Churn really knew, and then we'll follow him."

"Well done."

"One more thing…"

"What?"

"I saw the Nyia Chia's golden pearls. They were stunning."

His uncle agreed. "Yes, they are – and when you find the Tomb of El Dorado, we're going to have more them than we could ever spend in a lifetime."

Chapter Fifty-Two

Dìxià Chéng, Beijing – China

The Beijing Capital Airport was uniquely quiet despite its size.

Sam scanned the sea of people, all moving and walking in respectful silence. He and Tom grabbed their backpacks, made their way through customs, and stepped into the arrival's lounge. It had been a long time since Sam had flown commercial anywhere, but it was easier to do so than go through the onerous process of getting the necessary documentations and approval to fly into Beijing on his private jet.

And that was saying a lot, considering Sam and Tom had landed everywhere from the Amazon jungle to abandoned military air bases. Sam looked around. The only people there were a haggle of flight attendants that were clearly bored, and a lone tour guide. He walked up to the woman and reached his hand out to shake it. The guide ignored the gesture and buried her face in a brochure that was most likely intended for the visitors.

In the departures lounge, they were greeted by woman holding a sign with Sam Reilly's name on it.

Sam greeted her. "Miss. Liqiu Wu?"

She greeted him with a pleasant smile. "Yes, Mr. Reilly?"

He smiled politely. "Just Sam."

"Pleased to meet you, Sam," she replied, before turning her attention to Tom. "And you must be Mr. Bower."

"Tom will do fine. Pleased to meet you."

She gave both of them a cursory glance, as though trying to determine what sort of clients she was looking after today. "Welcome to Beijing. I hope your flight was okay?"

Tom said, "Fine. Slept the whole flight."

Sam sidestepped the question, by answering another. "I'll catch up on my sleep tonight."

"You're here to see the real Dìxià Chéng, is that right?"

"Yes," Sam said, returning to his business-like mode. "We're keen to find some information on someone who used to live there."

"That might be hard. There are many people living in Dìxià Chéng, and none of them have documented addresses." She spoke with near perfect English, with a slight trace of a North American accent. She suppressed a slight grin, licked her lips, and said, "But I'll try my best to help you find what you're looking for."

Sam said, "Thank you."

"You're welcome." Liqiu exchanged a quick glance with both of them. "Do you need anything before we go?"

"No," they both confirmed. "We're good."

She nodded, her eyes darting across their small backpacks, a wry grin forming on her elegant face. "That's all your luggage?"

"That's it," Sam confirmed. "We'd love to spend more time here on a tourist visa next time, but unfortunately, this is just a short stopover to try and find some details about a lost friend of ours."

"How long are you planning on staying?"

"That depends on how long it takes to find what we need, but hopefully no more than a few days."

She gestured toward the exit gates and said, "If that's the case, we'd better get started right away."

243

Chapter Fifty-Three

They took a taxi to Dìxià Chéng.

Sam watched the city go by as they sped along an eight-lane highway. The road was clear and well maintained. Liqiu explained that she didn't own a car, and even if she did, she wouldn't use it to take them where they wanted to go, because there was nowhere for her to park once they got there.

Twenty minutes later, the taxi stopped out the front of 62 West Damochang Street in Qianmen. Sam looked up at the rear-view mirror in front of the driver's seat. The taxi driver looked scared, with eyebrows furrowed into an expression of worry and wariness. The guide said something in Chinese, to which the driver nodded and took the money that she gave him for the fare. Sam, Tom, and Liqiu got out, and the driver sped off. In front of them stood a large red door. The tour guide opened it and they all followed.

At the height of Soviet-Chinese tensions in 1969, Chairman Mao Zedong ordered the construction of the Underground City during the border conflict over Zhenbao Island in the Heilongjiang River. The Underground City was designed to withstand nuclear, biochemical and conventional attacks. The complex would protect Beijing's population, and allow government officials to evacuate in the event of an attack on the city. The government claimed that the tunnels could accommodate all of Beijing's six million inhabitants at the time, upon its completion.

The complex was equipped with facilities such as restaurants, clinics, schools, theaters, factories, a roller-skating rink, grain and oil warehouses, and a mushroom cultivation farm. There were also almost seventy potential sites where water wells could easily be dug if needed. Elaborate ventilation systems were installed, with 2300 shafts that could be sealed off to protect the tunnels' inhabitants from poisonous gases. Gas and water-proof hatches, as well as thick concrete main gates, were constructed to protect the tunnels from biochemical attacks and nuclear fallouts.

There was no official disclosure about the actual extent of the complex, but it was speculated that the tunnels may link together Beijing's various landmarks, as well as important governmental buildings such as the Zhongnanhai, the Great Hall of the People, and even military bases in the outskirts of the city. It links all the tunnels that make up the underground city from areas of beneath central Beijing, from Xidan and Xuanwumen to Qianmen and the Chongwen district, in addition to the Western Hills. In the event of a nuclear attack, the plan was to move half of Beijing's population underground and the other half to the Western Hills.

Of course, a Soviet nuclear war never eventuated and the entire complex was abandoned. The majority of the solid concrete doors were closed forever, with walls and buildings being constructed in front of them to prevent the doors from ever being reopened. But some doors remained, and through these, people ventured into the deep, dark, and often eerie confines of Beijing's Underground City.

A place where an entire culture of people who call the tunnels home and the government has decided to ignore them. China has done census readings of the tunnels and it was estimated over 50,000 people live below in the tunnels.

Liqiu led them in through the concrete nuclear resistant doors and down into Dìxià Chéng. Outdated light bulbs hanging from wires barely compensated for the lack of natural sunlight. People left and right were hunched over going about their various businesses.

Liqiu turned to Sam and Tom and began to speak. "Welcome to Dìxià Chéng – the great Underground City. As you know, it was originally made as a nuclear bomb shelter. It was meant to hold half of all Beijing if necessary, but now the city's too big and there's no need for it anymore. There were hundreds of entrances, but most of them were destroyed by the government."

Tom took in the massive complex and raised his brows. He gestured to the sprawling subterranean secret. "So why wasn't this destroyed?"

"Officials wanted to keep a few for tourism and propaganda purposes. They thought they blocked off all the tunnels to the residential areas, but the hermits always find a way in. They're like rats… or troglodytes."

"So that's the people that live here – hermits?"

Liqiu smiled, but her lovely dark eyes were solemn. "Yes, and those who can't afford to live anywhere else." She wiped her nose, and Sam wondered if perhaps she had lived here, once… a long time ago. "The entire place was equipped with everything you would want in a city: wells, hospitals, malls, food stores, schools, even a skating rink. You name it, it was there. Now of course, most of it is in disrepair, but beggars can't be choosers. The hermits use some of them."

It still didn't make sense to Tom, and he said as much. "But how could it possibly protect millions? A nuclear blast is pretty strong."

"Really?" she snapped. "You would know, you Americans." Before Tom could open his mouth, she barreled on. "Did you miss the part where it's hundreds of feet underground? We don't build things like you do." She preened a little, on that rather ambiguous statement, and couldn't help adding, "It also has ventilation and double-walling to protect against water flooding or gas attacks from the surface."

"How big is this entire thing?" Tom asked.

"No one knows exactly. Since the Cold War bonanza died down, the government seems more inclined to forget about the entire system and won't say anything about it. But they say it's larger than Beijing itself. But a shame it only holds 55,000 people."

Sam redirected his attention to his surroundings. They'd passed dead-eyed druggies, clear-eyed clerks, and all manner of wares imaginable; he'd registered the terrain out of the corner of his eyes as they'd passed, out of old habit. They had been walking for a good deal of time, long enough for Sam to almost forget that they were completely, as she said, hundreds of feet underground. Now they emerged from a corridor and the somewhat snaking streets into a bustling square. Contrary to what the guide had told them, the people were dressed well, clean, and looked happy, as if their life underground was no different from the accepted one going on right above their heads. In the walls, several staircases were cut out of the stone, leading to what Sam assumed were the entrances of apartments. Signs posted all around the square directed customers to nearby restaurants and businesses and even showed the estimated walking distance and time it might take to get there. At least, Sam reflected, you didn't have to worry about traffic.

As the guide paused to let them take in the sight, Sam figured now was as good a time as any to ask the guide about any information about Churn's whereabouts. He grabbed the printout of the passport he'd taken from Nathan Sanchez and from the back pocket of his jeans and presented it to the guide, folding it open to the identification page as he did so.

"We actually came here to find any information on this person." The narrow-eyed guide squinted at the bad copy in the dim light. Sam held the book steady. "He was from China originally, but he went to another country looking for a place called El Dorado."

"El Dorado?" Her eyes narrowed further with distrust and she looked around as if someone might be watching her response. "I don't know anything about it. Maybe you can ask some people at the Sinchang."

"The what?"

"Dixia Sinchang. Underground Business. It's where all black market goes through in China. If you get anything illegal, chances are one of the middlemen at the Sinchang station has gotten their hands on your money and products."

Sam and Tom shared a look. Their search was about to turn way more dangerous than they had planned for. But they both knew there was no other option. Churn must have gotten his information and desire from somewhere, and they needed to find out who or what that was.

Sam spoke first. "Take us there, and we'll pay you extra." He held out ten 100-yuan bills, Mao Zedong's face staring disapprovingly at them.

The guide snatched the bills at the same time she said, "I'll take you, but I'm not going in." The bills disappeared in the pocket of her shapeless pants. She pulled the communist cap further down on her head in triumph. Sam and Tom exchanged a look above her head – what had they gotten themselves into?

No choice now, they seemed to say. They began to follow the guide through various twists and turns across the underground labyrinth.

Though Sam and Tom's foreign faces were met with either benign indifference or curiosity when they had first arrived in the subterranean city, now each turn led to fewer people, and fewer friendly expressions. As the light lessened and the glances turned downright hostile, Sam could feel loud and clear that they weren't welcome anywhere near this place.

Finally their tour guide turned abruptly right at a particularly shady alleyway. They were immediately met with a huge towering hulking mass of human. Even Sam had to tilt his head upward to meet the man's eyes. He must have some Mongol descent, Sam thought wildly, to be so tall. With his craggy jaw and deep-set eyes, he could easily picture the man hawking wolves from the back of a rugged mountain pony smaller than he was, feeding bloody bits of kill to his bird.

The mountain man pushed both of them with one hand each, sending Tom tumbling onto the damp floor and Sam barely maintaining his balance by holding onto a fire extinguisher fixed onto the stone wall. The guide began shouting at the man in rapid-fire Chinese. It seemed to Sam like she was denying all involvement, reassuring him they were just a paycheck and what was she supposed to do about that?

The mountain man replied in similar aggressiveness and started menacingly toward the startled pair.

Tom dusted his hands as he pulled himself to his feet. "What's he saying?"

She made a derisive comment in Chinese, then laughed. "You need Google Translate for that? He doesn't want you two going into the Market. White faces aren't trustable."

Sam sighed. Did he have to do this again? He procured a small stack of redbacks and fanned them out as if he were tempting an angry dog.

The man's distrusting demeanor instantly changed. Part disbelief and part distrust showed on his face as he counted each bill individually, his lips forming the numbers as he counted. He got to the end, folded them in half, and shoved the bills in his back pocket. He glared at them.

Then all of a sudden, he swept himself to the side and they stepped forward into one of the greatest black markets on Earth.

Chapter Fifty-Four

Sam's eyes darted furtively across the new landscape.

It was a completely different world than any of them could have ever expected. Directly in front was a plaza that closely resembled the town circle at the entrance of the underground city. However, instead of restaurants and other services around it, people had set up individual booths, each advertising something different with Chinese banners draped across the top.

Sam ambled over to the closest one on his left. On it lay the greatest arsenal of firearms he had ever seen. The collection was casually laid out, and spanned from every type of weapon from Australian police issued Glocks through to military grade heavy weapons.

"I'm not going any farther. I leave now. Good luck on the rest of your trip." The tour guide half-heartedly shook Sam's hand and hurriedly exited.

Tom said, "Well, time to get looking." He began to peer at each of the sign names. Finally, Sam saw something that might help. An inconspicuous brown sign labeled "Human Information" presented a booth that was filled with nothing but papers and folders. Sam had no idea what the sign meant, but seemed the closest they could get.

"Hello, I was wondering if you could help me find anything about a man named Churn Ng?"

A shrewd and thin man with his head buried behind a newspaper barely stirred. "What city?" he asked, flipping a page with a rustle.

Tom tapped his booted foot. "This city."

"What you need him for? Forced labor? Trafficking? We kidnap him very quick for cheap."

"Uh… Just trying to find information."

The man put down the newspaper and pulled a large green binder toward himself without another word and began flipping through the laminated pages. Churn Ng?"

"Yes." Sam put his hands on the table and leaned toward the man expectantly. "What does it say about him?"

"No information." The man threw the binder down on the ground and resumed his newspaper reading. "Go away."

Sam held onto his temper hard. "I understand there must be a lot of Ng, but there has to be some way to…"

The man's eyes peeked over the newspaper. "You got cash?" He smiled. "Like you said. Lotta Ngs."

Sam dug into his wallet, handing the man a not so meager gift.

Twenty minutes later, Sam's mind overflowed with despair and disappointment. They had bribed their way through two people to one of the most illegal and dangerous places he had ever been to be greeted with this? They'd gotten information, but there was no telling how accurate it was.

What was the point of coming to China in the first place? They were no closer than when they'd left Australia. Thanks, he thought bitterly.

Tom patted Sam on the back and gave a slight nudge, seeing his black look. "Come on," he said, "Time to move onto the next spot."

They suffered through the gauntlet as goons stared down their foreign necks as they navigated the warren back to the surface. Sam tried to move faster, but the weight of the underground city and his disappointment slowed his steps. By the time they reached the doorway that led topside, he was cursing everything Chinese he'd ever dealt with in his life, from his horoscope to fortune cookies.

As Tom squeezed through the narrow doorway of the Market, avoiding a crush of kids coming in who didn't see fit to make space for a big Marine, Sam's eyes lit on the crazy collage of posters and graffiti that adorn all city walls, papered and taped and stapled over each other until it becomes a topography of a place.

The door wasn't wood, but iron, he noted. Heavily rusted. His tired eyes skimmed, skimmed, then caught. Went back. A single yellowed piece of paper caught his attention but it took him a moment to understand why.

Hung on the frame with duct tape, with bold Chinese characters scrawled on the top, straight in the middle was a picture of a familiar landscape.

Under which, in English, read, "The Tomb of the Golden Man."

The landscape came back to Sam's head, last seen clearly from the air as the pilot joked with them in the tiny cockpit of the plane. Shortly before he and Tom had descended into Claustral Canyon and embarked on their rescue mission. The landscape which, was probably the last thing on the surface of the Earth that Churn had seen before he died.

Sam stared. Suddenly it became clear. It wasn't just chasing mythical beasts. The Chinese knew about the legend, and judging by the single note, so too, did a series of Treasure Hunters.

Someone had posted a US ten-million-dollar reward to locate the ancient colony of *Nyia Chía* or links to the Tomb of El Dorado.

Sam sighed… which meant the Treasure Hunters would be coming out in droves to seek their fortunes.

Chapter Fifty-Five

Sam ripped the paper off the doorway and folded it quickly into a small paper, slipping it inside his pocket. He had no idea what it was doing there. But they didn't have time to think about that now: first priorities first. They had to leave. If they stayed much longer, Sam had the distinct impression they might not be getting out again. He thought of that weapons station, the casual "Human Information" booth response: "We kidnap him quick for cheap."

He turned to Tom, only to find the other man frowning, folding his arms, and scanning the unsavory characters. It had been unsavory with the presence of the tour guide. Without her...

Tom quirked his brow at Sam. "You thinking what I'm thinking?"

"We've overstayed our welcome."

"Please tell me that memory of yours still works underground, in Chinese."

Sam grinned. "It's your lucky day." He scanned the scene, fixing the steps in his mind.

Left... straight here... right... another right...

Sam focused intensely as he tried to recall every single step. He was too engrossed in this task to see a small but steadily growing crowd of people following them out. They looked at the two white men inquisitively, but not with malicious intent It was too soon to tell if it was malicious or not. A few times children would try to run up to Sam and Tom and touch them, but the Chinese parents would quickly grab them and harshly reprimand them for trying to touch an *outsider*.

Tom looked out for Sam, anxiously looking for the large man that had stood in their way. But he was nowhere to be seen. Soon enough they were at the red door. Without looking back, they pushed it open and climbed back into the sunlight. Beside him, Tom gulped in the filthy air. Sam waited until he'd flagged down a taxi and they'd both climbed inside before he allowed himself to take his own deep breath.

Tom gestured at Sam's right pocket. "Let me see that paper." Sam reached in, grabbed the grimy poster, and handed it to him. Tom inspected it, frowning. "That's what I thought. There wasn't enough time to make sure in there, but…"

Sam leaned over. "What's up?"

"Take a look at this." Tom pointed at the bottom left corner. "It says 10 million with a dollar sign next to it."

"But this is China. Maybe they made a misprint," said Sam.

"Ten million yuan isn't that much, all considered. And I'm certain anyone selling wares in that market down there damn well knows the difference between yuan and dollars." He leaned back into the seat, glancing at the driver. You never knew if they spoke English or not. "This wasn't a Chinese assignment. I don't think so, anyway. Someone from another country who posted it at the Market knew his way around the place. Experienced enough to know all about these shady places." Sam nodded. "You still have Churn's journal and passport, right?"

Though he knew it would be there – Sam never lost anything – his hand instinctively went to his back pocket to check. The familiar imprints in the denim of his jeans confirmed it. Sam relaxed. "Still…"

At the same time, his other pocket began to shake violently, startling him. Sam dug in his pocket and pulled it out. The screen flashed with urgency.

The caller ID showed: Elise.

She said, "Having fun in Beijing?"

"A blast." Elise rarely did the chit-chat thing and never called without a purpose. He skipped any further preamble and smiled ruefully. "What have you found, Elise?"

"That remains to be seen. Who's your favorite person on the ship?"

"What've you got?"

"So you know how you told me to look for gold pearl dealers, right?"

"Yes..."

"Well. It took a bunch of digging and more hits on ugly jewelry than I ever want to see in my life, but I think I found some information for you. Or at least it's the best I could rustle up."

Elise's best was usually very good. Sam held the phone closer. "Tell me more."

"Let me find the file I made." He could hear the rustling of papers in the background. "Ah, here. Okay. There's a man in Europe who's been selling these exotic trinkets up until just a few years ago, when the shop transferred ownership. There's pretty much no trace of him online except for a German jewelry forum that mentions his unusual sales." Her voice held the ring of triumph. "You ready for the punchline?"

"I was born ready."

"So this goldsmith started selling golden pearls, describing them as man-made pearls of pure gold. He kept the numbers down and the prices high."

"Do you have his address."

"Yeah, it's in some city called Venedig." He could hear her pride in her voice. "I just got the hit now. You spent some time in the motherland, right? Have you ever..."

Sam shook his head, unable to fight his grin. For as smart as she was, Elise had some unusual blind spots. But then, Sam reflected, he'd found that most geniuses usually did.

"I hate to break it to you, Elise, but that's not German."

He had the rare pleasure of hearing her surprise, uncertainty. "What? But the forum was in German – I had to –
"

"Well, it is German, technically. But it's not in Germany. Venedig is the German name for another city. A foreign city." He glanced at Tom and slapped his thigh. Of course! The crossroads between the East and the West… the most important trading hub on the silk road…. It all made sense. "Venice, Italy."

Sam was grinning.

Tom asked, "I take you found a new lead?"

Sam nodded. "It looks like it. We'll see where it takes us."

"Where are we going now?"

Sam grinned. "Right now, it appears we're heading to Venice."

Chapter Fifty-Six

Venice, Italy

Through the tiny plane window, the sky spread above the canal like an old silk scarf, ragged around the edges and regal.

The city below was much the same.

Venice had stood at the crossroads between the Eastern and Western empires for centuries, a vital stop on the trade routes between the Orient and Europe. For hundreds of years she had witnessed scandals, murders, war, plague, death, and unbelievable wealth without flinching. Throughout which, she had earned her name – La Serenissima.

The Most Serene Republic.

Sam was not feeling particularly serene as the industrial belch of black smoke and gray fields of Mestre obliterated his plane window. The tiny plane banked with a shudder, however, and the utilitarian view was replaced by picturesque churches and canals. This was the contradiction of Venice – one side, dirty, filthy, functional with Mestre, the industrial suburb on the mainland of Venice, and the gateway into the island paradise, and on the other, floating on the waves like a vision, was the dream of eternal beauty. Sun sparkled on serpentine rivers, reflecting the perfect sky.

"Sir, please stow your tray table; we're preparing for landing."

The stewardess gave an odd look at the Chinese script in Sam's book. Apparently he didn't seem the type to be fluent in Chinese.

Sam smiled at her. "Of course, ma'am."

He stowed the book in his backpack and wiped his face as they began their turbulent descent.

From the airport they took a train to Venice. It was a short trip, lasting no more than ten minutes. They emerged from the Santa Marco train station, pressed in close by the crowd of tourists pouring through the station. The clamor of Italian and a dozen of other languages assaulted his ears; the scent of sweat and sewage assaulted his nose, and the warm Italian sun rose up like the plague to choke him as they got pushed toward the exit, hemmed in on all sides. Sam kept one hand on his wallet and the other gripping his bag tightly, in which was the book they could not afford to lose.

The doors opened, and stepped out into a spectacular view.

It staggered Sam every time he came here that the train station opened up directly onto the lagoon. He stepped quickly out of the way of some irate local, then cast around for Tom, only to find him fighting his way through the throng.

Tom reached his side with an expression of distaste, then took in the view. He gave Sam a crooked smile that took in everything. "Ah, Venice."

Their map said they were less than a mile from their hotel. Even so, it took them almost 45 minutes to find the Hotel Olimpia, in the Santa Croce district. The receptionist greeted them by name and presented them with a heavy brass key on an opulently tussled fob and pointed them up the stairs and to the end of the hall. Porters in white gloves carried their bags, despite Sam's insistence they could do it themselves.

The room was luxurious and equally brocaded, with gilded mirrors and a marble bathroom. From the open window, singing wafted up from the canal. Tom grinned. "Of course I find myself in the most romantic city in the world with you."

Sam threw a pillow at his chest.

They took a coffee at one of the street side cafes, shaded from the worst of the midday sun by a green awning emblazoned with a LAVAZZA logo. Sam stood at the counter, wedged in between a dapper gentleman arguing with a Rolex-sporting young man, and Tom, gulping at a bitter shot of espresso sweetened with two packets of sugar. Nearby, tourists paid double to bake in the sun, seated in wicker chairs and on the sidewalk so they could claim to be part of the elite. Tom looked ridiculous clutching his tiny cup of espresso, but Sam wasn't one to judge. After their adventures in China and half a world of travel, he was on his second cup as well.

Tom slid his cup and saucer across the counter where it was whisked away with a non-descript "Prego", twisted out of the way of a woman in a leopard stole ordering an aperol spritz and consulted the map.

"According to this, the shop we're looking for is just over the Rialto, in the Calle De L'Aquila Nera." He squinted. "But that might be the name of the canal. I can't tell." He scanned the street, already crowded. Sam felt the coffee take hold with a vengeance. He pushed away from the bar.

"Well? Should we go find out?"

Out of breath, sweating (and swearing) profusely, his pant cuffs wet from having been shoved off the narrow sidewalk at a sudden dead end, and over an hour later, Sam finally spotted the tiny sign- hidden up high on a building corner, behind several others saying contradicting things.

He nudged Tom in the side and Tom looked up from his phone, which, they'd discovered, was absolutely worthless as a GPS navigator, no matter how many times they tried. "There is a God."

Tom grinned. "Hallelujah."

They ducked into the street with relief. They had spent the past hour climbing over Venice's canals, edging down streets so narrow the passersby coming the opposite way had to wait for them to cross lest they be knocked off into the water below, and generally running in circles. When they'd finally found their way to the Rialto Bridge – guided by helpful arrows on the ground and on the edges of the buildings... sometimes – Sam had shouted in triumph.

Fifteen minutes later, as they struggled through the city's maze-like streets, he gritted his teeth in frustration and tried for serenity. It seemed that just where you wanted to go in Venice was the one place you were unable to get. No wonder the city had withstood so many invasions.

At last they found the shop tucked into the end of a narrow road. Sam got the impression of clean glass and dusty stone, ornate writing with that unique Italian flair that somehow mimicked the uneven cobblestones.

The bell chimed as they entered into the smell of history and polish.

And hopefully somewhere they might find answers.

Chapter Fifty-Seven

The shop was empty of tourists.

Sam and Tom wandered the pristine counters, decked out with exquisite work. It looked promising. Off the tourist path, this man didn't sell cheap stuff to foreigners. If there was a place the golden pearls had rested, it was possible it was here.

A door opened behind the counter. A clean-cut man, well-dressed even for an Italian, with elegant fingers, emerged, wiping his hands on a rag. He regarded them with a sharp intelligence behind his eyes. "Buona sera, signori. Come aiutare?"

Sam nodded at him. His Italian was limited, but he understood a little. "I'm Sam Reilly," he said. "I called inquiring about the…"

The man's razor gaze sharpened further. "Ah, yes. I remember," he said, replying in good English. He put his hand to his chest. "Jacopo Santini. Piacere."

Jacopo glanced outside at the slanting afternoon light. Then he walked around the counter without further comment and turned the open sign to closed. He locked the door from the inside.

Tom raised his brows. "What are you doing?"

Jacopo smiled, more with his eyes than his mouth. Still without a word, he poured three shots of grappa from an ornate Venetian glass bottle into matching exquisite glasses and handed one to Sam and one to Tom. "I will close for the afternoon and five minutes makes no difference." He wafted his own drink under his nose. "And this is a conversation that should not be interrupted, I think, yes?"

Sam and Tom sat in small, uncomfortable brocade chairs in a curtained alcove it seemed Jacopo used for design consultations. Sam shifted on the tiny seat, hoping it wouldn't break as Jacopo opened a locked cabinet with a tiny key. The key disappeared into some hidden pocket and he brought out an old wooden box, engraved with a single circle of gold.

He set it on the table and lifted the lid.

Sam and Tom leaned in instinctively, drawing their breath.

Two gold pearls nestled inside. It was something of a shock to see them without expecting them, and Sam appreciated Emily the archivist's reaction a little more, even accustomed as he was to their beauty.

Jacopo leaned back and crossed one immaculate leg over the other.

"These are the only remaining two, signori, and the story of their acquisition… *Va Bene*," he said using the Italian expression that mean, *goes well*. He shrugged off a tale of undoubted extremity with an Italian's typical acceptance of opera. "The previous owner of this shop was an immigrant – from China. He was an outsider. Venice does not take kindly to outsiders."

The man spoke from experience, it sounded. "In what way?" Sam asked. They were outsiders here, themselves. "You're not Venetian?"

Jacopo shook his head. "I come from Tuscany, Florence. I have worked this shop for over twenty years, and I am only now beginning to see an increase in business. I cannot imagine how it must have been for him."

"Where did the pearls come from?" Tom rolled the gems between his fingers.

"He never told me. All I know is that he imported them from his father, who had old connections along the silk road."

"What kind of connections?"

"Secret ones, apparently. The man left no record of his contacts, or his chain of supply. He told me simply that his father vowed to take the truth about his unique trade with him to the grave." Jacopo spread his hands. "And he did so. He died twenty-five years ago. I had just arrived in Venice."

Sam processed this. Dead end. He glanced at Tom. "That's a shame." He flicked some dust off of his pants. "Do you know where he was buried?"

Jacopo smiled, as if Sam's intent were transparent. "I do. He was buried in the catacombs beneath San Michele island."

"I didn't know there were catacombs on San Michele."

"Not many people do."

Tom leaned back, draining the last of his grappa. "This goldsmith. He was extremely successful, right?"

"Si."

"And he was rich?"

A sardonic eyebrow. "Yes."

"What are the chances that an extremely rich and successful gold merchant would have been buried with all the other mere mortals in the catacombs?"

"A foreigner? A Chinese?" Jacopo's brows rose. "He was lucky to be buried at all."

"Damn."

"Fortunately, his son loved him very much, and he had powerful connections to the Doges." Jacopo's lips stretched. "His son constructed him a grand tomb in the north section, beside the clerical leaders of the day."

Sam grinned. "That's great! We'll go have a look. See if that can give us any clues."

Jacopo shook his head. "I'm afraid that's not possible."

Sam got the sense that the man was deliberately enjoying the difficulty of their plight.

He reminded himself that the Italians had invented opera. "What? Why not?"

Jacopo rolled one of the gold pearls between his elegant fingers meditatively, as if he could see the future shining on its surface. "Because that entire area of San Michele – including the catacombs – was completely flooded in 1993." He looked at them with his sharp eyes. "Perhaps you have heard, signori? Venice has been sinking ever since."

Chapter Fifty-Eight

Island of the Dead – Venice

Sam raced the teak speed boat toward the north of the lagoon.

The bow galloped over the waves under the bright sky, headed toward the distant island. Sam trailed his hand in the spray, enjoying the burst of coolness as the spray of their transit splashed his face.

On the horizon, the lump of land grew larger.

The *Isola di San Michele* is Venice's island of the dead. It lies in the lagoon between the *Fondamente Nuove* and the glassmaking island of Murano, as if the furnaces give birth to the dead. Both are equally famous. Indeed, the view of the cemetery from the *Fondamente Nuove* is one of the most celebrated of Venetian waterscapes and had inspired artists from Tintoretto to Turner.

As the little boat bounced over the choppy lagoon, a surprisingly vast amount of water after the tight claustrophobia of the Venetian canals, the severe barracks-like red walls of the Isola di San Michele shone in stark contrast with the simple, elegant off-white stone of the Renaissance façade of the Church of San Michele and the adjacent *Cappella Emiliana*. Sam could see why the view had been so inspiring to artists. Approaching the island was like traveling toward something that had materialized out of the lagoon as if by magic.

And yet, San Michele's curiously rectangular shape suggested that the island was not a natural creation. According to their guidebook, there had been an island here since well before Napoleon's conquest of the lagoons. But the distance from the city made it ideal for dumping off the dead, especially during Venice's many brushes with the plague. As the dead piled up, San Michele achieved its current form in the 19th century, when the need for more space led to some land reclamation.

They docked the boat at the pier right in front of the church, tying its mooring lines tight. The building's simplicity was startling after the grandeur of Santa Marco and some of Venice's more opulently well-known monuments. Sam found it soothing, and yet somehow ominous. Saint Michael, Sam knew from his studies, was the angel of death. He remembered one of his priest's descriptions in the hopes to make the liturgy relevant to teenage boys – Saint Michael used his scales to pass judgment on who could and could not pass through the Pearly Gates. Like the bouncer of an exclusive Elysian discotheque.

Sam couldn't help but grin at the image as they stood in front of the serene facade. He hoped it contained more surprises than a disco.

They entered the huge doors and found the place almost deserted, the scent of incense heavy in the air. The church had a nave and two aisles, which were almost deserted, their colored marble decorations gleaming in the candlelight.

Sam noticed a priest lighting candles on the other side and approached with Tom, who crossed himself near the font. "Father." Sam smiled. "Buon giorno."

The priest noticed the men, his furtive eyes trying to determine where they had come from. "Good morning, my son. How may I be of service?"

Tom gestured. "We're looking for a friend of a relative who was buried here at the beginning of last century. How do we get to the northwestern section of the catacombs?"

The priest put on a contrite expression. "I'm very sorry, my son. But those grounds are inaccessible."

Sam's eyes narrowed. "Inaccessible?"

The priest spread his hands. "Alas, no. Nothing so temporary. This area suffered an earthquake in the 1993s – Venice is ever under siege from some kind or another. The levee which kept the lagoon out for over a century finally collapsed. The whole island flooded. The commune did the best they could to clear the water, and over time things improved, but there was no way to reverse the damage to certain parts and…" He gave a Catholic, Italian shrug. "It was god's will, it seems. The souls in the catacombs commune are with the lagoon, now."

Sam stepped forward. "Our friend mentioned he'd been to see his ancestor recently. If the area is flooded, how is that possible?"

The priest waved his hand back and forth, wishing to get rid of them. "It is possible, my son, if their ancestor was buried in the southeast section. If that is the case, then the crypt may still be accessible, after a fashion. The southeast end was constructed on higher ground, and some of it was spared the worst of the flood. Yes, that must be what he meant. You must have misunderstood. If it is in the southeastern section, I will show you."

Sam shook his head. "Unfortunately, we need to get to the northeastern section. He specifically mentioned the northeast."

The priest fought from rolling his eyes. "Then I'm sorry, but you are out of luck, my children." It was lunch time, and he was hungry, and he asked God's forgiveness for getting rid of them in such a flippant way. "That is, unless you can defy God's plan and breathe underwater."

Sam grinned, taking the old man totally by surprise. "As a matter of fact, Father, it just so happens we can."

Chapter Fifty-Nine

They descended a series of stairs at the back of the crypt and entered the catacombs. They didn't get far before reaching the flooded section.

The dark water threw disturbing light patterns up onto their faces as it swirled below. Sam fought the feeling he was in a cheap horror film and double checked his equipment. It was always the easy missions that got you into trouble.

Sam glanced at him. "Are you thinking what I'm thinking?"

"That you should have stayed in that hotel room in Ubuntu with Catarina and not dragged her out in the rain?"

Sam grinned. "But then we'd miss out on all the fun." He triple-checked and saw that despite his complaints, Tom was doing the same. "Remember what he said?"

"Northeastern side. Check. Flooded crypt of rich Chinese gold merchant – somewhere near the middle. Check. If we can even find the middle."

Sam held up his waterproof tablet. "That's why we have this baby. The priest gave me a map, since we're headed under, I photographed it."

Tom gave a theatrical admiring sigh. "Ah, I knew you were useful. Speed boat and equipment rental for twelve hours: eight hundred euro. Coffee and pastry: twelve euro. Facing certain death with your best friend in pursuit of treasure that will alter the course of history as we know it... priceless."

Sam grinned and pulled down his mask. He gave Tom the good to go symbol and they dropped face first into the dark water.

He switched on his flashlight. The beam shot through the dark water, carving its way through his poor visibility. Less than ten feet at most. The tunnels were tight and murky with decades of silt and garbage collected in every nook and cranny.

Far ahead, there was a darker gap, and a lighter one. Sam turned back to Tom and pointed. Tom shooed him on.

Sam went on.

The flooded catacombs twisted and turned as if to throw off any invasion. Nothing was simple in Venice, it seemed, not even for the dead.

Then they hit something unexpected.

Dry land.

Or close to it, anyway. It seemed they'd either gotten turned around in the tunnels, or… Sam checked his map. No, they were on track. They were in the northeastern section, as required. The priest hadn't said anything about only the passageway to the catacombs being flooded. Sam had assumed they'd be doing the entire mission underwater.

Beside him Tom was apparently thinking the same thing. "Why, the bastard. Thought he'd throw us off by making it harder than it is."

Sam laughed. "I don't think you're supposed to say that about a priest, are you?"

Tom crossed himself and looked around uneasily. "Sorry," he said to the shadows.

Sam understood – here it was particularly spooky. He pulled off the heaviest of his scuba gear and considered what to do. "What do you think? Leave it here?"

Tom shrugged. "It's not like anyone else is going to be coming by to steal it. We'll pick it up on the way back."

They tucked the gear behind a crypt, slogged up the mucky slope into the stone ground, and kept walking.

The walls of the catacombs closed in tight and musty as a tomb, the dank water splashing over their boots as Sam and Tom slogged across the broken floor. The rough walls scraped their shoulders, making a whistling sound on their wetsuits that made it feel they were being chased by ghosts.

Sam consulted the map. Nothing looked familiar, and he had no idea how they were going to find what they'd come to find. True, they'd both poured over the sketch in Churn's journal, but Sam knew of all things how much hoping to find something could distort reality. He tripped over a lintel and went sprawling.

Tom helped him up, panting. "Santini said it was somewhere toward the end. Well… we have to be getting toward the end."

Sam dusted himself off. "Well, I can't really say he's too reliable so far. In fact, nothing seems to have been…"

"Uh… Sam?"

Sam broke off.

Tom was pointing. "What about that?"

Confronted with the tomb, Sam concluded that Churn's grandfather was no artist. But there was a certain similarity in the curve of the lid and… he double checked. Yes. Yes! "Two lions on the face." He squinted. "Hopefully he was a better trader than he was an artist."

"We can't all be good at everything."

Sam's excitement fluttered in his breath and it wasn't just from the exertion. The thrill was always the same: treasure hunting was one of the most primal instincts known to man. Sam was sure of it. The seeking of something greater than ourselves, whether for our own glory or for its, was wired into our DNA. To seek was one of the seven primal emotions that were concentrated in the ancient subcortical regions of all mammalian brains – the other six, being rage, fear, lust, care, grief, and play.

He grinned at Tom. "Come on. Let's see what's inside."

As they neared, Sam's heart sank, however. The cover, ornately carved with lions and fish and all manner of symbols, must have weighed a ton. Though the lip clearly hung over the base of the tomb, there was no way he and Tom would be able to lift it themselves. He shook his head, feeling like an idiot. "I should have known it couldn't be this simple." He cast around his tool kit for the crowbar that he'd brought for that particular purpose. "Come on, Tom, let's see if we can move it an inch. If we go slow, we might be able to…"

But Tom wasn't paying attention. He was bobbing and weaving around the box. For a moment Sam thought he was appreciating the artistry, but Tom wasn't really an art appreciating kind of guy. He wasn't that subtle. Genevieve constantly teased him about it.

Sam shook his head. "Tom… what are you doing?"

But Tom grinned, lost in his search. Finally, he stepped back with a sigh. "Ah ha. Gotcha. Genius."

Sam's eyes narrowed. "Is it?"

Tom pushed on the lion's nose. Nothing happened.

Sam rolled his eyes. "Tom, come on. It's not going to be that simple…"

Tom grunted and pressed again. He ran his fingers around the edge of the nose and down into the jaw. Despite himself, Sam settled into wait. Tom had some of the most sensitive fingers of any man he knew. In fact, his lock picking skills had gotten them out of more scrapes than he cared to admit. You'd never know it to look at his big form, but Tom possessed some delicacy after all.

"Knife," Tom said, without taking his eyes off the nose.

Sam passed it over without a word.

After five minutes of scraping off centuries of mineral deposits algae and mud, Tom pressed again. A huge grating noise, and the nose pressed back into the tomb!

Sam's jaw dropped.

And so did the lion's.

A series of mechanical movements later, and Tom was beaming. "Come on," he panted, gesturing to the massive lid as it slid back against their efforts. It was difficult, but not impossible, to pivot it on the midpoint and rest it vertically alongside the tomb. Sam stared.

"How the hell did you know that?"

Tom grinned. "My grandpa served in Korea. Brought back a whole collection of puzzle boxes from Japan. Used to hide my allowance in them. If I wanted it, I had to figure out how to open them." He shrugged, modestly. "I learned a few things."

"Nice one. Let's see if we've done our chores."

They peered inside together.

There was a blackened corpse clutching a leather-bound book.

Sam had a closer look, opening the corpse's skeletal hands to extract it

Tom whooped in triumphed and picked it up. "Another book!"

He held it aloft, and Sam only barely succeeded in stealing it from him before he dropped it in his excitement.

"Careful!" he scolded, lifting the tome carefully into the light. "Do you think this one's locked, too?"

Tom shrugged. "Try it."

Sam gently slid the latch that sealed the leather-bound book. The latch looked like overly bright brass, but on closer inspected was much too heavy. He shined his flashlight at the metal, and it glistened back at him – it was made of gold.

He opened the book.

Its pages parted easily, as if the occupant had recognized that anyone clever enough to get through the tomb deserved to find what was hidden inside.

But whatever was hidden inside was written in Mandarin.

Sam flipped through carefully. Beautiful elegant script, and totally illegible to him. There were too many arbitrary strokes for him to decipher.

Somewhere nearby, something sloshed in the water, and the part of Sam's brain not taken up with disappointment was aware once more how vulnerable their position was – not to discovery, but to further flooding. San Michele was an island, and the lagoon, for all that it was protected, was still subject to tides. He'd forgotten to check those before they had dived.

Sam flipped some more, refusing to give up.

"Damn." Tom ran his hand through his hair. "I really thought that..."

Sam yelled with delight.

Tom stubbed his head in shock as the shout echoed in the narrow space. Dimly, Sam wondered if they could hear the shout above ground, but he didn't care. All thought of tides were forgotten, buried in a moment of triumph. For there in the book, in the pages of lines, were lines he recognized: awkward, like the writing of a child: El Tumba El Hombre Dorado – *The Tomb of the Golden Man.*

Sam beamed. "This is it!"

Chapter Sixty

They smiled at each other like idiots.

Tom shook his head. "I have to hand it to Churn. I never thought that old book would pan out."

Sam packed the book carefully in a sealed watertight bag and tucked it in his backpack.

"The world is full of surprises. Come on. Let's get out of here before the tide shifts and we have to swim the whole way."

"I couldn't have said it better myself."

Sam and Tom spun. Sam dimly realized that the sound he'd thought was the tide was not the tide at all.

Five men stood crammed in the narrow tunnel, completely blocking the exit. They all wore wetsuits and appeared Italian. The one at the front caught Sam's attention. He was larger than the rest of his men, and appeared to be in charge, but that wasn't what drew Sam's attention. It was the handgun the man held, trained on them without wavering.

The man smiled. He spoke with an accent that echoed in the dripping tunnel. For a strange second it seemed to Sam that the tomb itself was speaking. "Buongiorno, signori. A strange tourist stop, no? Mr. Sam Reilly!"

Sam shrugged. "We do have a talent for getting lost."

The man gestured with his chin. "And for finding." His voice hardened. "Give me the book."

The catacombs were divided into a series of north south and east west running stone passageways. Right now, they were at a crossroads. Their attackers, along with their SCUBA equipment were to the south of them. If they ran north, they would most likely end up shot in their backs. But east or west, they might have a chance.

Sam exchanged a glance with Tom.

The two of them had worked together long enough to just about read each other's minds.

Their attackers were talking, animatedly about the discovery of the book.

For a second Sam thought they were talking about the Chinese manuscript they'd just unearthed. And then Sam realized Tom was holding Churn's old journal.

He felt a surge of hope.

He lunged and grabbed the book out of Tom's surprised hand. "No way. You can have this book over my dead body."

The man grinned. "Suit yourself."

The head honcho leveled the gun at him.

Sam said, "This journal has been with the Caretaker of the colony of Nyai Chia since 1421, when the colony boarded one of Zheng He's Treasure Ships in search of new farming mountains."

The man with the gun said, "So what?"

Sam shrugged. "So, it's very delicate. If you shoot me and I drop it, the pages might literally implode, making them unable to ever reveal the secret location of the Tomb of El Dorado."

Their attacker lowered his handgun. His face filled with distrust, and a slight hint of fear. Somehow the thought of losing a treasure that had been quested over for centuries, after getting so close, seemed too much to stomach. "Okay, gently hand over the book."

Sam grinned. "Okay, here you go!"

He immediately flung the damp book into his attacker's face.

As Sam expected, his attacker reached for the book – Churn's journal, not the ancient Chinese manuscript – instead of firing his weapon.

In that instant, Sam and Tom switched their flashlights off and ran due east.

Their reprieve only lasted seconds.

Behind them, Sam heard the shouts of his attacker ordering the men to split up and find them. Tom and Sam moved quickly, fear driving them onward, covering nearly a hundred feet in a matter of seconds, before turning away from the main passage into a small alcove designed to support a large marble tomb.

They hid behind it.

In the distance, someone began taunting them. "Come out, come out, wherever you are…"

Sam waited in silence, cursing himself for not grabbing the crowbar when he had the chance, and keeping it for a weapon.

Another one said, "All we want is the book. You know, the Chinese manuscript… the one that leads to the Tomb of El Dorado."

More silence.

The man searched the alcove thirty feet away from them. "Right now, Mr. Reilly, you're probably asking yourself why come out when all we're going to do is kill you once we get the book, am I right?" Failing to gain a response, the man continued. "You see, you're right, we will kill you as soon as we have that book. But the question is about choices. Do you want to die begging to live?"

Sam waited in silence.

The stranger continued. "Or, keep the location of the book secret, and, by the time we're finished with you, you will be asking us to let you die. The choice is yours."

Sam dipped down, behind the tomb, with his back up against the marble. Previous water damage to the high mounted alcove, had caused it to develop a permanent lean downward toward the main passage of the catacomb.

In the dim light, he exchanged a glance with Tom, who gave a curt nod with a grin, in acknowledgement. They both knew what had to happen.

Their attackers continued searching, stopping at each alcove, their flashlight beams flicking off the walls as they continued to hunt.

Sam could hear their breathing.

They were getting closer.

Sam spotted the two men enter the alcove directly opposite the one they were hiding in. The adjacent alcoves were separated by nearly six feet of height, most likely representing their owner's wealth. Kind of like on a residential street where the high side has the views and the low side didn't.

"Now, Tom! Now!" Sam said, his voice kept low.

They both heaved their backs against the marble tomb and pushed.

If the ground had been level, it would have been impossible for them to shift the massive tomb. But it wasn't level. The ground was uneven, and the tomb already teetering on a delicate balance. One that Sam and Tom just shifted, sending nearly two-tons of stone tomb on its downward journey. Spurred on by gravity.

It began to race toward the alcove below.

The two men screamed, but there was nowhere to go.

The tomb crashed into them, wedging both men between the marble and the stone wall of alcove and a permanent fixture of the catacombs.

Chapter Sixty-One

Sam shouted, "Quick! Let's go!"

They bolted down the tunnel, heading farther east until they reached another flooded section.

He knew their splashing would give away their location, but there was nothing to do but go forward. Unless...

He had no idea how familiar these people were with the tunnels. He also had no idea who these people were. But if he could make them think they'd gone on, when in reality they'd gone nowhere...

He grabbed up a handful of small stones and threw them down the tunnel. With a little luck their attackers would hear them and think they'd gone on ahead. He gestured frantically to Tom and as quietly as they could they ducked behind a massive tomb, half-buried in broken marble. Trying not to pant, he waited, reached out and grabbed the nearest piece of broken marble, barely even looking at it.

Footsteps passed, shouts.

Tom raised his brows, but Sam shook his head. He knew the ruse wouldn't work for long but it might buy them enough time to take stock of the situation.

Sam gripped his weapon and waited.

Chapter Sixty-Two

Sam tried not to breathe in the damp cold air.

He gripped the marble, forcing his fingers not to go numb. Numb fingers didn't fight well, he knew that from experience. Sam cast around for more help, and came face to face with a grinning skull. He jerked back in surprise. In shock, he looked down at his weapon and realized that what he was holding was not marble, as he'd thought – but a decaying human femur.

Beside him, Tom swung round to see the problem and his face went blank. Sam shook his head. The whole situation was so outrageous, all he could do was grin back.

"Thanks, Buddy," he whispered to the skull. "A little help would be great."

Footsteps in the tunnel, a passing shadow barely distinguishable in the dim light. Sam gestured. Tom nodded, and snuck out of hiding, moving as quickly as he dared. When he was sure to get the man's attention, he did the most outrageous pratfall Sam had ever seen.

But it was effective – their attacker pun around. He raised his gun, charging after Tom as Tom struggled in the rising water to get to his feet. Their attacker grinned, aimed...

And Sam smashed him across the back with the skeleton.

The man gave a shout, a grunt, and went sprawling. The handgun went flying. Tom, no sign of slipping now, grabbed it. A Tanfoglio T95 – Italian 10mm automatic. Beautiful gun. Sam barely even saw his finger move, just registered the sound of the shot without even hearing it, felt it in his gut, a known fact as he'd felt it so many times before, and the man's face returned to the water and the water ran red.

The Tanfoglio made a very small hole. Now the entrance wound, too, started to bleed. The red an opulent burgundy in the dark.

Sam flexed his fingers. "Nice. It wasn't the leader. He's still…" Footsteps raced up the tunnel. "Out there."

They squared their shoulders, Tom with his gun, Sam with his femur. He felt ridiculous with the weapon, but it was lighter than the crowbar, and easier to wield in the tight space.

The men, including the leader, swung around into view. When he saw Sam's weapon, he started to laugh. He said something in rapid fire Italian, and without warning, opened fire. Tom fired back and they ducked for cover. They exchanged a few volleys, dangerous in the narrow tunnels. The man's eyes narrowed with renewed and wary respect. He barked something again, brandished the journal, grinned at Sam, and disappeared down the tunnel.

Sam and Tom looked at each other. "If they go for the gear, we're done for."

"Way ahead of you. You still have that…"

Sam brandished the map, his tablet glowing in the dark tunnel. "Right here. Come on!" They thundered back down the corridor, stealth be damned. Now there was no question: the tide was rising, and Sam had no desire to be trapped in flooding tight spaces. Again.

Tom skidded to a stop outside a tomb, but Sam raced by. "Not that one!"

Tom shook his head, fury on his face. "I recognize the carvings – this is where we left the gear." He spread his hands. "And this is what we get!"

A half-burned cigarette taunted them from the ground. The gear was gone. Sam swore. Then he swore some more and kicked at the unyielding stone.

"Bastards." He spun on Tom. "Why didn't you stop them?"

Tom threw up his hands, a half-grin plastered across his face. "With what?"

The fight was forestalled by a massive explosion that felt like it was no more than two feet away. Sam and Tom ducked reflexively, showered by water and slimy stone.

When the smoke cleared, they were confronted with a terrible sight: the tunnel back to the church and to the surface was totally blocked. Life, he knew, was made in split second decisions. Civilians often have the luxury of forgetting such a simple truth. Sam glanced around, then zeroed in – the water up ahead was a steady stream, and growing.

Flowing fast.

He grabbed Tom's sleeve and beckoned. "There! Let's go!"

Tom shook his sleeve free. "You want to get us drowned?"

Sam shoved him, gesturing again. He hurled his finger at the flowing water. "That water isn't stagnant, it's flowing. That means that that water reaches the outside of the catacombs. You want to stay here and keep our skeleton friends' company, by all means. But I'm getting out."

Tom shook himself into action, then settled himself. "Okay."

They sloshed forward, through broken marble and the rising water. The tomb occupants floated, now, their light bones buoyed up by the sea. The dead watched their progress as Sam hit the dead end. He shook his head, gasping. "No good. There's…" He consulted his tablet and his map. The glow lit the space with an eerie blue light, but his position was clear. "We'll have to back track…"

Voices echoed in the tunnel behind them.

"Someone's coming!" Tom warned.

Sam switched off the tablet, and the eerie glow disappeared. He took shallow, quiet breaths, wondering whether or not he'd been seen.

A second later, a shot fired.

Sam flinched away as the shot hit the wall where his shoulder had been seconds before. He threw out his arm to halt Tom as the ancient stone, weathered from centuries of damp and rot, crumbled with a muted roar, unable to withstand the modern impact.

They stood panting in the dust, deafened by the collapse.

A shot whizzed by again and Sam clutched instinctively at his stomach where the artifact pressed tight into his bone.

Tom spun, fear in his eyes. "You okay?"

Sam shook his head. "Not hit – come on!"

The catacombs passed in a blur.

At every turn, it seemed they hit dead ends. Hollow openings in the bony skulls of previous occupants watched them from the walls, slimy with mold and algae from their damp grave. The low light of Sam's flashlight gleamed on the algae, making them seem alive. Sam didn't spook easily, but if he let himself think of where they were, the weight of the stone above them made it hard to breathe. He shackled his focus to the present and let all other distractions go.

They came to a fork in the path and stalled, panting. Sam frantically checked his tablet. The screen flickered, but the image shone. It was enough. Left, right, straight, then left again – Sam fixed the route in his mind and pocketed the slim tablet. In the uncertain terrain, it was possible they could lose the pursuit. He pushed the thought that their attackers knew more about these catacombs than he did out of his mind.

"Come on," he said to Tom, ducking into a narrow path and dropping into water up to his thighs. "Almost there."

"Whatever you say." Tom fired a wild shot behind them, more as a scare tactic than any real threat, and the red light glowed hellishly on the damp stone. Shouts of pain echoed in the narrow walls, indecipherable anger.

The water was up to Sam's waist now and it was like wading through half-set concrete. Sam felt the panic of the dead and the depth underground closing in around him. His lungs burned and he longed for fresh air. He thought of their recent experiences in Claustral Canyon. No one knew they were under here except that priest."

"We have to be getting close," Tom gasped behind him. "You still got it?"

Sam checked the book again, tight against his belt. Safe. "Got it." Step one accomplished, but they weren't out yet. A shot sent a fountain of water blasting up by their knees. Sam pushed on harder, praying that their pursuers were having as hard a time as they were seeing in the dark.

Behind him, Tom gave a grunt of pain and Sam spun. "You hit?"

Tom shook his head, wincing. "Stubbed my toe." Sam had no way of knowing if he was telling the truth. In this dim light, water and blood looked the same. He pulled Tom in front of him by the slick, skin-tight arm of his dive suit. If his friend was going to collapse, he wanted to know when it happened. Tom resisted.

More shots spattered water behind them like killer rain. They were all packing weapons.

Their eyes met.

His lungs burned and his legs turned to pillars of heavy fire, Sam pushed away the possibility of death. Focus on the moment at hand. Keep Tom in sight; keep the book safe. If the people behind them got possession... well. A little pain in his legs would be the least of his problems.

Thirty feet... twenty feet... a hard right and a struggle over a pile of rock...

And a dead end. The tunnel was completely closed. A nearby crevice was open, though, and Sam had to make a choice.

Call it.

Tom swore with the fluency of a military background and life at sea combined.

"Tunnel," Sam panted. Now. They didn't have the firepower for a standoff, and stray bullets were deadly in such tight space.

Panic flared briefly in Tom's eyes. "We stick to the map. If this tunnel doubles back…"

He started pulling down rocks from the blocked passageway, wasting precious seconds. Sam recognized the symptoms of a fear that could swamp you under and take you down. He'd seen it happen to the best of them. He grabbed Tom's shoulders and shook him hard. His friend's eyes flew open and he coughed.

"Tunnel. Trust me."

Tom wrestled away the panic and pushed it down hard. Then he nodded and pushed his big form through the tight crevice.

Sam followed, praying he was right.

Twenty feet. Ten feet. Ahead of them, the water deepened. Sam hoped this was a good sign. The underground entrance had seemed a blessing, a way to prevent outside intrusion. Now it had become a death trap. As Sam barreled through the catacombs, he hoped their mission wasn't going to make them permanent residents.

They pushed on toward the lighter dark of the exit. Tom was panting, stumbling. Sam hoped it was the exertion, not something more sinister. There wasn't time to check. Their rough breathing echoed harsh against the walls. His heartbeat blasted loudly through his consciousness, drowning out pursuit. Sam moved, completely focused.

Without warning, they stepped off the edge of the world.

Sam was forced out of his spinning thoughts to see Tom pointing. In the distance: another wall of rock that Sam had missed in his panic. And in it, another crack. They could make it. Make it out if they were quick. And on the other side, the Venetian lagoon. They were both strong swimmers, but they had no gear. Could they make the three hundred yards to the surface? Could they make it if the bullets came?

A shout behind them made him spin.

There were four of them in black coats, the picture of menace. He and Tom couldn't hold off five. Guns raised. Sam and Tom looked at each other.

The question was, do they stay above water and be targets but have a sight line to their possible salvation? Or dive and be faster, but have no idea when bullets rained from above, wasting precious oxygen for god knew what was waiting on the other side?

Another burst of shot hammered the tomb next to them.

Tom gave Sam a curt nod.

They dived.

They entered the church at a squelching run into the tranquil scent of frankincense and the flickering candlelight. Stray tourists and worshippers were just settling in for the evening mass; out of the corner of his eye, Sam saw the same priest was preparing to give the homily. He spread his arms, the light gleaming on the gold stitching, then stared as Tom and Sam raced up the knave, covered in mud and dripping the sludgy lagoon. It was, after all, the shortest distance to the pier.

The priest gaped. "How did you get here?"

"Thank you, father!" Sam shouted as he raced by, ignoring the stares and the whispers of those seated in the pews. "Your directions were most illuminating!"

They pushed out into the spectacular Venetian sunset and the doors of San Michele, church of the island of the dead, swung closed behind them.

The priest gawked after them as the shock of the doors echoed with finality. He cast his gaze heavenward and said a prayer.

His candle trembled in his hand.

Chapter Sixty-Three

The water taxi skipped across the Venetian Lagoon.

"Let's recap," Sam said, holding up one finger, glancing at their attentive driver, and kept his voice low. "We've just been attacked." He held up another finger. "We don't know by whom, but we know they wanted us dead." Sam tossed his whole hand out, in what was unmistakably an Italian gesture. "And all that after following the advice of a priest! Hell, Venice is the city of love and luck!"

"I guess those guys and the gods don't want us to get what we're after," Tom observed. He held out his hand and Sam surreptitiously slid the book they'd uncovered in the Chinese tomb into his friend's palm. Tom turned it over with his long and muscular fingers. The leather journal looked miniscule in his hands. "Any idea who they might be?"

Sam scrubbed his face. "Beats me. You have any theories?"

Tom glanced at the cabbie, then away. "They looked Italian, right? Maybe the Mafia?"

Even with all the insanity that they had experienced, Sam couldn't help but laugh. "The Mafia? What the hell would the Mafia want from us? The two hundred soaking-wet dollars in my bag?"

"What about more than that?"

Sam snorted. "If you've got more than that, you've been holding out on… me. Oh." His waterlogged brain started to work. "You feel it might be related to the poster we found, back in China? The one with the…" He dropped his voice. "Million-dollar offering to find the *Nyia Chía*?"

"You mean the ten million dollar offering? And yeah, it might. Anyone with enough money to offer a fortune that big probably has the means to send killers after us for whatever reason they want."

"Right." The two men subsided into themselves and the ride was quiet for some expanse of time as they enjoyed the open-air view out of their respective windows. Sam looked out at mazes of canals and gondolas, while Tom saw modern fashion storefronts adapted into 17th-century Renaissance-era structures.

A cell phone ring broke the silence in unceremonious fashion, startling Sam. He was set to be jumpy for any damned thing by now.

A man said, "Good afternoon, Mr. Reilly."

Sam recognized the voice of the Nyia Chia caretaker. "Ramirez!" Beside him, Tom's brows rose. Sam shrugged, as his memory supplied information of his last memory of the caretaker and the quest to find the Nyia Chía. It felt like months ago they'd parted ways in Colombia instead of just over a week.

"I'm sorry to have been so out of touch. I haven't forgotten entirely about you, it's just that I… well. It's been a busy past few days and service has been slim." Sam felt a twinge of guilt, even so. Ramirez was the reason they were here in the first place. The urgency of it all returned with a vengeance. "I should've updated you on everything somehow."

Ramirez chuckled on the phone. "Please, no offense taken. You are doing the work that I've begged you to do – please do not apologize for how you are doing it. Besides, I am somewhat at fault. I'm not even calling you from the phone number I gave you, for safety reasons."

It seemed he wasn't the only one having a rough week. "I see."

"Speaking of safety." Ramirez's voice turned concerned. "I heard you got attacked. I hope you and Tom are all right." Sam was momentarily surprised, but maintained his composure. The man was wealthy. Who knew what means Ramirez had at his disposal to keep them safe? He had to know nearly everything about anything happening to keep them safe. Sam cocked a brow at Tom and grinned. "News travels fast. Wish I had your sources."

"I couldn't agree with you more – we could have saved ourselves some grief."

"How did you hear of it?"

Ramirez's voice dismissed his worry. "I have connections everywhere, my eyes and ears in the jungle – even the flooded lagoons of Venice. A couple of my associates called me after hearing of some gunfire in Venice. Two men attacked in a church, on the hunt for… something. Fired on by two of the shadow men."

Sam blinked. "Two of the what?" Tom sat up in interest. "Wait, you know who they are?"

Ramirez paused momentarily. "Eh… just a little. They tend to get in the way of Caretakers and anything related to the *Nyia Chía*. They've been doing everything to get their hands on the golden treasure the creatures produce for centuries. Over the years we've become… acquainted."

Sam shook his head. "They didn't give us the most friendly greetings."

The voice on the other end took an unexpectedly somber edge. "It won't be happening any longer."

"Why? What's happened?"

"The last *Nyia Chía* has died."

They both said nothing for a good ten seconds. Tom gestured, demanding to know what was being said. Sam waved him down as Ramirez cleared his throat and spoke again.

"You see, they're incredibly social creatures. They need to be with their own kind, their colony, to survive. I thought that my company would be enough – I stayed with him as much as possible – it had been ten years… but it wasn't enough." Sam waited through the obvious emotion in the other man's voice. "It wasn't enough. I've failed. If we don't find the main colony, they'll go extinct."

The man's voice turned brisk. "How far away from the airport are you?"

Sam glanced at Tom. "How did you…"

"I heard the planes take off in your phone. They have a very distinct flight pattern." Sam's brows rose as he reassessed exactly who the hell this Ramirez was.

There wasn't much to do about it now. Sam glanced up at a rapidly passing sign on the freeway. "Three miles. Almost there. Why'd you ask?"

"We're running out of time. It's time to leave the jungle. After all, there's not much reason to stay anymore. I've chartered a private jet to get you wherever you need. I'm in the air on it right now and I'll be down at the Venezia Marco Polo in… one hour."

Sam's expression must have betrayed his shock, because Tom stared expectantly at him. Sam mouthed "private jet" at him. He seemed to get the idea. His big brows rose. Sam turned his attention back to the phone. Ramirez was speaking again.

Sam asked, "I'm sorry, what was that?"

"I said some of my associates in the Chinese Market informed me you were looking for some extensive translation. A friend of mine is fluent in many dialects of Chinese; I've brought him along should you require his assistance."

At this point, Sam didn't even question where Ramirez got his information: he was just glad the Caretaker was getting them what they absolutely needed. "That's perfect. Thank you very much."

Ramirez's voice smiled over the phone. "I'll do whatever it takes to find the colony, Mr. Reilly. These creatures cannot be allowed to go extinct on my watch."

The water taxi pulled up along the closest jetty to the Venice Marco Polo Airport just as Sam hung up the phone. "Is everything okay, signore?"

Sam leaned forward, breaching the screen. "Please take us to the other end," he said. "Our plans have changed."

The taxi swung up next to a small private jet. Sam peered out the window, already shouldering his backpack. He pressed a 50-euro bill into the man's hand as he and Tom exited, already looking toward the plane. The sooner they got out of Venice, the better, as far as Sam was concerned.

The Caretaker looked exactly the same as Sam remembered him in El Dorado. He was maybe even wearing the same muted linen clothes. The man extended a hand as Sam skipped up the steel steps, Tom clunking behind him. Sam shook the weathered grip.

"Mr. Reilly. A pleasure to see you again," he said with infinite sophistication and delicacy, at odds with the roar of the plane, which looked ready for takeoff.

Sam shook his head. "I just wish it were in better circumstances," he shouted. Ramirez made a gallic gesture and escorted them into the fuselage. The door closed behind them, encasing them in blessed silence.

The interior of the plane was elegant with no frills, much like the Caretaker himself. The first thing Sam noticed, apart from the bottles adorning the leather tables, was the small Chinese man, impeccably dressed, who sat at the bolted side bar. He smiled a perfunctory greeting as Sam slung down his backpack. A steward hurried to take it, but Sam waved him down. "I'd prefer to keep it with me, thanks."

The steward backed off with an apologetic murmur. "I'll be up front should you require anything else, sir."

Ramirez nodded graciously and said something in Spanish. The steward retreated behind the partition that blocked the cockpit. Sam's brows rose. Ramirez smiled, seeing it. "Andrews is also the pilot. Pays to keep the crew light, I've found. He'll take us anywhere we want to go."

Tom hooked his thumbs in his belt in appreciation. "You've thought of everything."

"I hope so." Ramirez gestured to the Chinese man. "Gentlemen, this is Alex, my translator. He's been a friend of many years, and is well versed in a number of Chinese dialects. I do hope you'll forgive the liberties. But I've brought some supplies that should help as well."

Sam eyed the bottle of wine. "Well, it's a little early in the day for a glass, normally, but after the day we've had, I won't say no."

Ramirez laughed. "Please, you're more than welcome." He opened the wine with an expert hand. "But I was referring to more scientific pieces. LIDAR, SONAR, and Ground Penetrating Radar." He shrugged at their surprise. "We have no time to waste. If Alex can help us find the location, there was no use in not being prepared."

Sam accepted the glass the Caretaker handed him with a smile. "I'll drink to that."

They sat around the table and the bottle was almost gone, along with a tray of meat and cheese, by the time Alex leaned back.

"You're sure?" Ramirez asked, piercing. "We can't afford to be wrong."

"I'm sure. And I'm not wrong." He tapped the journal. "It's labeled here, clearly. "The Tomb of the Golden Man." He quirked his lips. "From all you've told me, it doesn't get much clearer than that."

Sam set his glass aside carefully. "That sounds like the place, all right. Does it say where it is?"

The translator nodded. "It does, Mr. Reilly. The tomb of the golden man is hidden in the Yellow Dragon Cave."

Tom grinned. "Great!" He glanced around at them all. "Any idea where that is?"

The translator tilted the book, as if it contained more secrets. "I've never been there myself, but I know the location well. Yellow Dragon Cave is buried beneath the Zhangjiajie national forest park."

Though they tried to hide their incomprehension of the tongue-twisting language, Alex translated anyway, with just a trace of smugness. "Most people have heard of this park, only they don't know that they have."

Sam pursed his lips. "Where?"

Alex grinned. "Most westerners know it as The Floating Mountains of China."

Chapter Sixty-Four

Zhangjiajie, China

At Beijing Capital International Airport, the Learjet was traded for a more robust AG600 amphibious aircraft, known as a Monstrous Flying Dragon.

The plane was Chinese built and amphibious. When Tom had expressed disbelief at the caliber of the transportation, the Caretaker had explained that he wanted the ability to land on the various rivers within the Chinese jungles nearby Zhangjianjie, if necessary. Tom couldn't agree more – in his experience, more preparation for jungle excursions was always better than less.

The aircraft had a single body flying boat fuselage, high wings that had been cantilevered in addition to four WJ-6 turbo-propellers, complete with tricycle retractable landing gear, totally stable. Despite its mammoth size, the aircraft was capable of landing in just eight feet of water.

It had been designed to conduct Sea State 3 operations with ten feet tall waves, but was mostly developed for aerial firefighting, able to collect 26,000 pounds of water in twenty seconds, and transporting up to 820,000 pounds of water on a single tank of fuel. As for search and rescue, it held the capacity to retrieve up to fifty people lost at sea.

She was a beauty, Tom thought, as the twin propellers churned the air into fluid silver storms as he peered out the window. He grinned. He loved new toys.

The AG600 had ample space to spread out, and he and Sam had been making good use of it, pouring over topographical maps of the area since they'd taken off from the private hanger in Beijing. The Zhangjiajie national park covered eighteen and a half square miles, and although Tom didn't distrust the translator's assessment, the past few weeks had taught him to do his own homework.

Plus, even if the translator was right, the Yellow Dragon Cave was massive.

Tom had no desire to get lost again. According to the dossier on the cave, it covered 120 acres almost 9.5 miles in length, with four levels – divided into dry and wet sections – thirteen chambers, three underground waterfalls, two underground rivers, three pools, ninety-six passages, and, as if that wasn't enough for them to sift through, an underground lake. According to the guide book, the largest chamber in the cave covered an acre and the tallest waterfall fell a hundred and fifty feet. The guided tour through the cave lasts about two hours and includes a boat ride down one of the underground rivers.

That's about how long they'd been flying from Beijing, Tom reflected. And, based on the maps, the information from the Chinese government pertaining to the caves, and what he hoped would be corroboration from the SONAR equipment, they'd worked out that the Tomb of El Dorado was buried somewhere within a series of unsearched passageways at the back of the Yellow Dragon Cave – in an underground labyrinth potentially accessible through a large sinkhole in the karst mountain behind the cave.

That was the theory, anyway. He tapped the paper. "You're sure?"

Sam shrugged. "Sure as I can be from the air, I guess." He gestured out the window. "Looks like we'll get to test it soon."

Tom slid to the window and peered out. He'd seen some pretty incredible sights in his life, but this one took his breath without asking and refused to give it back.

Giant sandstone pinnacles rose skyward from the valley floor, taller than skyscrapers, with tufts of evergreen shrubs clinching to their narrow summits. Tom recognized them from Chinese paintings- they must have seemed like deposits from the gods to the ancient inhabitants. In reality, the huge pillars were the result of centuries of erosion from expanding ice in the winter and the plants that grow on them, the erosion carried away by mountain streams.

His eyes drifted to the south where he spotted Moon Hill, a natural arch a few miles outside Yangshuo in southern China's Guangxi autonomous region. It was named so for its wide, semicircular hole through the hill, and all that remains of what was once a limestone cave formed in the phreatic zone. Like most formations in the region, it was karst. A single rock climber dangled from a rope some sixty feet off the ceiling of the arch.

This magnificent nature always made Tom reconsider life.

In doing so, in the distance he spotted something mechanical, out of sorts in the rich nature. What the- Ah. Tom remembered reading about this- but it was quite something to see it in person. The Bailong Elevator looked like it had come straight from Gustav Eiffel's notebook, oddly futuristic in a non-futuristic setting. Built in 2002, it could rocket fifty travelers at a time to the best panoramas in the park in less than two minutes. Tom pressed a hand to the glass. Unlike his friend Sam, Tom had a natural love of heights. If they lived through this, he thought, without getting shot, lost, or otherwise incapacitated, he was treating himself to a ride. He wanted to be at the front of the long queue when the doors opened, to stand against the car's glass walls to get an unobstructed view as he shot up three hundred and ninety feet from the valley floor.

He grinned. Maybe he could get Genevieve to come.

The plane banked and he glimpsed steps carved into solid rock. He pressed close to the glass. "Is that what I think it is?"

The translator saw him looking and smiled. "Their people call it the *Sky Ladder*, and it kept them safe for centuries. Then, in the seventies, the village elders decided to break down. They carved the road with nothing but hand tools and thirteen men. It took them five years and now it's a tourist attraction."

Tom leaned in for a closer look. "That's incredible."

"That's the Chinese. It's all tunnels through solid rock and leveled cliff face for the entire length of a mile." His lips quirked. "They even made it wide enough for tourist buses. Once you get to the village, it's entirely made of stone. It's beautiful and harsh. The canyon below is narrow and deep and you can see the layers of colored rock. For some time, even after the road was built, it remained a secret, difficult to get to. But then the government realized it could turn a profit and the village is getting famous. There are hotels, now, and restaurants. A few years ago, the villagers fought back, claiming the government had swindled them. Now it's stuck in limbo." He waved his hand at the breathtaking scenery, the distant metropolis. "China."

The plane moved past and they left the village behind as if it didn't exist. They swooped over it into the mountainous jungle behind, past the Gallery of Watermills that marked the entrance to the Yellow Dragon Cave.

Tom looked at the translator in confusion. "Wasn't that the entrance?"

The translator shrugged. "It's impossible to land here. We're aiming for a river on top of the mountain."

"Okay, nice."

Between the trees a snaking thread of silver shot into existence and the plane zeroed in. Tom thought they'd never make it through the tall canopy and flinched as the branches seemed to scrape the very fuselage. He'd been shot down in the middle east once, and he had no desire to use what he'd learned. But the plane lived up to her specs and they hit the river with a triumphant splash, as precise as an Olympic diver off the board. Tom leaned back, impressed. Whoever manned this bird knew how to handle her, that was sure.

He collected his bag.

They emerged into the morning. Tom squinted. It looked like they were to the north of the Zhangjiajie mountains. That would put them at… He glanced at Sam as the men tied up the plane and pushed a zodiac into the river. "Going in by the back door?"

Sam shouldered his backpack. "Looks like it. From what the translator says, there's a sinkhole in the back that's been roped off by the park system as being too dangerous. But it drops you directly into the back of the cave system."

Tom narrowed his brows. "Too dangerous, eh?" He watched the amiable translator rattle off instructions in Chinese with a smile to their small army of workers. Bills changed hands and were stashed so fast you had to be looking to see them.

Tom was looking.

He folded his arms. "I wonder how he knows about it?"

Chapter Sixty-Five

Sam lugged his bag on his shoulder, as did the rest of their party. It was the waterproof one, the one he brought everywhere, and it contained, apart from the journal that Alex had translated on the plane, but a digital version of Churn Ng's grandfather's journal.

Now, Sam wasn't taking any chances. They needed all the information they could get.

He wiped his brow and surveyed the caravan hiking to the mouth of the sinkhole. Apparently, the translator was more than just a translator – he had connections. Within minutes of their arrival a dozen locals had materialized out of the jungle to help transport their dive equipment, RADAR, and underground sonar. There was very little as humbling and inspiring as Asian efficiency. He said as much to Alex as they trekked toward the entrance to the cave.

The translator smiled. "We'll need all the help we can get, Mr. Reilly." He pointed to a narrow jungle path that disappeared up the mountain. "If we're going to reach that."

He was right. Sam was stuck with sweat and covered with bugs by the time they reached the sinkhole. From here, they had an equal view of sky and canopy and his legs burned. They took a welcome break as the locals unpacked their equipment at the edge of the raging river. They had to shout to be heard over the roar of the water, and Sam guessed that anything they said couldn't be heard even ten yards away. It was probably the only place possible they could shout at will on a top-secret mission.

Sam stopped at the sinkhole.

It was roughly ten feet wide, and so deep that he couldn't see where the fall ended. The whole area was surrounded by a thick canopy of jungle that somehow reminded him of Sierra Nevada de Santa Marta in which the Tairona had once inhabited and built the now lost city of El Dorado. On the opposite side of the sinkhole, it there was a short cliff, that rounded a fast-flowing river.

Tom approached. He jerked his chin at the unloading frenzy, then at the sinkhole. "Looks like they got everything except the scales."

Sam blinked. "Scales?"

"We go in there and we find the tomb... you do realize that all these *Niya Chia* have been living there for centuries. There's been no mass influx of golden pearls on the market, and I can't imagine anyone transporting them down this mountain just for kicks." He shrugged. "This whole place is going to be filled with centuries of golden vomit. Thought they might want to weigh it."

Sam stalled for a moment. Then he grinned. "I wonder if it has to solidify into the pearl, or if it comes up fully formed," he said, wrapping the cord to rappel in around his waist. "You know, like a hairball. We should ask Ramirez."

He looked around for the Caretaker, but didn't see him.

Over the course of the next half an hour, they set up a rappelling tripod over the sinkhole that could be used to abseil from, or haul heavy equipment, or gold back from the depths of the ancient cave system.

Tom was on the opposite side of the sinkhole, finalizing a secondary set of rigging ropes and knots as a set of redundancies in case the first system failed.

Sam tightened his backpack, making sure it was well secured, and gripped the rope, before gesturing to the massive sinkhole. "Looks like it's now or never."

Ramirez stepped into the small clearing and grinned, holding a Glock level with him. "I couldn't have said it better myself."

Sam swallowed hard, realizing he'd been betrayed.

And behind Ramirez, a ghost appeared.

Ramirez watched Sam's eyes dart toward the new arrival. He lips twisted maliciously with pleasure. "Ah, I see that you have met my associate, Churn Ng."

Chapter Sixty-Six

Sam glanced at Churn Ng.

The man wore a malevolent grin.

Sam turned his palms skyward. His eyes narrowed, locking with Churn's. "You faked your death, didn't you?"

"Guilty as charged," Churn replied.

None of it made any sense to Sam. "Why?"

Churn shrugged. "Because I never would have survived the investigation by the Australian police once we reached the surface. The gold would have been confiscated and more important yet, a formal investigation into the Tomb of El Dorado would have commenced – and that we couldn't have."

Tom said, "But we saw you disappear into the river. No one could have survived that!"

Churn nodded and his lips parted in a wry grin. "I was carrying a pony bottle."

Sam said, "Thus, you stayed underwater until we presumed you were dead, and continued to the surface."

Ramirez fixed his Glock at Sam and said, "Yes, yes... whereupon you followed the old journal – the one Churn was carrying – to China and then to Venice, before finally leading us to the Tomb of El Dorado."

Sam grinned. "Hey, we haven't found it yet..."

"But we will. We no longer need you, Mr. Reilly," Ramirez said. "Good bye, Mr. Reilly..."

Tom waved his arms, crisscrossing his hands. "Wait! You still need us."

Ramirez turned the barrel of his Glock toward Tom. Even at the far end of the sinkhole, it was an easy shot to take. His eyes narrowed. He licked his lips, paused and bit his lower lip, as though considering the inconvenience of being drawn into what was most likely an attempt to stall their deaths. Doubt was plastered across his face. He spoke slowly, with the sound of finality, only someone holding the handgun could muster. "Tell me... why do I need you still?"

Sam grinned. "Because the tomb itself is locked."

Ramirez studied his face, trying to determine whether or not to shoot them both dead. "Then I unlock it."

Sam crossed his arms and made a winning smile. "I doubt it. The tomb has a coded trap, designed to cause the entire cavern in which it's housed to collapse, burying it permanently in a tomb of ruble that will take decades to reach."

Ramirez met his eye. "Or, you might just be lying in an attempt to stop us killing you."

Sam shrugged. "It's a possibility, but are you willing to risk it?"

"Churn," Ramirez said to his strongman, "Bring him here."

Churn nodded, opened up a flick knife, and bared his teeth maliciously. "My pleasure, Ramirez."

"Don't kill him!" Ramirez warned. "We're going to need him alive if he just happens to be telling the truth."

Churn switched the knife so the blade pointed backward, opening the blade for to slice. "I'm sure I can keep him alive... not very well, and very uncomfortable, but alive."

Sam gripped the rope with one hand and braced for his attacker.

Churn moved forward slowly. His lips parted in a curious grin. His eyes tracing Sam's projected movements to the other side of the sink hole. "Where do you think you're going to go?"

"Who knows, but I don't think I'll be going with you," Sam replied. "I just don't like your attitude."

"That's okay, you don't have to like my..." Churn never finished his sentence, he lunged and sliced at Sam's chest.

Sam shifted his position to the left and the blade skimmed the side of his left arm. Adrenaline surged, his heart raced, and he knew that Churn meant it when he said Sam was going to be very uncomfortable by the time he finished with him.

Churn stepped back, his blade held out in front of him, his eyes greedily searching for the best location to place his next strike.

Sam gripped the rope in his hands, slowly pulling in a small bite – or coil – in the rope.

Churn studied him, and then lunged.

Sam shifted his weight forward, leaning in toward the knife attack, in a move that defied logic and startled Churn.

Churn, afraid that he might mortally wound Sam in the process, turned his wrist so that the angle of the knife no longer aimed at Sam's gut.

With his other hand, Churn tried to lock onto Sam's throat, while sending a small barrage of punches into Sam's solar plexus.

It drove all the air out of his lungs, winding him as the muscles of his diaphragm spasmed.

Locked together, like a pair of boxers awaiting their opponent's next move, Sam dropped the hangman knot that he'd been forming over Churn's neck, and pulled it tight.

Churn's eyes went wide.

An instant later, Sam pushed back, dragging Churn with him as he swung across the sinkhole. The hangman's knot was roughly three feet lower than where Sam had gripped on the rope, meaning that Churn fell farther down the hole before the noose took his weight with a sickening crunch sound.

With Churn's weight below him, Sam failed to reach the other side, instead swinging back toward the middle of the sinkhole, where, like a pendulum, he finally lost momentum and now dangled dangerously above a seemingly endless abyss.

Despite the crunching sound, the fall hadn't killed Churn.

The knot restricted his breathing, and he dropped his knife, his fingers grabbing at the rope around his neck in a violent attempt to remove the constriction to his throat.

Sam kicked at him, ramming his knees into the man's head.

But still the man kept fighting. Built of solid muscle, the man seemed immune to the volley of collisions his head was taking.

In the background, Ramirez was laughing like a school bully at a playground fight.

Tom gripped his dive knife, helplessly unable to provide any assistance.

To Sam's horror, Churn began to climb the rope.

Tom shouted, "Sam! Take this!"

Sam glanced toward Tom, who threw his dive knife toward him.

He caught it and in one quick movement severed the taut rope below him.

Churn screamed in abject terror all the way down, until the screams turned to silence.

Chapter Sixty-Seven

Free of his dead weight, Sam swung the rope, like a child on a swing until he got close enough for Tom to pull him across.

Standing on the opposite side of the sink hole, away from Ramirez and his goons, Sam searched frantically for his next move.

Ramirez still laughed. "Thank you, Mr. Reilly. Because of you, it now appears that I no longer have to share the fortune from the Tomb of El Dorado with Churn."

Sam and Tom backed away right to the ledge of the cliff. Sam's eyes flicked between the raging rapids far below, and Ramirez.

When Ramirez stopped laughing, Sam said, "Now what? Are you going to send another one of your thugs to try and bring us in?"

Ramirez shrugged. "No. I think I'm going to take the gamble that you're lying and about the Tomb of El Dorado."

Tom said, "So, you get us to do your dirty work and then you off us in the jungle, is that it? I hate to break it to you, but that's the oldest story in the book."

"There's a reason old stories persist, Mr. Bower. You taught me that." Ramirez raised the gun again. "Because they're true."

Sam's eyes darted toward the fast-flowing, white-water rapids far below.

He and tom exchanged a glance.

Ramirez shrugged. "If you'd prefer to die that way, be my guest..."

Sam's eyes darted between Tom and Ramirez.

Tom made the slightest of nods.

Two of Ramirez's goons were trying to circle around the sinkhole to reach them.

A second later Ramirez fired a shot.

It went wide, missing them by inches.

And Sam and Tom jumped.

Chapter Sixty-Eight

Sam swung his arms the whole way down...

His feet hit the water and he plunged deep into the shallow river, striking the rocky ground below with jarring force.

Despite the pain in his ankles, he pushed off the ground, kicking hard until his head reached the surface.

He gasped for air.

The fast-flowing current swept him downstream immediately, his eyes scanning the surface for signs of Tom.

Tom popped up a second later, taking a breath as casually as he would going on a recreational snorkel. "You okay, Sam?"

Sam's ankles were tender, but undamaged. "Yeah. You?"

"Never better."

He turned his gaze downriver, trying to work out where they were headed. "Tom, I don't suppose you noticed where this river's going to spit us out?"

Tom opened his mouth to reply, but he didn't get to speak.

Instead, the water next to him, suddenly erupted with the onslaught of bullets raking its surface, sending a spray high into the air.

Sam ducked underwater, letting the current whisk him downriver, and trying his best to protect his head from being smashed on any number of submerged boulders that lined the riverbed. He dropped down the small chute of a waterfall, plunging into the deep water of the punchbowl below. He stayed underwater until his lungs burned and then he waited longer, before eventually being forced to surface.

His head broached the surface and he took a couple deep breaths, turning around and trying to orient himself to the cliff where Ramirez and his goons were trying to take shots at them. Discombobulated, he squinting his eyes, but couldn't even see where they had entered the water.

The movement of the water, tugged at him, and pulled him down the next section of rapids. The

"Tom!" he shouted, grabbing onto a boulder to avoid being swept downstream. He looked around wildly, clearing spray from his eyes, only to seeing the back of Tom's head bobbing farther downstream. All he got was a hand above the surface.

And then the hand disappeared.

Sam had no way of knowing if Tom was all right or not, but he was downriver, and that was enough. Sam let go of his boulder and was immediately swept along by the raging flood. Floating, buffeted into unseen stones hard enough to bruise and too numb to know if he'd broken anything, Sam fought to keep his head above the surface. His injured leg had barely had time to heal and he kicked with it in agony as he fought to ride the current that was dragging them toward nothingness.

Nothingness in a river was never good.

He risked a glance backward and saw Ramirez and his goons fast shrinking along the shore far behind them. At the moment they were no threat. Sam turned his attention to more important matters.

Like the churning precipice of the lethal waterfall that was fast approaching. The waterfall had looked so picturesque from the air.

It had also looked huge.

It looked infinitely larger up close.

Tom shouted, "Sam!"

Sam twisted at the shout, to see Tom clinging to a massive fallen tree branch wedged between some boulders, just near the edge, through the mad swirl of eddying river and sky. Sam felt a surge of hope.

Sam forced himself into surrender. He sensed the current, and assessed the flow hurtling toward him. At the right moment, praying he was right, he let go.

The current swept him like a battering ram straight into Tom's outstretched hand.

Tom shifted, sliding his grip so Sam could find some purchase on the slick bark.

Sam coughed. "Thanks."

"You're welcome," Tom replied, amiably.

He raked the river, trying to work out how they could possibly avoid going over the massive waterfall at the end. The current was too strong to swim across in the amount of distance they had.

Sam frowned. "You got any ideas?"

Tom jerked his chin at the edge of the world. "I think that's our ticket."

Sam shook his head. "Are you crazy? Those falls are nearly a thousand feet high!"

The head-shake cleared his vision and he saw what Tom had seen.

The remains of an old military float plane that had become stranded on an island of rocks at the very edge of the waterfall right in the middle of the fast-flowing river. It was an old Chinese turboprop, most likely left over from its service during the Korean War. It was badly dilapidated. There were no visible markings and nothing to identify the type of aircraft.

Whatever it was, Sam didn't recognize it.

Its wings and fuselage were mostly intact, but the tail had long since broken off – either being the cause of the aircraft's original demise, or after decades trapped on its precarious perch above the waterfalls and being battered by the river. Thick jungle vines now encapsulated most of the wreckage.

Sam glanced at Tom. "Are you serious?"

Just then, their branch jerked and Sam almost lost hold.

"Why not?" Tom asked, as he reclaimed his grip in desperation. "This thing won't hold both of us for long. It's that or we both go over."

"Where would we even climb onto it?"

"Over there, on the starboard wingtip. There are number of vines hanging off it. We can climb those onboard."

Sam's eyes narrowed on the thousand-foot plunge directly past the wing. "You know we're only going to get one chance at this."

"Agreed."

"If we manage to get on board that old warplane, then what?" Sam asked. "It's not like we can get it flying again."

Tom nodded. "No, but it's something. Right now, there's no chance we can reach the bank of the river. At least on board there we can buy ourselves some time. I still have my backpack with the satellite phone inside. We just need to survive long enough to get someone to retrieve us."

Sam was about to protest, when then the branch snapped, and the decision was made

Chapter Sixty-Nine

Tom's head ducked underwater for a second.

As soon as he surfaced, he swam with all his might toward the starboard wingtip. He was a strong swimmer, but only an insane man would be delusional enough to believe that his strength could overcome the flow of the current.

He swam diagonally so that as he was swept toward the waterfall by the river, he would also traverse the river horizontally simultaneously. If he timed it just right, he would end up reaching that series of vines just at the right moment.

That was the plan, but the river gods took no pleasure in giving such a plan to mere mortals. Instead, the turbulent waters shifted him in the wrong direction. He tried to fight it, but failed. Just before being shot past the wreckage of the aircraft, two waves collided, creating a shallow vortex.

For a few seconds he was trapped, spinning round and round, uncontrollably destined to follow the whims of the sea, while slowly dragging him under. When Tom could no longer fight it and was about to drown, he stopped fighting. Kicking and paddling hard, he dived through the vortex and was shot out the starboard side.

It took him right where he needed to be.

Tom reached up and grabbed a dangling vine and hauled himself out of the water and onto the island of steel, using the rusted engine nacelle to step on.

Safe, on top of the warbird's steel wing, Tom urgently searched the turbid water for Sam. The entire river was a sea of discombobulated waves, eddies, and whirlpools, but there was no sign of Sam. Tom's eyes narrowed, his mouth was set firm, and his eyes piercing as they raked the sea. It seemed impossible that Sam might have gone off the waterfall already.

From the river that lapped the portside wing, Sam cried out, "Tom! Over here!"

Tom turned to face him. His eyes locked onto Sam, who was being drawn, despite his best efforts, to the river that flowed beneath the portside wing. Sam was paddling as hard as he could to avoid it, but had already missed the tail of the plane, and was now committed to the wrong side. Refusing to give up, Sam was paddling hard, trying his best to combat the current which cruelly and serendipitously had decided to drag Sam down the wrong side of the old warbird.

Tom cursed and without even considering if the wing was structurally safe to hold his weight, he started to run along the top of it.

Sam dropped down a small crest of a wave and was shot out toward the farthest tip of the wing.

Tom dived to the end reaching down as far as he could with an open hand.

Sam rolled to his right side and took it.

Their thumbs interlocked and Tom pulled Sam out of the raging torrent.

Chapter Seventy

Sam clambered onboard the old Chinese warplane.

The plane looked like it had been there for years – maybe even since the local village had built that road through the mountains. Most of its frame had been destroyed by the water and the resulting rust. They crawled crab like across the length of the wings, deafened by the roar of the falls, trying not to look down, but it was no good – as Sam stared into the blinding white spray, it became inescapably clear – there was no way they were getting off their island refuge without going over the eight-hundred-foot falls.

Trapped on the wing, unable to reach either side of the river, they climbed down through the open hatchway and into the main fuselage. With the tail missing, river water was able to enter the bottom half of the cargo bay.

Sam said, "See if you can find anything we can use."

Tom ran his eyes across the empty fuselage. It looked like it had been cleared out by the elements long ago. "Like what?"

Sam grinned. "Well, a nine-hundred-foot length of rope would be just perfect."

Tom laughed. "That might be asking a little too much."

They continued to search the aircraft but found nothing that could be used to help them reach either side of the river.

Tom removed his backpack and found that the satellite phone had been damaged by an impact since jumping in the water. He held it up, but the screen and the keys had all been shattered. "Sorry."

"Not your fault," Sam said. "I lost mine, so I can't complain."

"Yeah, but now we're really up the creek without a paddle."

"We'll find a way out this… we always do."

Outside, a short burst of bullets pelted the aft section of the warplane.

Afterward, a man started to shout across the roar of the river. "Sam Reilly! Come on out here…"

Sam carefully sneaked a glance from the hatchway.

On the starboard bank, Ramirez and several of his thugs armed with machineguns looked at him. Ramirez shouted, "I know you're in there, Reilly! You're trapped. There's nowhere for you to go. Why don't you come out and we can have a chat?"

Sam bit his lower lip, grinned. He shouted back, "We're happy where we are, Ramirez… why don't you come over here and join us?"

"I don't think so," Ramirez replied. "I'm a little worried that your aircraft doesn't look stable. Maybe it won't last there much longer? What do you think?"

"I think it's been here since the Korean War. No reason for it to go anywhere now while we wait for our friends to come get us… and when they do, we'll be coming for you Ramirez, so maybe you'd better take that head start you've been given, because we're not going to stop until you're dead."

"That's so harsh. After all we've been through, I expected more from you Mr. Reilly. I'm disappointed."

Sam shrugged. "You'd better get used to disappointment. There's going to be a whole lot of it where you're going."

"Maybe… maybe not?" Ramirez laughed. "I think you'll get there before me. You'd better hope that old warbird can still fly."

A few seconds later, Ramirez lobbed a grenade in their general direction.

Sam dropped back into the fuselage and yelled, "Grenade!"

The grenade landed in the water thirty feet from the wreckage of the warbird and exploded beneath the water, causing a large wave in its explosive wake.

Sam and Tom held on to the internal steel skeleton of the aircraft.

The entire plane shifted, bobbing up and down like a small boat disturbed by the wake of a large ship. The entire cargo hold shuddered and echoed with the sound of metal scraping rock as the plane readjusted its position in the river, before finally settling back into the riverbed...

Before two more grenades exploded.

When the blast waves settled down, Sam said to Tom, "I don't know how much this old bird can take of this. We need to go."

Tom set his jaw firm. "Ah, Sam, I don't mean to be the bearer of bad news, but... you do realize we're trapped here right?"

Sam wasn't ready to give up, just yet. "Come with me, I've got a plan."

"You're kidding me," Tom said. "What have you got?"

"Just come with me and you'll see."

Sam scrambled into the cockpit. It was already occupied, and he shoved the skeletal remains of the pilot out the window without ceremony. The bony remains, fell through the window to the ground far below. If he was wrong, they'd be joining him shortly. No point in fussing.

He looked up from strapping himself in to the pilot's chair to see Tom staring at him like he'd gone crazy. Sam raised his brow. "You'd better strap in tight, too. This might be a bumpy ride."

They exchanged a quick glance.

"Hey," Tom said, raising his hands as if talking to a madman, "I'm not casting any dispersion on your piloting skills, Sam – I remember what you're capable of in the air – but I really don't think you're going to be able to get this old bird to fly."

The plane gave a massive lurch and they both instinctively threw themselves backward to prevent their momentum from being the thing that pushed her over the edge. Their additional weight had already tipped the nose of the plane forward enough.

Sam grinned. "You were saying?"

With an oath Tom strapped in tight as around them the plane creaked and groaned like some stone dragon coming to life.

Tom had barely strapped himself in and checked the latch when the plane lurched forward like a rollercoaster. Sam felt the contents of his gut rise as the plane tipped forward, overlooking the eighty-hundred-foot fall below.

He swallowed and a split second later, the aircraft began its final journey into oblivion.

Sam yanked on the twin ejector lever.

Nothing happened.

He pulled it again – hard.

Tom swore…

A small explosion blew what remained of the cockpit away.

And an instant later they were shot out into the air.

Chapter Seventy-One

Ramirez raced along the path after the pair, dodging vines and boulders in panic. He had seen their mad dash toward the plane, and their desperate salvation. Now he watched in horror as the two ejector seats shot off into the air like a missile firing on fair day. He tracked their progress intently, bringing the binoculars up. Through them, one parachute deployed. He scanned frantically for the second.

The body fell. Tumbling repeatedly.

But the chute never showed.

Then, finally, just before the body hit the trees, at the last possible second, the tiny white scrap blossomed into existence, and the falling body jerked and slowed.

It disappeared behind the canopy with the elegance of a jellyfish.

Ramirez lowered the binoculars and rubbed his chin. It was an unexpected problem.

He turned to one of his men. "Did you see what I saw?"

The man said, "Yes, sir."

Ramirez jerked his chin toward the jungle. "It seems they've survived the explosion, no?"

"Yes sir."

"Well? What are you doing just standing there? Go!" He gestured to the trees. "Do what you're hired to do. They might be injured from the fall. It will be difficult to make it back through this jungle." He turned to the man with a steely glare. "See to it that they don't."

The boy bowed. "Very good, sir."

He disappeared into the jungle and Ramirez put his hands in his pockets. He never could stay still when anxious, though. He lit a cigarette instead. The smoke calmed his nerves as it sailed toward the clear, blue sky.

He motioned to two of his men. "Make sure they don't survive their landing!"

Chapter Seventy-Two

The old warplane used a Martin-Baker zero-zero ejector seat.

It was designed to safely extract upward and land its occupant from a grounded stationary position – thus, its designation, zero altitude and zero airspeed. Or at least that was what it was designed to do back in the fifties and Sam prayed it still worked.

Zero-zero technology used small rockets to propel the seat upward to an adequate altitude and a small explosive charge to open the parachute canopy quickly for a successful parachute descent, so that proper deployment of the parachute no longer relied on airspeed and altitude. The seat cannon cleared the seat from the aircraft, then the under-seat rocket pack fires to lift the seat to altitude. As the rockets fired for longer than the cannon, they do not require the same high forces. Zero-zero rocket seats also reduced forces on the pilot during any ejection, reducing injuries and spinal compression.

For a split second, Sam floated in the air and heard nothing but the pristine nature and calmness of the jungle. Before him was an endless blanket of green from the canopies of the tall jungle trees. To see them like this, it was almost possible to believe that he could safely land on the verdant layer like a bed.

The delusions of the moment were instantly shaken out as the parachute pack on his back unfurled, jerking him painfully by the armpits with a jolt so hard it took the breath from his body. The chute made a terrifying woosh sound as it caught the wind. Pain and relief washed over him. The wind pushed against him with the force of the sea and he tried to breathe with it, tried to breathe at all, sucking in tiny sips of air around the force of his relief.

Maybe they'd make it, after all.

But there was something wrong. Sam's extensive military training, tours, and even some of his more extreme recreation adventures had given him experience with the various sensations of hurtling through space. Now, he noted, fighting not to panic, his body seemed to be tumbling to the ground faster than he expected.

Sam instantly expected the worst. Fighting the awesome weight of gravity and wind, he craned his neck back and looked above him to the parachute.

Well, it had opened, as he'd thought. That was something. Except it was riddled with holes of varying sizes. One especially large one stared back at him, its rough edges flapping violently in the wind. He cursed his own hope, naiveite, and desperation.

Was it much better to plummet to the ground or die going over a waterfall?

In this moment, he wished he'd never found that damn transom, heard of El Dorado, or seen those golden pearls.

"Those damned..." was all Sam could manage before his fight-or-flight reflexes set in. He swore violently, fluently, and at length. Some abstract, shock-riddled part of his brain noted that, if Tom were around to hear him, even he would be impressed.

As he flailed in the open air, desperately trying to slow his inexorable journey toward the canopy, Sam could hear the blood pounding in his ears as he searched for any way out of his situation. Two voices, as different as could be, came unexpectedly to his aid: the first, his tenth grade algebra teacher, Mr. Preston, a weedy man, ex-hippie, who had drummed into their heads that the rate of gravity was 9.8 feet per second. The second was the raspy yet solid iron voice of his drill instructor, during basic of his first year of training, right before Sam's first base jump: If your parachute AND your reserve don't work, you're probably mincemeat! But just in case, make sure to steer to a soft landing platform! Then, make yourself into an "I" shape and land on your feet!" When Sam had expressed the very real concern that a landing like this might break both his legs, the man had laughed in his face. "Of course you'll break them! Better your legs than your spine!"

Sam could feel his muscles move into the landing position on their own: his mind remained frozen in fear.

He closed his eyes.

The world silenced: thick fronds of foliage gave way to Sam's body as he crashed through layer after layer of jungle. Branches hammered him like battering rams and he could see the green flash all around him. Tiny twigs ripped through his clothes, seeking skin; he felt the sting of sweat enter a thousand open wounds.

Whether it was from tree interference or from exhaustion, he didn't know, but Sam lost his form. His feet began to rapidly bend and straighten as if they had a mind of their own and his arms, wrenched from the centrifugal force that had kept them pinned to his side by a particularly hard hit with a tree limb, refused to go back in place as he bounced from branch to trunk to leaves. The only coherent thought he could muster in the chaotic descent was: protect your neck.

His legs hit something hard and he yelled in pain as his injured leg throbbed anew. Next his arms. All the breath knocked from his body and he knew that paralyzing panic of being completely conscious and equally completely incapable of movement, no matter how desperately you try. It was one of Sam's biggest fears, and he fought it hard.

He forced himself to take stock: not dead. Hard thing. Ground. Hard thing: ground. Under him. The ground.

Ground.

Ground.

All of a sudden, the chaos gave way to the same silence he had experienced before the parachute opened.

Sam gave himself to the clarity, grateful.

Slowly, shakily, he stood up, careful of any massive injury. He took his right arm and gingerly ran it over every single limb. Then he did it again in disbelief.

He seemed improbably whole.

Why am I not broken and bleeding? Am I hallucinating? Surely I must be. Blood loss causes the brain to lose consciousness and function, he thought as he stood there dumbly. He checked once again, just to be sure. The only pain and blood he was feeling radiated from the cuts on his arms and an ache, bone deep in his injured leg- but surely those were manageable. They would have to be, he thought. Neither he nor Tom had brought medical supplies with them, and in these woods, they-

Tom.

Where the hell was Tom?

"Tom!"

The shout was out before he could control it, and he clapped his hand over his mouth, cursing himself for his stupidity: they would hear the calls and track both of them down, like wolves hunting a deer. He stood there, trying to breathe, listening to the happy calls of birds.

Birds.

He remembered the bird calls they had devised together for situations just like this. Sam cupped his hands around his hands, took a lungful of humid jungle air, and cried,

"Coo, coo!"

He counted carefully to three, slowly, as agreed on. Then he continued with three "Caw!" cries in rapid succession.

Then he cupped the hands around his ears and awaited a response.

Nothing. Just jungle sounds. Jungle sounds and... birds?

To his left, he heard a faint echo of his call. He waited again; the call was repeated, carefully counted. Even his luck wasn't that sadistic. Sam grinned.

Sam detangled himself from his useless parachute, left it behind him. He felt oddly free from its weight as he began to navigate the vines and roots overflowing on the ground to reach Tom.

He'd gone about three hundred feet when he reached a small clearing in the jungle. Here, even though the plants were growing on the surface, the canopy of leaves and branches seemed to have opened up, allowing sunlight to reach the ground.

As he traced and retraced his steps, in the back of his head, he swore he could hear Tom's voice whispering to him to hurry it up. Sam shrugged it off. He'd been stuck with Tom for weeks now and they'd just been through a shocking ordeal. It wasn't any surprise he was hearing things.

But as he looked, the voice became louder, harder and harder to ignore. Was he going crazy? Sam shook his head. No, he wasn't going crazy. It sounded... real?

Sam stalled. No. Could it be...?

His gaze swung up.

There was Tom, hanging off a thick branch by his parachute. Sam noticed with some resentment that the dirty canvas of Tom's parachute had no holes.

He folded his arms. "You got a better parachute than me."

"Well, at least you got to take it off!" Tom flailed, and nearly lost his grip on the branch. He clutched it again, tangled in canvas and lines. "You wanna help me get down from here?"

Sam grinned. "Well, I don't know. This is a rare..."

"Will you save it, already? Did you forget there's people trying to kill us?!"

Sam bit back his humor. Shock, he told himself, turning his attention to the situation at hand. The branch from which Tom was suspended was at least fifteen feet above him- too far to fall without risk of serious injury, and Sam was in no shape to try a dead man's catch.

He followed the trunk down to the ground with his eyes. The thick, straight trunk of the tree was nearly buried by layers of vines, some dead and some alive- all thick from years of uninterrupted growth. Sam's eyes narrowed.

He grabbed a handful of greenery, found a solid toe hold, and began climbing. The task was surprisingly easier than he had anticipated; the vines stayed exactly in place, held to the trunk by determined roots and years of undisturbed growth. In quick succession he was at eye level with Tom.

He grinned, barely out of breath. "Just like the wall at the gym."

Tom glowered at him. "I hate that wall." He held out his hand, awkward given his situation. "Just give me a knife and I can cut out the ropes."

"Yeah? And then?"

"And then I'll climb down after you!"

"I thought you hated that?"

"Sam! Just give me the damn knife before I lose feeling in my legs!"

Sam adjusted his grip, and then, hanging off the tree by one hand, he fished into his pants, praying it hadn't gotten lost in the river.

He found the slim knife in relief and pulled it out. "How am I going to get it to you? You're at least ten feet away from me, and I honestly don't trust this to hold both of us if I go any further."

Tom raised a brow. "You could throw it."

Sam couldn't tell if he was joking or not. "Are you serious?" When Tom said nothing, he held the knife hard. "What if you don't catch it? We'd lose it and you'd be stuck up here forever."

Tom shrugged. "I won't. It's just like tossing car keys."

"You have one good idea and now you're full of it?" Sam shook his head. But the more he looked, the less options looked open. He inched forward on the branch and gave an experimental tug. The branch snapped, sending a shower of tiny twigs down to the ground.

Sam retreated to the safety of the trunk and the vines. He brandished the knife, raising his brows. "You better catch this, then. We only get one chance"

Tom gripped the branch with his legs, then raised his hands and placed them in front of him with the fingers in a diamond.

Sam adjusted his grip. Was that the target? "Overhand or underhand?"

"My god, man! Did you never you play football?"

"Not well. Overhand it is." Sam threw the pocket knife.

In the longest second of his life, the small tool sailed across the gap, turning over and over in the air.

Tom caught it convincingly, both hands "Told you. Ye of little faith."

Taking the blade, he began working on the ropes with an expert hand. The knife was small for this kind of work, but the ropes were worn and Tom cut directly opposite of the grain, making it easier to cut through the strands. He shook off the last of the rotting parachute, leaving it behind him in the branches like a ghost.

In no time Tom was climbing down the thick vines alongside Sam, getting the dirt from his passage stuck in Sam's eyes.

"So, now what?" he asked when they hit the ground, as Tom stretched out his numb legs and slapped some feeling back into his wrists. "Where are we headed? Where ARE we?"

Though Sam had the ability to think on his feet and get the two out of tough situations such as the one back in the underground tunnels of Venice, Tom had always been the one who planned ahead and thought everything out logically. Even if one of their journeys was meant to be laissez-faire and have no rules, Tom would spend weeks before their departure studying up on possible locations they would visit and form contingency plans for disasters even Sam couldn't think of. He'd been that way as long as Sam had known him, and truth to tell, it was one of the reasons Sam was so glad to have Tom on the team. Elise often joked that she was unnecessary because of it.

"You've phased me out, man," she would say, pointing at Tom. "We already have a human computer here."

Tom would then stalk off to do more calculations in peace.

Elise. Sam squinted into the trees and wondered if he'd see her again. Her, or-

Tom's voice brought Sam back. "While I was flying through the air, I did a panoramic sweep." He scanned the greenery, as if to get his bearings now that he was ground level and not above the trees. "Looks like the jungle ends not too far from here. There's a road that cuts through, to the west." He squinted in the sun, then flicked his wrist inward to check the compass on his watch, and pointed straight ahead of him. "That way."

Sam wavered. "We want a road?" Road meant visibility.

Tom straightened his shirt. "We've got a better chance finding our way back to the cave along a road than we do through uncharted jungle.

Sam slapped at a mosquito. It was a point.

It wasn't long before they found themselves squinting through the relentless sun down the asphalt, into the distance along the Guoliang Road. "Well, it's consistent with the GPS, anyway," Sam said, returning his wallet to his pocket after thanking a local for directions. "Let's just hope the timeline is as…"

He jerked, off balance, as Tom suddenly crouched down behind the bushes at the shoulder and pulled Sam down with him.

Sam shook off his arm and went still. "What's the matter?"

Tom jerked his chin toward the mountainous lane. "Look down the road," he whispered, barley moving his lips.

Sam tentatively complied, peering through the small spray of leaves.

Out in the distance, he could barely make out two figures walking toward them on the path. Could just be locals, he thought. But as they figures moved closer to them, the familiar uneasiness bubbled in Sam's stomach. Tom gripped his arm, and he saw the trademark black suit and Brownwood pistols they symmetrically clutched in their right hands, out of sight by their sides.

"Damn," he whispered, moving further back into the leaves. Maybe they could sneak back into the jungle at the side of the road without being seen.

A twig snapped.

Sam's gaze snapped back to the road.

There, the worst of his suspicious were confirmed: the two men had most certainly seen Sam and Tom: their brown-coated forms were sprinting at full speed to them.

Tom and Sam glanced at each other. They didn't have to say anything. Tom quirked a brow, scrambling to his feet.

A deceptively innocent sounding pop splatted into the gravel behind them. Sam jumped, then ducked, scrambling forward along the scrubby grave.

From behind them, more bullets popped and whizzed into trees, into rocks. He smelled hot metal and sulfur. He thought of the beach. It seemed that the jungle had come alive all of a sudden. Exotic birds cried in sounds Sam had never heard before as Tom's military boots crunched.

Tom was shouting something, but Sam couldn't make out the words.

Then he saw what Tom was pointing at, and grinned.

There, along the side of the road was a pair of Kawasaki Ninja 1000cc motorcycles.

Sam looked apologetically at the two riders, his knife in his hand. "I'm sorry, we're going to need to borrow your bikes."

Chapter Seventy-Three

The dirt road gave way to highway, but it wasn't much to look at, Sam thought as he clutched the handlebars with absolute focus blessing the Guoliang Road's tourist boom, and the enterprising motorcycle rental place that sought to profit from selling tours of the stunning scenery. It had been a while since Sam had had to hot-wire a bike, but the Kawasaki Ninja wasn't too different and it was over in a matter of minutes.

Kawasaki Ninja 1000, Sam thought. I love it.

The last thing he'd seen before the dust obliterated the mirror as the wheels spun in the gravel, eager for the purchase of the paved road, was the owner rushing outside, mouth opened in shock, shouting after them in torrent of Chinese.

"If we live through this, remind me to pay him!" he shouted as he and Tom careened down the narrow mountain road.

"You got it!"

Their furious pace spun dirt from their wheels into their faces, stinging his arms and body, hard enough to bruise. There wasn't that much traffic this afternoon, not this remote, but Sam wasn't sure if this was good or bad- there wasn't enough to get a rhythm down to weave, and just enough that they couldn't blast off however hard they liked.

Bullets spattered up stones behind. That didn't help, either.

Sam swerved hard, praying the baddies shooting at them would follow him and spare the family of four he passed. A young boy gaped at him out of the back window. Sam could barely spare him a glance, let alone a reassuring smile.

The road ahead narrowed dangerously.

He dragged his eyes from the passage toward Tom. "Mosul?" he shouted.

"Roger that!" Tom shouted back, and immediately put on a tremendous burst of speed, peeling off toward the narrow canyon.

The nearest baddie put in a similar burst of speed, clearly intending- from what Sam could tell in his tiny rear-view mirror – to slam him into smithereens as they rounded the corner.

It was going to be tight…

He let his instincts take over as he throttled the bike. Like riding the wind, he thought. Ride it. Ride it.

He hurtled around the corner, hoping, hoping… this whole thing was terribly dangerous if they didn't time it right…

He glimpsed a bike ahead – a clear hand signal he'd been watching for.

Sam pushed the bike hard and then jammed on the brakes.

It handled like the dream he'd been praying for. Startled, their pursuer jammed his brakes, locking his wheels, sending him skidding in an uncontrolled slide. His wheel hit a stone and went crooked, throwing him off the edge of the cliff. There was no way they'd hear the impact, not over the roar of the road, not two thousand feet down.

Probably for the best.

Sam slowed to a stop in the bushes in the brief reprieve, hurled himself off the bike, grabbed the wheel pump attached to the frame of the bike and gripped it hard like a shiv.

Soon the roar of the bike announced their attacker. Sam waited… waited…

The bike screamed into view. The man, elegantly dressed, saw them waiting at the side of the road, as if helpless. Sam kept the pump out of view. The baddie gripped the bike one handed, raised his gun as if he were jousting, and fired in one fluid motion, faster than Sam was expecting.

Sam ducked. The man had good reflexes- and good aim. Anyway- he just had to hold off a little longer. Just a little longer... he couldn't afford to let him slow down.

Before he could order, Tom took off running, confusing him enough that Sam could lunge from hiding.

He lunged out, shoved the pump out into the fork of the bike as the man zoomed past, sending him flying.

The would-be assassin launched himself like a gymnast and rolled with his bike. He ducked into himself and hit the ground hard on his shoulder, coming to his feet in the same move like a professional athlete – or in this case, a mercenary.

The man's cold gaze met Sam's with a grin.

There was nowhere to run, and Sam was useless with his bike pump. Throw it at him in the chance it would hit, but leave Sam defenseless if it came to hand to hand combat? Or wait and use it in close combat?

In his split second of hesitation, the man squeezed the trigger.

Sam's entire world shrieked.

For a minute he thought he'd died, and then he saw the truck rumbling around the corner, blinded by the tight curve. It tried to break when it caught sight of the scene ahead, but no luck – it was too heavy and there was not enough time.

The assassin spun at the sound of the truck, threw his arms up, and dived – but he wasn't fast enough.

The truck lumbered right over him, impervious, leaving the man a bloody ruin in its wake.

The truck shuddered to a stop some distance down the road, Sam noted dimly, its tire tracks stained red. He wondered where Tom was.

Sam went to the messy, bloody roadkill and found the man's gun, close by his lifeless hand. It was a Tanfoglio T95 – Italian 10mm automatic – the same beautiful, and familiar one he'd seen before. Sam turned it over in his hand, remembering their fight in the catacombs.

The truck door opened. The driver climbed out, babbling frantically in Chinese.

Sam waved the gun in his face. "Go!" He shouted, trying to sound menacing. In his current state, it wasn't hard. "Go! Gone! Kill you too!"

The babbling driver couldn't get into his truck fast enough. It sputtered to life and hurtled down the mountain road.

Sam panted in the sudden quiet. Tom limped into view. Tom tossed him something; Sam caught it in reflex.

Keys.

Sam grinned. "Let's go."

Chapter Seventy-Four

The Guoliang Tunnel links the village of Guoliang to the outside through the Taihang Mountains. The isolated village is nestled in a valley surrounded by towering mountains cut off from outside civilization.

Guoliang Tunnel is named after a local villager who led a troop of villagers to fight against oppression from government in the Later Han Dynasty. The fight waxed and waned, and the villager troop was besieged without food. The fight ended with Guoliang's leading the troop to a safe place where they rebuilt a village. In memory of Guoliang, a hero to the villagers, the village is named Guoliang Village. The village has a long history of more than one thousand years since then.

The Guoliang tunnel road was about four thousand feet long, fifteen feet high, and twelve wide. It was sixteen feet high, and twelve feet wide, which is of great significance to the villagers, and gives much convenience to villagers' planting, economic business, social activities and other activities.

None of this made it convenient for a high-speed motorcycle run. Especially not when you're possibly being pursued by villains of unknown number.

Those five thousand feet past by in a blur, and, as pursuit didn't seem to be coming, and it seemed, in fact, riskier to keep up their speed and alert the locals to something untoward, Sam slowed to a regular putter. Tom followed his lead, and then to the side of the road as Sam pulled over and pulled out his computer tablet. He checked their location in the spotty signal and shook his head.

Tom raised a brow. "We damned well better be close."

Out of breath, all Sam could do was point.

Sam and Tom peered through the bushes toward the edge of the sinkhole. To his military eye, nothing about this place looked remarkable, or remarkably dangerous. It just looked like jungle.

If that was the case, why the dead feeling in the pit of his stomach? Sam fingered the stolen gun, remembering the way it had felt in Venice.

He jumped at the crack beside him, and spun soundless.

Tom held up his hands.

Sam lowered the gun and they both sank back into the brush, returning their gaze to the cave entrance.

Tom spoke, barely moving his lips. "You were right-there's at least seven of them. Bastards."

"Armed?"

"Armed. From what I could see, all of them are."

Sam's stomach dropped again. He turned the gun over in his hand, then eased off the trigger. "There's no way we're getting in there with just this, then."

Tom shook his head. "Afraid not." Sam was surprised to find him grinning. Tom had a thing for extreme situations. "We'll just have to find another way inside."

Chapter Seventy-Five

Yellow Dragon Cave

The entrance to the cave was guarded by a picturesque system of watermills, wooden and ancient but definitely still in use. Each was topped with a painted, roofed pagoda, as if some kind of shrine to the elements. The water spun through their intricate system of gears and wheels, each turning the other as the river sluiced slot by slot, turning the gears like a child's toy.

Sam and Tom snuck past, sending prayers of thanksgiving that the roar of the water hid the sound of their passage.

Often, it is the smallest things that yield the biggest changes. Yellow Dragon Cave was a prime example of this. Over ninety feet high, the cave was formed as drop by drop, water seeped through any available cracks into the karstic layer and dissolved the limestone, thereby extending the gap. As in any karstic cave, over years, the gap had widened. Over centuries, the gap had become very large. Over millennia, if gone unchecked, the gap had reached enormous proportions.

Before entering the cavern, as Sam studied the internal map of the canyon, topside, he hoped some similar inevitable revelation would reveal itself. The cave system was immense. From his brief glimpse now, plus relying on his memory from their study on the plane ride over, he could make out two underground rivers, two pools, four waterfalls, at least ten large halls and too many galleries to count- and probably too many to even be shown on the map. Not to mention hundreds of thousands of stalagmites, columns, stalactites, cave stones and other formations inside the cave that definitely weren't shown on the map, and which he knew from experience could cause all kinds of havoc.

Sam tapped the map. "If I learned anything from Claustral, it's that maps lie. And if the labyrinth here is anything like what we found in Australia, the best way in (or out) will be through this river here."

Tom thought. "You think Ramirez's going to be in there?"

"Don't know. I do know he's risked a hell of a lot to find this place, and I have a hard time imagining he'd miss his magnum opus."

"I have a hard time imagining he'd get his hands dirty." Tom fiddled his fingers. "Might mess up his suit."

"There's that, too."

They thought in silence a while longer.

Finally, Sam shook his head. "There's no way around it. If they're all armed, we have to get them into a situation where they won't be able to use their weapons."

"What might that be?"

"In the water."

Tom started, then stared. "What- you mean?"

"If we go down, if we SCUBA in the cave and up the river section, we can take them by surprise in that hidden section. It's not too much space in there- we might be able to draw them into the water if we can get a head start and they see that we're in the lead." He shook his head.

"Wishful thinking."

Sam shook his head, and pulled the map closer. "Think about it. This cave system receives more than a million visitors a year. You got any ideas how old El Dorado kept his tomb secret?"

Tom studied the map of the underground system. It had been mapped all the way up to the northern end, where any progress was blocked by a down-flowing river.

When Tom looked up, Sam saw he understood by the dour expression on his face.

"The only way the Tomb of the El Dorado could possibly stay hidden is if you could only get to it from under the water."

"Great. Venice all over again."

Sam shrugged. "It's our only chance at an even fight."

Tom shook his head, and then he shrugged. "I hate it when you're right." He sighed. "I wish I could see other options. I can't."

Sam nodded. "So we'll take dive gear, and explore up this river."

Tom raised a brow. "Where will we get the dive gear?"

Sam ran a hand through his hair, glancing around at the immense jungle, the nearby village cut off from civilization, where the Ramirez's AG600 amphibious aircraft was currently moored. On board there were plenty of SCUBA diving equipment.

Tom followed his gaze. "Oh no, we're not going back there."

"Not us, we wouldn't get within a hundred feet of that plane."

Tom crossed his arms. "So then, how do you suggest we get some dive equipment?"

Sam leaned against the bike in anticipation and talked to a local boy who worked selling knickknacks to tourists at the Yellow Dragon Cave. The kid spoke good English and was keen for the opportunity to make good money. Sam explained where the aircraft was and the large team working from it.

The kid asked, "How do I get them to give me the dive gear? I don't even know what it looks like."

Sam nodded. "Just tell him that Ramirez ran into some water and need more gear." If they give you a hard time, just say "That's all they told me. They don't have time to argue.""

The boy nodded, and scampered off, promising to grab some friends to help.

Tom watched the kid go. "This is never going to work."

"You have any better ideas?" Sam asked. "We can't get gear, we can't get in. He doesn't get it, we're no worse off."

They waited an hour for the boy to return.

Finally, Sam spotted a figure lugging two full bags almost his own size. He fought to keep from punching the air in triumph as the boy dumped them, breathless.

"I went the wrong way," the boy panted, but he didn't sound apologetic. "To throw them off your trail. Then I doubled back through the pass. They'll never find the track." Eyes bright, cheeks flushed, he looked delighted to be part of a spy mission.

Tom and Sam beamed at him.

Sam said, "You did great, kid. You're a regular Indiana Jones."

Chapter Seventy-Six

The Huanglong Cave means "The Yellow Dragon Breath Cave" in Mandarin. It was guarded by a system of wooden watermills which, though antiquated, were still fully functional and presented a picturesque opportunity for tourists to take photos.

Covering a total area of 128 acres, the cave system extends to nine miles in length and was divided into dry and wet levels. There were four levels, thirteen chambers, three underground waterfalls, two underground rivers, three pools, ninety-six passages, and one grand subterranean lake.

The typical way to see the cavern is with a cruise along an underground river in a small boat. After that you can move from hall to hall along the paths and bridges. The guided tour lasts about two hours.

It was somewhat lacking in amenities of a cruise boat, but as Sam drifted down at eye level with the water, in awe of the soaring majestic limestone cathedral above him, he wouldn't trade their method, despite the dire straits that made it necessary.

The glittering and translucent limestone gleamed in the semi-darkness and the water moving over its smooth surface, trickling in and out of crevices, made a lovely, unearthly, ethereal music the likes of which Sam had never heard before.

It was a strange soundtrack to what they were about to do, but in this moment, as they entered this cathedral like space with this otherworldly symphony, Sam felt they were entering a sacred space. He could see why the El Dorado would want to be buried here.

As he pulled his mask down over his face and took his first breath of recycled air, and Tom gave him the thumbs up nearby, Sam devoutly hoped they would not be joining him in eternity.

They plunged beneath the icy water in a riot of bubbles.

Chapter Seventy-Seven

As his head plunged beneath the surface, Sam braced for the deep freeze into his bones and managed to conserve his energy. He had some experience diving in caves by now, he reflected ruefully. Unlike the other times, though, the water was pitch-black, limiting Sam and Tom's ability to look. The goggles that came with the SCUBA gear didn't help, either. In their haste to get up the river and into the labyrinth, they had put on their air tanks and skin suits so hurriedly that he'd forgotten to spit in the mask and now the goggles were fogging up.

"Exactly what I don't want," he muttered to himself, a tiny stream of bubbles fleeing through the regulator. The visibility would become a bigger issue later on as they began their search for the tomb of the El Dorado, through the cavernous subterranean labyrinth.

Though both Sam and Tom had gone over their plan by scouring over the maps and discussing possible locations for the underwater cavern, Sam struggled to sort them all out now that he was on site, disoriented by the taxing physical excursions and close calls they had experienced up until this point. The ride in the plane and Alex's description of the cave seemed like it had been weeks ago instead of just this morning. Still. Determination and the icy water shook everything into focus. He had one goal – to reach the Tomb of El Dorado before Ramirez.

They had been shot at, dodged death in a series of violent rapids, barely managed to avoid plunging to their deaths over a waterfall taller than most skyscrapers, been catapulted from a decaying plane, and narrowly escaped death by fall and death by motor accident – not to mention bullets – to find this tomb, and Sam would be damned if he let Ramirez get the gold and the glory.

Sam and Tom systematically paddled through the dark water, sweeping their high-beam flashlights back and forth for any sign of anything out of the ordinary. Something more unusual than diving in a huge and deep underground river, at least, sneaking up on a centuries-old tomb. The beams of light cut through the murk with a glow like butter, but revealed nothing. On the bottom of the river, wooden planks stuck out from underneath layers of sediment, probably undisturbed for centuries.

They passed over the ancient wood and continued, Sam wondered where it had come from. Maybe the Chinese had used this river as a method of burial for the nobles when they died. When he was in Egypt, he had learned of the rich traditions of the Egyptians and how they had dealt with their dead. When a relative of the Pharaoh died, they would place their bodies in a decorated boat and send it off down the Nile. Sam couldn't see why the Chinese wouldn't do that too.

The water was cold and dark as a tomb, and even more empty. There was not even so much as a single fish in the wide expanse of water. The only movement was the dirt particles brought up by the slow-moving current, and Tom's form swimming ahead of him.

All of a sudden, Tom stopped swimming. Sam back-peddled immediately to avoid running into him. He waited. On point, Tom floated aimlessly, staring straight ahead at something Sam couldn't see. Then, in one quick motion, Tom's tall figure swooped onto the flashlight fixated onto his SCUBA helmet and flicked it off.

He turned around by beating the water to his left, wriggling until he faced Sam. Sam, confused, shrugged and gestured in the universal sign of "I have no idea what you're doing." Bubbles temporarily obscured Tom's face; he was glaring when they cleared. The bubbles risked giving away their position.

Tom brought his right hand up and urgently poked at the flashlight. What the hell is this about? thought Sam. His partner continued the same motion. Sam's flashlight played on Tom's face through his goggles, revealing his wide eyes that made him look like a deer caught in headlights. Something told Sam that Tom was being serious in his vigorous movements. Sam switched it off, and paddled over next to Tom. Tom pointed to the right in a 30-degree angle, and Sam saw it instantly.

Six people in full SCUBA gear were swimming through the river downstream, in the same direction as Sam and Tom. Without a doubt, they were the same group that had shot at them and tried to get them killed in the jungle. Sam swore, though he hadn't really expected anything else. He'd hoped, but he'd been naive in thinking that they'd given their pursuers the slip.

Even in the dark – or maybe because of it – their forms looked bulky and muscular, as if whoever was sending them had hired the scariest bouncers to not only intimidate Sam and Tom, but to crush them into tiny pieces. The 30-pound air tanks looked like children's backpacks on their bodies. Sam squinted. In at least two of the thugs' hands, harpoon guns were gripped, glinting in their LED light beams. They clearly weren't concerned about stealth.

Unless it was a diversion…?

No way we can take these guys on, Sam thought, as his well-trained brain automatically ran through various combat scenarios and not liking any of the results. We're going to end up dead. He felt a tap on his shoulder through the skin suit, and turned. Tom jerked his head toward the group, and raised a fist. He then began gesturing in rapid-fire fashion. For a few moments, Sam was taken aback, but simultaneously remembered what Tom was doing: sign language they had learned in their military stint. He caught onto the rest of the message.

Not as hard as you think. Stealth, Tom signed. Albeit a bit rusty, Sam began to move his arms and fingers in the water.

No way. Too dangerous. He made the motion forward, for them to continue toward the tomb. We-

Caretaker. With them.

Sam raised an eyebrow, even if Tom couldn't see, as wordlessly and without permission Tom ducked back the way they'd come.

He sure as hell knew Sam well, Sam thought, pivoting in the dark water with barely a ripple.

He followed.

By the time he reached Tom, the group was closer than they'd been when he first saw them. They appeared completely oblivious, sweeping their own flashlights in search of the temple for themselves. But Sam knew that obliviousness rarely meant stupidity, and it wouldn't necessarily remain that way. Oblivious or coy, either way, Sam and Tom could only move ahead by using the light cast from Ramirez's team's lights. Turning on their own would instantly draw attention to them. And very likely draw some harpoons, or bullets, into their bodies.

The perfect balance of speed and silence was necessary. When the thugs stopped moving to inspect something on the riverbed, Sam and Tom stopped moving. Splashing water would alert them. Errant bubbles where no bubbles should be would alert them. Currents under the water counter to their own movements would alert them.

With infinite care, Sam and Tom crept closer, closer… until Sam could almost reach an arm out and touch the hulking mass in front of him. He instinctively looked at Tom to his right, muscles tense, eager to get in on the action. Tom sent him a fierce grin. Swept up by the moment, Sam grinned back.

In a lightning-fast movement only possible with a decade of killing memory dug into his muscles, Sam hooked his left arm over the thug's neck and pulled.

As expected, his arms and legs started flailing and Tom spared no time in restraining his limbs in submission holds. The thug opened his mouth to scream, but it came out as a low moan and sheets of bubbles from his respirator. Without a second thought, Sam jerked his arm and hands to the left, breaking his victim's neck. He held the neck in place until the body went limp, and Sam let the body sink to the river floor.

Swift, deadly, efficient, he thought. Like wraiths in the night.

Sam pulled back, and looked at Tom.

One down, five to go.

So far, it seemed none of the men suspected a thing. They continued on downriver, glancing back, glancing forward. But in the dark, it was hard to see, and even harder to count with the shadows moving on the water like men, moving like magic. Sam shook his head and pulled his wits about him. If he gave into the feeling of doom inside these deep stone walls, they were all done for.

Sam dragged his eyes away from the sinking body, realizing with a jolt that it was no longer even visible.

For a moment he stalled, disoriented – then caught sight of Tom casting him a quizzical brow.

Sam left the dead to the dead and swam on.

Tom gestured ahead, where Sam could barely make out a black flipper in the gloom. A tiny trail of bubbles trickled from a mouth he couldn't see- but he focused instead on what he could see: the SCUBA tank and the regulator pipes.

Tom flicked open Sam's own pocketknife, and Sam felt a flash of surprise. Had Tom never returned it to him?

Good thing, now. He nodded, and Tom drifted closer to the man, closer with his long limbs, silent, not breathing, deadly in the dark.

The knife flashed down.

While Sam knew the SCUBA system was designed to withstand anything from fish biting on it to getting the pipes stuck on stray rock formations, the thin plastic regulator pipes were no match for Tom's expertly precise and strong knife-cutting skills.

A whoosh rocked through the river, and Sam flung up his hands to protect his face from the bubbles. The thug's air tank completely detached, the lines connecting it flailing in the water.

So much for stealth.

Two previously oblivious thugs now turned around and looked at Sam and Tom, but in the bubbles and the black, it was unclear how much he could see. What Sam could see was the unforgiving cold gaze of their scuba masks, the flashlights trained directly on their faces.

The thugs took no chances- they brought up their harpoon guns and fired into the bubbles.

Sam instantly formed himself into a tight ball to minimize his surface area as much as possible.

It worked. The harpoon cut through the water harmlessly past him.

When he opened his eyes, he saw the closest thug paddling backwards, already reaching to reload from a harness slung over his shoulder.

Another split-second decision. Sam pointed straight downwards. Without delay, Tom shot straight down, using his hands for extra speed. Sam refocused his attention on the thugs. He flicked on his flashlight directly at their masks in quick succession. The men, disoriented, attempted to shield their eyes from the bright light, flailing and thrashing as they tried to stay afloat and not sink into the black water.

Sam jumped on the window of opportunity he had given himself. He groped below him on the riverbed and found what Tom had brought him: he hauled the now-lifeless body of the man whose neck he'd broken and hurled it with his all his might at the duo, who were still recovering from the flash.

He shut his flashlight, rendering all in blackness, and the men ahead uncertain of their attacker. He shot forward, following Tom beneath the two men, using the darkness of the depths to their advantage. Tom had already gotten the idea: he lunged from behind at the thug on the right, grabbing at the harpoon gun. In a panic, the thug fired off his harpoon. The bolt whizzed uselessly through the river.

The thug on the left moved to help his comrade, but Sam was already on him, arm tight around his throat in a headlock. He'd trained for this, both in the military, and then in recreation, where he played rugby and water polo with his father's friends.

The body went limp and Sam dropped it without a sound.

At a flurry of ripples in the dark water, Sam snapped his attention to Tom. He was fighting a losing battle. Tom had lost his element of surprise, and the thug wrestled hard, attempting to get full hold of Tom's arm. Thankfully, their slippery suits hindered his progress, but Tom was losing his strength. Soon, he would be no good to any of them.

Sam shot forward and grabbed the arm of the thug he had submitted and aimed the harpoon himself. Then he hesitated. As Tom and the thug rolled in the water, he gripped the harpoon in indecision. In the writhing black suits and the black water and the bubbles blazing white, Sam had no idea where to shoot.

Then Tom punched the thug in the stomach with a force Sam thought impossible underwater.

The thug grunted, jerked back, and momentarily floated backwards in shock. The bubbles followed him and Sam pulled the trigger.

The harpoon shot from the gun and hit the man's body with a thud, silent underwater. All Sam heard was the thud of his own heartbeat and his harsh pant of breath like a sci-fi villain. The spear penetrated the man's suit and body and he suddenly fell silent, a cloud of black like ink rising around his chest.

The blood pounding in Sam's ears died down. Tom trod water, gathering himself, panting in relief, suspended over the body as it slowly sank below.

They looked at each other and Tom exchanged a glance. Tom cocked a brow toward the surface. Sam glanced up.

Above, a faint golden glow wavered. Was it daylight? Had they reached the exit?

Together, they kicked toward the surface and broke into the air with a rush of cold.

Tom shook his hair out of his eyes. "Counted five. That was all of them, I think." He grunted, rueful. "Should have known Ramirez wouldn't have come and done the dirty work himself."

Sam had to laugh. "Yeah, I owe you ten." He treaded water, breathing hard. "Wonder what he'll say when he finds out that all his men were taken out by two."

A small click echoed in the cavern like a gunshot.

Tom blinked. Sam stared.

There, standing on the shore, the Caretaker held a pistol. Sam thought for a second his aim wavered, but it was just the shadows cast by the water.

"He would say thank you, gentlemen." Ramirez glanced between them both. "But he would say he doesn't need both of you."

Sam and Tom didn't take their eyes from Ramirez. Tom spread his hands, treading water in the deep river. "You do need us, if you want the gold. We haven't found the tomb yet, but we know where to look!"

Ramirez clicked the safety off and aimed the gun at Sam. "Then I would say I don't need either of you."

Sam braced himself to dive, but the finger didn't pull.

Instead, Ramirez grinned and the gun swung.

Centered straight on Tom.

The finger squeezed.

"Stop!" Sam shouted. It echoed in the massive cavern as if it had originated from an army.

The finger stopped.

Ramirez turned to Sam with perfect poise and grace. "Yes, Mr. Reilly? You have something to say?"

Sam gulped. "I know where it is."

The gun never wavered. "If you're lying, Mr. Reilly..."

Sam shook his head, the cold water trickling into his wetsuit. "Tom doesn't know. I haven't told him. But I worked it out. He's always been slower than me at figuring out clues. He hasn't had time to..." Sam bought time, furiously- but as he thought, it all made sense. They'd thought the odd ascension in the topographical maps had just been a line of karst in the cave, that the machines had got a hit on an abnormal mineral thread, but what if... as he saw the tunnel leading away from the main cavern, he knew he was right. It hadn't been a mineral thread. Or if it had, it had been exploited centuries ago and transformed into... something else?"

He spread his hands, then pointed to the shadowy passageway that lurked behind Ramirez in the dark. "There. The tomb is there. We have to go... up."

Ramirez turned to see where he was pointing, and Sam could have kicked himself, his stomach sinking as he realized there was absolutely nothing he could do. There was no gamble he could make- without weapons, any surprise attack from the water on Ramirez while his back was turned would be more than useless- he'd hear the splash, turn with that gun, and fire at them like fish in a barrel without a second thought. He saw the same frustration reflected in Tom's face as they looked at each other as Ramirez watched the tunnel that led away.

Their only chance was to lead him to the tomb.

Sam shrugged at Tom, quirking a brow. Tom nodded.

Ramirez turned back around with a smile. He beckoned them with his gun. "Well, gentlemen. It seems you are still useful after all. Lead the way."

Chapter Seventy-Eight

Sam squelched up the twisting, turning passageways, his flashlight of the scuba suit lighting the way. He distinctly felt the gun trained on his spine as Ramirez followed in his wake, sending shivers up his spine. The path was narrow, unused, and the footing uneasy. It hadn't been walked in centuries, Sam thought.

Back in the river, with the gun trained on Tom, this seemed like the lesser of two evils. He would have given up the secret to anything to save Tom's life. Now, as he led the caretaker toward the tomb of El Dorado, knowing he would probably be shot the moment the caretaker saw the edifice, he wondered what the hell he was doing.

Nice work, genius, he thought. Then he tightened his resolve. He'd have to improvise. Think about that when the time came.

Though, if he was being honest with himself, and when you were on the verge of death always seemed like the right time to be honest, he was having a hard time seeing a way out of this.

Tom nudged him. "Sam…"

"Working on it," Sam muttered.

Tom nudged harder. "Sam!"

"I'm improvising."

He saw where Tom was pointing, and stared.

To the left of the cavern hall they were walking in, Sam saw the slightest traces of light leaking out from cracks in the wall. The light was brilliant and bronze, like gold…

This was it. They had found the tomb.

"What are you doing? Get a move on. I don't have all day!" Ramirez shouted at them from behind Sam and Tom. For a second, the thought of surprising the caretaker and overpowering him crossed his mind. He then looked behind him. The man had put a good amount of distance between them, the pistol still trained dead onto Tom. Sam shook his head. He had always looked for a way out of every situation he found himself in. Now, doing so would get his best friend killed, and undoubtedly Sam next.

Sam assessed the options. Clearly, Ramirez had not seen the light that led to the tomb. They could feign ignorance and keep moving forward, acting like they were looking for it but couldn't find the tomb. Alternatively, they could concede defeat and allow the caretaker to take the gold, then pray that Ramirez didn't have any need to kill the two after finding his goal.

Yeah, right.

"To your left. Look – there. Look closer." It was Tom's voice that carried through the dark narrow stairwell.

Tom was defeated, as if he had already given up and resigned his life to Ramirez's gun.

Sam swung around and stared at him in disbelief. "Tom, what the hell are you-"

Tom just shrugged, listless. He left one hand open, palm out. "He's won, Sam. There's no point in pretending." He laughed, bitter. "We're trapped miles underground, no one knows where we are, there's probably a hundred armored tank creatures down here who want to rip our throats out and we have no idea where they are except that they probably carved this tunnel we're going to die in. Does it look like we've got a choice?"

Sam's eyes narrowed and he studied the walls, trying to be as unobtrusive as possible. Now he knew what had looked familiar about the passageway – the top had that groove that Sarah had noticed in Claustral Canyon in Australia. As if…

His thought cut off abruptly as Ramirez's head instantly snapped west.

"Looks like you guys are pretty good explorers, after all," Ramirez chuckled so evilly that Sam wanted to just drop everything and strangle the man right there. Did people really laugh like that in real life?

Ramirez flicked his gun to the left, directing Sam and Tom to enter first. But as Sam approached, he saw the problem with this plan. There didn't seem to be anything to enter.

The cracks that had drawn Tom's attention appeared to actually be from the deterioration of the thick stone door intended to look exactly like the rest of the wall surrounding it. Maybe when it was first made, Sam reflected, it would have been impossible to find, but after centuries of erosion, the passageway had revealed its secrets. Sam studied the door. That still didn't mean they could get through it. Visible cracks or not, he didn't see a handle anywhere on it.

He stepped back and dusted his hands on his suit, leaving muddy smears. "There's no way in. Unless you want to…"

Ramirez slapped his pistol, and the sound of flesh against metal echoed through the cave. Sam fell silent, reminding himself that they were underground with an armed madman. No matter how long they delayed or stalled, this fact did not change, unless they miraculously found weapons from somewhere.

Weapons!

He thought about the dive knife Tom was carrying.

He glanced down. That Tom was holding loosely in his palm, the point peeking out from under the long sleeve of his SCUBA suit.

Jesus. They were going to take on an armed madman with a five-inch blade. Which of them, exactly, was the crazy one, here?

Better to wait. See what presented itself. Buy as much time as they could. His gaze slid up to Tom's face, where he saw perfect understanding. The communication that had helped them survive countless firefights together passed between them without words.

The tiny blade disappeared, leaving a small bump under the sleeve. It was obvious, but in the dark, you'd have to be looking for it. And Ramirez had other things on his mind. At least Sam hoped he did.

Better make sure.

"Hey, Tom- do you see what I-"

Tom beckoned at Sam from the other side of the door, playing along.

"I thought so, too. Check this out." Sam stood up and walked to Tom, acutely aware of Ramirez's gun, which was still trained on the two. But Sam had lived most of his adult life around guns, and now he filed the sensation away where it belonged and did the job.

He studied the ancient door, crouched down by the base. Right by the base, on the left-hand side, there was a tiny crack in the stone that looked different. Instead of looking like a crack, it looked like an... incision.

It was just the kind of thing that would lever a door like this open, concealing a secret latch.

They'd found it- Sam was certain of it. He felt it in his gut.

There was just one problem, though.

The incision was too narrow for fingers.

But for a pocket knife blade...

He glanced at Tom, who crouched down next to him, reading his thoughts.

Sam shifted to block their work from Ramirez as Tom slid the tiny blade from his sleeve and wedged it inside.

"What's the hold up?" Ramirez's voice was rough, angry. Impatience, Sam wondered, or fear?

"There's a crack here," he said, turning around so he could gauge how best to hide Tom's work. He schooled his face into the appropriate mix of apprehension and excitement and resentment. "It looks like it might be a secret latch."

A glance down told him that Tom was still working the slim metal blade inside the stone. Come on, Tom…

"If we can just…"

A click, and then a screech of stone.

Sam's heart lurched in relief, in excitement.

The door groaned with the pain of an old man that had not moved for days and lurched outward. It was slow, but beautifully engineered. With every moment, the light that spilled around the crack shone brighter and brighter…

And then it stopped.

The crack was not wide enough to admit a man.

Ramirez glowered. "What? Now what? What are you…"

Sam, with certainty from some unknown instinct, pushed to his feet. He touched the side of the door with one finger for dramatic flair, and the massive slab slid aside as if that's what it was made to do.

"The Tairona were excellent stonemasons," he said. "They hid their dead well."

All three of them turned toward the now open door. His eyes used to the dark cave, the sudden glare of his scuba flashlight shining off a reflective surface suddenly blinded all of them.

It was his one chance to take Ramirez unaware.

Sam missed it.

The sight of the tomb took his breath away. For an impossible moment, all three of them forgot about any animosity and stared.

Under the harsh light of their headlamp, the Tomb of the El Dorado glowed. Sam forgot about the gun, about their situation as triumph surged through his veins. He'd waited his entire life for a find like this.

Gold coins of every shape and size spilled out of piles to litter the floor. As Sam took in the sight, he saw that not only were there coins. But what looked like every treasure imaginable: ruby and emerald- encrusted necklaces sprawled out over the coins, and some were even hanging off silver hooks placed into the walls. Gold drinking vessels. Gold amulets. Gold talismans shaped like birds and strung on gold collars with gold beads and bone. Spilling everywhere, piles upon piles of them, casual as bat shit, were the stunning golden pearls that had started all of this. Wildly, Sam thought of what archivist Emily would have to say about this.

Hundreds of shells inlaid into the wall reflected the light like eyes. It was as if the spirits of all the Tairona dead watched them, waiting to see what they would do.

Then there was the tomb itself.

It wasn't large, but it radiated a power that was impossible to ignore. Covered in sheets of beaten gold, it was inscribed with symbols. Sam remembered the Tairona didn't have a written language. Somehow, though, he got the sense of a story or prayer.

He remembered the Muisca custom of throwing their valuables into rivers and streams, of the chieftain being rowed to the middle of the lake and diving in to symbolize death and rebirth.

Looking at all of the riches spread before him surrounding the dead, Sam couldn't help but wonder what exactly would be waiting for them at the bottom of the river that flowed through the cavern, if anyone ever bothered to dredge it.

He tore his eyes away from the tomb to Tom. Tom was still staring at the treasure, but when he felt Sam's gaze, he turned. They shared a grin that was pure excitement, the grin of two boys.

Then Ramirez broke the silence. "Well. I can't thank the two of you enough for your help. I couldn't have done it without you."

Sam shot a look at Tom. All trace of excitement had left his face, and he'd resumed his slump -shouldered depression. So he was going to be the compliant one, Sam thought. Better, maybe, if they were going to try and take Ramirez by surprise.

Sam folded his arms and glared. "We didn't have much of a choice."

Ramirez laughed. "Well, of course, you didn't have much of a choice! But I like to be polite." Ramirez's voice, once sophisticated and warm, now dripped with sarcasm and vitriol. Ramirez tilted his gun hand in an expression of balance.

Sam gestured to the tomb – conspicuously lifeless. "But the *Niya Chia* – there's no sign of them. These pearls could have been here for centuries. They might all be dead. Shouldn't we try to find them?"

Ramirez brushed this off with a shrug, but a frown spread between his brows. "They'll come when they're called. I wanted them mainly for farming the pearls, you understand. Apart from that, they don't have much value. Big, smelly things."

"But they're so rare! You can't just let them die out!" Tom's shock sounded genuine. Ramirez laughed.

"Oh, a tree hugger. Mr. Bower. This is worth millions. Yes, it would be nice to have a lifetime supply of golden pearls. But where would I keep them? Frankly, I've gotten tired of taking care of the bastards." He surveyed the hall again. "No… this should last me quite a long time."

"We trusted you," Tom spat.

Ramirez laughed. "Oh, signor." The accent affected, patronizing. "Trust is like cigarettes. So alluring, but bad for your health." He lit a cigarette now, and the smoke unfurled in the small space.

"You want to share?" he asked. "You owe us that much. One cigarette." He gestured. "For all this."

But the caretaker just laughed. "I do, do I? Brilliant adventurer, but not too bright, are you. Hopelessly naive. Clearly, I convinced you enough that I was really doing this for all of us. For history and posterity, I presume. But let me tell you something, Mr. Reilly. In the real world, none of that matters. No one cares. Take a look around you. Artifacts destroyed, UNESCO World Heritage sites defaced for more cities and malls. Rainforests ravaged so that palm oil can rule the world. Arctic tundra- what's not melting, anyway- mined for oil to fuel the cars that will only hasten our world-wide suicide." He pulled on his cigarette. "But they have a point. What is nature? What's it worth? This entire cave system is useless to society once I remove this gold here. It'll get flooded and renovated to be some stupid water park or ride."

Anger burned in Sam's gut. "Useless? It's beautiful. People thrive on beauty. It's what makes the world a little more bearable, a bastion against evil like you."

Ramirez grinned and spread his hands. "Oh, Mr. Reilly. Beauty is meaningless. Did you miss the memo? Cash is king." He grinned. "But, since you guys were nice enough to lead me here, I have one last present for you."

The gun lowered; Sam didn't think.

He took three aggressive steps toward Ramirez. "Let us go."

Ramirez was faster than he looked. The caretaker stepped back with the grace of a dancer and raised his weapon. "I was going to give you your pick of the treasure, but now I might reconsider."

Tom stalled in surprise. He shot a glance at Sam. "Wait – what?"

Ramirez laughed with genuine warmth. "You didn't really think I'd shoot you, did you? Or let you leave unrewarded? One small thing. You can take one small thing with you, and we'll call it even." His smile twisted. "You sure you still just want that cigarette?"

Sam and Tom glanced at each other. Ramirez looked between them, enjoying their hesitation. "Of course once you take it, I'll shoot both of you, pop pop, and leave your bodies here. All this gold IS a little cold. It could use a little life... Success demands sacrifice. That way, you guys can die and stay in the tomb you worked so hard to find. I think that sounds like an excellent plan. Don't you?"

Tom glared. "Why you unimaginable-"

Ramirez fired.

The bullet hit the ground by his shoe, making them both jump.

"You really want to finish that sentence?"

Sam and Tom looked at each other. Were they really out of options?

Tom clenched his right fist, where Sam knew the pocket knife rested invisibly. Tom was ready for a suicide mission.

In the shadows, something moved.

Sam fought to keep his face still, unreadable. But Tom caught the change.

Sam shook his head, minutely. Tom glared.

Sam's gaze flicked to Ramirez, who was watching them suspiciously. Sam shook his head. "Call them. Can you call the *Nyia Chía?* I want to know how big a mug I am. Were they ever really here, or was it all just a lie?"

The caretaker's face twisted in distaste. "I wouldn't give you the satisfaction, Mr. Reilly. I don't want to see another of those brutes as long as I live – not even for all this." He gestured to the unimaginable wealth. "Better just to assume it was..."

He broke off, glancing to the shadows. A frown descended on his brow. His gun wavered. Sam watched him closely.

"Is everything okay?"

Ramirez collected himself. "Trust me, Mr. Reilly. Whether I'm okay or not is the least of your concerns."

He broke off again, glancing around. This time, fear filled his face and his hand shook.

Now Tom heard it too. Unmistakable rustling. The air in the canyon thickened and took on the stench of wet fur and stone.

Sam braced himself out of the corner of his eye, Tom did the same.

The *Niya Chia* charged out of the darkness, directly toward the caretaker.

"STOP!" he shouted, as he'd done in the ruined city of Colombia. "STOP!"

But these creatures, feral without a caretaker for centuries, had never been trained to obey commands. And even if they had, they probably would not have spoken Spanish. And Ramirez didn't speak Chinese.

The massive creature bore down on the terrified man. Sam had to hand it to him- he never tried to run. He fired again and again, though, into the armored hide, even though he knew it must be useless. Desperation makes us hope impossible things, Sam thought dimly as he leapt aside and the creature descended with a crunch.

He grabbed Tom's arm and pulled him to his feet. "Come on! We can make the door if-"

Tom pulled his sleeve, hard.

"Uh- Sam?"

That's when Sam saw it, too. The shells in the walls were... moving.

As the *Nyia Chia* abandoned Ramirez and turned its glowing gaze to them, Sam saw it clearly – the shells weren't shells at all.

They were eyes.

Chapter Seventy-Nine

The creatures closed in.

Stealthy, inexorably, they crept closer, surrounding Sam and Tom in a circle, predatory.

Tom glanced at Sam, gripping the knife. They stumbled closer to each other, herded back to back.

Sam adjusted his footing, having no other weapons. His SCUBA suit gave him some extra protection against the wicked claws he'd just seen slash Ramirez's throat as if it were a stuffed pillow, but... not much.

Beside him, he heard Tom gulp. "Sam." It was rare to hear Tom so utterly defenseless. But in the face of this ring of Niya Chia, Sam completely understood.

"Just- don't. No." He caught Tom gripping the knife from the corner of his eye – the creature in front of him growled, tensed, and its eyes darted to Tom. Sam raised his arm slowly, not taking his gaze off the creature before him. It was strangely captivating. He had the sudden thought that this must be what birds felt, watching the dance of a cobra just before they got eaten. "No... sudden... movements."

He turned his head to face the horde before him.

The nearest *Niya Chia* squinted, recoiling in pain at the bright light from the SCUBA lamp.

That's it! They're cave dwellers!

They don't know what to do with so much light – crank it up and they would be gone. But he had no idea if that were true or not- for all he knew they came and went as they pleased. The *Niya Chia* in Colombia certainly had no problem seeing above ground.

And to blindside them somehow felt… ignoble… for such magnificent creatures. He couldn't explain it, maybe it was stupid – he knew it was stupid – but he got the sense that, as with most predators, they would not attack unless provoked.

Slowly, slowly, Sam raised his hand to his SCUBA lamp. With infinite care, he dialed down the light to as low as it would go – stopping just short of off.

"Sam," Tom sputtered. "What are you doing?"

"Shh…"

Gradually Sam lowered his hands in what felt like a ridiculous pose of surrender. Then he settled his shoulders, and looked into the eyes of the creature before him. He didn't even have to duck, much.

He was totally unprepared for what he saw.

As the dim glow of the lamp hit the face in front of him, the eyes shone in dazzling colors and combinations he never even knew existed. Sam tilted his head just a bit and the creatures eyes changed colors. It was more than the way a dog or a deer's eyes reflect odd colors when caught in headlights at night. This was… magical. It was unexplainable.

He couldn't help it. His mouth opened in awe.

The brilliant eyes were interrupted by a strong protruding snout that barely covered razor teeth, revealed as the creature panted in the dark. Blood shone wetly on its snout and saliva dripped casually from its mouth, but it didn't feel sinister, despite the fact that it had just committed a kill. It felt like what it was a justice far beyond the realm of man.

The face was covered in short, brownish colored fur, but underneath, Sam could make out thousands of small overlapping scales that also seemed to shimmer in different colors. The facial armor looked significantly less developed than the iron-looking scales that covered the rest of the tank like body, armadillo style. Maybe it was an evolutionary measure, Sam thought, somewhat irrationally, meant to protect the *Nyia Chía* from the new, man-made threat of guns the creatures had no doubt experienced as the Spanish invasion ravaged the entirety of their natural habitat in Central and South America.

The whole creature was at least eleven feet long, he thought, with a tail almost as long as Sam, which lazily flicked back and forth, like a cat assessing prey. Interestingly, the only portion of the animal without their natural scale-like armor appeared to be the ankles, which were instead surrounded by mahogany-colored fur. These surprising tufts reminded Sam of the tribal anklets he and Tom had seen when they had stayed a night at a village in Peru that still maintained their traditions by performing spiritual dances at night before a bonfire. It made the creatures feel primal, half human, half animal, and Sam could well see why the Tairona would revere them, even thinking the golden pearls were worthless.

Three fingers protruded from each foot, ending in wicked, curved talons. Though they seemed at rest, now, Sam had no doubt they could unsheathe in a moment's notice to shred, just as they had when they mauled Ramirez.

Beside him, Tom relaxed, slightly.

He seemed as awed as Sam.

One by one, more Nyia Chía padded up from behind the tomb and treasure and surrounded the two men. Each one had the similar eyes of ambiguous color, but they were all unique. The first Nyia Chía's pupils pulsated between a mellow burgundy and a sunflower yellow, while another's pulsated in shades of blue.

Soon, the two were completely surrounded.

Sam realized that his back was now directly against Tom's, and they circled around and around. The creatures seemed to be assessing the pair, just as they were taking in the creatures.

In some dim part of his mind, Sam wondered why the creatures had not attacked, and yet had gone straight for Ramirez. There was nothing so different about them. Perhaps the creatures were a good judge of character, perhaps? Who knows, Sam thought with a small smile. At this point, with everything else they were capable of, it would not surprise him if they could sense the good and the bad in people. Animals had a sixth sense like that. It was humans that seemed to miss it, he thought wryly.

He bowed his head to the Niya Chia in recognition, humbled as he understood their judgement.

Sam felt Tom's right shoulder tense up: there was no doubt he was clutching the pocketknife tightly, just in case. For a minute, electrical tension between man and animal, man and nature, held the room hostage. Not a thing moved, and the only sounds were the shallow yet slowing breaths of Sam and Tom, and the slight whirring emanating from deep in the *Nyia Chía*.

Then without warning, the one *Nyia Chía* blocking the route to the door outside stepped backward, its huge muscles rippling beneath its scales.

Sam and Tom looked at each other in confusion.

Sam brought his gaze back to the claws. Could they just- leave, then? Without getting mauled by those foot-long claws?

He raised his eyes to the creature's face, scanning the room. Despite the ripple coursing down his own spine, they did not look tense at all. In fact, their eyes, though completely different from human eyes, betrayed curiosity. Somehow Sam knew they wouldn't hurt them. If they were going to attack, they would have done it by now.

Backs still turned against each other, Sam spoke over his shoulder. "I think we've disturbed them long enough. What do you think?"

Tom laughed. "Read my mind."

Chapter Eighty

The way out was much better than the way in.

They slid down the passageway wet from their previous ascent until they reached the river, which flowed as inexorably as ever, the walls washed with weird water-shadows and gleaming stone.

Sam and Tom hauled themselves out of the river into the shadow of the waterwheels. Sam sat on the bank and kicked his feet in the water.

"Well…" He grinned at Tom. "I guess this is another one for the history books."

Tom shook his head, slicking back his hair. "Can't say I'm too disappointed it's over. Good thing, too- the girls would give us hell if we were away too much longer."

Behind them two people moved in the shadows.

Sam spun.

There, standing in the cavern of the Yellow Dragon Cave, were the last two people on Earth Sam expected to see.

Nathan Sanchez folded his arms with a smug, cocky smile, and Gordo Rojas, watching them with that cold, snakelike gaze of his.

Tom asked, "What the hell do you think you're playing at?"

When Nathan pulled the gun out of his shorts and aimed it at them.

Sam and Tom spread their hands.

Sam turned to Gordo. "My goodwill only went so far?"

Gordo nodded. "Afraid so, Sam. The Tomb of El Dorado is worth a lot more than any amount of goodwill."

Sam shrugged. He shouldn't have expected more from him. "And the original etchings of El Dorado within the Colombian Salt Mine?"

"What about them?"

"The other miners… the ones you said were killed in a tunnel collapse?"

"Yeah?"

"That was all a lie, wasn't it?" Sam said. "You killed them so that you could keep the gold!"

Gordo grinned malevolently. "Guilty as charged."

Sam waved him down and folded his arms. He jerked his chin at Nathan. "How much exactly did he pay you, Sanchez? Promised you a part of the treasure, did he?"

"Bullshit. The treasure was just the bonus." Nathan laughed. "You think it was money that drove me? It was the adventure! You should know, Sam – you're just the same. Why did you come charging after two people you'd never met, to rescue them? Was it for the reward?"

He laughed. "Who am I kidding. It was the gold! Of course it was for the gold! God, you're one of the most idiotic morons I've ever met. You're on this mission, hush hush, and you lead us right here!"

Sam raised his brows, everything suddenly becoming clear. "Ramirez said he had connections all over the world." He jerked his chin at Sanchez. The man seemed an unlikely agent of espionage, but then, those were always the best. "You?"

Nathan shook his head. "I don't know any Ramirez. I'm not…" He raised his hands as Gordo turned to him with that cold, snakelike gaze. "I'm not like Gordo."

Sam asked, "How many pockets are you in, Mr. Sanchez?"

Nathan threw up his hands. "Nice try, Sam – frame me for stuff I know nothing about!" He pointed a finger at Sam. "We'd been looking for weeks for this stupid cave, breaking our backs and getting nowhere. Then you show up, all Lancelot on us in Claustral, and I knew. I'd heard of you – famed treasure hunter. There was no way you were in that cave by accident – no one is that noble! Then when you started asking about the tunnels, Churn and I knew we were after the same thing."

Sam raised a brow. "And we knew more than you did."

Nathan's mouth tightened, to have his moment of triumph turned against him. "I put a tracker in the journal!" he shouted, waving his arms. "I put a GPS tracker in the journal, told you it could lead you to the cave, but that I was too dumb to figure it out!" He spread his arms. "And voila here we are! Who's the chump now?"

Sam raised his hands. "Yes, you're very smart. So smart that when you go in there and find the tomb, you'll find a dead man. Seven dead men, to be exact." He raised Tom's cell phone. "And I've already called the authorities. What do you know? There's been a murder."

Nathan's face contorted with rage. "Damned right there's been a murder!" He lunged forward with his gun. "Yours!"

Chapter Eighty-One

Sam ducked. Then, without thinking, he lurched for the nearest water mill pole and began to climb.

Nathan grabbed onto his leg, but Sam kicked out and got the other man in the nose. Nathan's face immediately spurted blood, and he snorted. "You bastard!"

Nathan gripped the nearest pillar close to him and hauled himself up to climb after Sam.

Sanchez was a climber, Sam thought, as the man gained on him, unfazed by the awkward footing and uneasy terrain. He had to remember that.

He gained his feet at the top, the water sluicing down the channels designed for it- much faster than it looked from below. From below, the mills seemed like a picturesque tourist attraction, akin to log rides at amusement parks. Now, standing level with them, Sam was forced to admit they were exactly what they were designed to do – mill hard pieces of grain or wood into very tiny pieces. Bones would be no deterrent to this piece of engineering.

Sanchez stood in front of him, panting. He aimed the gun at Sam. "Admit it, Reilly. You lost."

Sam shook his head. "Not today, Sanchez."

Nathan laughed. "And how do you plan to stop me?"

Sam kicked at the lever by his foot, diverting the flow of water directly over Nathan's feet. Nathan jumped back in surprise, swearing.

"Sam!"

Sam risked a glance down, where he saw Tom, arm poised to throw. He didn't have time to think about what it might be- it was already hurtling toward his face.

Sam caught the Tanfoglio pistol in surprise. He cocked the trigger, spun, and aimed it on Nathan in one fluid move.

As they stood off on top of the mills among the clank of gears and rush of water, Sam wondered where the hell all the tourists were. Why didn't anyone put a stop to this?

Nathan grinned, as if he'd read Sam's mind. "Tuesday," he said. "Not open on Tuesday."

"Sanchez!" The shout came from below. Sam risked a glance to the edge to see the tiny, ferocious Gordo aiming a pistol steadily at Nathan. "Leave this. Only the tomb matters. If they have not sealed the entrance and the Niya Chia escape..."

Nathan rolled his eyes. "Always with these damned creatures! Enough already!"

He fired down at Gordo just as Nathan fired up.

Whether blinded by the spray or the mist, or deceived by the awkward perspective, Gordo missed.

Nathan didn't.

Gordo crumpled to the ground and didn't move again. Nathan rolled his shoulders in relief, grinning. "Man, that's a weight off my back. And my ears! Thank you, lord. What an insufferable git. Always the *Niya Chia* this, the *Niya Chia* that... what about my fucking gold?"

It was then Sam realized that Gordo had not told Nathan the crucial fact that the *Niya Chia* were, in fact, the ones that produced the gold.

"So now we get to the real point..." Nathan Sanchez re-steadied his aim on Sam. "I don't need any of you. I've got your tracker." He brandished something in his left hand. "I've been tracking you since you arrived in China. You've left a trail right to the tomb. All I have to do is go in and find it."

Behind Nathan... Sam kept his face perfectly blank. Slowly, behind Nathan, Tom was climbing up the scaffolding. "I wouldn't do that, if I were you."

Nathan laughed. "Why is that?"

"Because they'll kill you like they killed Ramirez."

Nathan waved the gun, and a full magazine of bullets. "Oh yeah? I'll take my chances."

Tom was almost up. Gordo on the ground was in no condition to warn anyone.

Slowly, slowly, Tom took Nathan's untied shoe lace and tied it stealthily to the track as Nathan lowered his gun. "Any last words, Mr. Reilly?"

Tom raised his own gun. "On three."

"Oooh, a duel. How honorable." Nathan grinned. "On three it is." He bowed, mockingly. "One... two..."

Nathan fired.

Sam, who had been halfway expecting such an underhanded move, flung himself out of the way. As he spun in space, his finger, already half depressed, squeezed all the way.

He was met with a click.

Was the gun really empty?

Sam dived down the narrow waterway as if his life depended on it. Behind him he heard Nathan lunge, then curse – he must have discovered his tied shoe. Sam skidded, risking a glance back. Tom was punching Nathan in the face, but Nathan was giving as good as he got. His tied shoe lace snapped and he charged at Tom.

Tom dodged and raced after Sam, gesturing to something in front of Sam, panic and determination in his eyes. "Go!"

Up ahead was a junction of three other mills, the massive cogs moving in sync as the water from different parts of the river was funneled into one powerful fall. If he could get to that, there was a good chance he could give Nathan the slip.

There was also a better than good chance he'd get crushed to death between those massive gears if he lost his footing even a little.

Don't think about that now.

Sam went.

As he slid and skidded across the slick wood and cold water, blessing the fact that he was still wearing the cleated boots of the SCUBA gear, he spared Tom one last, final thought, and then put him out of his mind.

Through the spray, Nathan was gaining on them.

And then, the worst happened – he hit a dead end. The falls spilled down, and he could go no farther. They spun, backs to the drop off.

"Jump?"

Nathan broke into view, gasping in triumph. "Nowhere to run, now, is there?"

Sam held up his hands. "Please, don't do this…"

The gun lowered. "You must think I'm…"

Then Sam saw it. The water was dragging Nathan's untied shoelace toward the crushing gears. If it got caught, it would drag him under and crush him in its massive jaws.

"Your shoe!" Sam shouted, despite himself. "Your shoelace is untied! It's getting…"

Nathan just laughed, wiping his smile with his gun hand. "You think I'm going to fall for that again? Fat chance. You're exhausted, you're out of bullets."

In desperation, Sam lunged and grabbed the lever – reversing the flow of water.

The waterwheel kept moving in the same direction, until the water built up, and enough momentum was produced to change the direction of the waterwheel.

Nathan charged at him.

Sam clambered over the giant waterwheels. There were three of them in a row. Each one spinning slowly in a clockwise direction.

Sam climbed the first one like a ladder.

Stepped over the second one and jumped from the third one.

Nathan was a rock climber and he moved with the quick, nimble body movements of an athlete. Up and over the first wheel, across the second.

And then the water reached its pressure limits, and the wheel reversed its direction – suddenly jolting in a counterclockwise direction.

Nathan fell backward into the deadly gear mechanisms.

All Sam heard was the scream, which soon came to pass.

The watermill ran red.

Chapter Eighty-Two

Sam dropped to the ground beside Tom, flexing his blistered fingers. Panting, he wiped his soaked hair out of his eyes and glared.

Tom caught the pistol Sam hurled at his chest, barely. "What were you thinking, giving me an empty gun?"

Tom shoved it in his pants before anyone could see it. "Yeah, really glad we're not dead, too! Thanks for saving my life, friend!" He threw up his hands. "It was the best I could do! I thought it had one shot left. Poetic, and all that. But I guess I lost count..."

He broke off, strangled by Sam's embrace.

For a moment they stood there, wet together.

"Glad you're not dead." Sam smiled at him. "Friend."

Sam glanced at the bleeding form of Gordo. He knelt down and took his pulse, but it was as he suspected: there was nothing they could do. He rested his wrists on his knees, squinting up at the watermills and their merciless turn.

"Poor bastard," he said. "He was already a rich man."

Tom shook his head. "Greed never pays."

"That so?" Sam glanced at the entrance, thinking of the treasure beyond. "What about being a good guy?"

Tom shrugged. "Speaking of that..." He jerked his chin at the cave. "Now that Sanchez isn't a threat, or Ramirez, or El Gordo... what do we do about the *Nyia Chia* and the Tomb of El Dorado?"

Sam sighed, fingering something in his pocket. Then he pushed himself to his feet, feeling both oddly somber and light. "Let them be. Humans have interfered enough in their lives. They just want to exist as they were meant to, unendangered." He grinned, small. "Who knows. Those pearls are still out there, if you know where to look." He took one from his pocket and tossed it to Tom, who caught it in surprise. "Someone might get curious, put the pieces together and find them, some day. Until then…"

Tom turned the small, exquisite golden sphere over in his hands. "And the Tomb of El Dorado?"

Sam thought about that for a moment, squinting into the sun. Then he held out his hand. Tom dropped the pearl into it and Sam put it in his pocket as they turned to go. "Let's let El Hombre Dorado finally rest in peace."

Epilogue

Sam Reilly's House, Lake Oswego, Portland Oregon – Three Months Later

The birds chirped outside. It was a calm day on the lake, and the summer scents of barbecue and sunscreen slicked the breeze.

Hot as hell inside, though.

Sam gripped the wrench harder and wedged it around the stubborn bolt. His arm muscles went taut and turned the wrench as hard as he could. His tendons stretched and his teeth ground together, but deep in the core of the thing he felt some imperceptible shift and knew he was going to win.

Sam coaxed the bolt loose and finished it off with his fingers. It took a few times to get some purchase what with the oil, but Sam didn't mind getting his hands dirty. Eventually the bolt turned free, and Sam sat back with a satisfied sigh and regarded the Thunderbird. He wondered again how things got so tight when it hadn't been used since he first discovered Excalibur more than six months ago.

Sam's moment of triumph was interrupted by the ring of his cell phone.

It took him a moment to understand what he was hearing, still lost in the hum and puzzle of his old car. Then he shook his head and came back to himself. He eased himself out from under the belly, groping for the rag nearby. He wiped his hands as he got to his feet, wringing hard at the oil that coated his fingers.

He dropped the towel on his workbench as he reached the receiver and picked up the phone.

Sam still felt the grease on his fingers despite washing them as quickly as possible as he strode into the house from his workshop attached outside.

The cell phone kept ringing.

Whoever they were, they were persistent.

Catarina, still wet from her swim in the lake, stepped down the hallway and handed him his cell phone. Sam mouthed the words thank you, his eyes glancing at her with a mixture of lascivious desire and affection, and he wondered why he'd felt the need to work on the T-Bird when he could have been swimming with her.

He smiled, contentedly smitten to have her in his life.

Catarina gestured toward the phone. "Are you going to answer it?"

Sam nodded.

He wedged the cell phone under his chin, reaching for a kitchen towel off the stove and wiping his hands as he answered. "Hello?"

The voice was curt. "Thank you for finally answering your phone, Mr. Reilly."

Sam's brows rose. "Madame Secretary. Good afternoon." Sam wracked his brains for the reason behind the call. "To what do I owe this pleasure?"

"What do you know about Palmyra?" she asked without further preamble. It was something he liked about the secretary of defense. She didn't waste any words.

"Syria?" He tossed the towel. "I read the papers and I hear the news about the war, but if I'm to be honest, not a great deal at all. Why? What should I know about its ancient capital, Palmyra?"

He could almost see her smile as she spoke. "A small deployment of Navy Seals stationed there discovered something that I... well. I think you'll be interested in."

Sam pivoted and sought the window, phone against his ear. Outside, the breeze blew stiff ripples across the lake. "Really? I'm not that kind of soldier anymore... what happened?"

"A group of three men stationed in Palmyra got engaged in a firefight with some insurgents two days ago. They got caught in some ruins outside of the city, hard pressed."

Sam frowned. "Enemy fire?"

"Yes… and heavy, too. They fought their way out but during their escape one of the men got separated from his companions and found himself under the ground."

"Go on."

"You need to know what he found."

"What makes you think that?" Sam frowned. "I mean, what does this specifically have to do with me?"

She smiled through the phone. "Everything, Mr. Reilly. Everything."

The breeze picked up through the windows off the lake. Sam thought of his car and his project, half-finished in the garage. Maybe he wouldn't get to finish it this trip, after all. More importantly, he wondered if there would still be time to spend with Catarina. "Why?"

"I could tell you, but it's easier if I simply show you. Are you near a computer?"

Sam tossed the towel on his counter, put the phone on speaker, and moved toward the laptop that he'd left on the low wooden coffee table, where he'd been enjoying coffee and the news earlier in the afternoon. He settled behind the screen and opened his email. "I am now. What do you want to show me?"

"Open your email."

Sam did so.

In an unsettlingly brief amount of time, an encrypted email arrived. It wasn't his first time receiving a communique from the higher-ups at the Pentagon, but their efficiency never failed to impress and intimidate, no matter how he tried to hide it.

Sam clicked on it and almost immediately a photograph loaded.

It was a picture taken inside what appeared to be a stone tomb. For a moment he thought it was a low-res image taken from some kind of hand held surveillance recorder, and he was surprised at the rare shoddy quality. Then the photo fully loaded into stunning resolution and he stared.

Along the wall was a detailed drawing of indeterminable age. Carved in stone and painted. Sam leaned closer to see. There at the center of the wall drawing was a depiction of a labyrinth, with a strange key at the center.

"Mr. Reilly? Did you receive the file?" The sharp voice cut through his amazement.

"Yes." Sam struggled to process what he was seeing. "I got it."

She said, "I believe you know what this means?"

Sam Reilly swallowed hard and nodded to himself. "It means that my history has finally caught up with me."

The secretary said, "The question is, Mr. Reilly... what are you going to do about it?"

Sam Reilly took a deep breath.

He knew the answer to that question, as much as he disliked it.

"It's time for me to return to where this all began... where I first heard about the Master Builders – and as much as I don't want to, it's time for me to dig something up that I had hoped would remain buried for all of eternity."

The secretary of defense said, "I'm sorry it's come to this Sam. I had hoped that it wouldn't."

He'd hoped so, too. But sometimes your past has a way of catching up with you. "I understand, Madam Secretary. I'll be ready for the flight within the hour."

He ended the call.

Catarina looked at him. Noticing the change in his demeaner, her brow furrowed with worry, and her piercing gray eye locked onto his. Her lips thinned. "Is everything all right?"

Sam took her hands affectionately into his, kissed them, and then kissed her on the mouth. He closed his eyes and enjoyed the moment. He could happily spend the rest of his life with this woman, and forget about his obligations…

He would do it too.

If only his obligations would forget about him and leave him alone.

She pulled back from him. Her trim eyebrows arched and her lips parted questioningly. "Tell me, Sam… what's happened?"

He took a deep breath. "I'm sorry. I need to go pack. There's something I need to do. I'm really sorry." He kissed her on the lips once more, a long slow, and passionate kiss. "I'll try my best to be as quick as I can."

"Sam, you're scaring me. What the hell is going on?"

He had already returned to his equipment room and begun packing two large duffel bags with what appeared more like military equipment than something a maritime salvage expert or archeologist might need.

Catarina grabbed his hand, and stopped him. "Sam!"

"I'm sorry. I'll try and make this as fast as I can."

Her eyes narrowed. Confusion and concern, plastered across her beautiful face. "Where are you going?"

"Palmyra, Syria, Washington DC, Nevada… among other places."

"Why?"

Sam ignored her question, continuing to pack.

She persisted. "When will you be finished?"

"Soon. No more than a few weeks. That is, if I survive."

"Sam!"

He stopped what he was doing and looked at her. "Yes?"

"I'm scared. Why won't you tell me what's going on? What is this all about?"

Sam closed his eyes and bit his lower lip. He swallowed hard. He knew she had a right to know. But all the same, he wanted to protect her as much as he could. But she needed to know the truth.

He opened his eyes and said, "Because it's time I go back to Hell – and retrieve the Labyrinth Key."

The End

Printed in Great
Britain
by Amazon

31575066R00229